THE HONOR STUDENT AT MAGIC HIGH SCHOOL 6

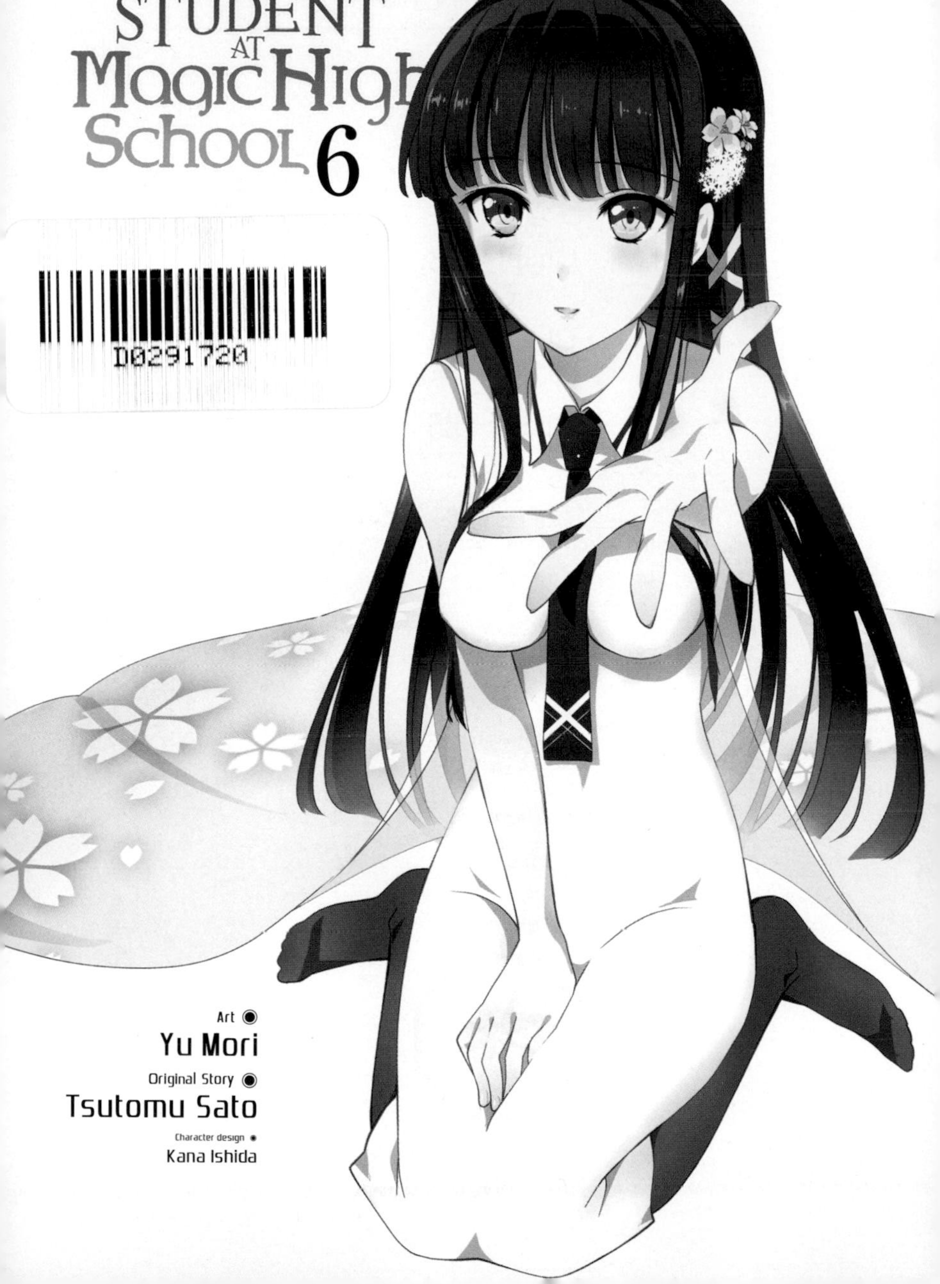

Art ◉
Yu Mori
Original Story ◉
Tsutomu Sato
Character design ◉
Kana Ishida

CONTENTS

The Honor Student
at Magic High School

CHAPTER 31

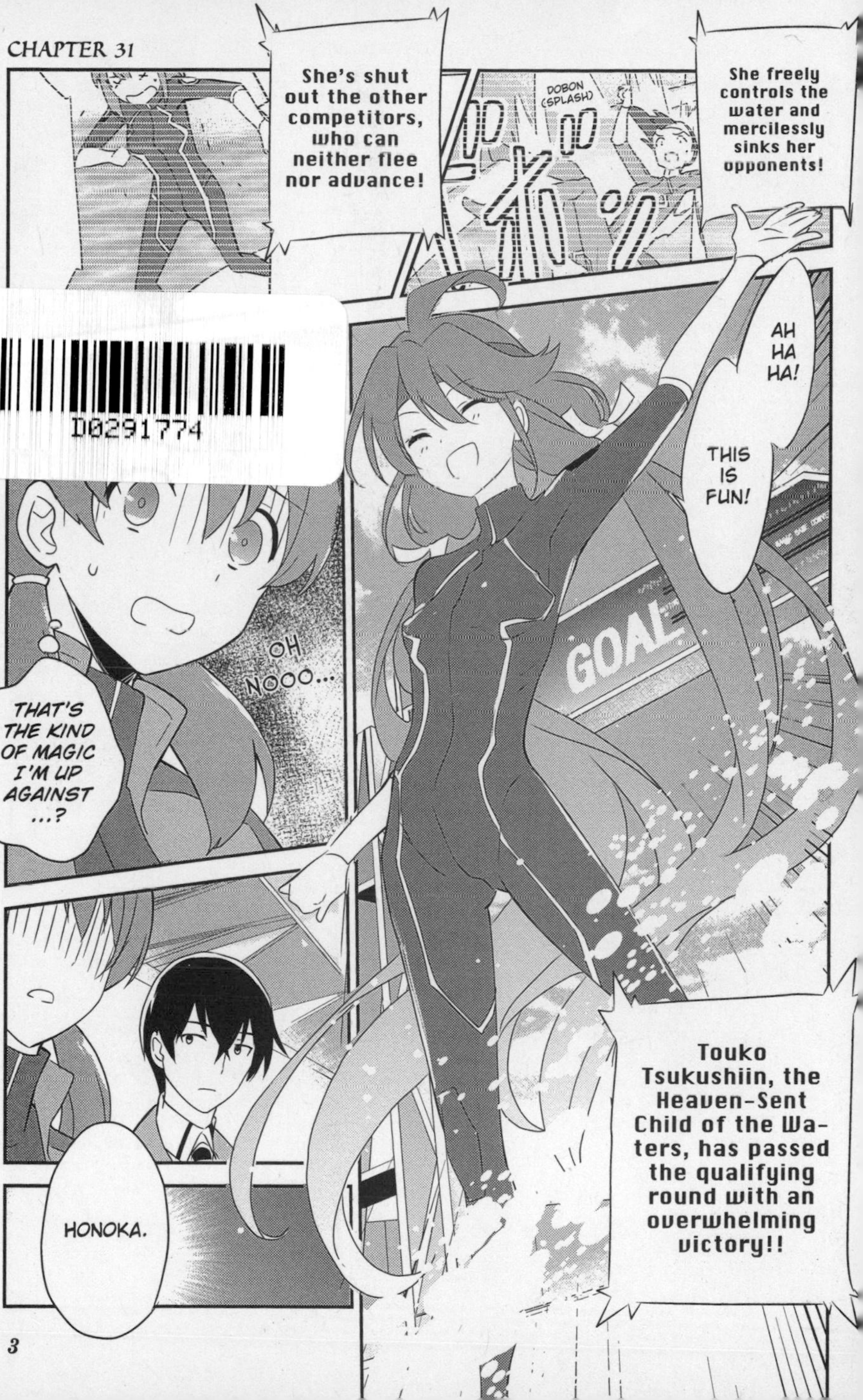
She freely controls the water and mercilessly sinks her opponents!
DOBON (SPLASH)
She's shut out the other competitors, who can neither flee nor advance!
AH HA HA!
THIS IS FUN!
GOAL
Touko Tsukushiin, the Heaven-Sent Child of the Waters, has passed the qualifying round with an overwhelming victory!!
OH NOOO...
THAT'S THE KIND OF MAGIC I'M UP AGAINST ...?
HONOKA.

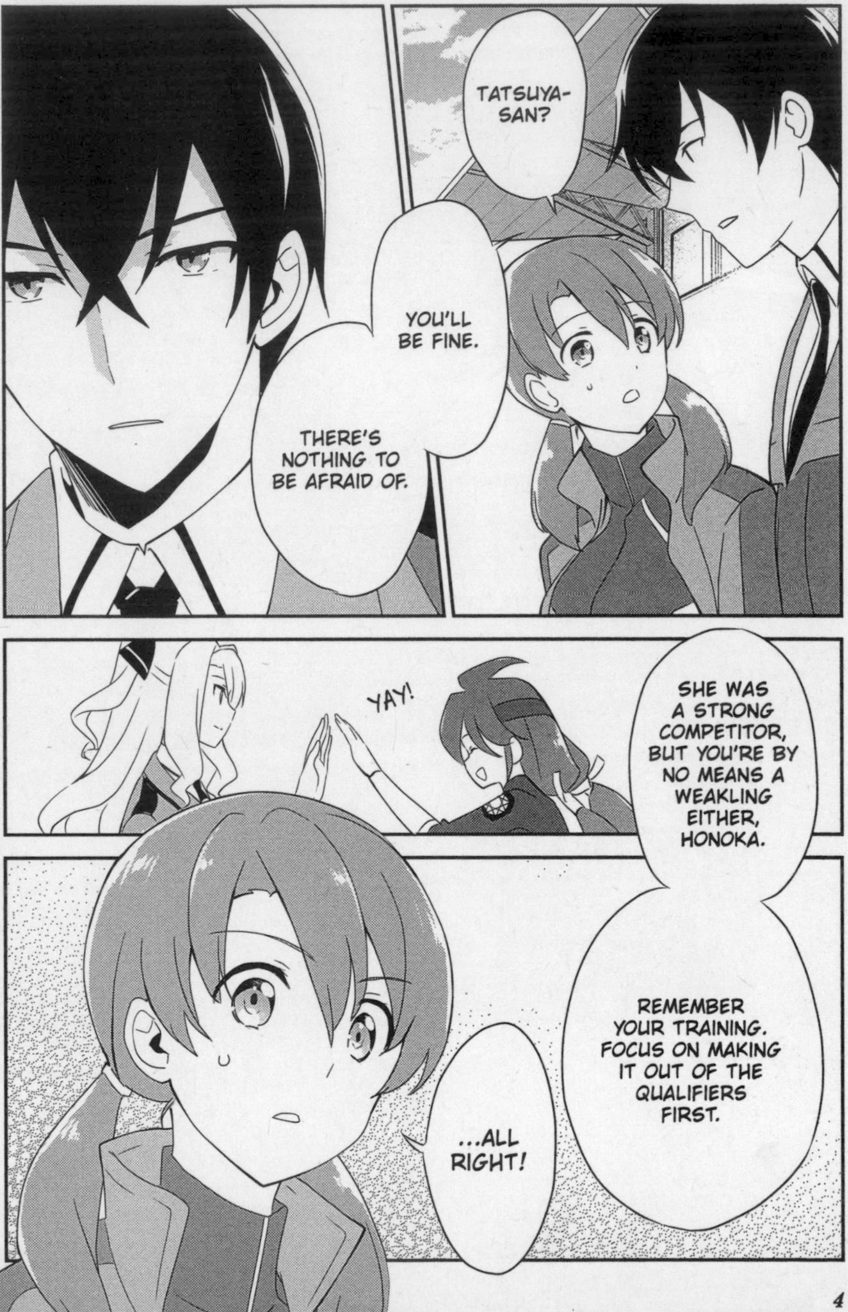
TATSUYA-SAN?
YOU'LL BE FINE.
THERE'S NOTHING TO BE AFRAID OF.
SHE WAS A STRONG COMPETITOR, BUT YOU'RE BY NO MEANS A WEAKLING EITHER, HONOKA.
YAY!
REMEMBER YOUR TRAINING. FOCUS ON MAKING IT OUT OF THE QUALIFIERS FIRST.
...ALL RIGHT!

CHAPTER 31

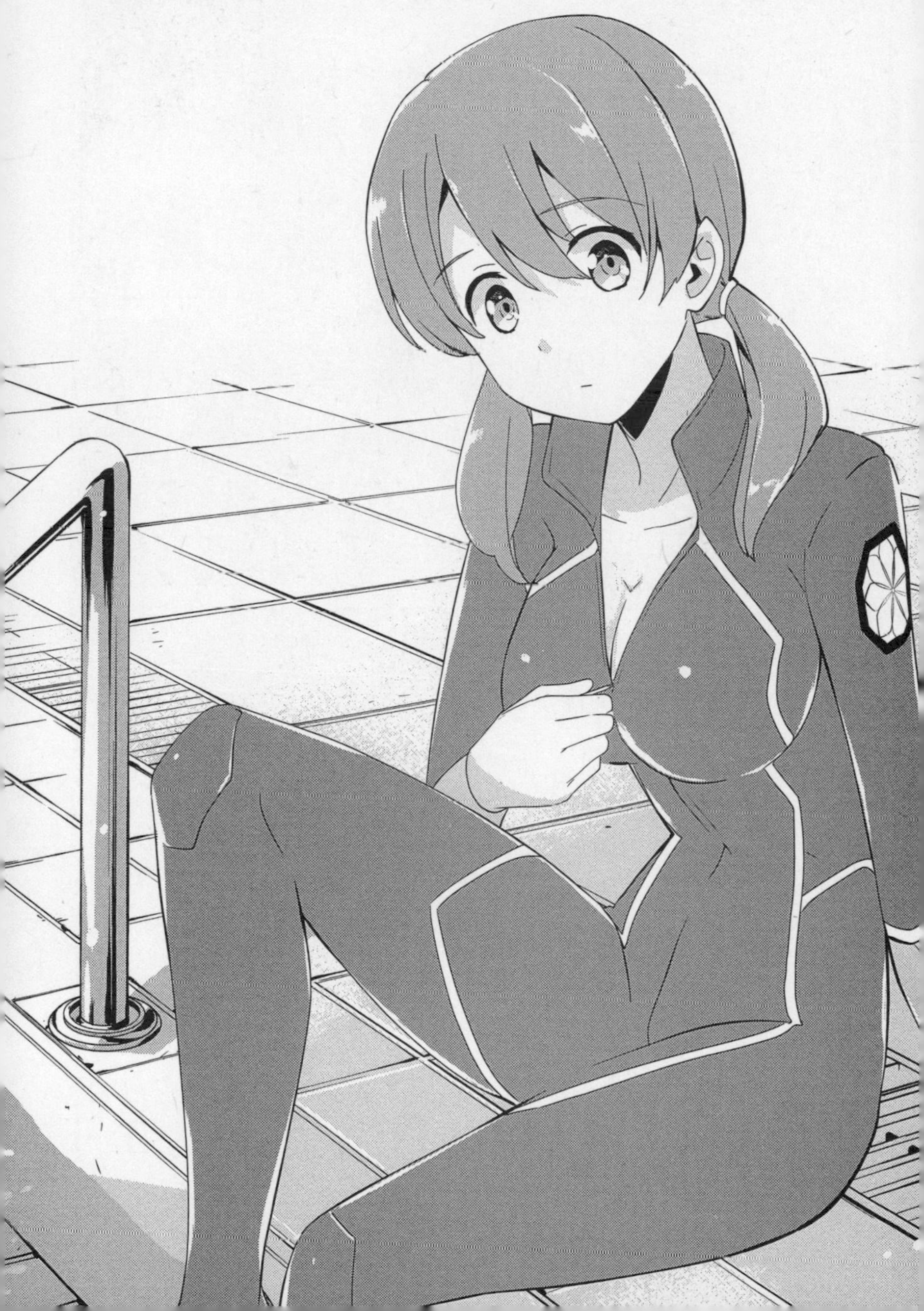

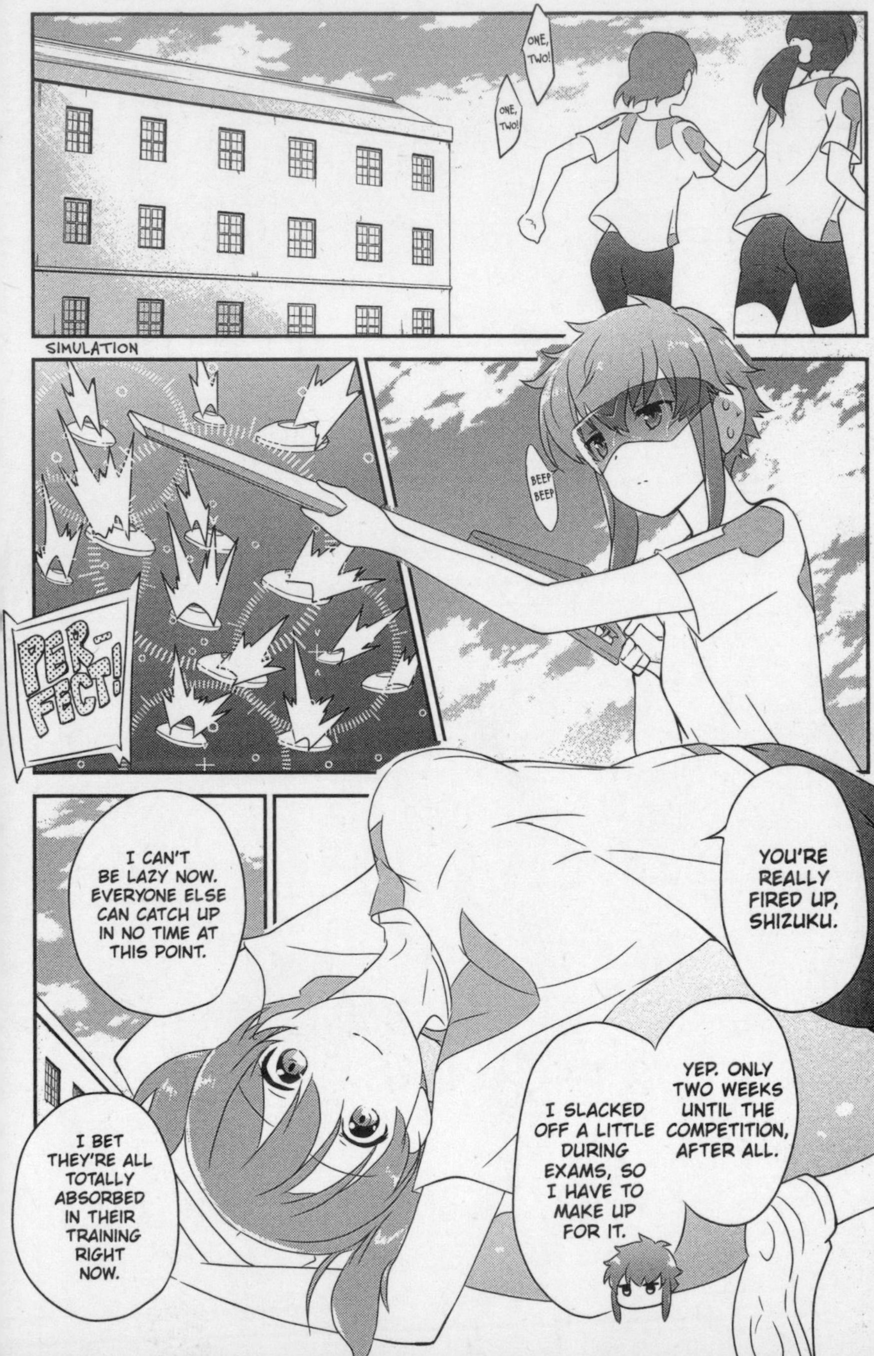

ONE, TWO!
ONE, TWO!
SIMULATION
BEEP BEEP
PER-FECT!
YOU'RE REALLY FIRED UP, SHIZUKU.
I CAN'T BE LAZY NOW. EVERYONE ELSE CAN CATCH UP IN NO TIME AT THIS POINT.
YEP. ONLY TWO WEEKS UNTIL THE COMPETITION, AFTER ALL.
I SLACKED OFF A LITTLE DURING EXAMS, SO I HAVE TO MAKE UP FOR IT.
I BET THEY'RE ALL TOTALLY ABSORBED IN THEIR TRAINING RIGHT NOW.

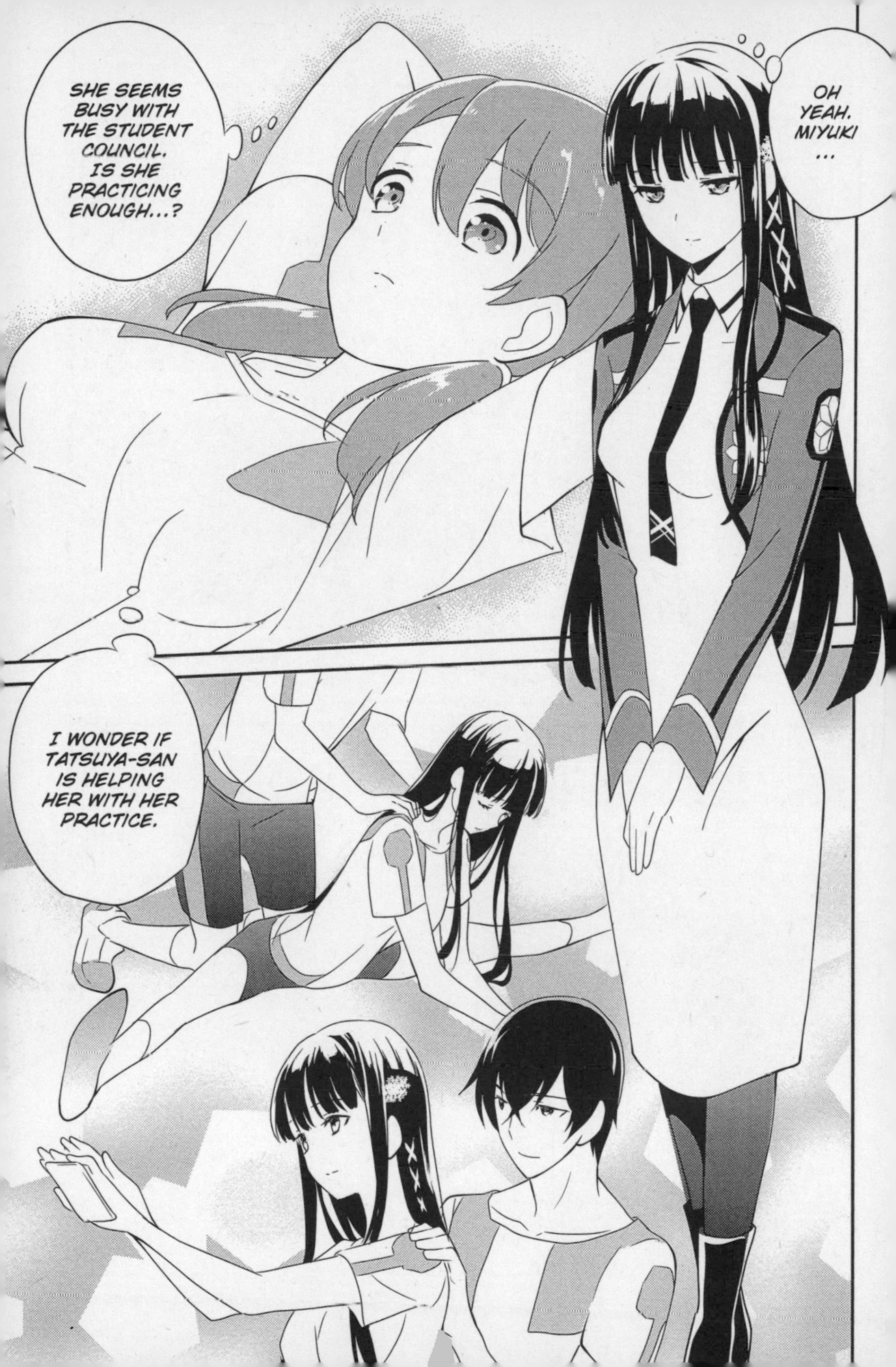
OH YEAH. MIYUKI ...
SHE SEEMS BUSY WITH THE STUDENT COUNCIL. IS SHE PRACTICING ENOUGH...?
I WONDER IF TATSUYA-SAN IS HELPING HER WITH HER PRACTICE.

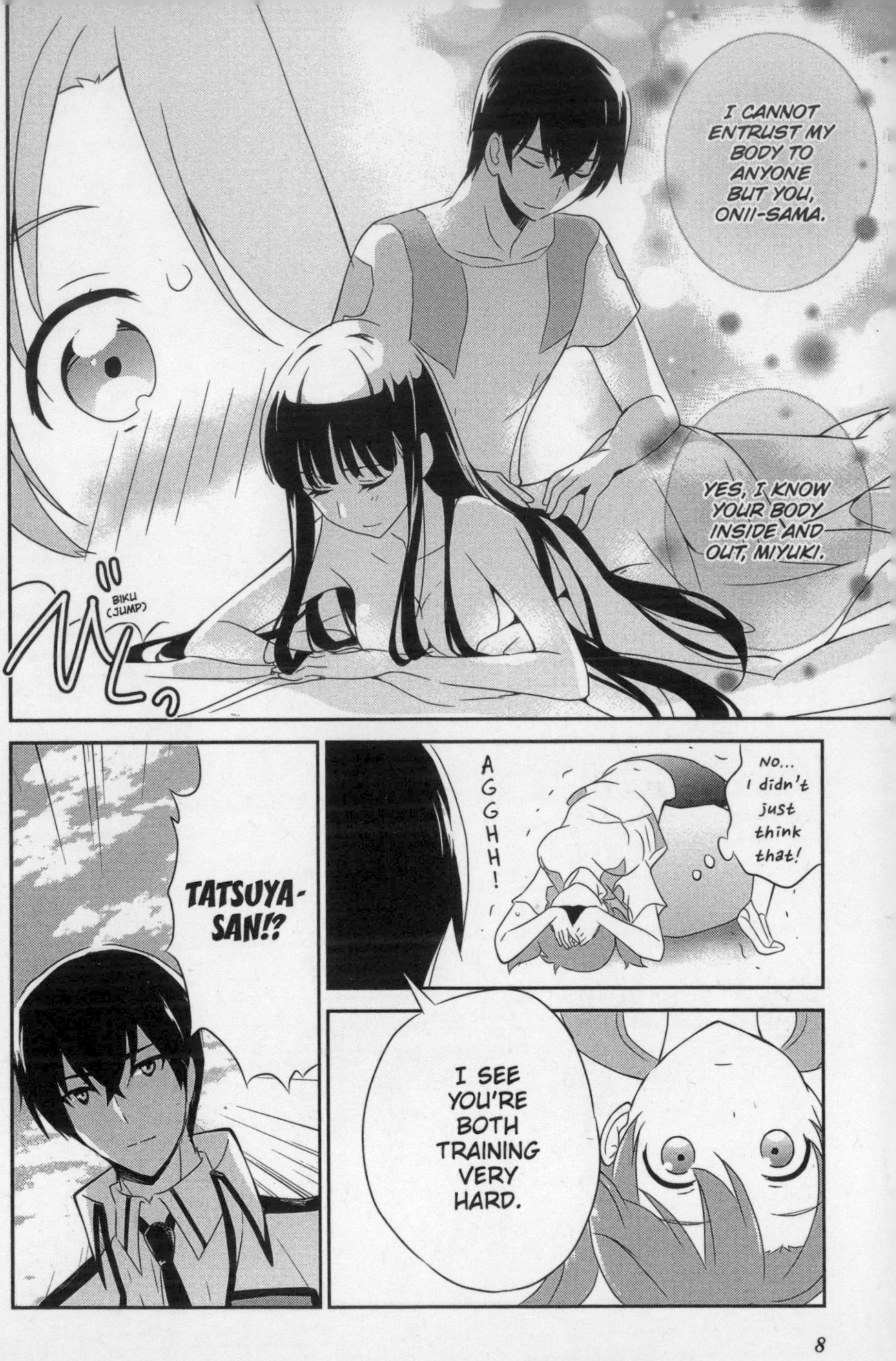
I CANNOT ENTRUST MY BODY TO ANYONE BUT YOU, ONII-SAMA.
YES, I KNOW YOUR BODY INSIDE AND OUT, MIYUKI.
BIKU (JUMP)
No... I didn't just think that!
AGGHH!
I SEE YOU'RE BOTH TRAINING VERY HARD.
TATSUYA-SAN!?

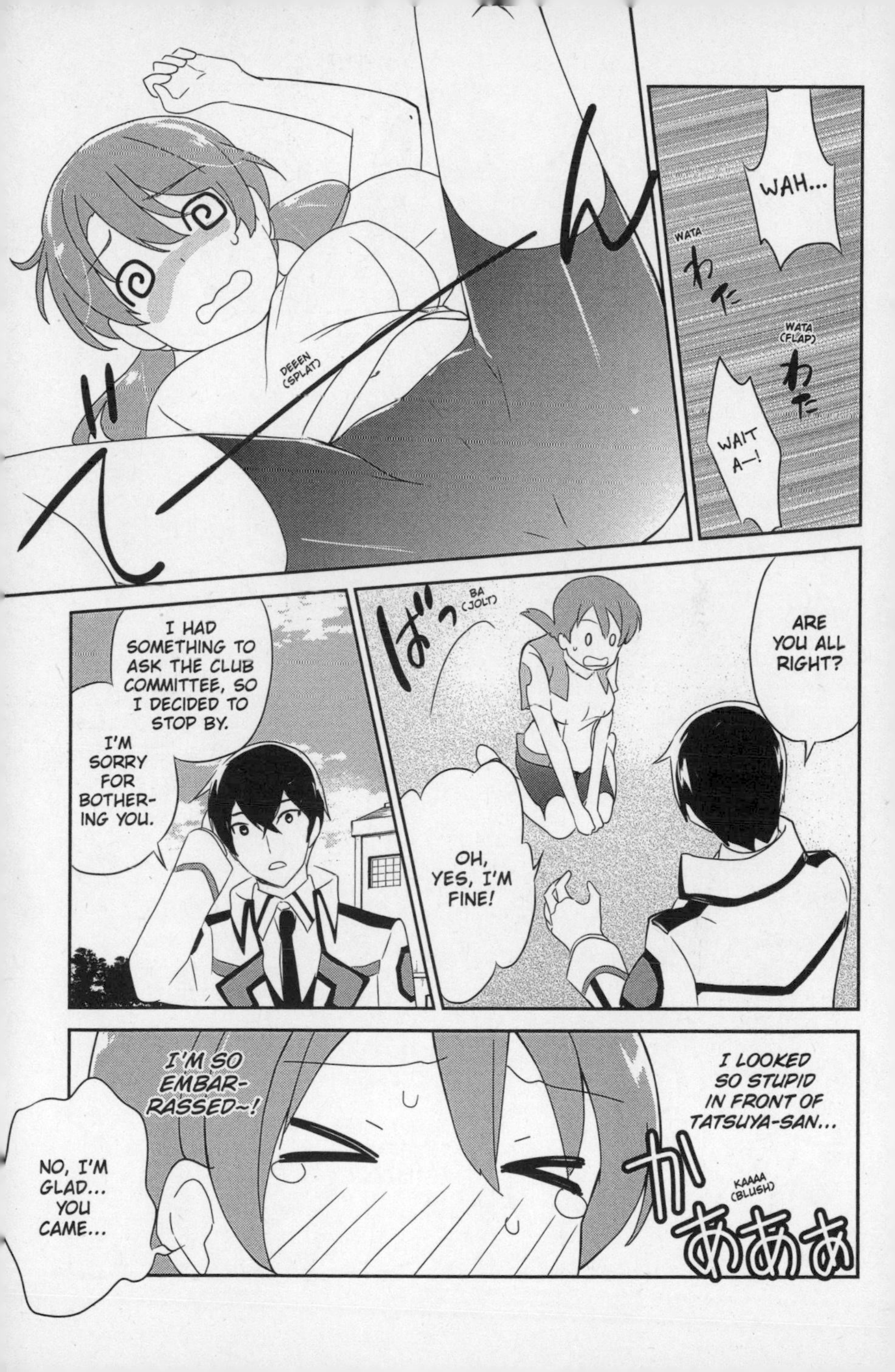
WAH...
WATA
WATA (FLAP)
WAIT A—!
DEEEN (SPLAT)
ARE YOU ALL RIGHT?
BA (JOLT)
OH, YES, I'M FINE!
I HAD SOMETHING TO ASK THE CLUB COMMITTEE, SO I DECIDED TO STOP BY.
I'M SORRY FOR BOTHER-ING YOU.
I LOOKED SO STUPID IN FRONT OF TATSUYA-SAN...
KAAAA (BLUSH)
I'M SO EMBAR-RASSED~!
NO, I'M GLAD... YOU CAME...

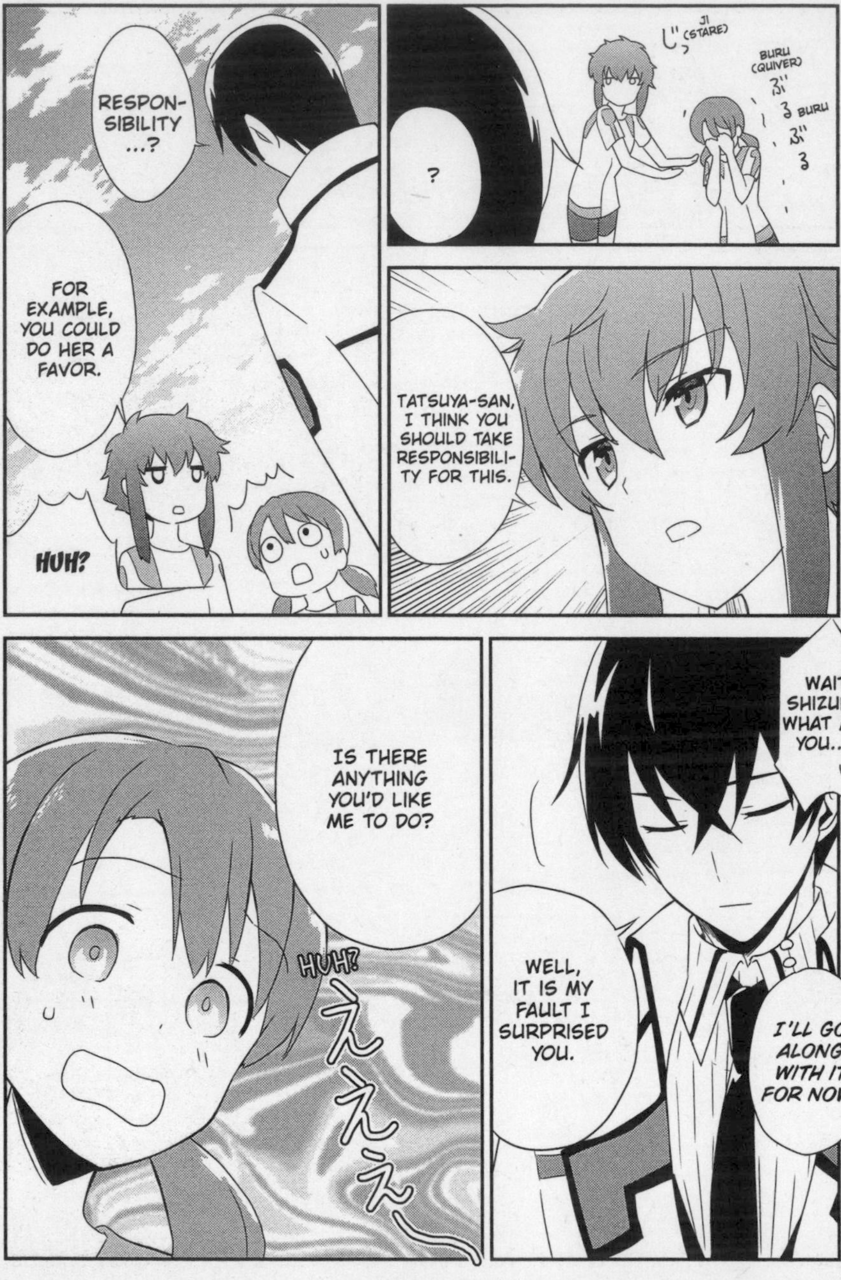

JI (STARE)
じっ
BURU (QUIVER)
ぶる
BURU
ぶる
?
TATSUYA-SAN, I THINK YOU SHOULD TAKE RESPONSIBILITY FOR THIS.
RESPON-SIBILITY ...?
FOR EXAMPLE, YOU COULD DO HER A FAVOR.
HUH?
WAIT, SHIZUKU, WHAT ARE YOU...?
WELL, IT IS MY FAULT I SURPRISED YOU.
I'LL GO ALONG WITH IT FOR NOW.
IS THERE ANYTHING YOU'D LIKE ME TO DO?
HUH?
えええ～

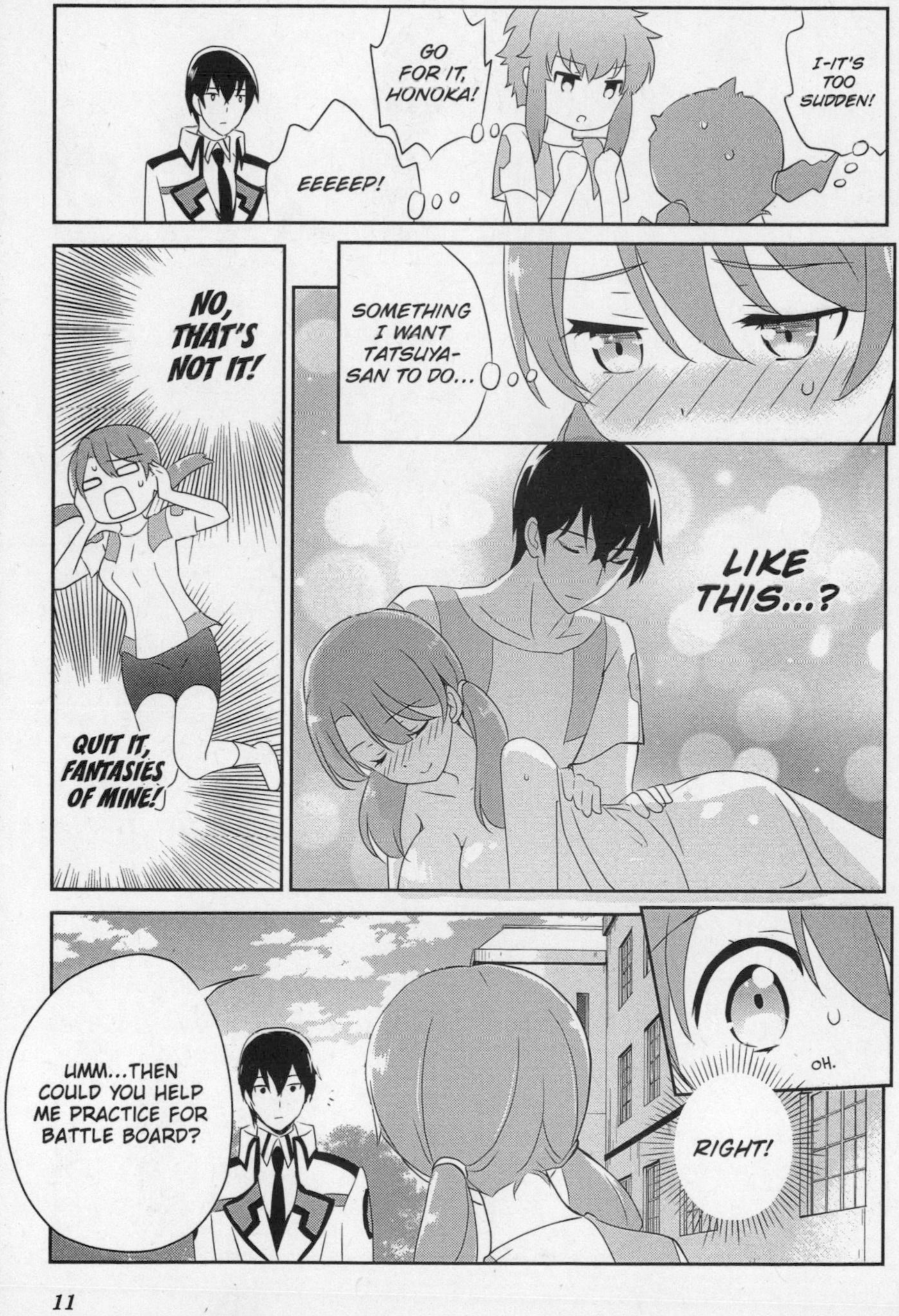
I-IT'S TOO SUDDEN!
GO FOR IT, HONOKA!
EEEEEP!
SOMETHING I WANT TATSUYA-SAN TO DO...
LIKE THIS...?
NO, THAT'S NOT IT!
QUIT IT, FANTASIES OF MINE!
OH.
RIGHT!
UMM...THEN COULD YOU HELP ME PRACTICE FOR BATTLE BOARD?

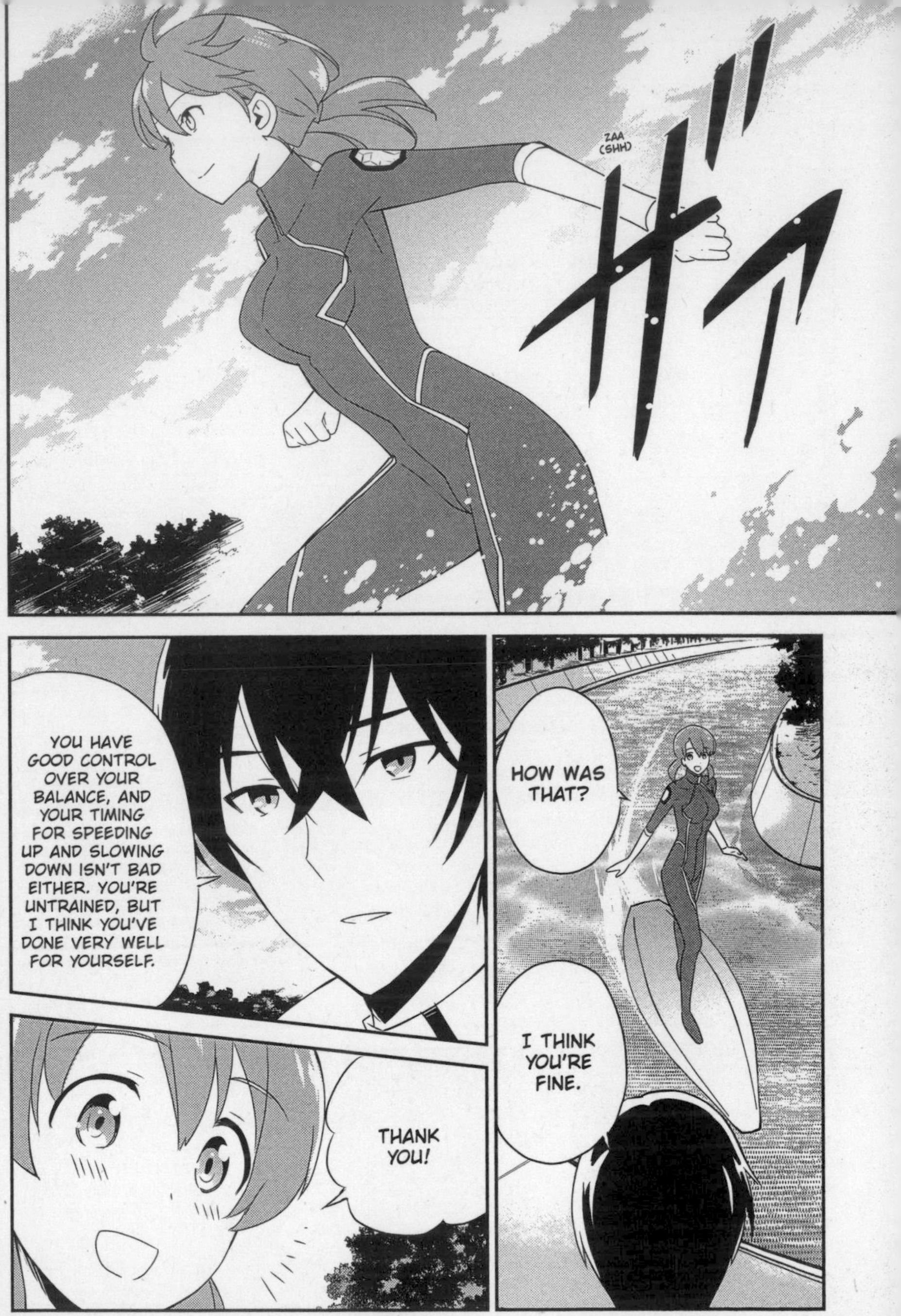
ZAA (SHH)
HOW WAS THAT?
I THINK YOU'RE FINE.
YOU HAVE GOOD CONTROL OVER YOUR BALANCE, AND YOUR TIMING FOR SPEEDING UP AND SLOWING DOWN ISN'T BAD EITHER. YOU'RE UNTRAINED, BUT I THINK YOU'VE DONE VERY WELL FOR YOURSELF.
THANK YOU!

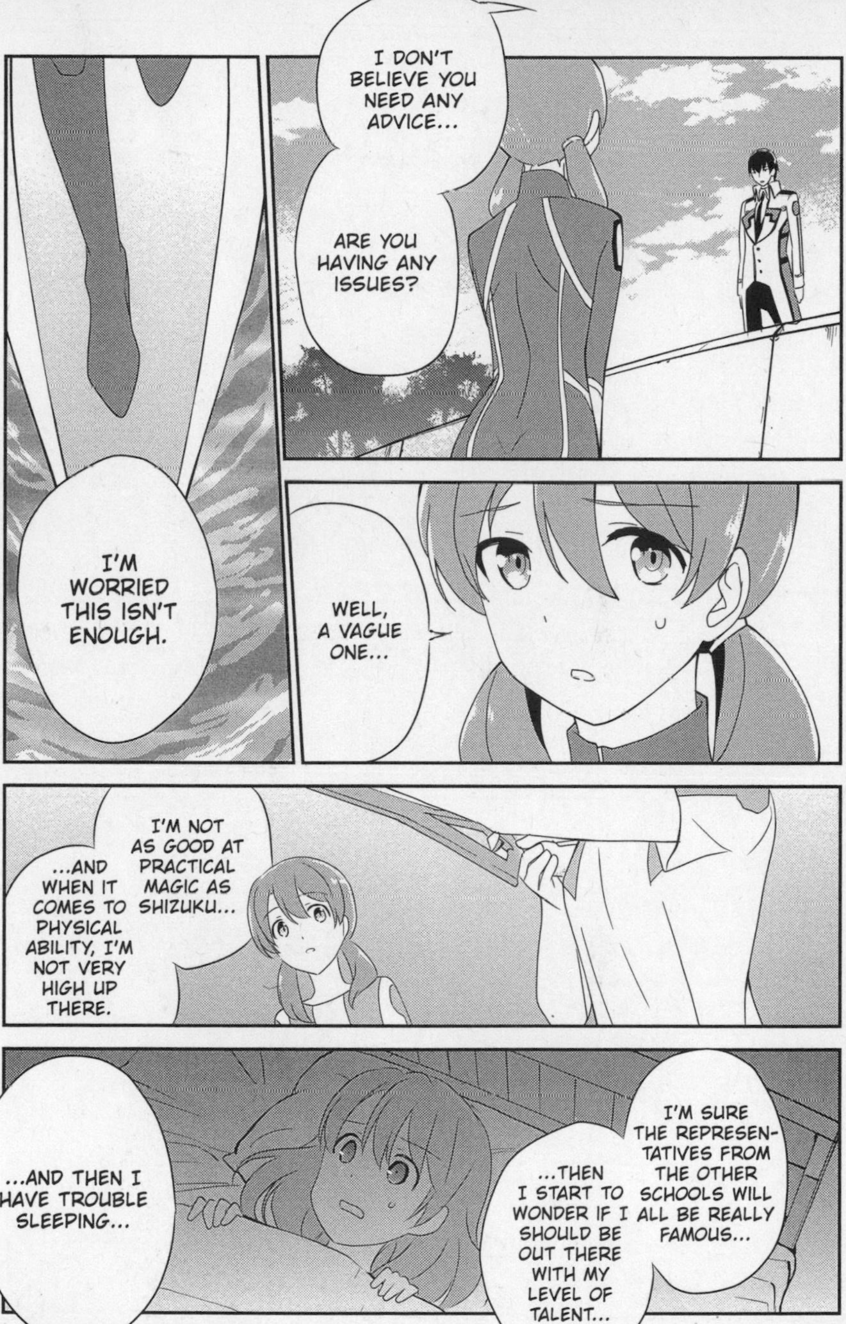
I DON'T BELIEVE YOU NEED ANY ADVICE...
ARE YOU HAVING ANY ISSUES?
WELL, A VAGUE ONE...
I'M WORRIED THIS ISN'T ENOUGH.
I'M NOT AS GOOD AT PRACTICAL MAGIC AS SHIZUKU...
...AND WHEN IT COMES TO PHYSICAL ABILITY, I'M NOT VERY HIGH UP THERE.
I'M SURE THE REPRESENTATIVES FROM THE OTHER SCHOOLS WILL ALL BE REALLY FAMOUS...
...THEN I START TO WONDER IF I SHOULD BE OUT THERE WITH MY LEVEL OF TALENT...
...AND THEN I HAVE TROUBLE SLEEPING...

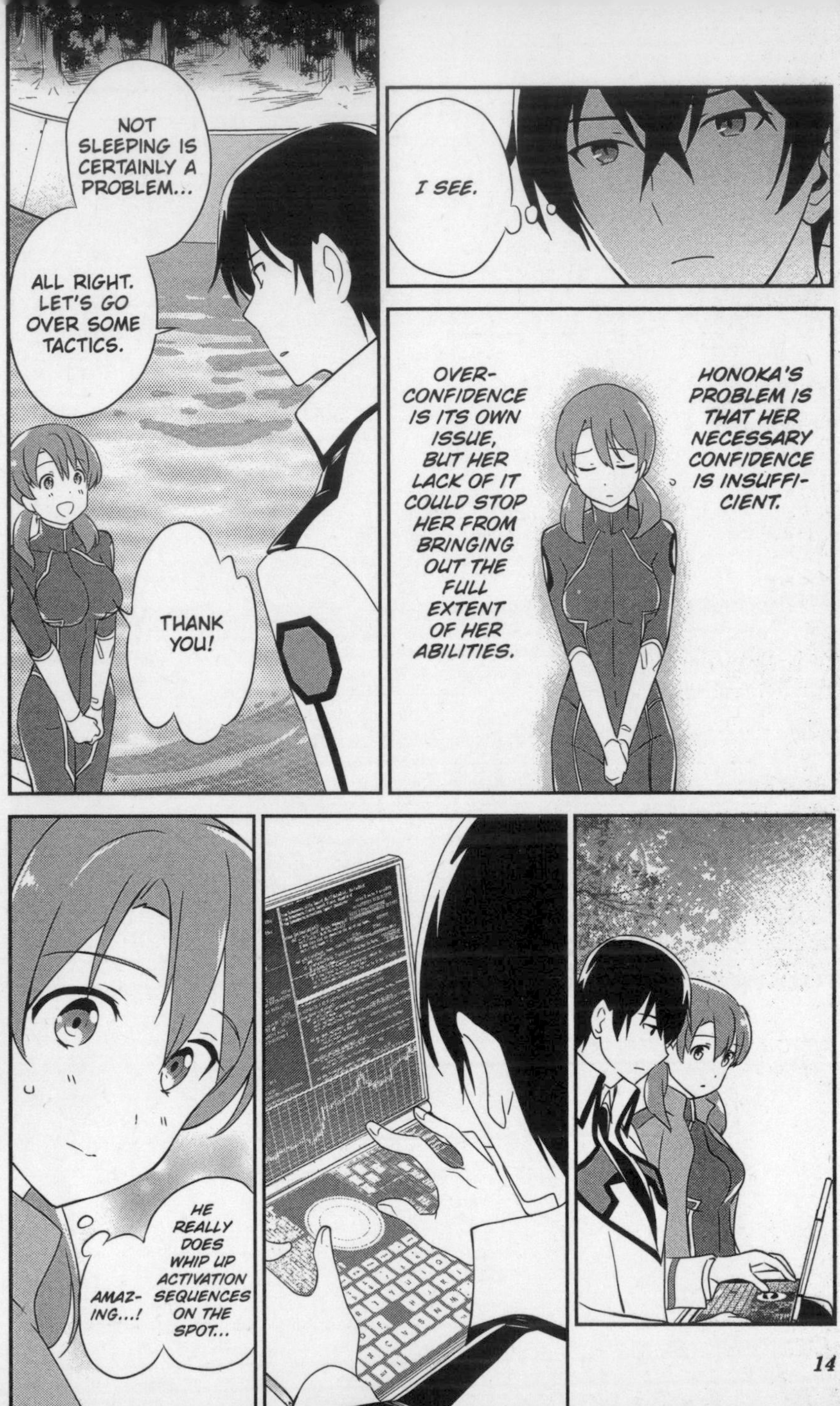
I SEE.
HONOKA'S PROBLEM IS THAT HER NECESSARY CONFIDENCE IS INSUFFICIENT.
OVER-CONFIDENCE IS ITS OWN ISSUE, BUT HER LACK OF IT COULD STOP HER FROM BRINGING OUT THE FULL EXTENT OF HER ABILITIES.
NOT SLEEPING IS CERTAINLY A PROBLEM...
ALL RIGHT. LET'S GO OVER SOME TACTICS.
THANK YOU!
HE REALLY DOES WHIP UP ACTIVATION SEQUENCES ON THE SPOT...
AMAZING...!

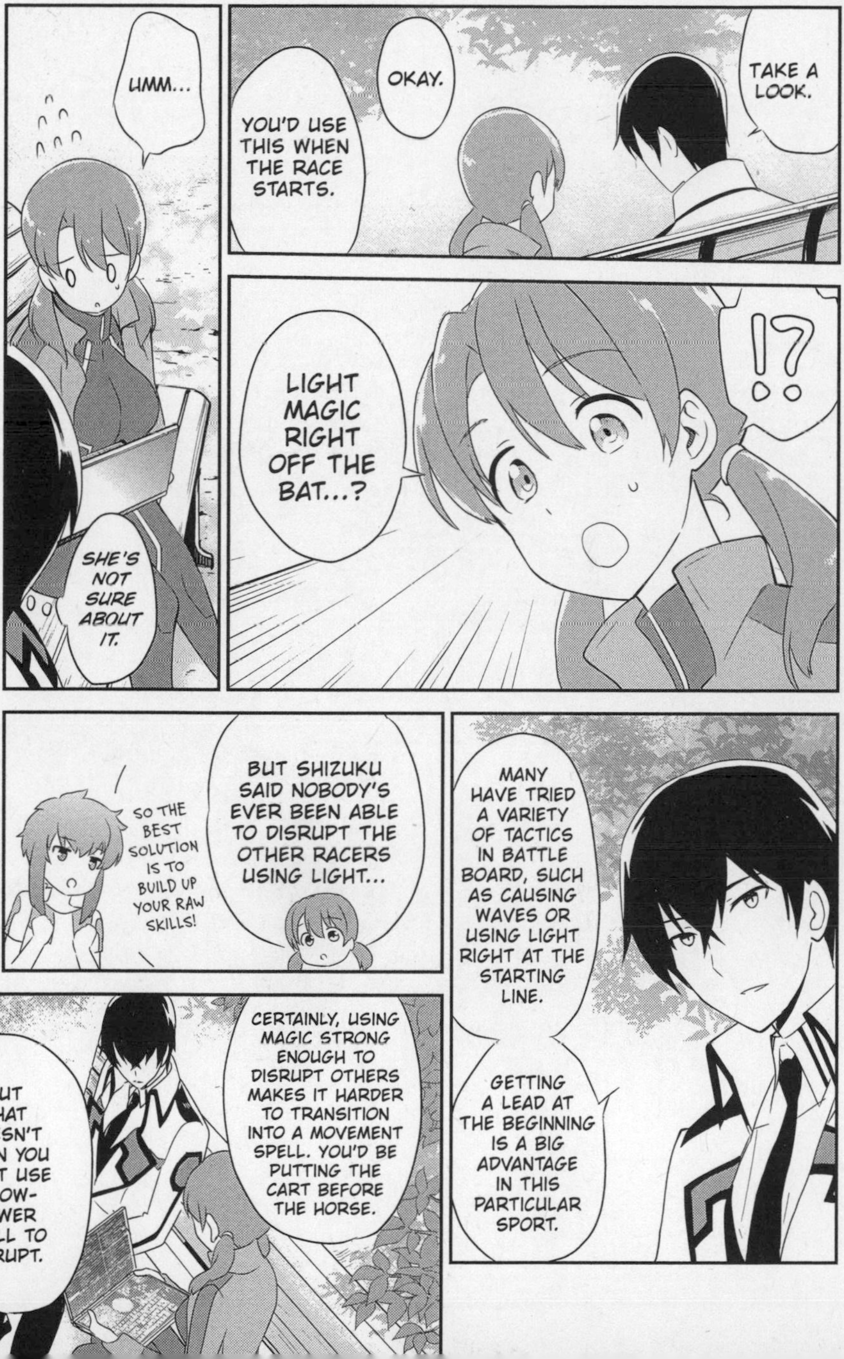
TAKE A LOOK.
OKAY.
YOU'D USE THIS WHEN THE RACE STARTS.
!?
LIGHT MAGIC RIGHT OFF THE BAT...?
UMM...
SHE'S NOT SURE ABOUT IT.
MANY HAVE TRIED A VARIETY OF TACTICS IN BATTLE BOARD, SUCH AS CAUSING WAVES OR USING LIGHT RIGHT AT THE STARTING LINE.
GETTING A LEAD AT THE BEGINNING IS A BIG ADVANTAGE IN THIS PARTICULAR SPORT.
BUT SHIZUKU SAID NOBODY'S EVER BEEN ABLE TO DISRUPT THE OTHER RACERS USING LIGHT...
SO THE BEST SOLUTION IS TO BUILD UP YOUR RAW SKILLS!
CERTAINLY, USING MAGIC STRONG ENOUGH TO DISRUPT OTHERS MAKES IT HARDER TO TRANSITION INTO A MOVEMENT SPELL. YOU'D BE PUTTING THE CART BEFORE THE HORSE.
BUT THAT DOESN'T MEAN YOU CAN'T USE A LOW-POWER SPELL TO DISRUPT.

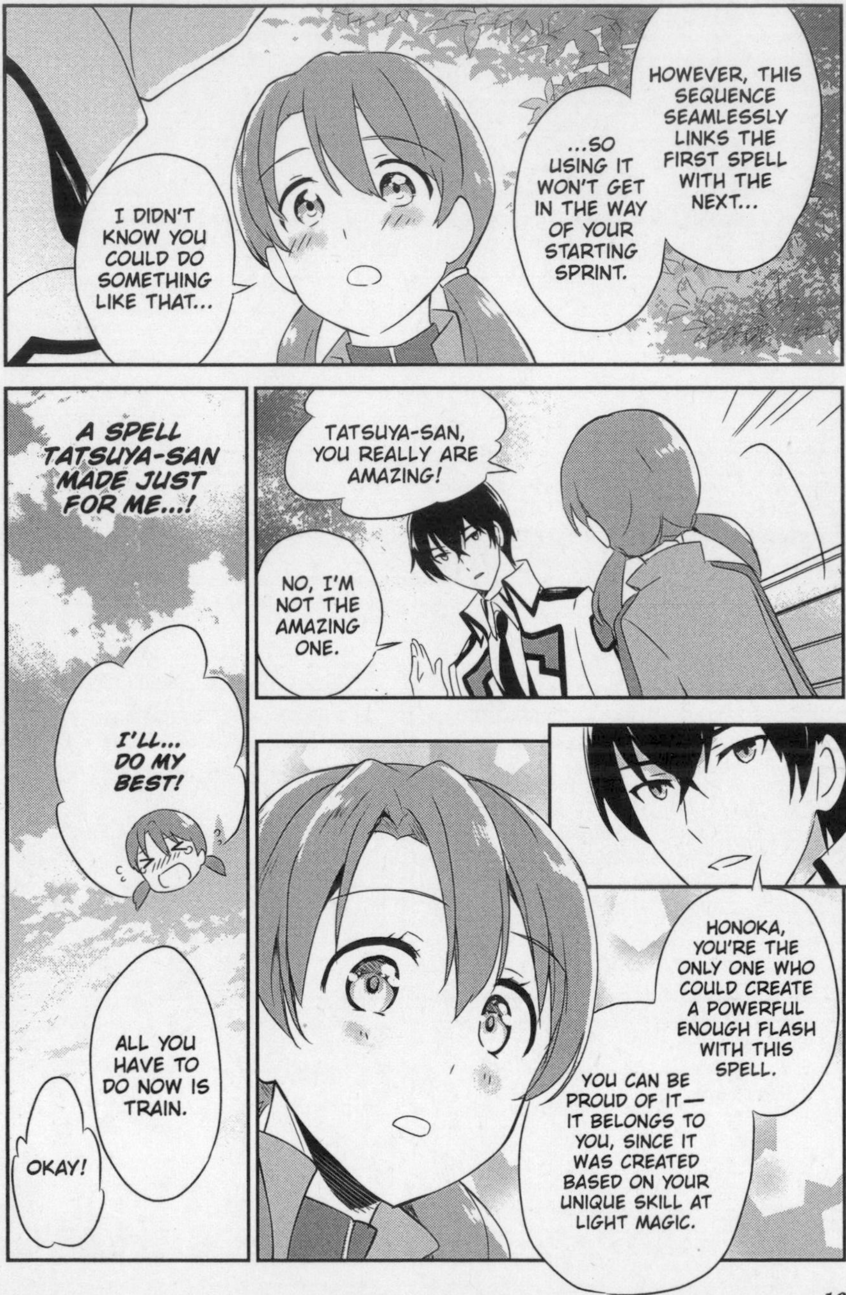
HOWEVER, THIS SEQUENCE SEAMLESSLY LINKS THE FIRST SPELL WITH THE NEXT...
...SO USING IT WON'T GET IN THE WAY OF YOUR STARTING SPRINT.
I DIDN'T KNOW YOU COULD DO SOMETHING LIKE THAT...
TATSUYA-SAN, YOU REALLY ARE AMAZING!
NO, I'M NOT THE AMAZING ONE.
HONOKA, YOU'RE THE ONLY ONE WHO COULD CREATE A POWERFUL ENOUGH FLASH WITH THIS SPELL.
YOU CAN BE PROUD OF IT—IT BELONGS TO YOU, SINCE IT WAS CREATED BASED ON YOUR UNIQUE SKILL AT LIGHT MAGIC.
A SPELL TATSUYA-SAN MADE JUST FOR ME...!
I'LL... DO MY BEST!
ALL YOU HAVE TO DO NOW IS TRAIN.
OKAY!

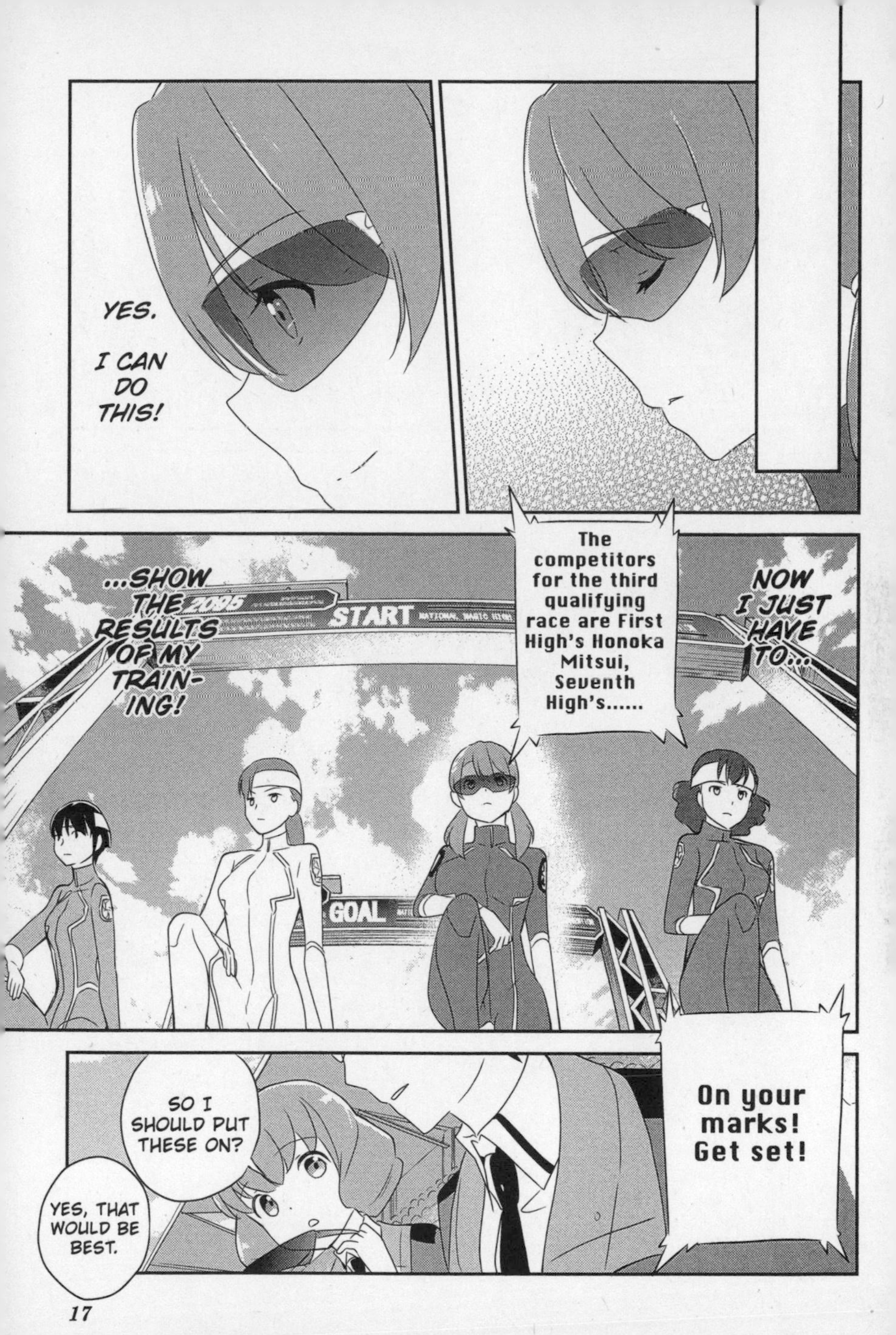
YES.
I CAN DO THIS!
NOW I JUST HAVE TO...
The competitors for the third qualifying race are First High's Honoka Mitsui, Seventh High's......
START
...SHOW THE RESULTS OF MY TRAIN-ING!
GOAL
On your marks! Get set!
SO I SHOULD PUT THESE ON?
YES, THAT WOULD BE BEST.

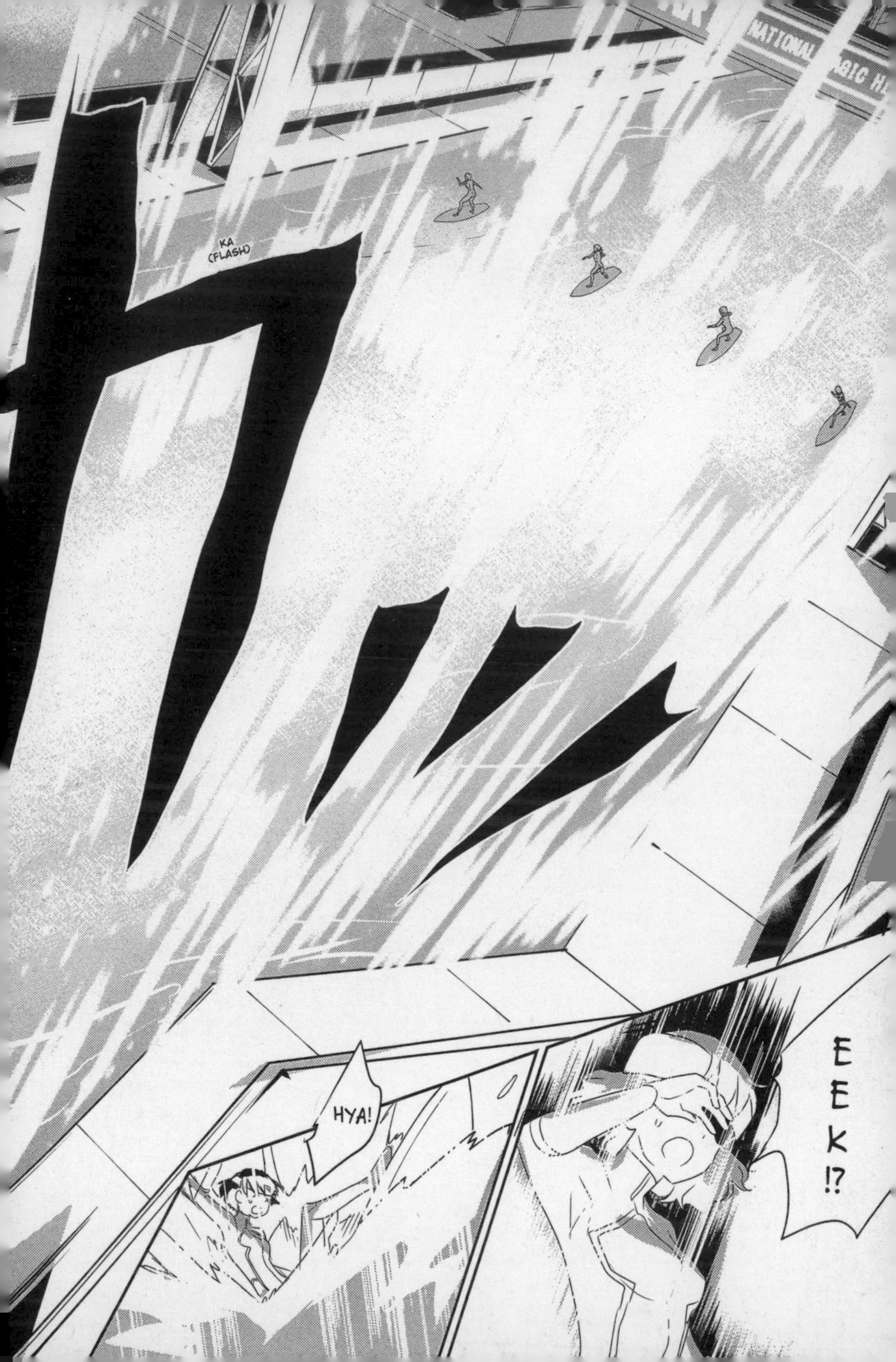
NATIONAL
KA
(FLASH)
EEK!?
HYA!

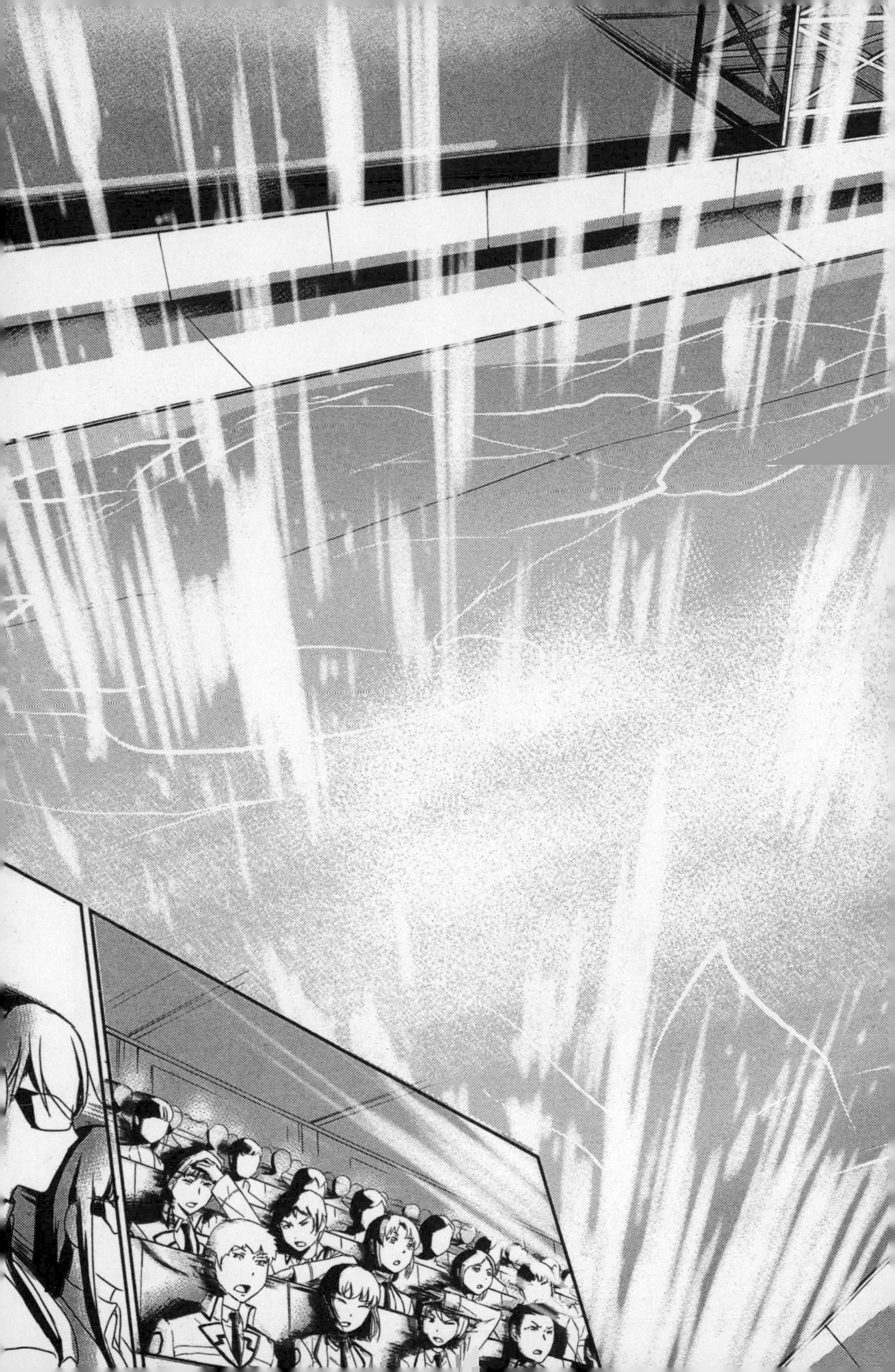

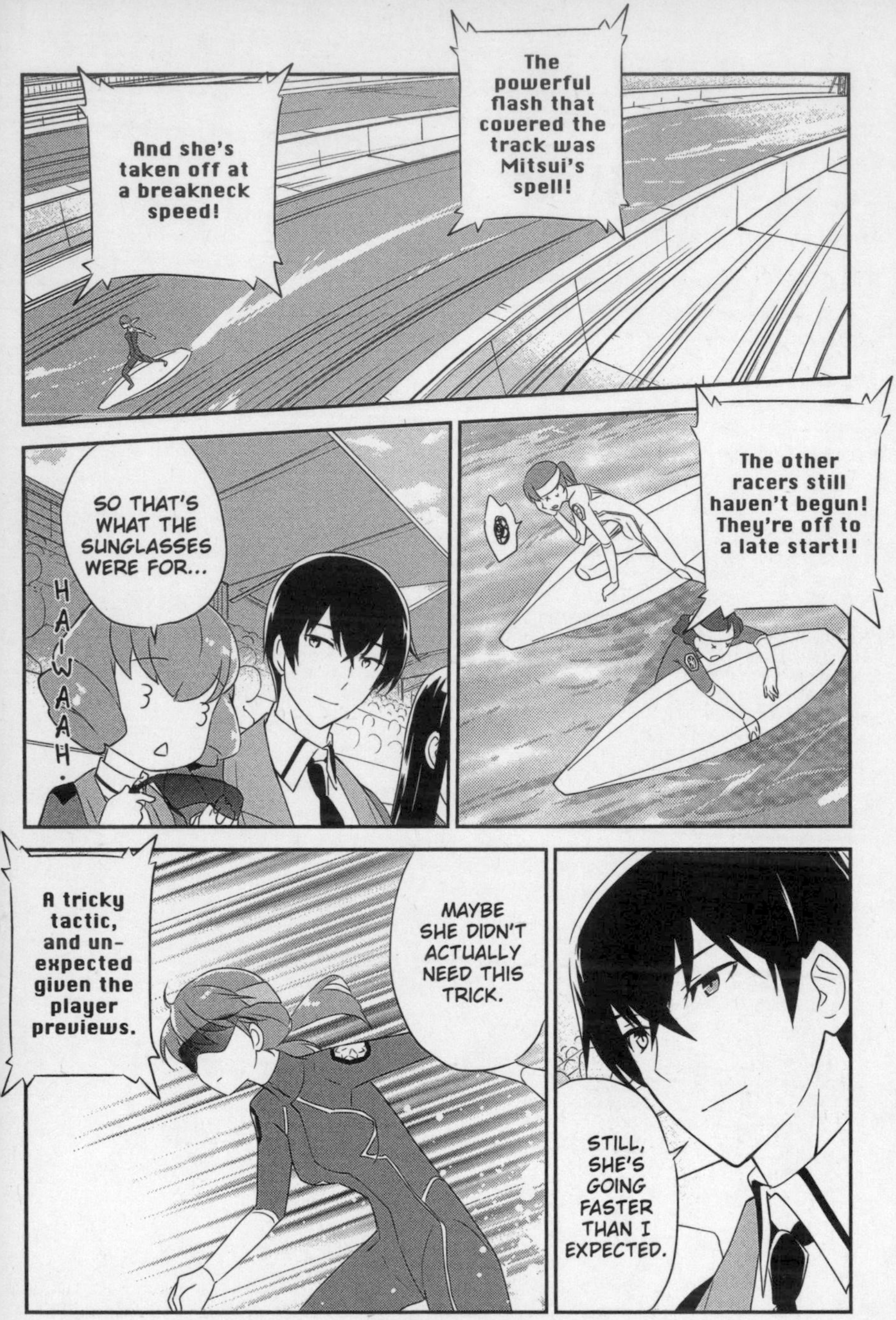

The powerful flash that covered the track was Mitsui's spell!
And she's taken off at a breakneck speed!
The other racers still haven't begun! They're off to a late start!!
SO THAT'S WHAT THE SUNGLASSES WERE FOR...
HAWAAAH.
STILL, SHE'S GOING FASTER THAN I EXPECTED.
MAYBE SHE DIDN'T ACTUALLY NEED THIS TRICK.
A tricky tactic, and un-expected given the player previews.

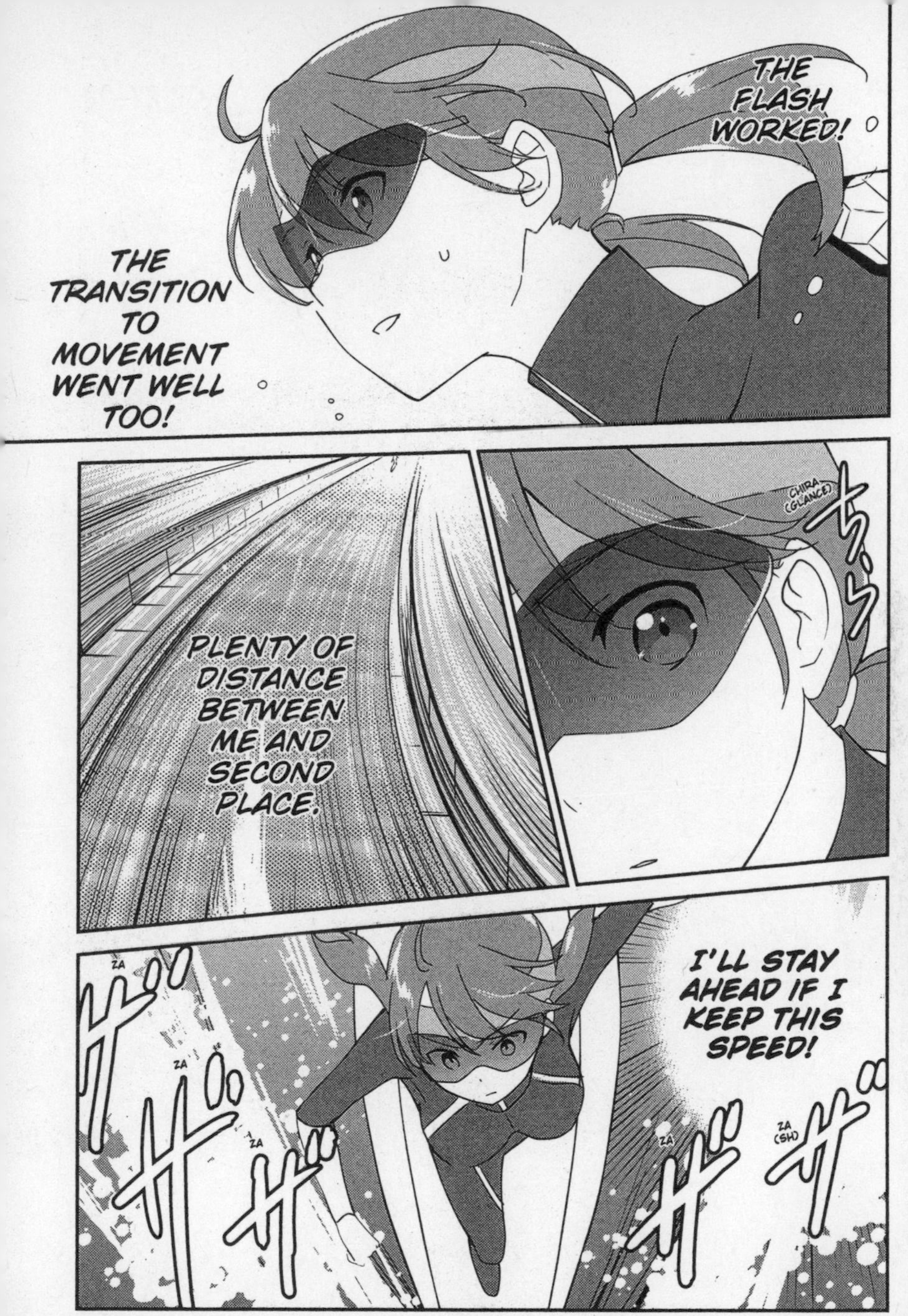
THE FLASH WORKED!
THE TRANSITION TO MOVEMENT WENT WELL TOO!
CHIRA (GLANCE)
PLENTY OF DISTANCE BETWEEN ME AND SECOND PLACE.
I'LL STAY AHEAD IF I KEEP THIS SPEED!
ZA (SH)
ZA
ZA
ZA
ZA

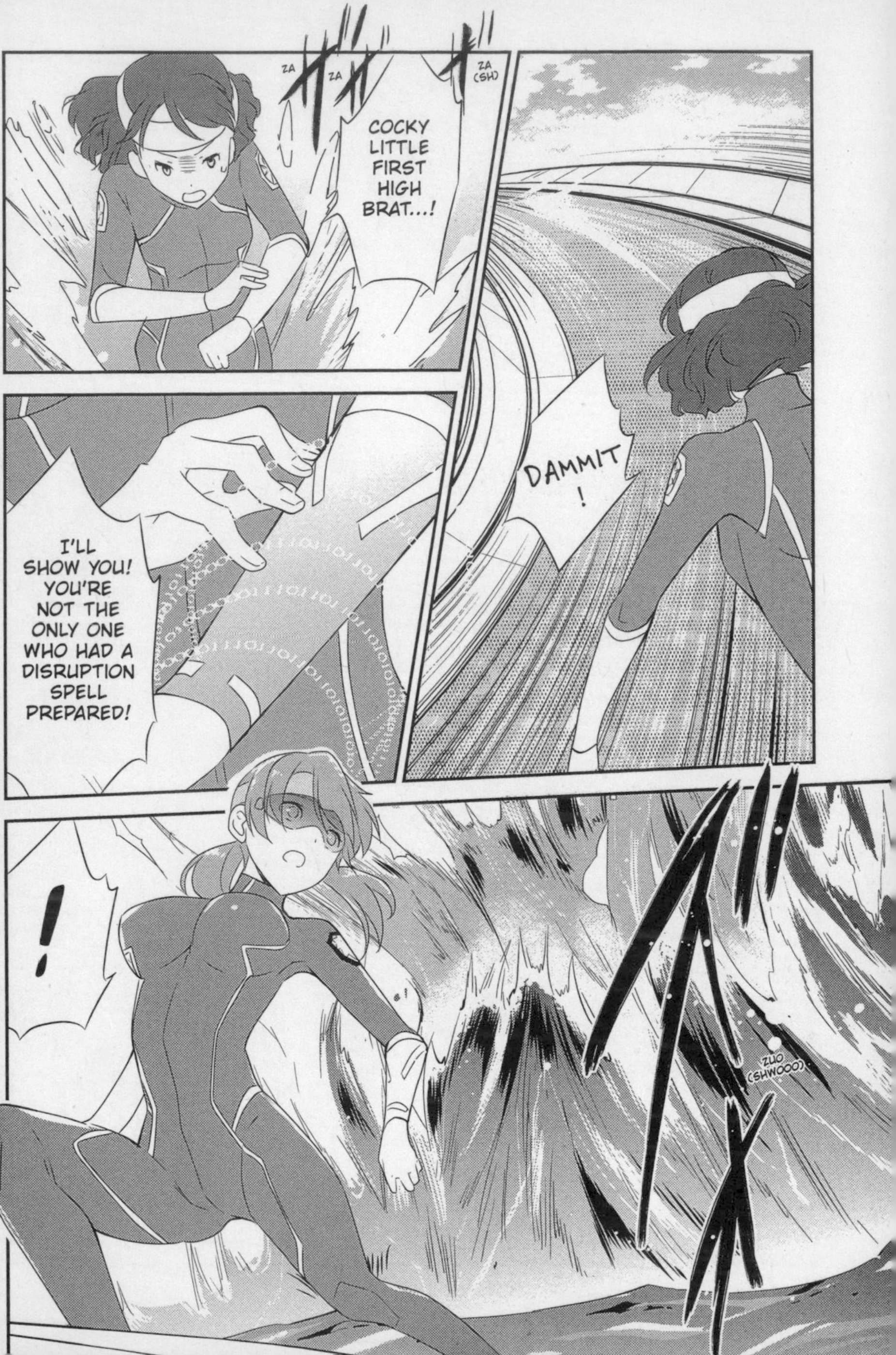
DAMMIT !
ZA ZA ZA (SH)
COCKY LITTLE FIRST HIGH BRAT...!
I'LL SHOW YOU! YOU'RE NOT THE ONLY ONE WHO HAD A DISRUPTION SPELL PREPARED!
ZUO (SHWOOO)
!

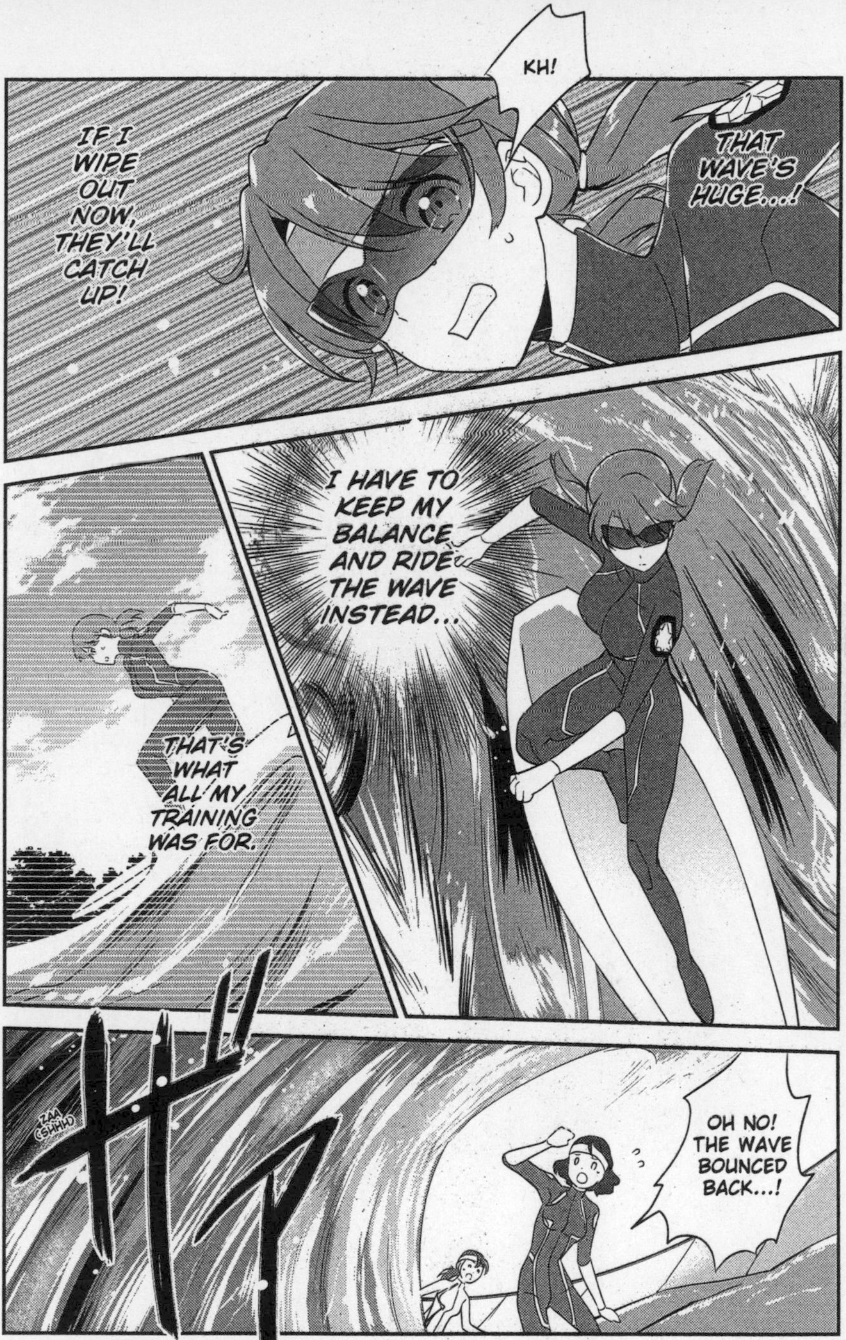
KH!
THAT WAVE'S HUGE...!
IF I WIPE OUT NOW, THEY'LL CATCH UP!
I HAVE TO KEEP MY BALANCE AND RIDE THE WAVE INSTEAD...
THAT'S WHAT ALL MY TRAINING WAS FOR.
OH NO! THE WAVE BOUNCED BACK...!
ザァ
ZAA (SHHH)

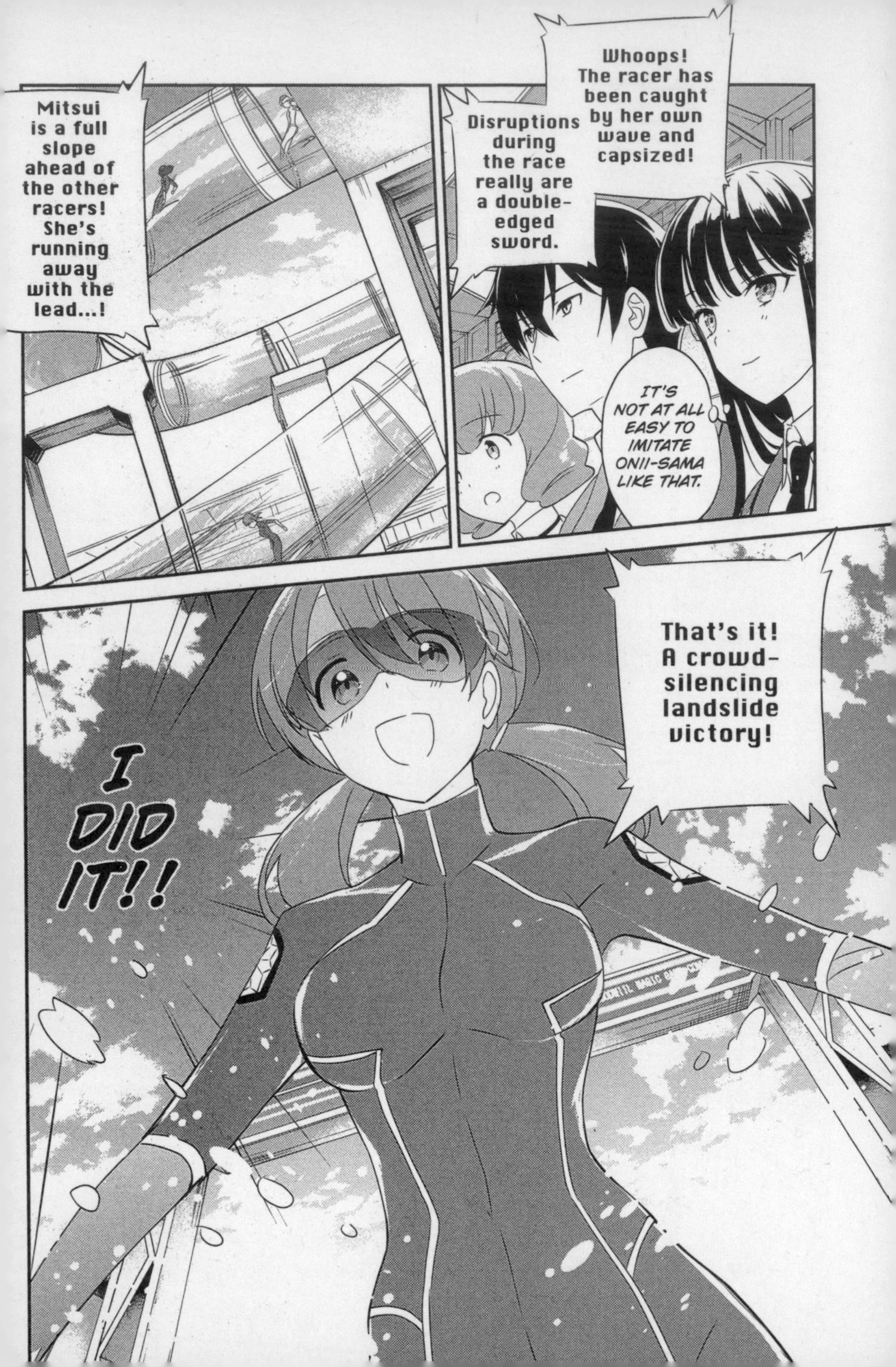
Whoops! The racer has been caught by her own wave and capsized!
Disruptions during the race really are a double-edged sword.
IT'S NOT AT ALL EASY TO IMITATE ONII-SAMA LIKE THAT.
Mitsui is a full slope ahead of the other racers! She's running away with the lead...!
That's it! A crowd-silencing landslide victory!
I DID IT!!

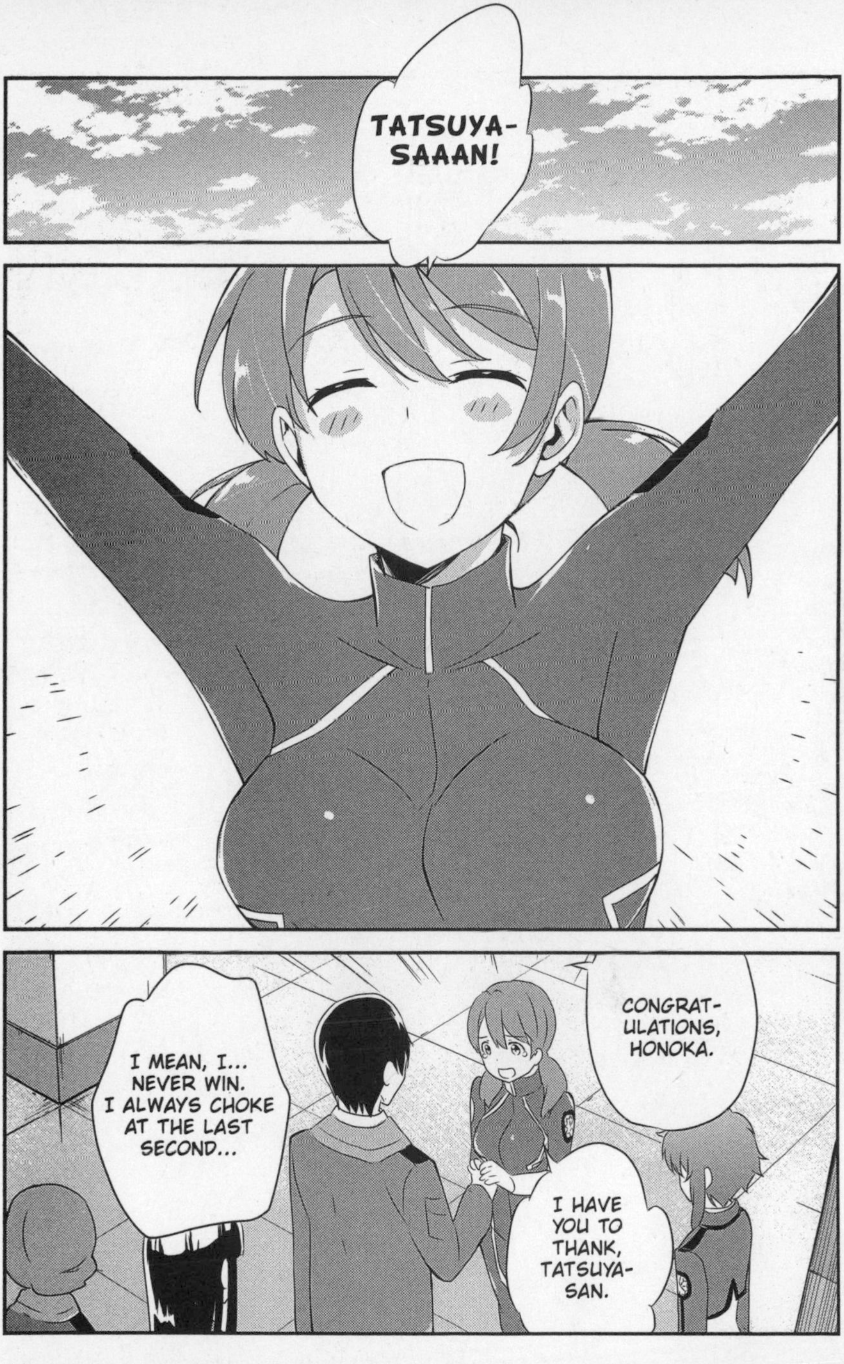
TATSUYA-SAAAN!
CONGRAT-ULATIONS, HONOKA.
I HAVE YOU TO THANK, TATSUYA-SAN.
I MEAN, I... NEVER WIN. I ALWAYS CHOKE AT THE LAST SECOND...

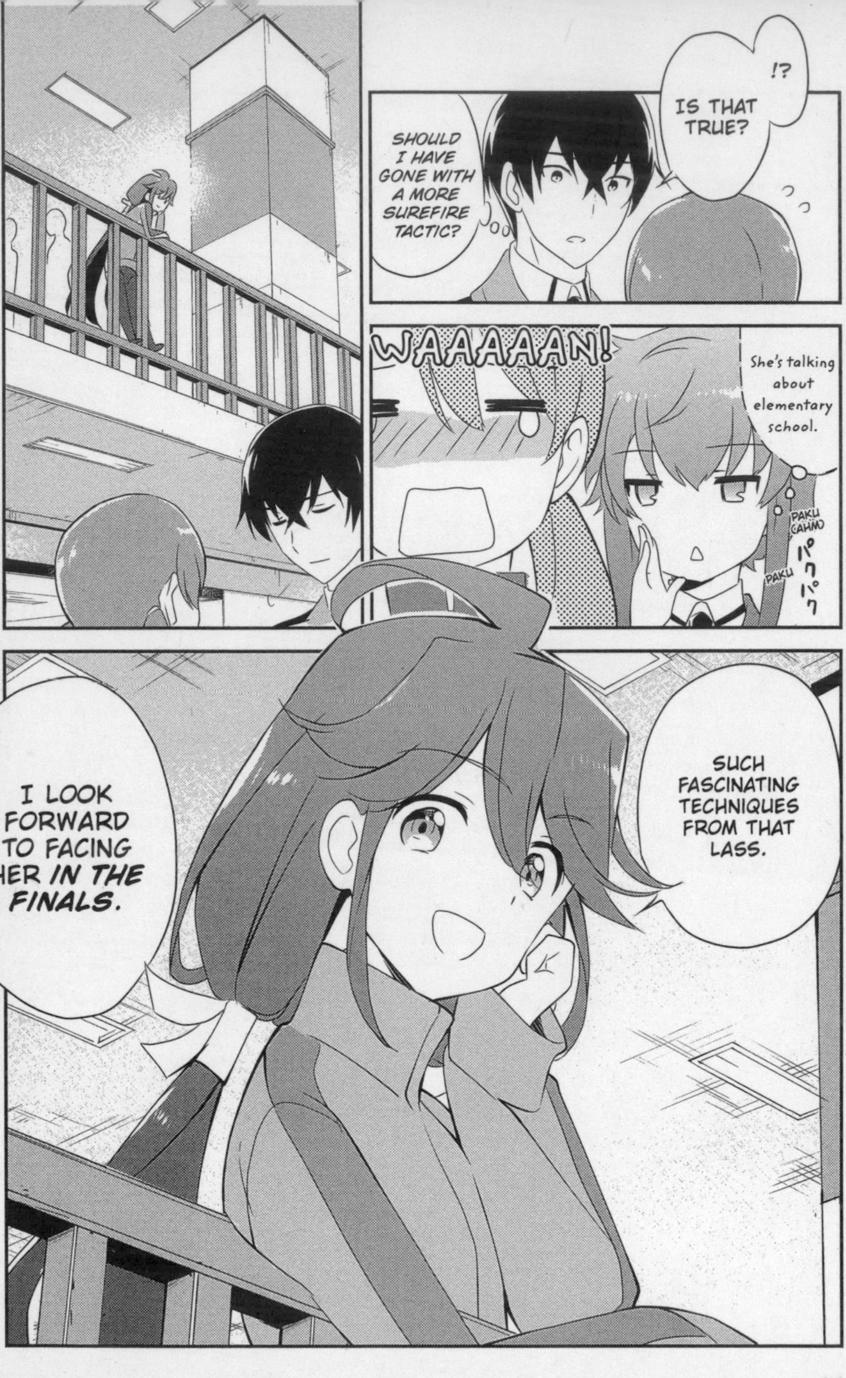

!? IS THAT TRUE?
SHOULD I HAVE GONE WITH A MORE SUREFIRE TACTIC?
She's talking about elementary school.
PAKU (CHOMP) パク
PAKU パク
WAAAAAN!
SUCH FASCINATING TECHNIQUES FROM THAT LASS.
I LOOK FORWARD TO FACING HER *IN THE FINALS*.

THE
HONOR
STUDENT
AT
Magic High
School

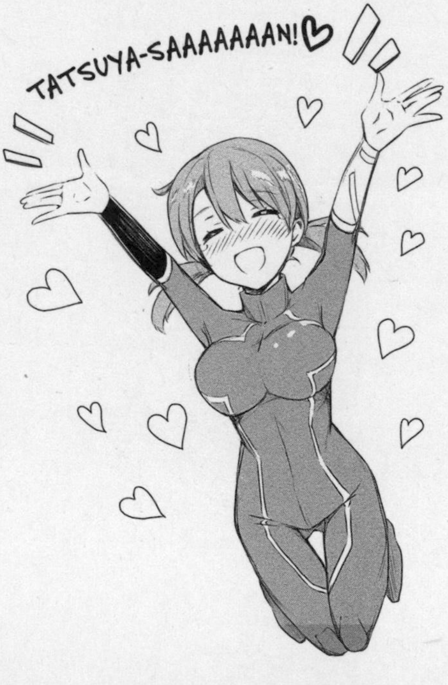
TATSUYA-SAAAAAAAN!♡

CHAPTER 32

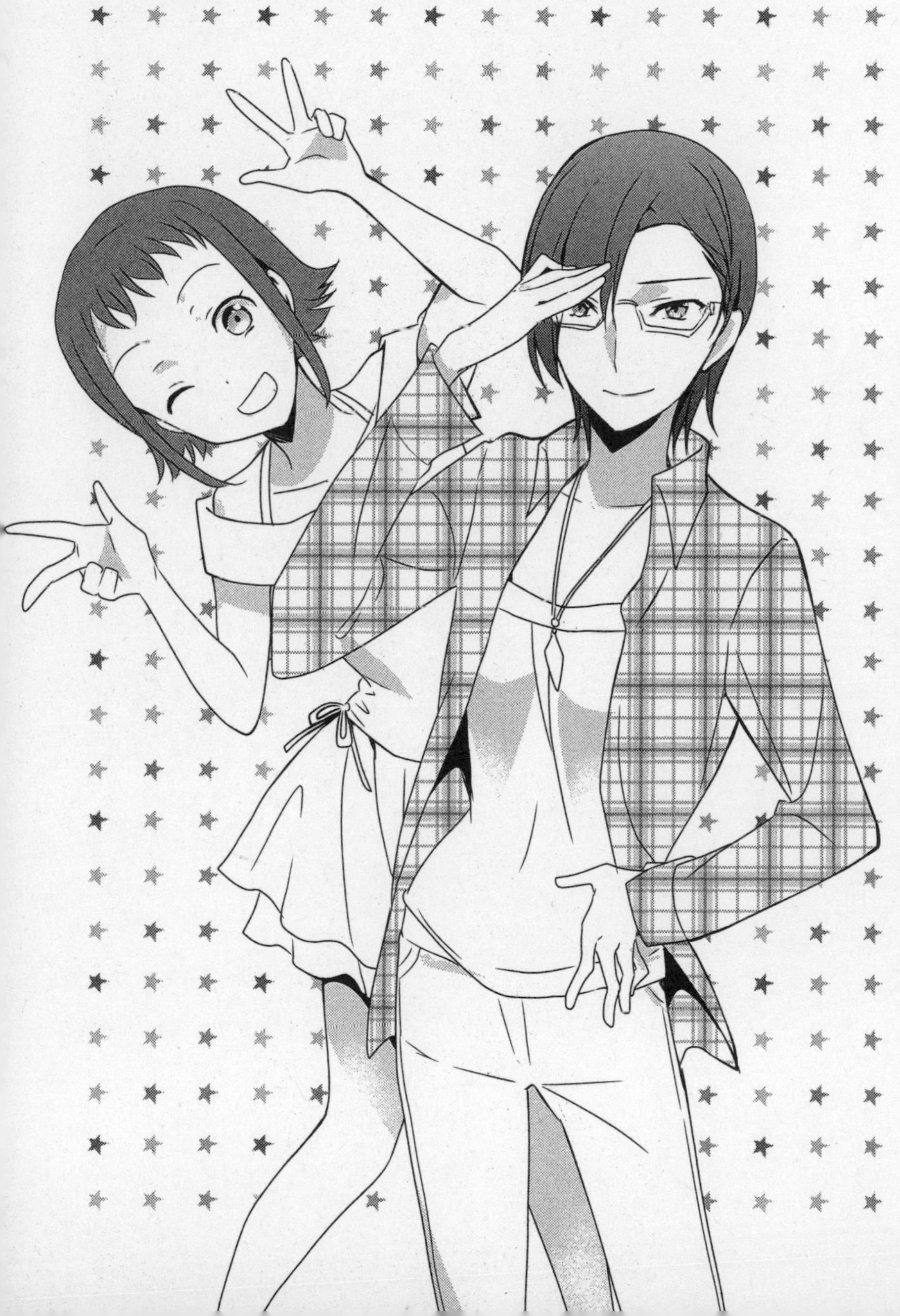

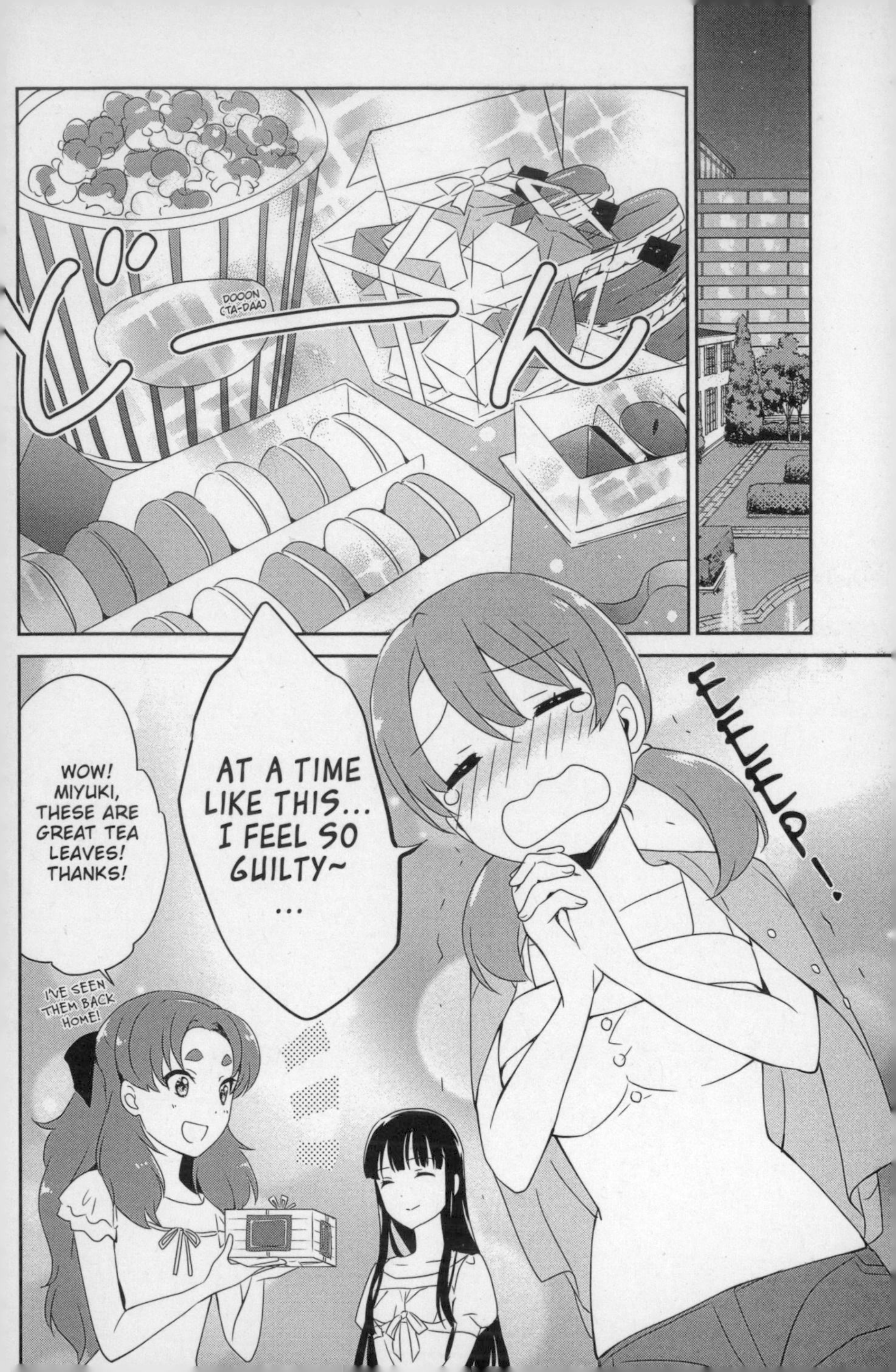
どーん
DOOON (TA-DAA)
EEEEEP!!
AT A TIME LIKE THIS... I FEEL SO GUILTY~ ...
WOW! MIYUKI, THESE ARE GREAT TEA LEAVES! THANKS!
I'VE SEEN THEM BACK HOME!

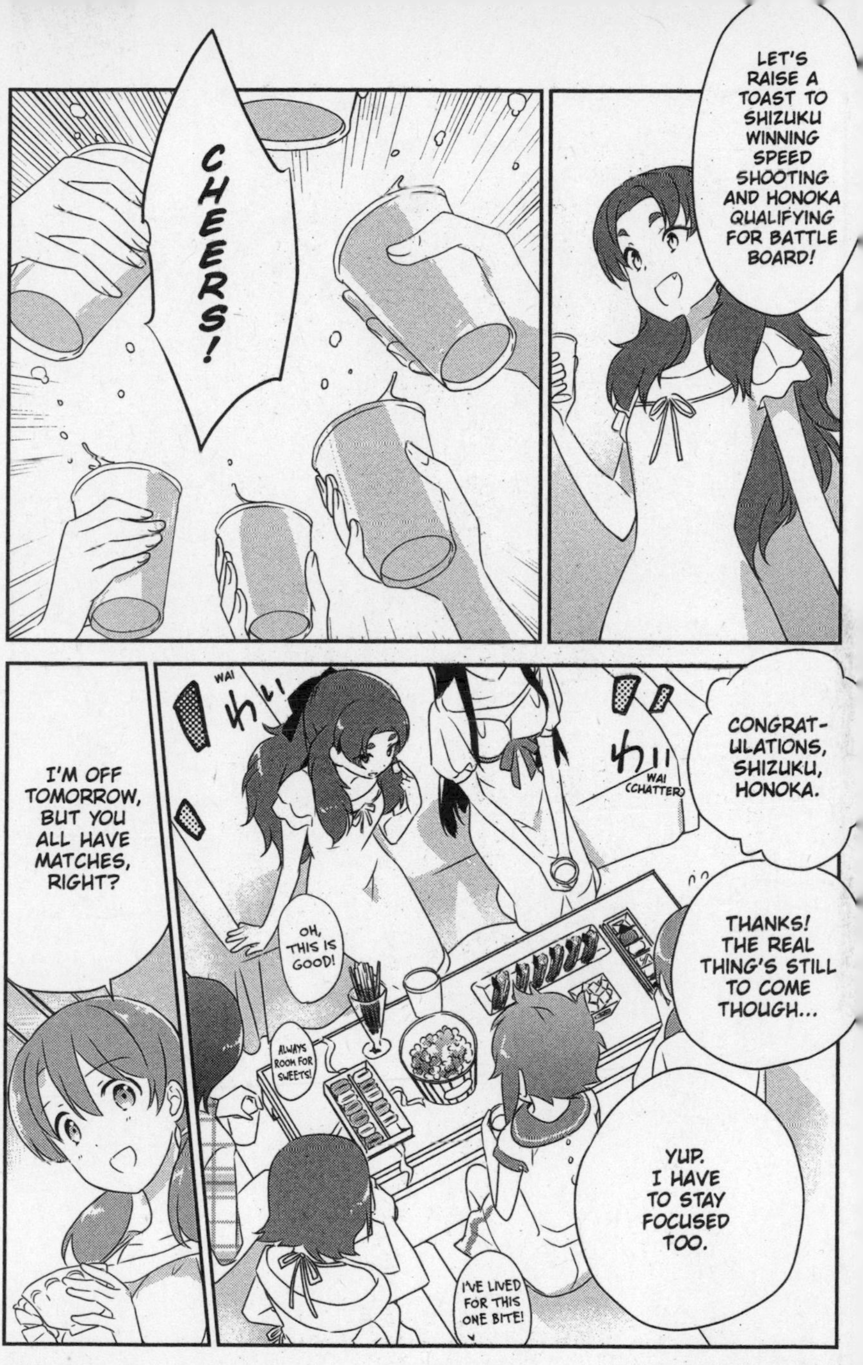
LET'S RAISE A TOAST TO SHIZUKU WINNING SPEED SHOOTING AND HONOKA QUALIFYING FOR BATTLE BOARD!
CHEERS!
わい WAI
わい WAI (CHATTER)
CONGRAT-ULATIONS, SHIZUKU, HONOKA.
THANKS! THE REAL THING'S STILL TO COME THOUGH...
OH, THIS IS GOOD!
ALWAYS ROOM FOR SWEETS!
YUP. I HAVE TO STAY FOCUSED TOO.
I'VE LIVED FOR THIS ONE BITE!
I'M OFF TOMORROW, BUT YOU ALL HAVE MATCHES, RIGHT?

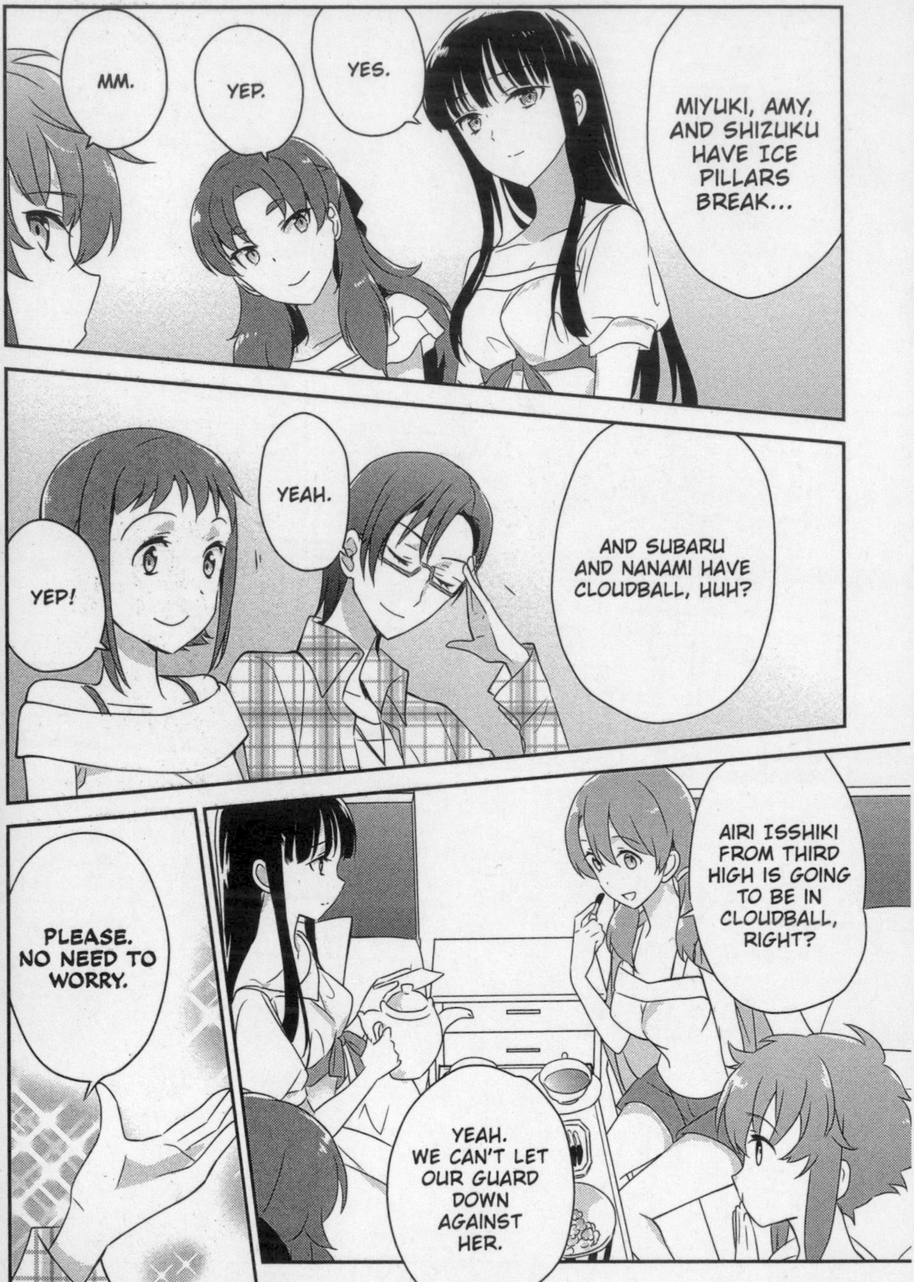
MIYUKI, AMY, AND SHIZUKU HAVE ICE PILLARS BREAK...
YES.
YEP.
MM.
AND SUBARU AND NANAMI HAVE CLOUDBALL, HUH?
YEAH.
YEP!
AIRI ISSHIKI FROM THIRD HIGH IS GOING TO BE IN CLOUDBALL, RIGHT?
YEAH. WE CAN'T LET OUR GUARD DOWN AGAINST HER.
PLEASE. NO NEED TO WORRY.

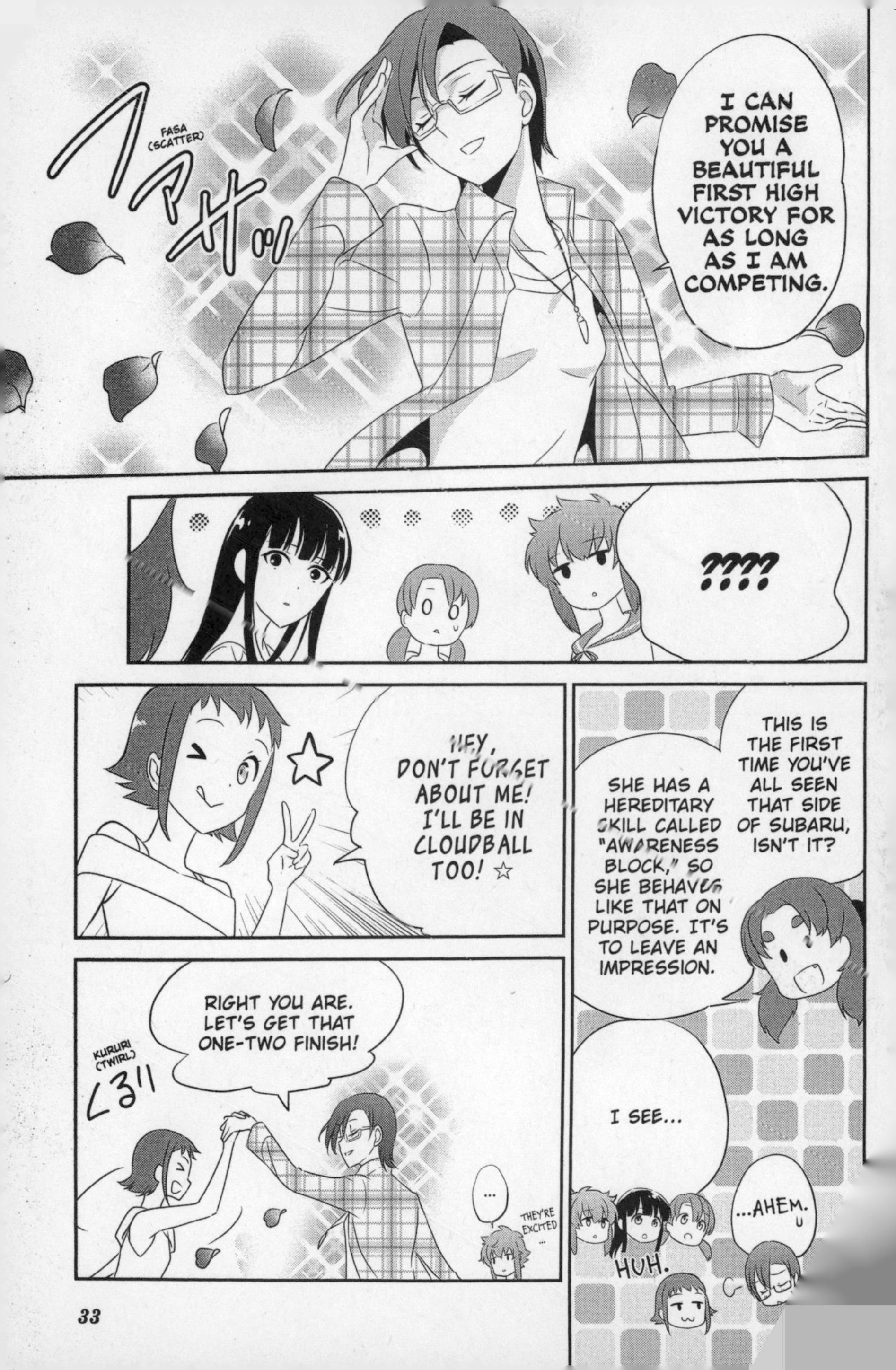
I CAN PROMISE YOU A BEAUTIFUL FIRST HIGH VICTORY FOR AS LONG AS I AM COMPETING.
FASA (SCATTER)
ファサッ
????
THIS IS THE FIRST TIME YOU'VE ALL SEEN THAT SIDE OF SUBARU, ISN'T IT?
SHE HAS A HEREDITARY SKILL CALLED "AWARENESS BLOCK," SO SHE BEHAVES LIKE THAT ON PURPOSE. IT'S TO LEAVE AN IMPRESSION.
I SEE...
...AHEM.
HUH.
HEY, DON'T FORGET ABOUT ME! I'LL BE IN CLOUDBALL TOO! ☆
RIGHT YOU ARE. LET'S GET THAT ONE-TWO FINISH!
KURURI (TWIRL)
くるり
...
THEY'RE EXCITED ...

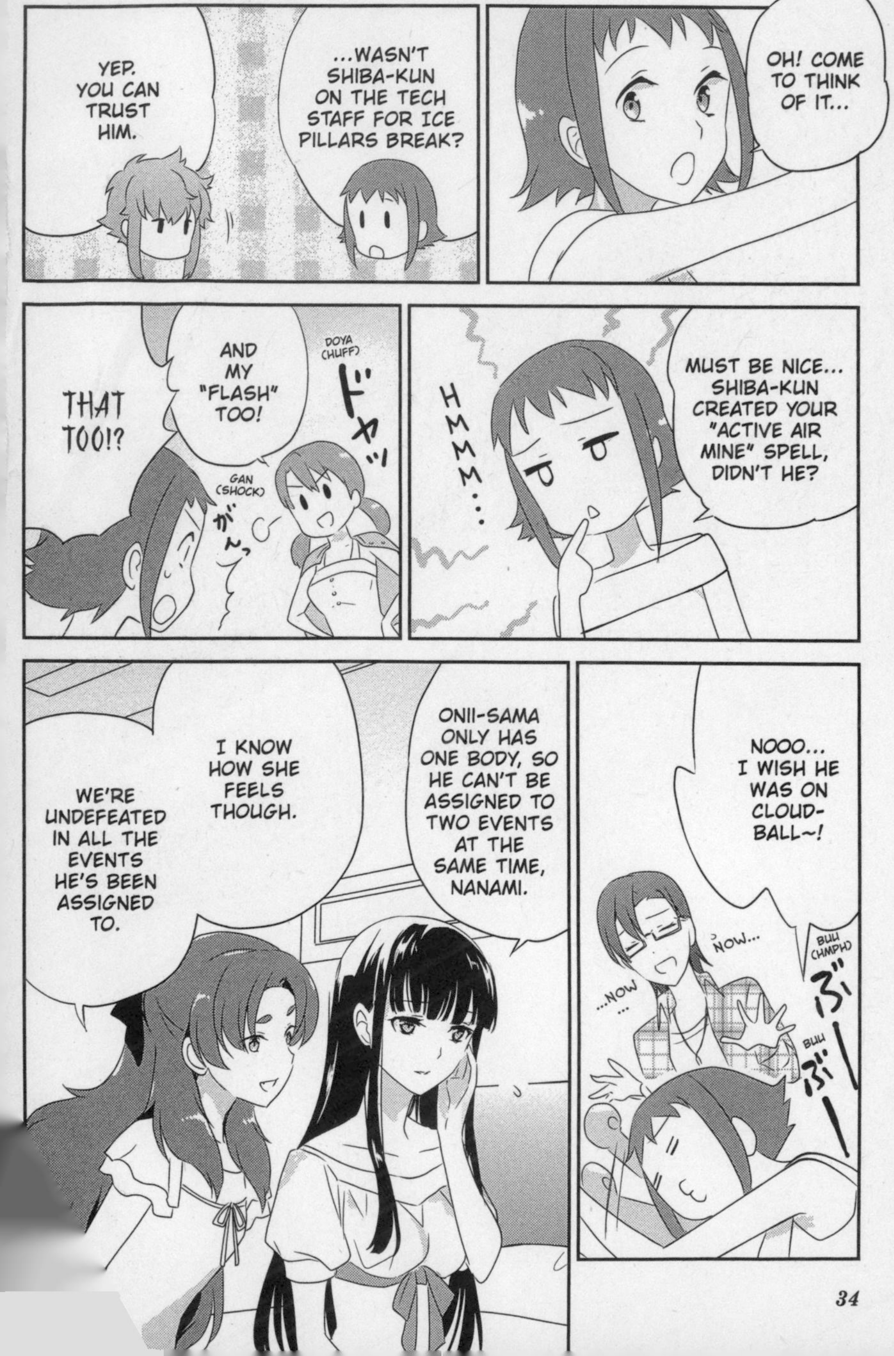
OH! COME TO THINK OF IT...
...WASN'T SHIBA-KUN ON THE TECH STAFF FOR ICE PILLARS BREAK?
YEP. YOU CAN TRUST HIM.
MUST BE NICE... SHIBA-KUN CREATED YOUR "ACTIVE AIR MINE" SPELL, DIDN'T HE?
HMMM...
DOYA (HUFF)
ドヤッ
AND MY "FLASH" TOO!
THAT TOO!?
GAN (SHOCK)
がんっ
NOOO... I WISH HE WAS ON CLOUD-BALL~!
BUU (HMPH)
ぶー
NOW...
BUU
ぶー
...NOW ...
ONII-SAMA ONLY HAS ONE BODY, SO HE CAN'T BE ASSIGNED TO TWO EVENTS AT THE SAME TIME, NANAMI.
I KNOW HOW SHE FEELS THOUGH.
WE'RE UNDEFEATED IN ALL THE EVENTS HE'S BEEN ASSIGNED TO.

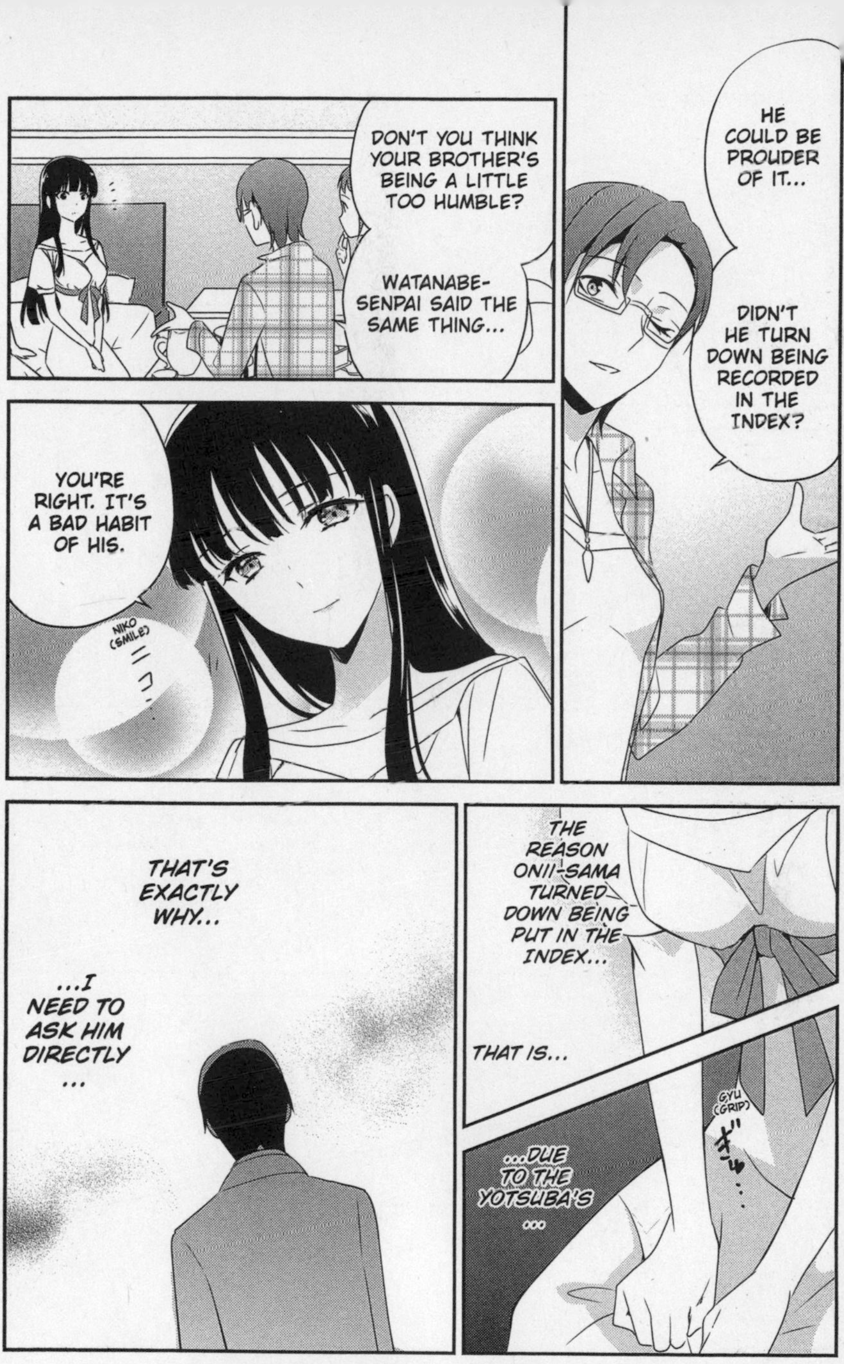
HE COULD BE PROUDER OF IT...
DIDN'T HE TURN DOWN BEING RECORDED IN THE INDEX?
DON'T YOU THINK YOUR BROTHER'S BEING A LITTLE TOO HUMBLE?
WATANABE-SENPAI SAID THE SAME THING...
YOU'RE RIGHT. IT'S A BAD HABIT OF HIS.
NIKO (SMILE)
THE REASON ONII-SAMA TURNED DOWN BEING PUT IN THE INDEX...
THAT IS...
...DUE TO THE YOTSUBA'S ...
GYU (GRIP)
THAT'S EXACTLY WHY...
...I NEED TO ASK HIM DIRECTLY ...

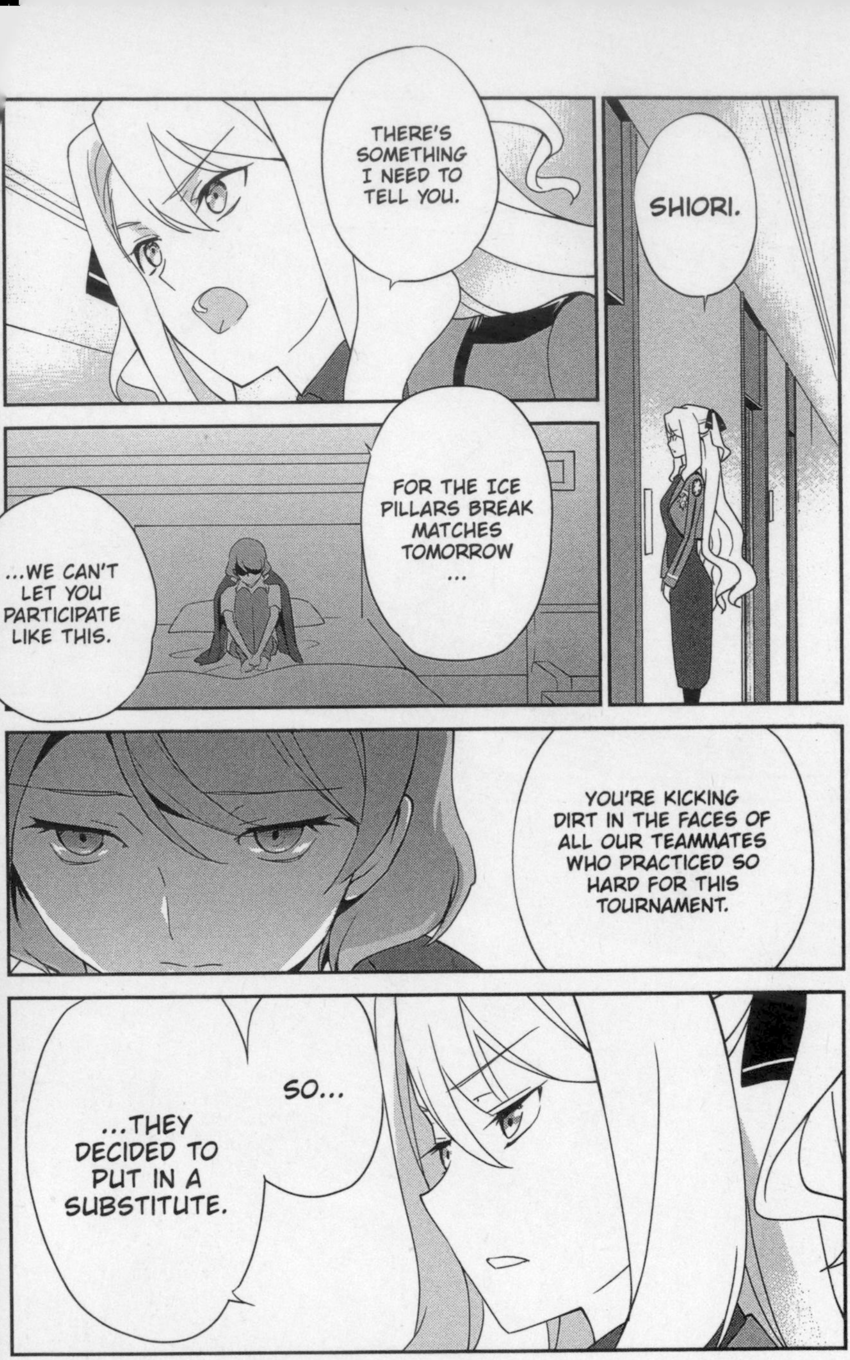
SHIORI.
THERE'S SOMETHING I NEED TO TELL YOU.
FOR THE ICE PILLARS BREAK MATCHES TOMORROW...
...WE CAN'T LET YOU PARTICIPATE LIKE THIS.
YOU'RE KICKING DIRT IN THE FACES OF ALL OUR TEAMMATES WHO PRACTICED SO HARD FOR THIS TOURNAMENT.
SO...
...THEY DECIDED TO PUT IN A SUBSTITUTE.

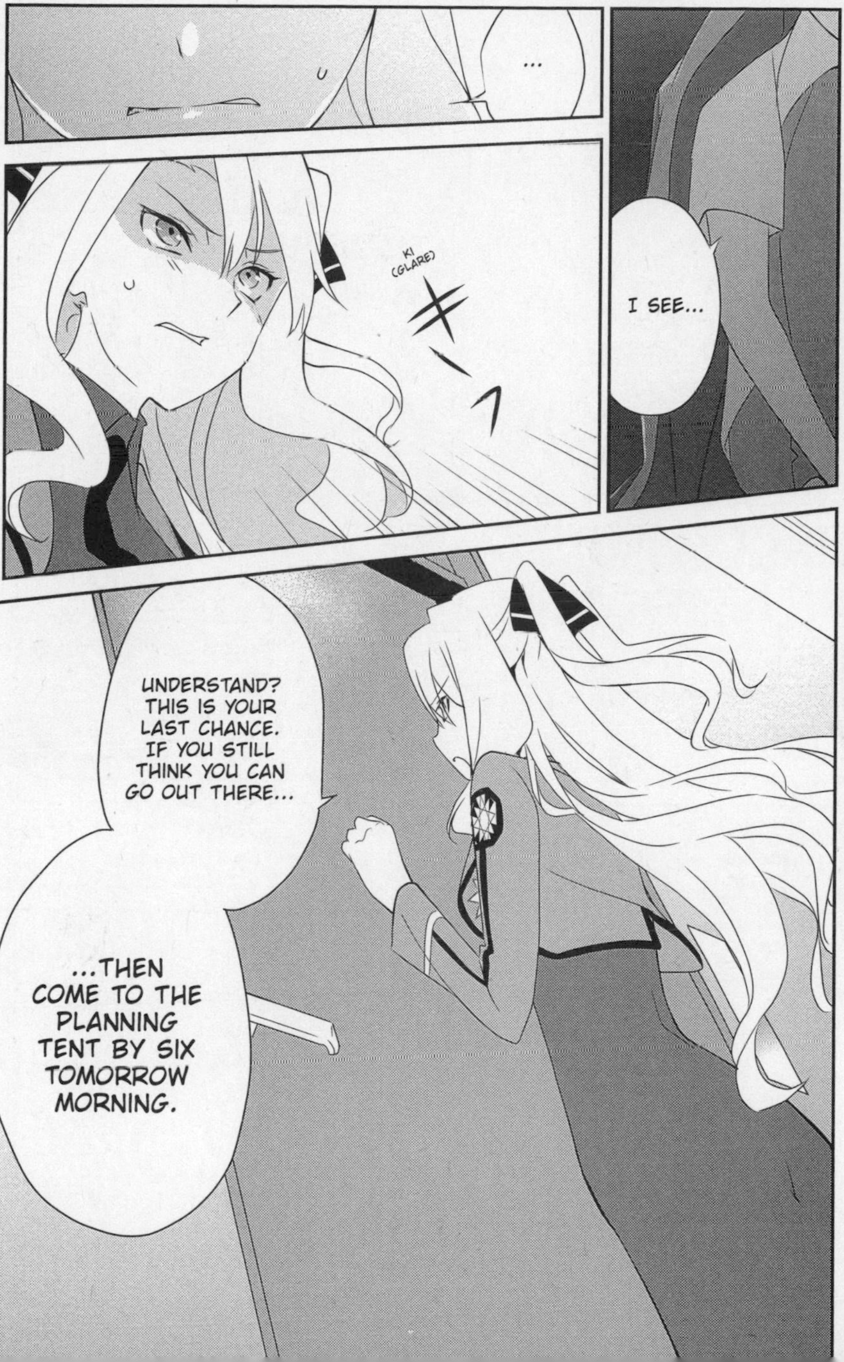
I SEE...
...
KI (GLARE)
UNDERSTAND? THIS IS YOUR LAST CHANCE. IF YOU STILL THINK YOU CAN GO OUT THERE...
...THEN COME TO THE PLANNING TENT BY SIX TOMORROW MORNING.

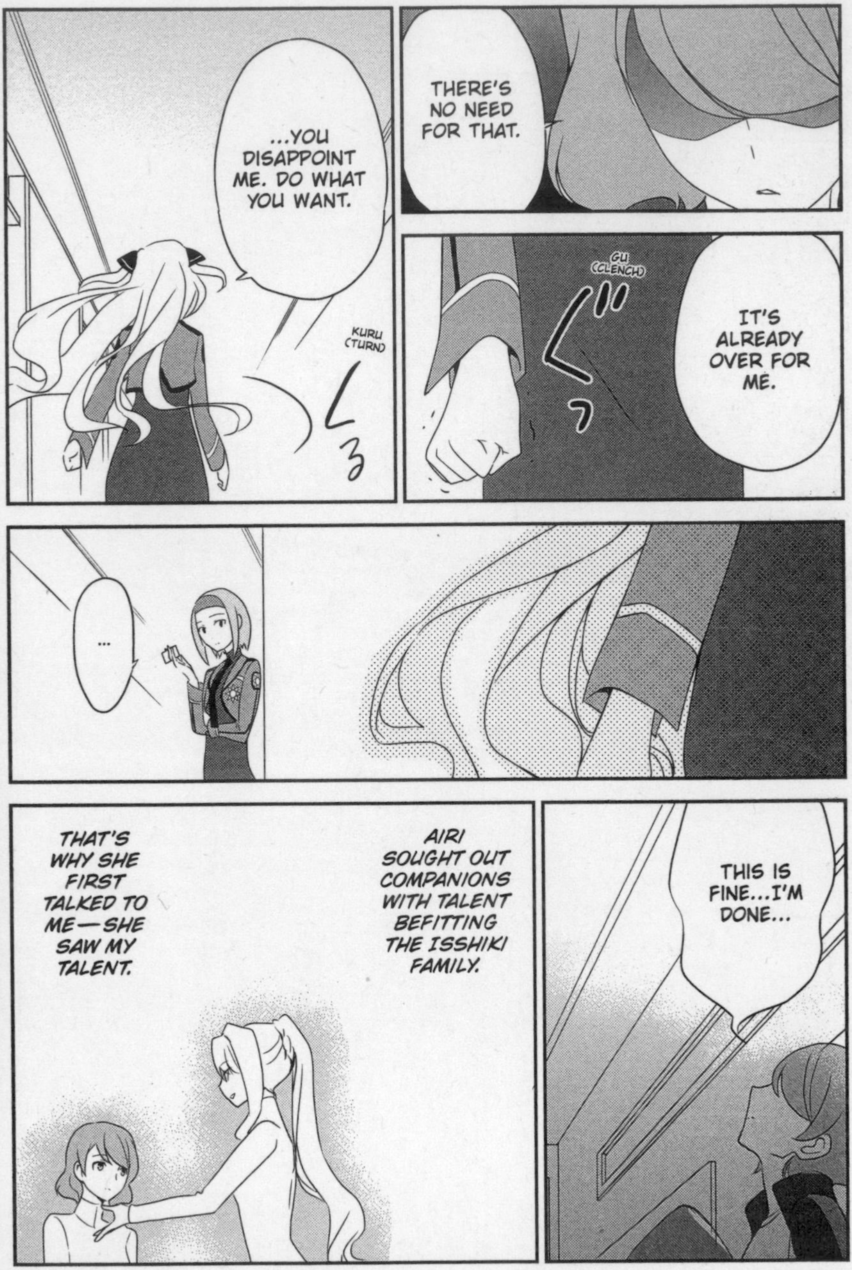
THERE'S NO NEED FOR THAT.
GU (CLENCH)
IT'S ALREADY OVER FOR ME.
...YOU DISAPPOINT ME. DO WHAT YOU WANT.
KURU (TURN)
...
THIS IS FINE...I'M DONE...
AIRI SOUGHT OUT COMPANIONS WITH TALENT BEFITTING THE ISSHIKI FAMILY.
THAT'S WHY SHE FIRST TALKED TO ME—SHE SAW MY TALENT.

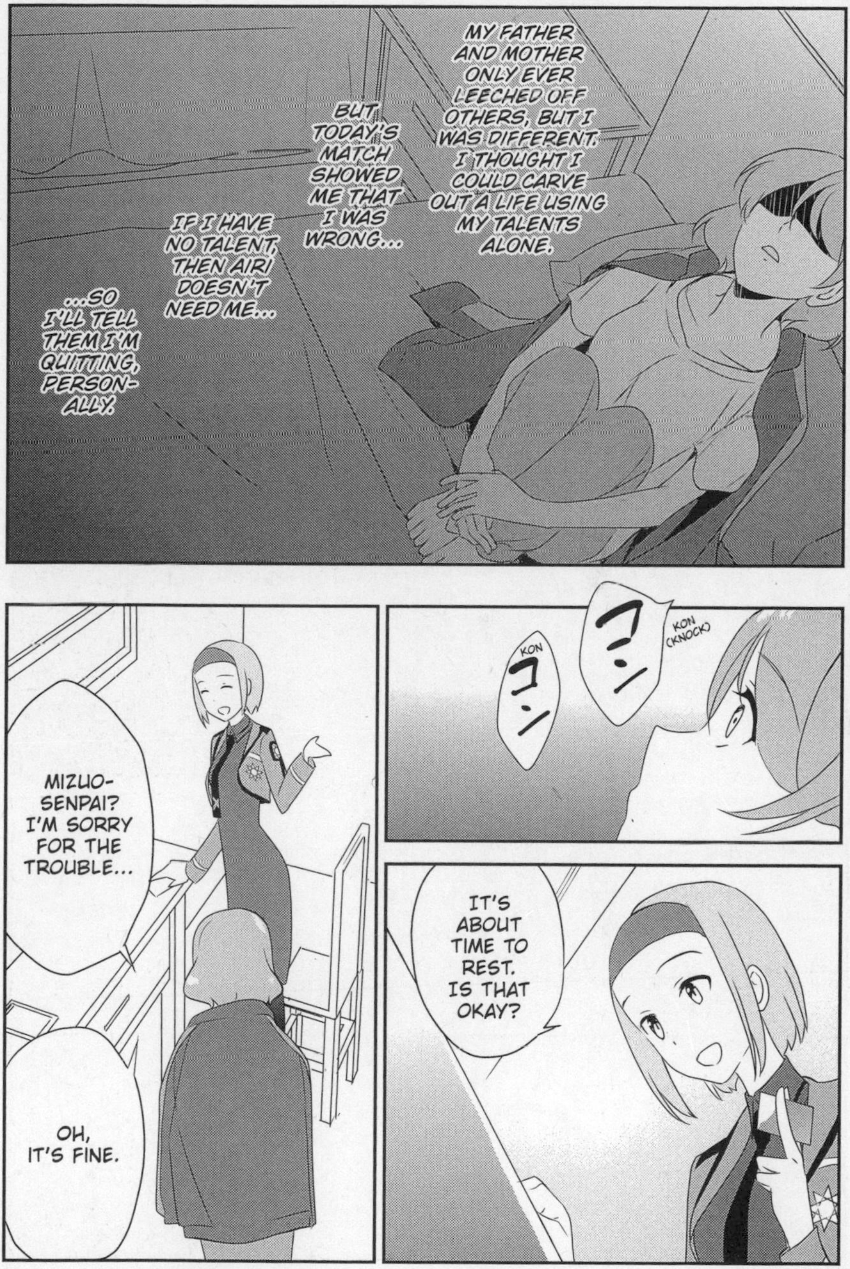
MY FATHER AND MOTHER ONLY EVER LEECHED OFF OTHERS, BUT I WAS DIFFERENT. I THOUGHT I COULD CARVE OUT A LIFE USING MY TALENTS ALONE.
BUT TODAY'S MATCH SHOWED ME THAT I WAS WRONG...
IF I HAVE NO TALENT, THEN AIRI DOESN'T NEED ME...
...SO I'LL TELL THEM I'M QUITTING, PERSON-ALLY.
KON (KNOCK)
KON
IT'S ABOUT TIME TO REST. IS THAT OKAY?
MIZUO-SENPAI? I'M SORRY FOR THE TROUBLE...
OH, IT'S FINE.

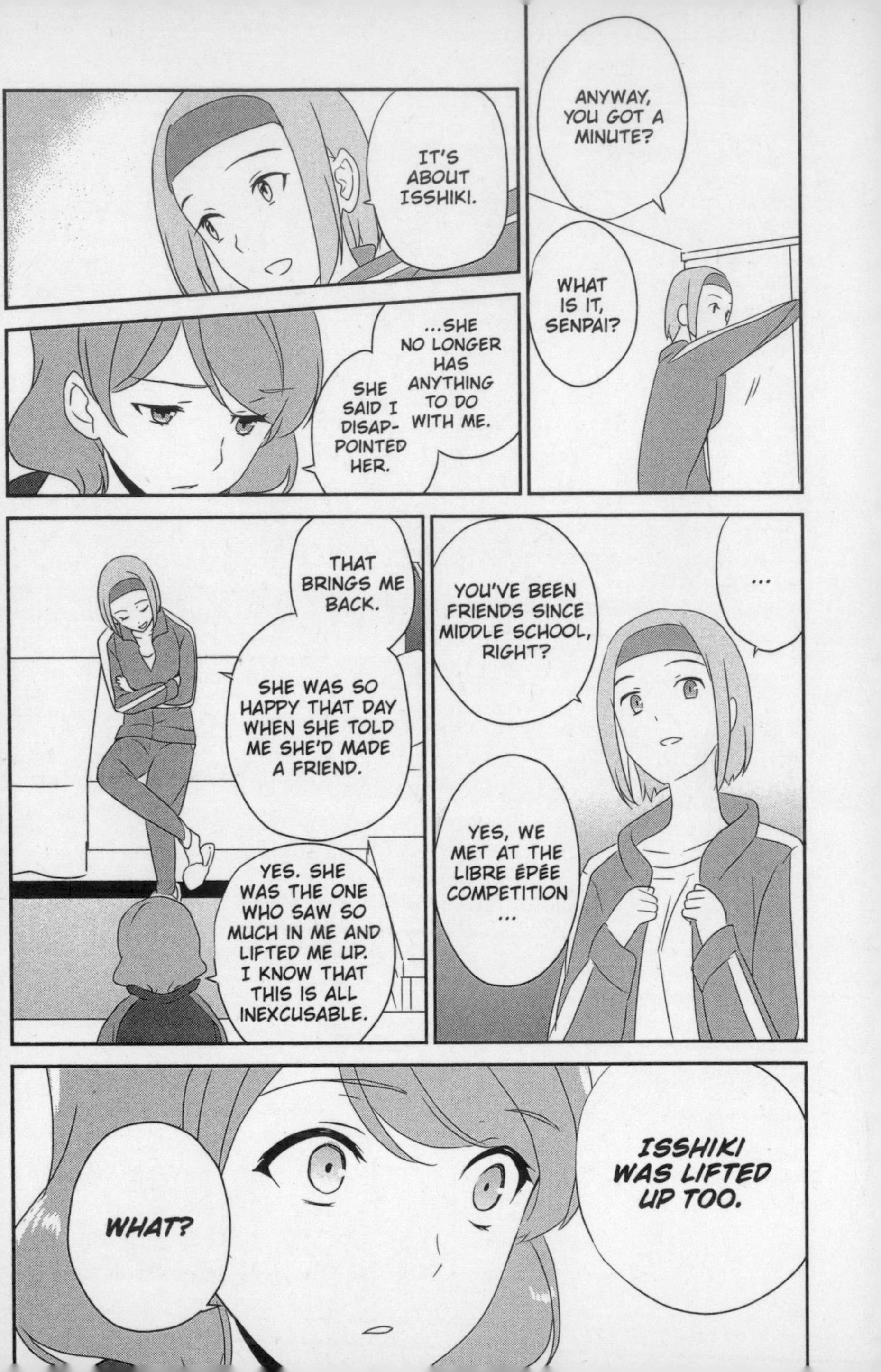
ANYWAY, YOU GOT A MINUTE?
WHAT IS IT, SENPAI?
IT'S ABOUT ISSHIKI.
...SHE NO LONGER HAS ANYTHING TO DO WITH ME.
SHE SAID I DISAPPOINTED HER.
...
YOU'VE BEEN FRIENDS SINCE MIDDLE SCHOOL, RIGHT?
YES, WE MET AT THE LIBRE ÉPÉE COMPETITION ...
THAT BRINGS ME BACK.
SHE WAS SO HAPPY THAT DAY WHEN SHE TOLD ME SHE'D MADE A FRIEND.
YES. SHE WAS THE ONE WHO SAW SO MUCH IN ME AND LIFTED ME UP. I KNOW THAT THIS IS ALL INEXCUSABLE.
ISSHIKI WAS LIFTED UP TOO.
WHAT?

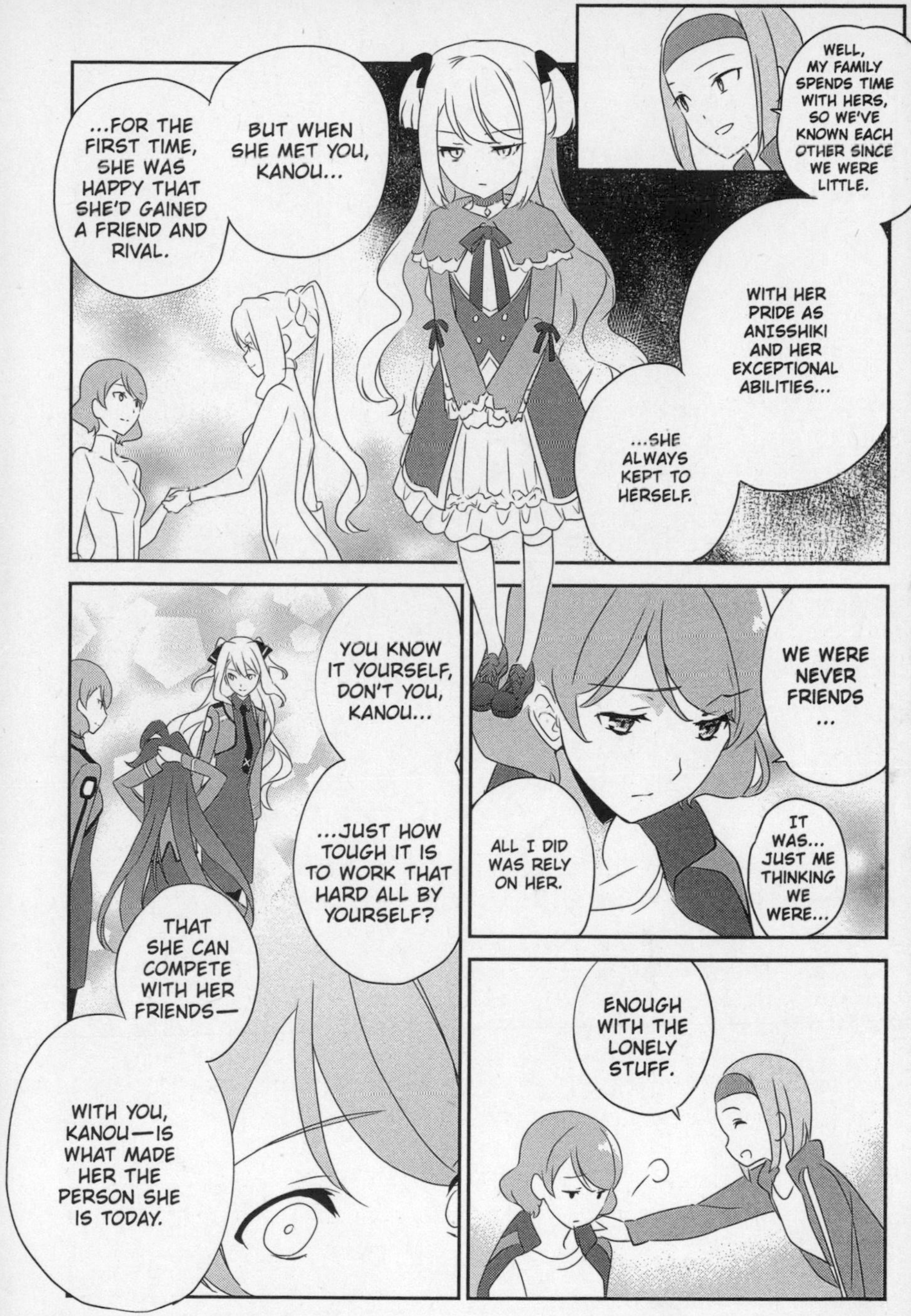
WELL, MY FAMILY SPENDS TIME WITH HERS, SO WE'VE KNOWN EACH OTHER SINCE WE WERE LITTLE.
WITH HER PRIDE AS ANISSHIKI AND HER EXCEPTIONAL ABILITIES...
...SHE ALWAYS KEPT TO HERSELF.
BUT WHEN SHE MET YOU, KANOU...
...FOR THE FIRST TIME, SHE WAS HAPPY THAT SHE'D GAINED A FRIEND AND RIVAL.
WE WERE NEVER FRIENDS...
IT WAS... JUST ME THINKING WE WERE...
ALL I DID WAS RELY ON HER.
ENOUGH WITH THE LONELY STUFF.
YOU KNOW IT YOURSELF, DON'T YOU, KANOU...
...JUST HOW TOUGH IT IS TO WORK THAT HARD ALL BY YOURSELF?
THAT SHE CAN COMPETE WITH HER FRIENDS—
WITH YOU, KANOU—IS WHAT MADE HER THE PERSON SHE IS TODAY.

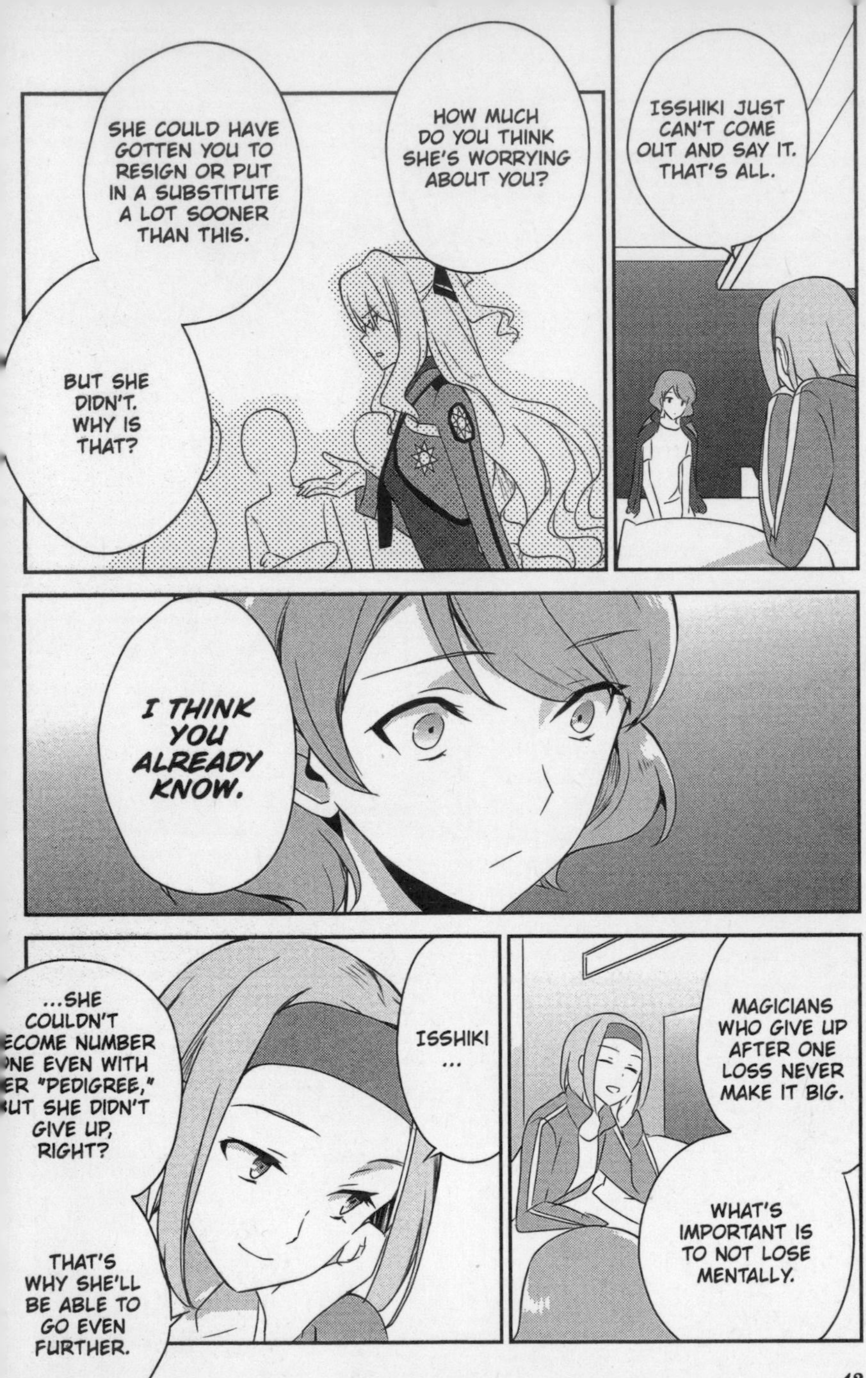

ISSHIKI JUST CAN'T COME OUT AND SAY IT. THAT'S ALL.
HOW MUCH DO YOU THINK SHE'S WORRYING ABOUT YOU?
SHE COULD HAVE GOTTEN YOU TO RESIGN OR PUT IN A SUBSTITUTE A LOT SOONER THAN THIS.
BUT SHE DIDN'T. WHY IS THAT?
I THINK YOU ALREADY KNOW.
MAGICIANS WHO GIVE UP AFTER ONE LOSS NEVER MAKE IT BIG.
WHAT'S IMPORTANT IS TO NOT LOSE MENTALLY.
ISSHIKI ...
...SHE COULDN'T ECOME NUMBER NE EVEN WITH ER "PEDIGREE," UT SHE DIDN'T GIVE UP, RIGHT?
THAT'S WHY SHE'LL BE ABLE TO GO EVEN FURTHER.

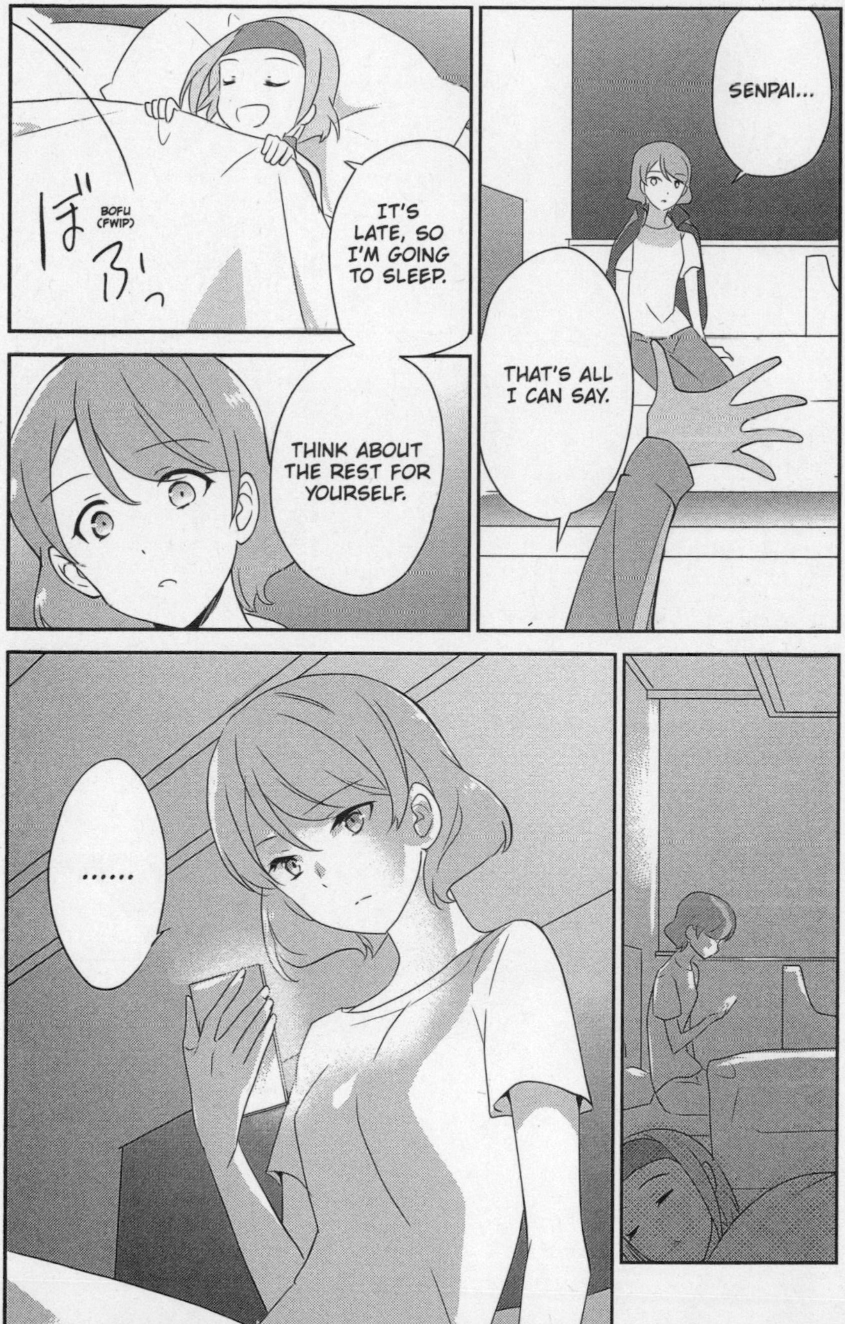
SENPAI...
THAT'S ALL I CAN SAY.
IT'S LATE, SO I'M GOING TO SLEEP.
ぼふっ
BOFU (FWIP)
THINK ABOUT THE REST FOR YOURSELF.
......

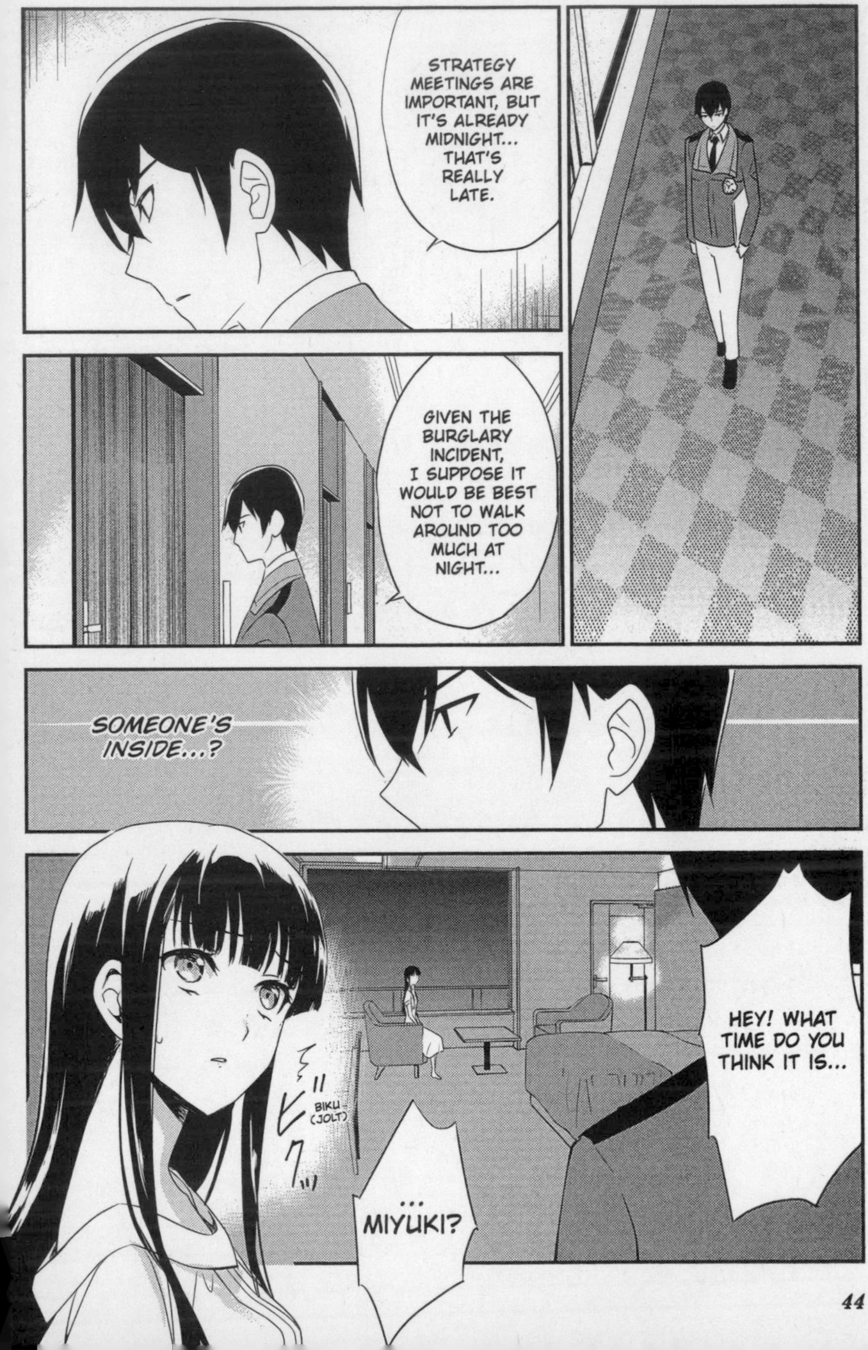
STRATEGY MEETINGS ARE IMPORTANT, BUT IT'S ALREADY MIDNIGHT... THAT'S REALLY LATE.
GIVEN THE BURGLARY INCIDENT, I SUPPOSE IT WOULD BE BEST NOT TO WALK AROUND TOO MUCH AT NIGHT...
SOMEONE'S INSIDE...?
HEY! WHAT TIME DO YOU THINK IT IS...
BIKU (JOLT)
... MIYUKI?

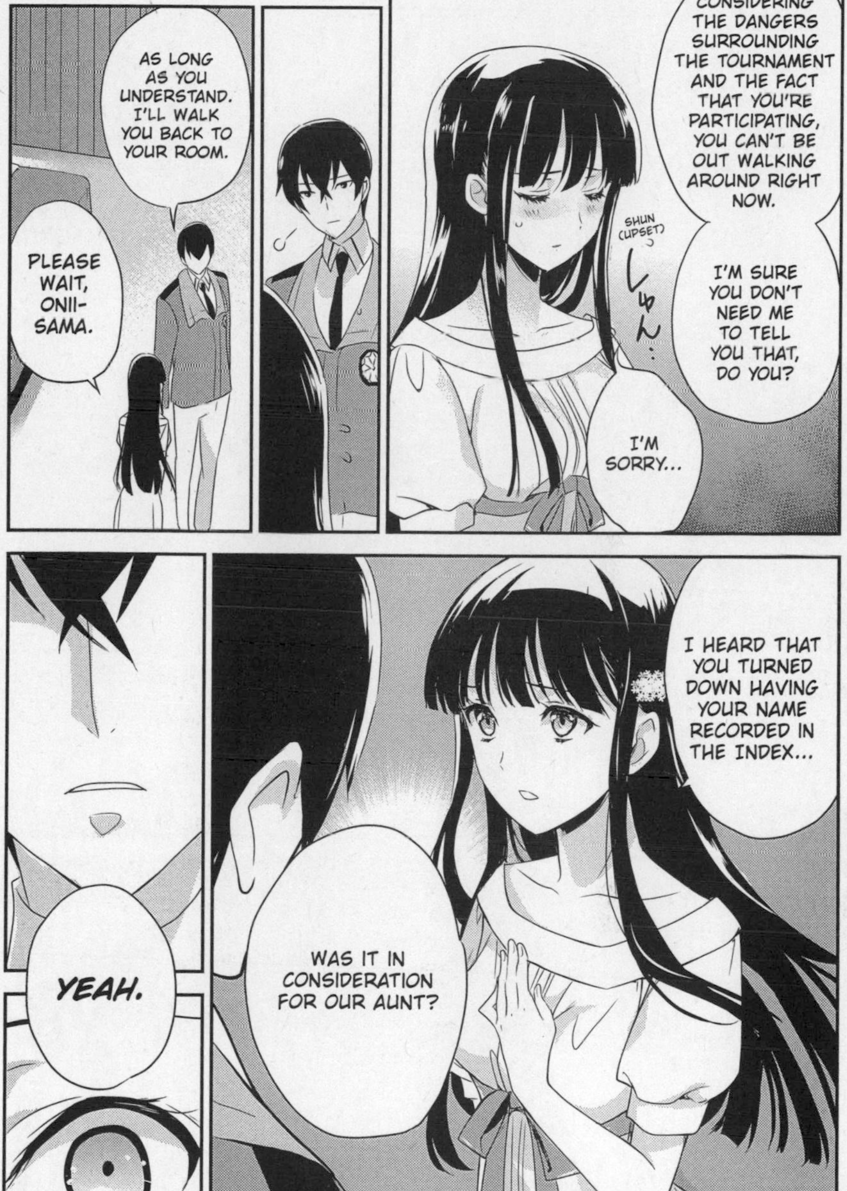
CONSIDERING THE DANGERS SURROUNDING THE TOURNAMENT AND THE FACT THAT YOU'RE PARTICIPATING, YOU CAN'T BE OUT WALKING AROUND RIGHT NOW.
I'M SURE YOU DON'T NEED ME TO TELL YOU THAT, DO YOU?
SHUN (UPSET)
しゅん…
I'M SORRY...
AS LONG AS YOU UNDERSTAND. I'LL WALK YOU BACK TO YOUR ROOM.
PLEASE WAIT, ONII-SAMA.
I HEARD THAT YOU TURNED DOWN HAVING YOUR NAME RECORDED IN THE INDEX...
WAS IT IN CONSIDERATION FOR OUR AUNT?
YEAH.

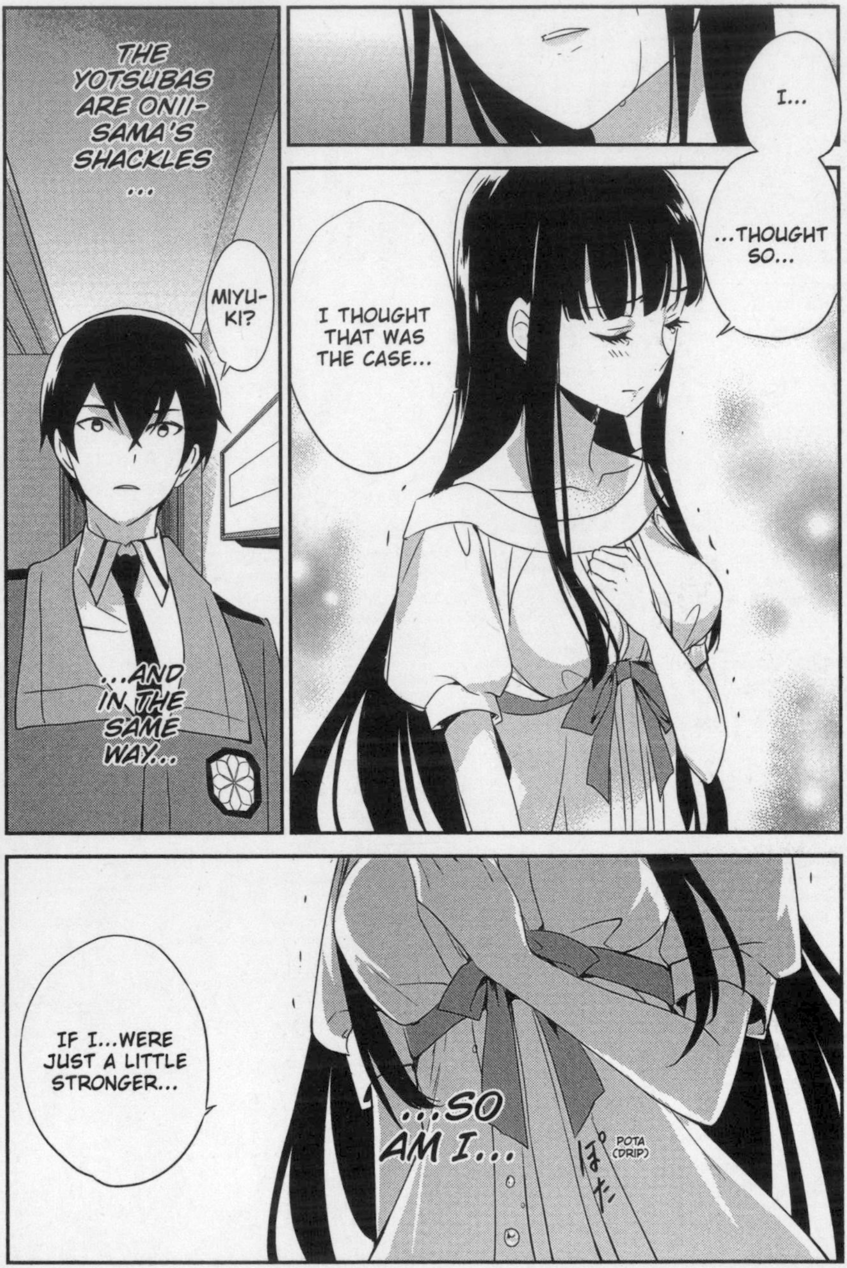

I...
...THOUGHT SO...
I THOUGHT THAT WAS THE CASE...
THE YOTSUBAS ARE ONII-SAMA'S SHACKLES...
MIYU-KI?
...AND IN THE SAME WAY...
ぽた
POTA (DRIP)
...SO AM I...
IF I...WERE JUST A LITTLE STRONGER...

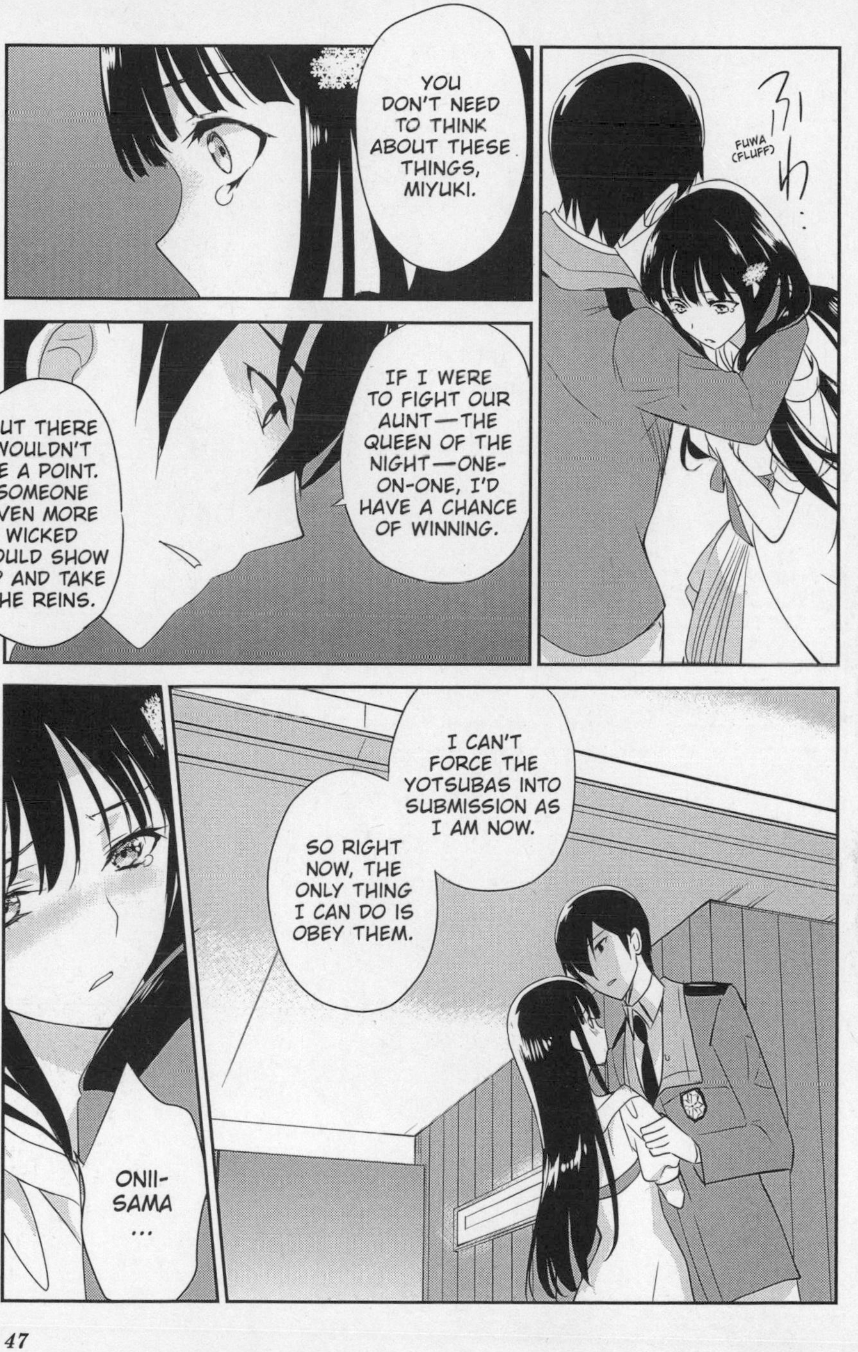

ふわ
FUWA (FLUFF)
YOU DON'T NEED TO THINK ABOUT THESE THINGS, MIYUKI.
IF I WERE TO FIGHT OUR AUNT—THE QUEEN OF THE NIGHT—ONE-ON-ONE, I'D HAVE A CHANCE OF WINNING.
BUT THERE WOULDN'T BE A POINT. SOMEONE EVEN MORE WICKED WOULD SHOW UP AND TAKE THE REINS.
I CAN'T FORCE THE YOTSUBAS INTO SUBMISSION AS I AM NOW.
SO RIGHT NOW, THE ONLY THING I CAN DO IS OBEY THEM.
ONII-SAMA...

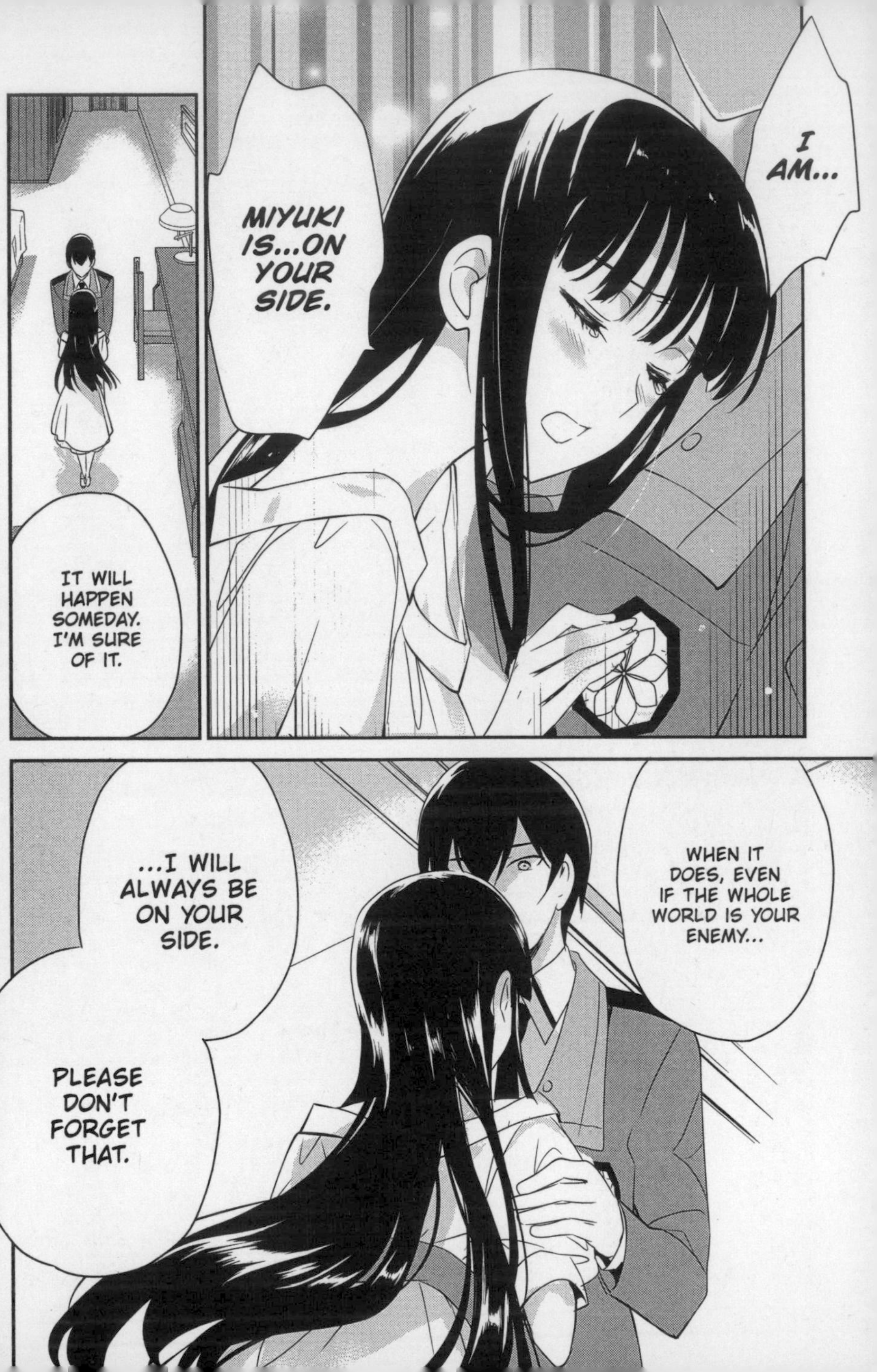
I AM...
MIYUKI IS...ON YOUR SIDE.
IT WILL HAPPEN SOMEDAY. I'M SURE OF IT.
WHEN IT DOES, EVEN IF THE WHOLE WORLD IS YOUR ENEMY...
...I WILL ALWAYS BE ON YOUR SIDE.
PLEASE DON'T FORGET THAT.

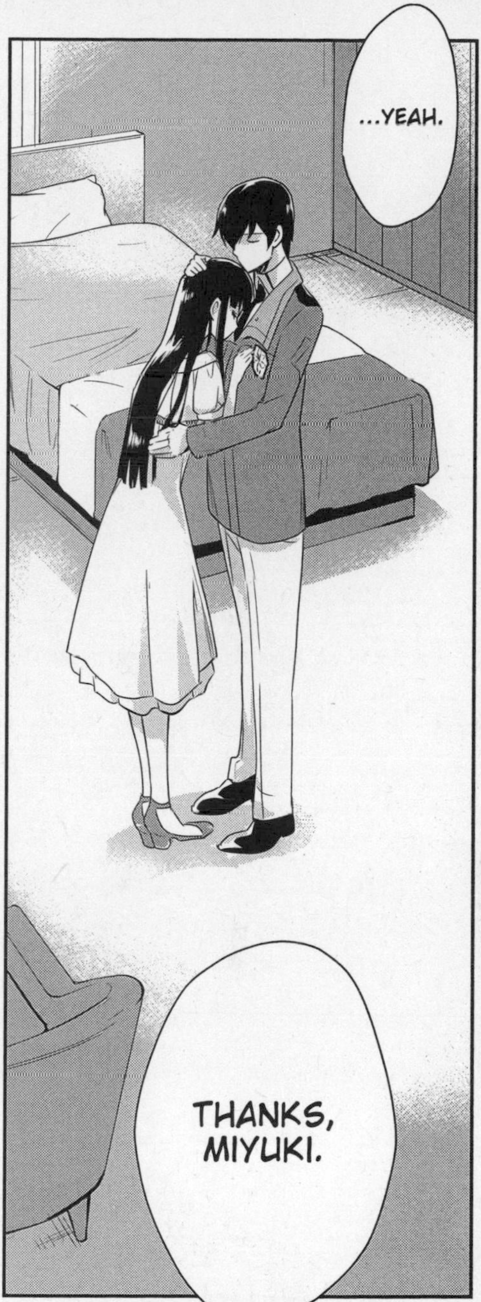
...YEAH.
THANKS, MIYUKI.

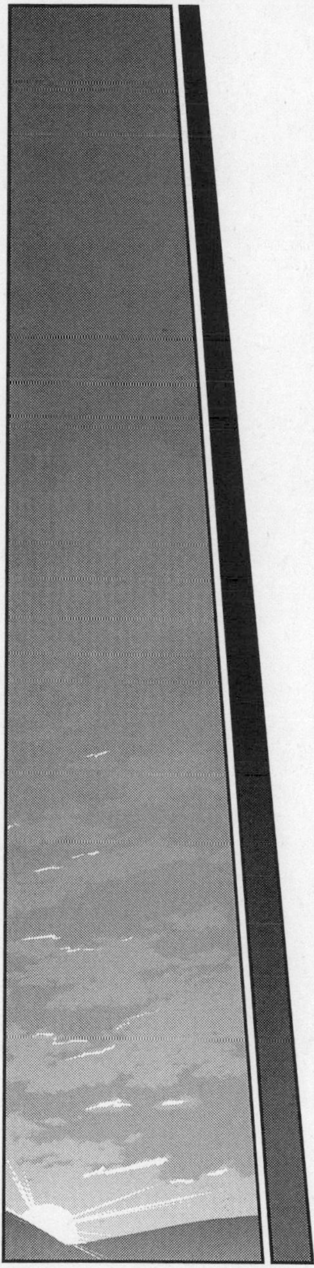

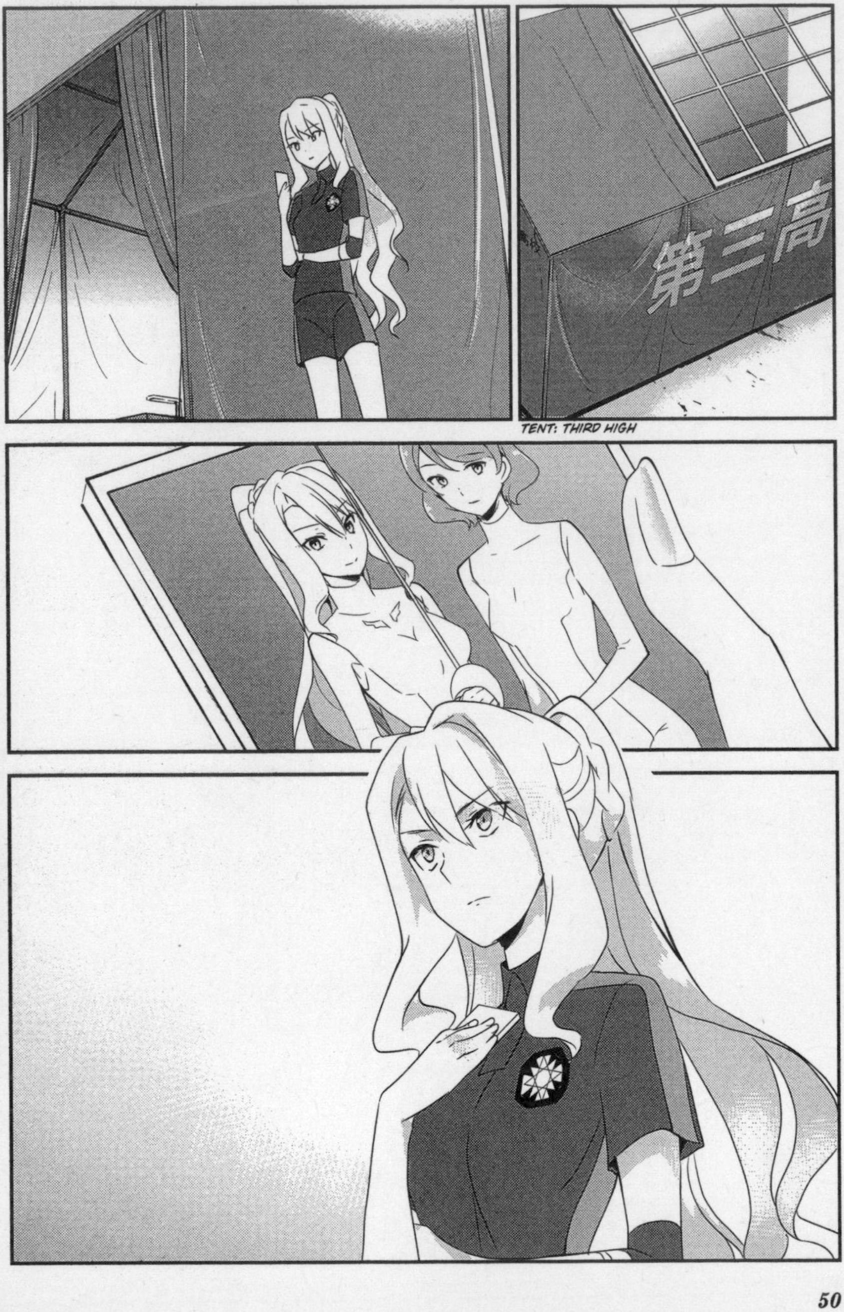
第三高
TENT: THIRD HIGH

THE HONOR STUDENT AT MAGIC HIGH SCHOOL

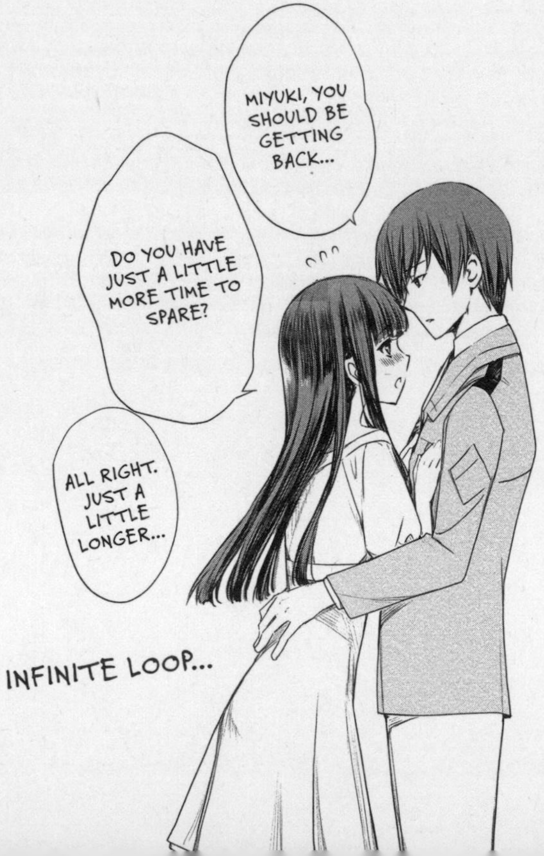
MIYUKI, YOU SHOULD BE GETTING BACK...
DO YOU HAVE JUST A LITTLE MORE TIME TO SPARE?
ALL RIGHT. JUST A LITTLE LONGER...
INFINITE LOOP...

CHAPTER 33

CHICHI (CHEEP)
CHUN (CHIRP)
CHUN
TENT: THIRD HIGH
YOU'RE LATE.

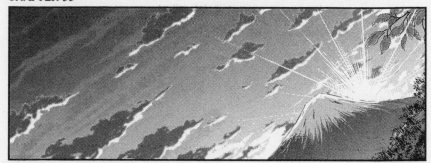

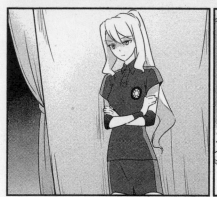

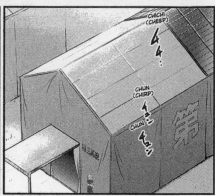

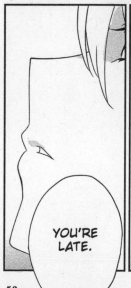

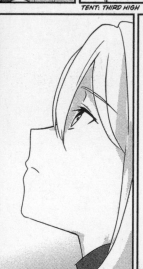

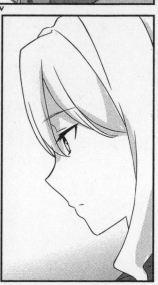

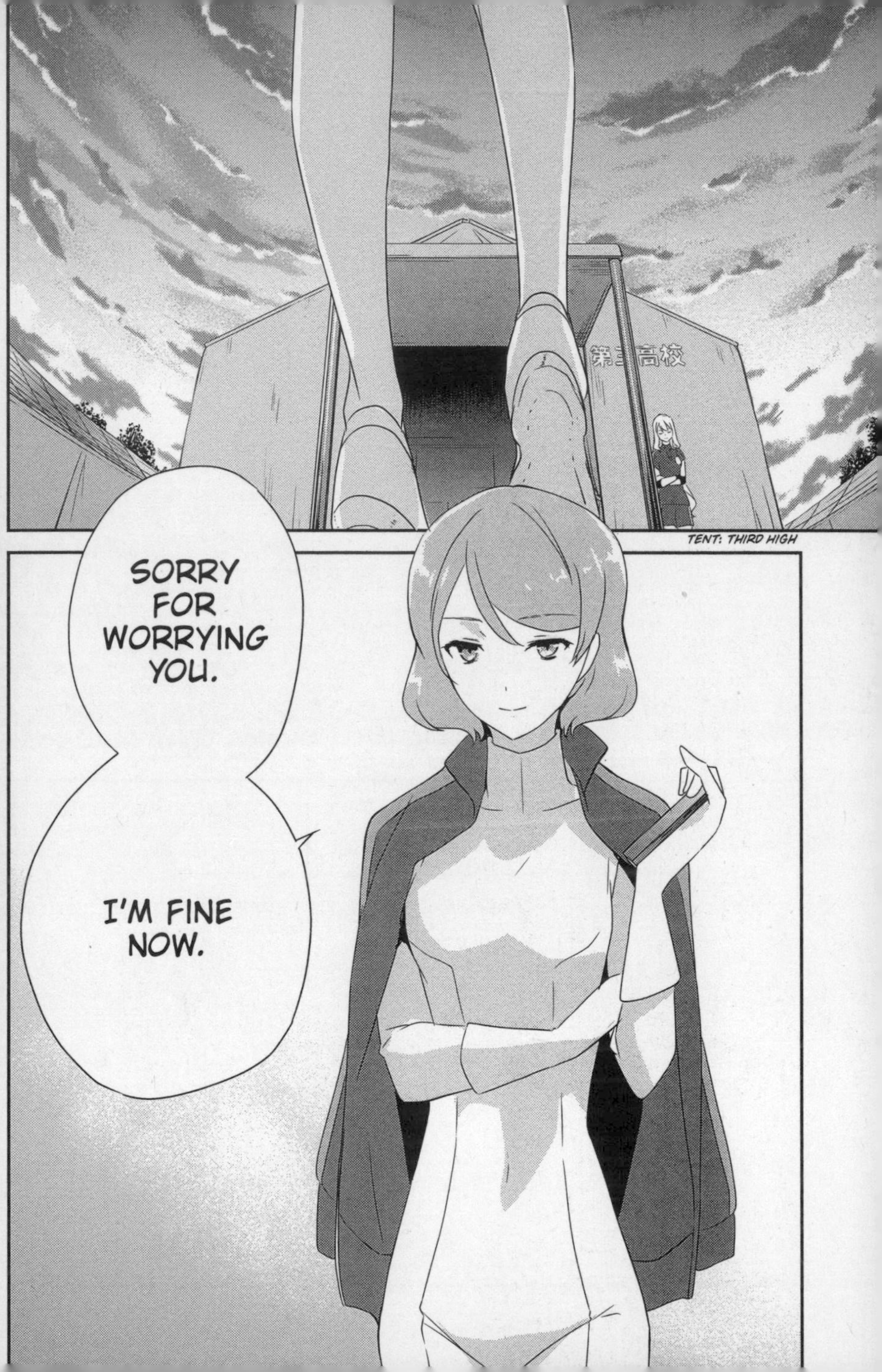
TENT: THIRD HIGH
SORRY FOR WORRYING YOU.
I'M FINE NOW.

CHAPTER 33

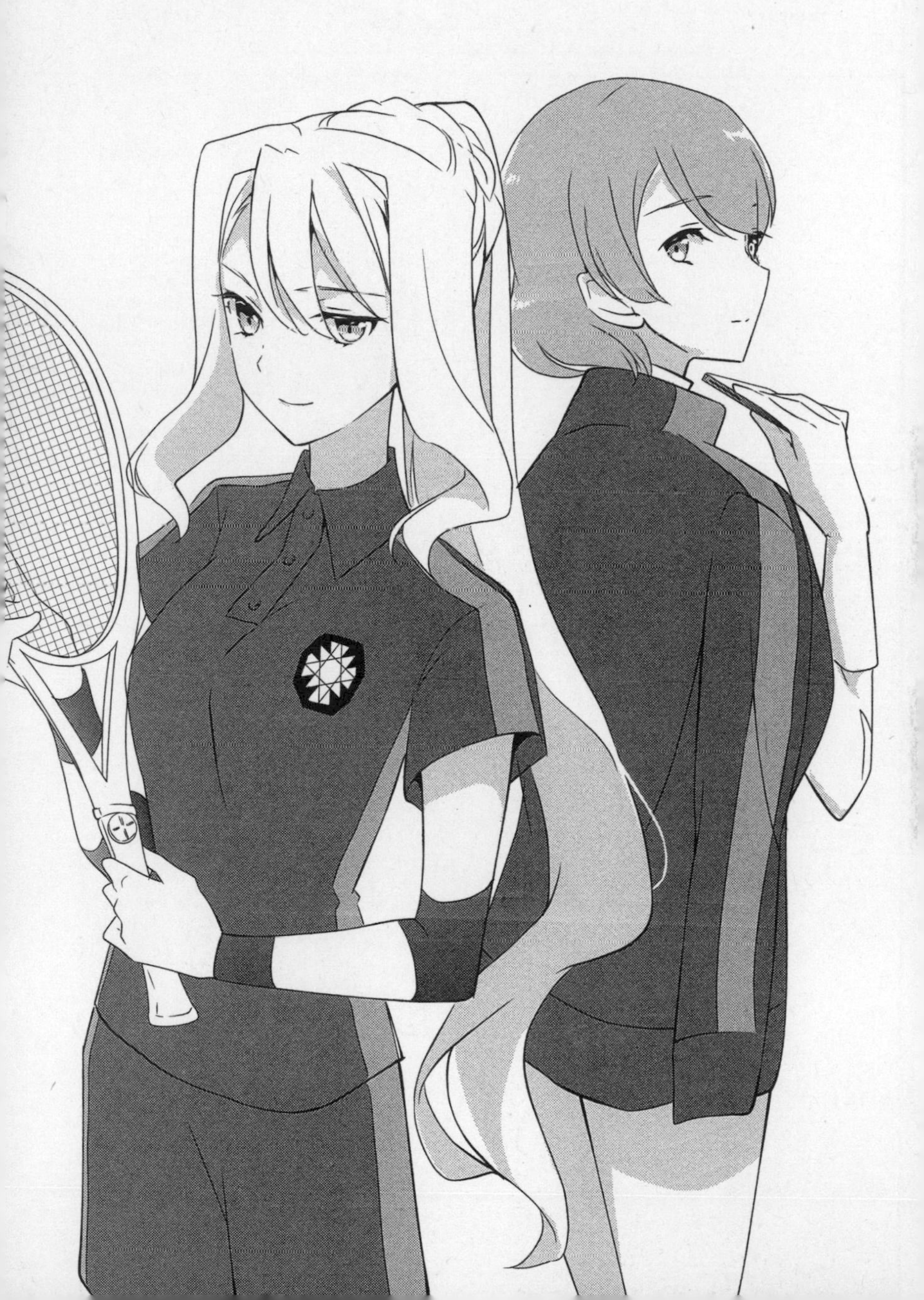

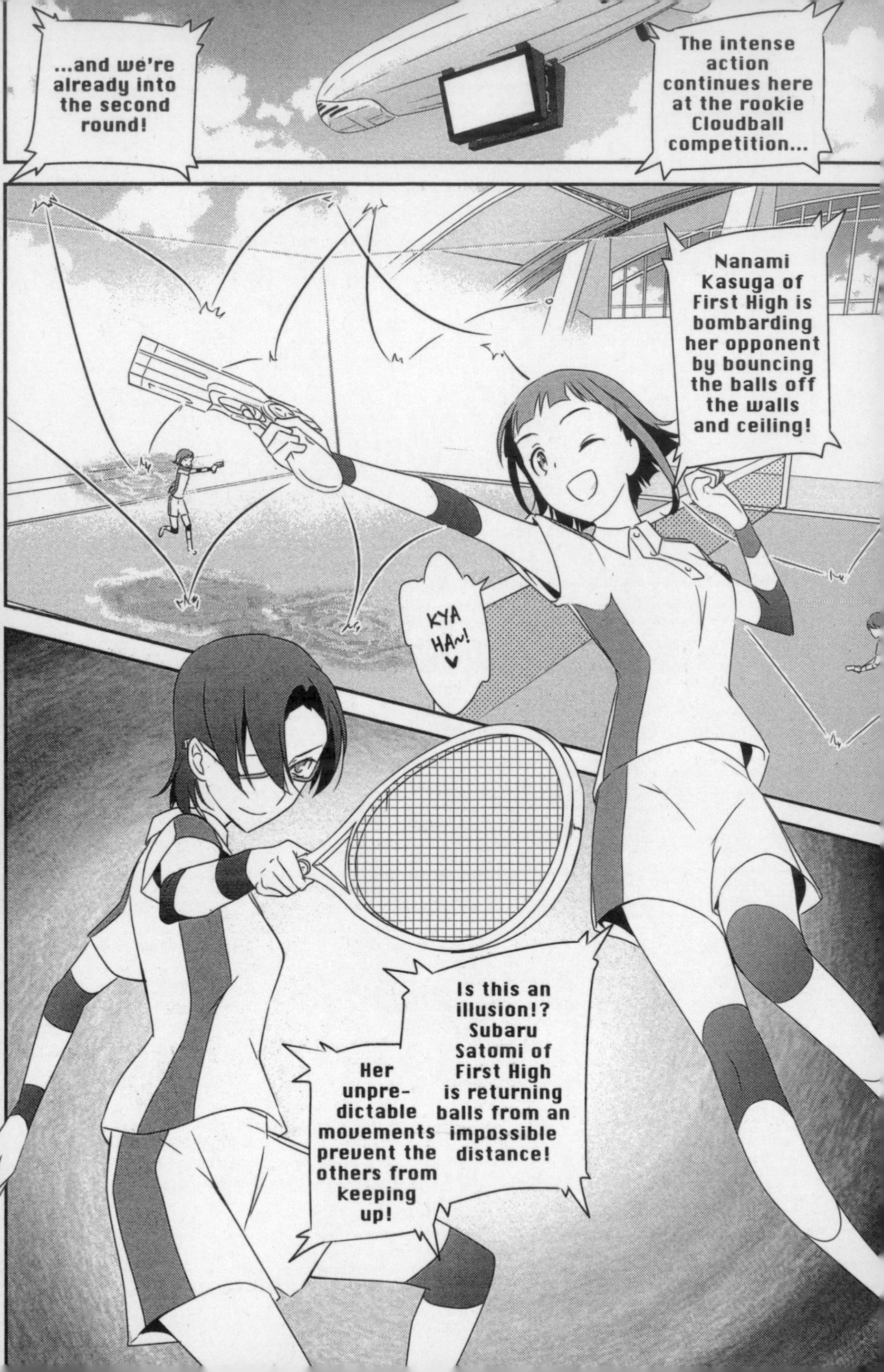
The intense action continues here at the rookie Cloudball competition...
...and we're already into the second round!
Nanami Kasuga of First High is bombarding her opponent by bouncing the balls off the walls and ceiling!
KYA HA~! ♥
Is this an illusion!? Subaru Satomi of First High is returning balls from an impossible distance!
Her unpre-dictable movements prevent the others from keeping up!

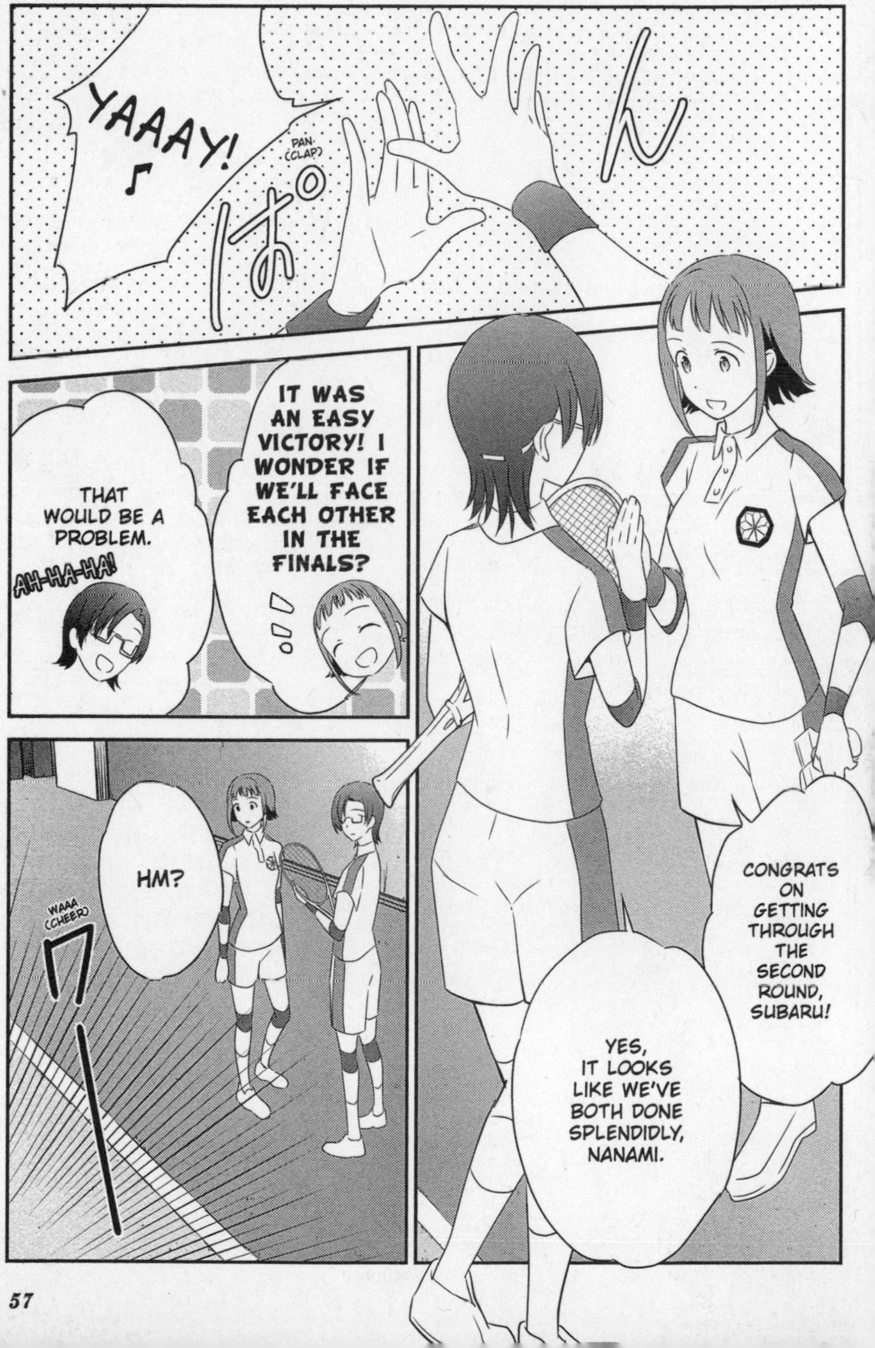
ぱん
PAN (CLAP)
YAAAY! ♪
CONGRATS ON GETTING THROUGH THE SECOND ROUND, SUBARU!
YES, IT LOOKS LIKE WE'VE BOTH DONE SPLENDIDLY, NANAMI.
IT WAS AN EASY VICTORY! I WONDER IF WE'LL FACE EACH OTHER IN THE FINALS?
!!
THAT WOULD BE A PROBLEM.
AH-HA-HA!
HM?
WAAA (CHEER)
ワー

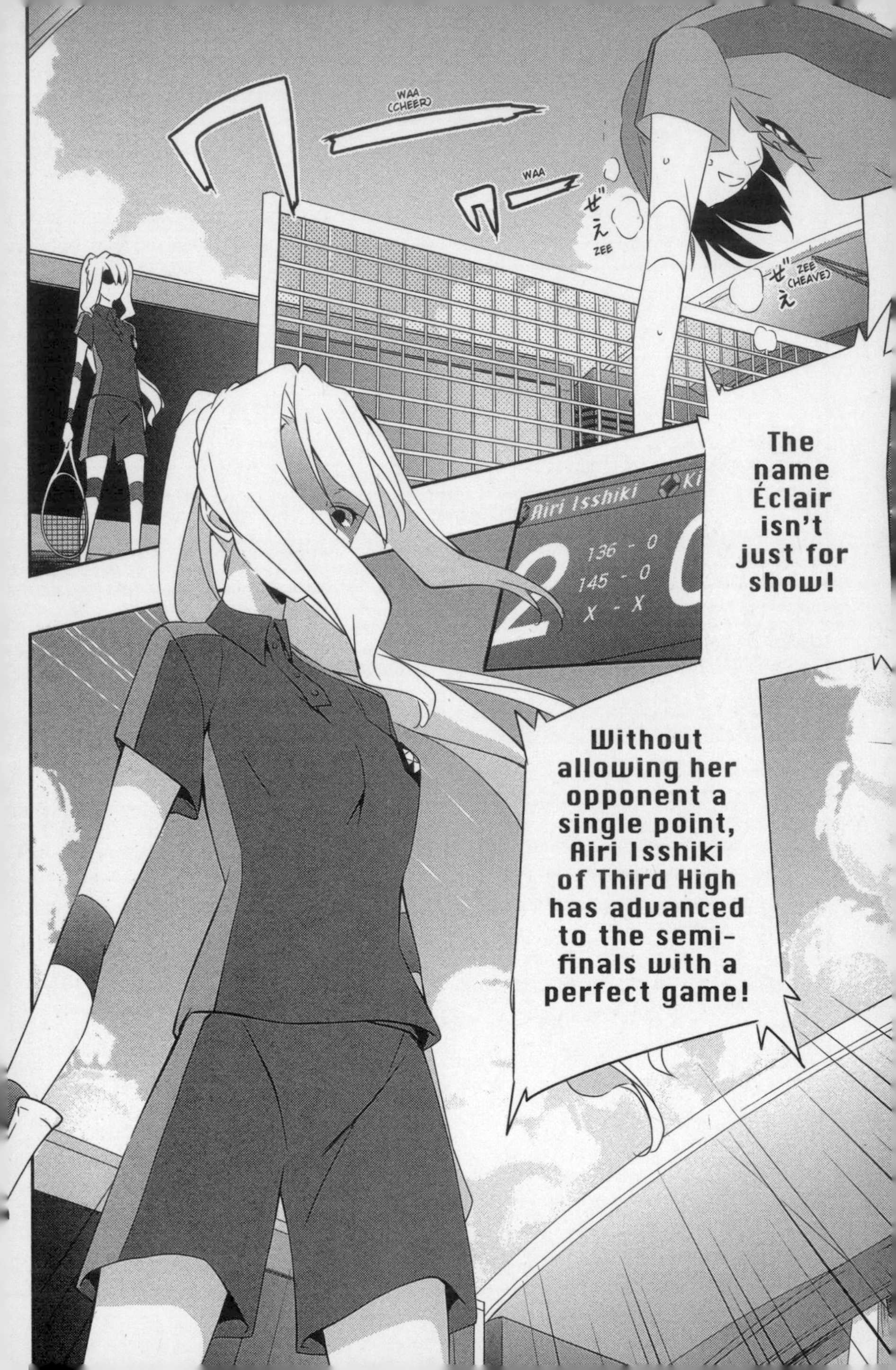

ぜえ ZEE (HEAVE)
ぜえ ZEE
WAA (CHEER)
WAA
Airi Isshiki
136 - 0
145 - 0
X - X
The name Éclair isn't just for show!
Without allowing her opponent a single point, Airi Isshiki of Third High has advanced to the semi-finals with a perfect game!

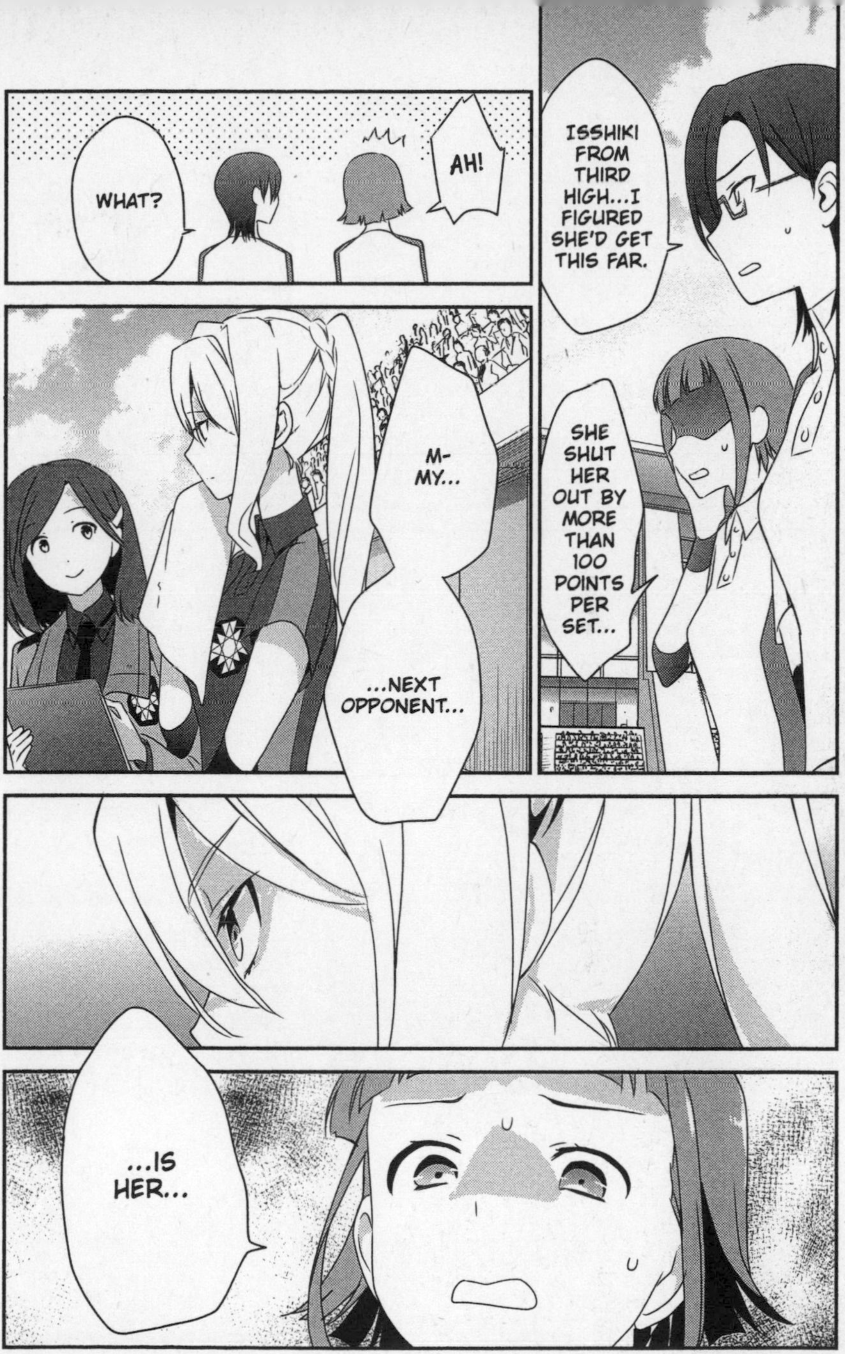
ISSHIKI FROM THIRD HIGH...I FIGURED SHE'D GET THIS FAR.
SHE SHUT HER OUT BY MORE THAN 100 POINTS PER SET...
AH!
WHAT?
M-MY...
...NEXT OPPONENT...
...IS HER...

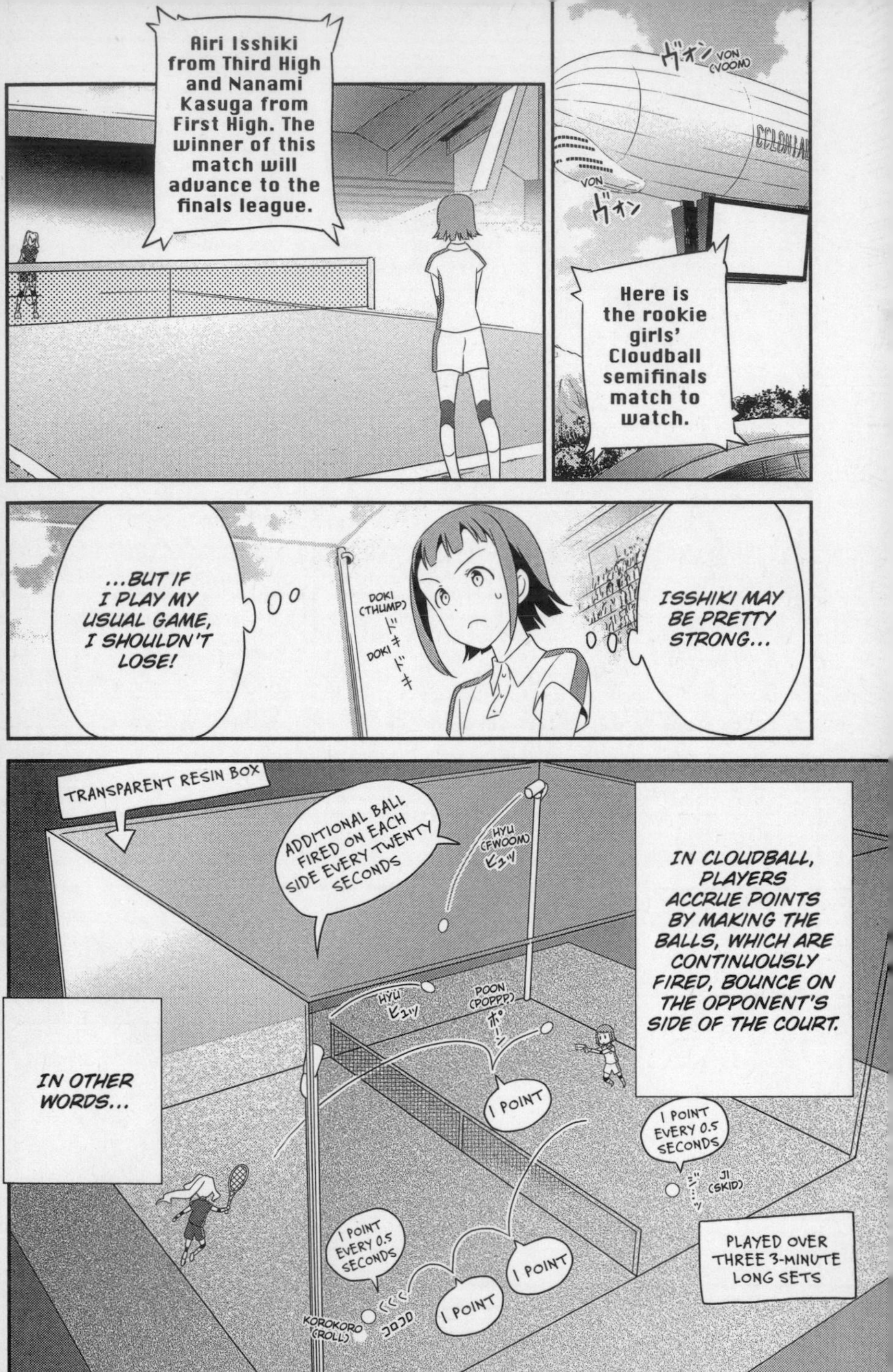
VON (VOOM) ヴオン
VON ヴオン
Here is the rookie girls' Cloudball semifinals match to watch.
Airi Isshiki from Third High and Nanami Kasuga from First High. The winner of this match will advance to the finals league.
ISSHIKI MAY BE PRETTY STRONG...
DOKI (THUMP) ドキ
DOKI ドキ
...BUT IF I PLAY MY USUAL GAME, I SHOULDN'T LOSE!
IN CLOUDBALL, PLAYERS ACCRUE POINTS BY MAKING THE BALLS, WHICH ARE CONTINUOUSLY FIRED, BOUNCE ON THE OPPONENT'S SIDE OF THE COURT.
HYU (FWOOM) ヒュッ
ADDITIONAL BALL FIRED ON EACH SIDE EVERY TWENTY SECONDS
TRANSPARENT RESIN BOX
POON (POPPP) ポーン
HYU ヒュッ
1 POINT
1 POINT EVERY 0.5 SECONDS
JI (SKID) ジーッ
IN OTHER WORDS...
PLAYED OVER THREE 3-MINUTE LONG SETS
1 POINT
1 POINT
1 POINT EVERY 0.5 SECONDS
KOROKORO (ROLL) コロコロ

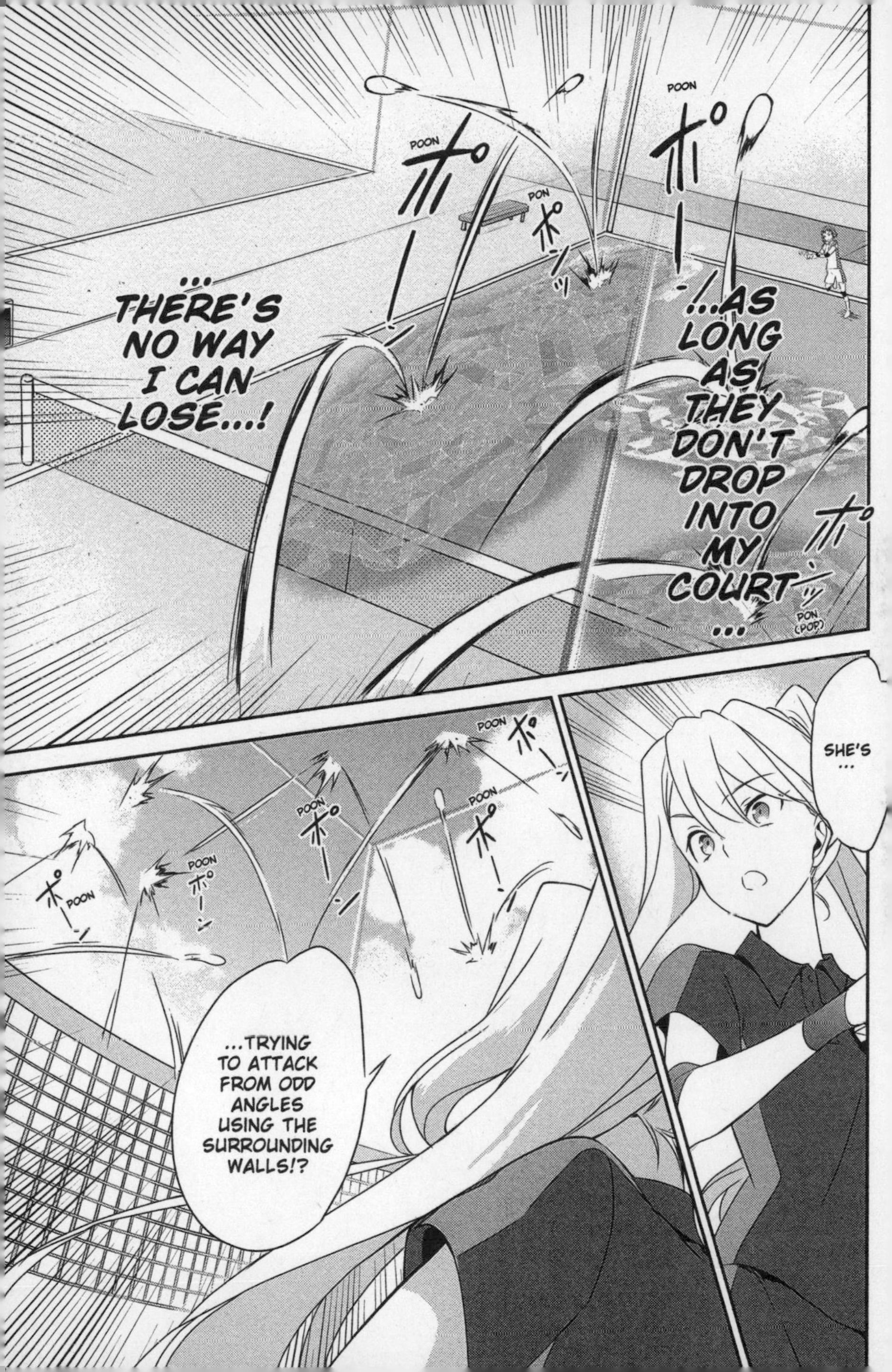
POON
...AS LONG AS THEY DON'T DROP INTO MY COURT...
PON (POP)
POON
PON
...THERE'S NO WAY I CAN LOSE...!
SHE'S...
POON
POON
POON
POON
...TRYING TO ATTACK FROM ODD ANGLES USING THE SURROUNDING WALLS!?

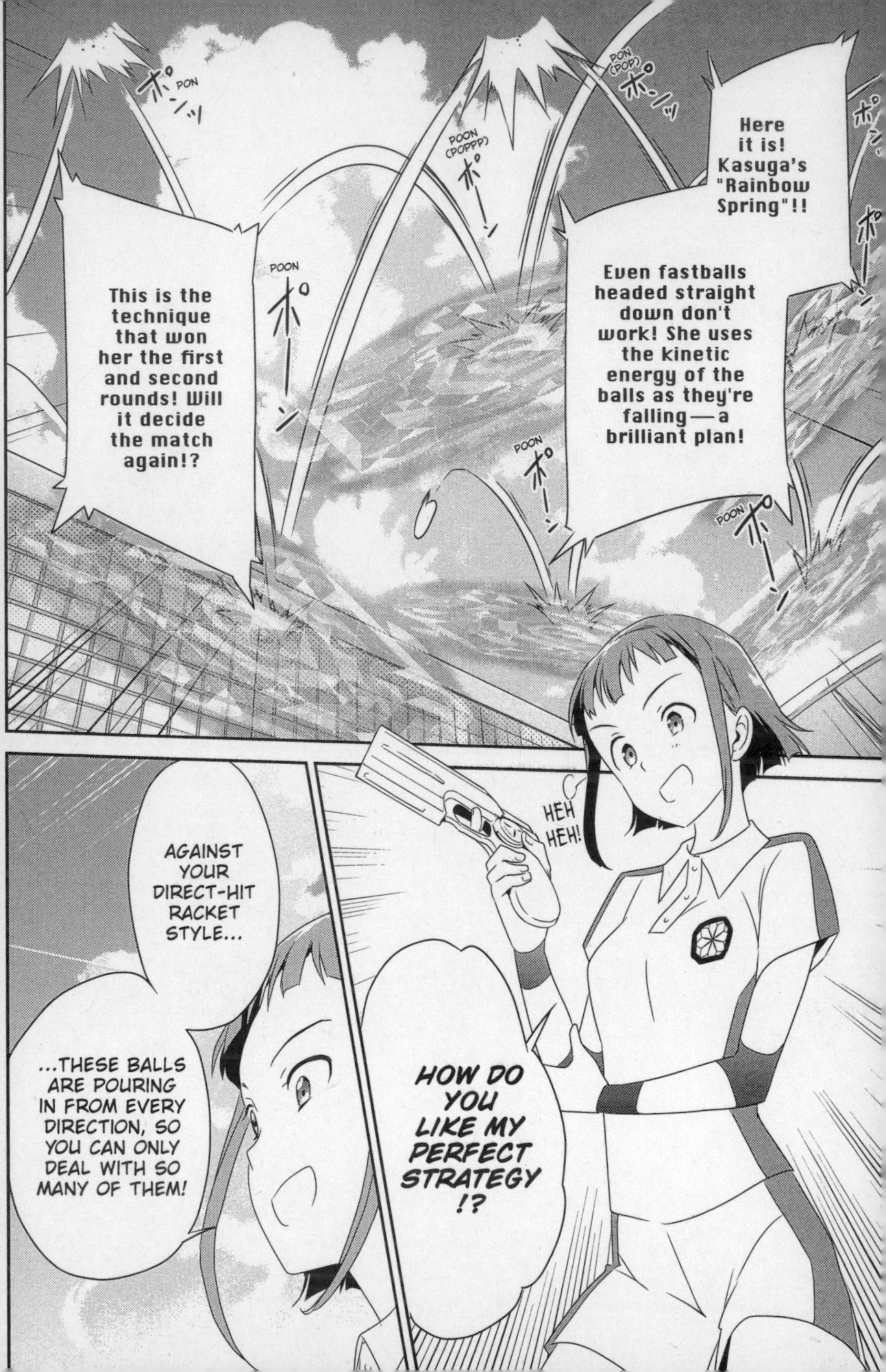
PON (POP)
PON
Here it is! Kasuga's "Rainbow Spring"!!
Even fastballs headed straight down don't work! She uses the kinetic energy of the balls as they're falling—a brilliant plan!
POON (POPPP)
POON
POON
POON
This is the technique that won her the first and second rounds! Will it decide the match again!?
HEH HEH!
AGAINST YOUR DIRECT-HIT RACKET STYLE...
...THESE BALLS ARE POURING IN FROM EVERY DIRECTION, SO YOU CAN ONLY DEAL WITH SO MANY OF THEM!
HOW DO YOU LIKE MY PERFECT STRATEGY!?

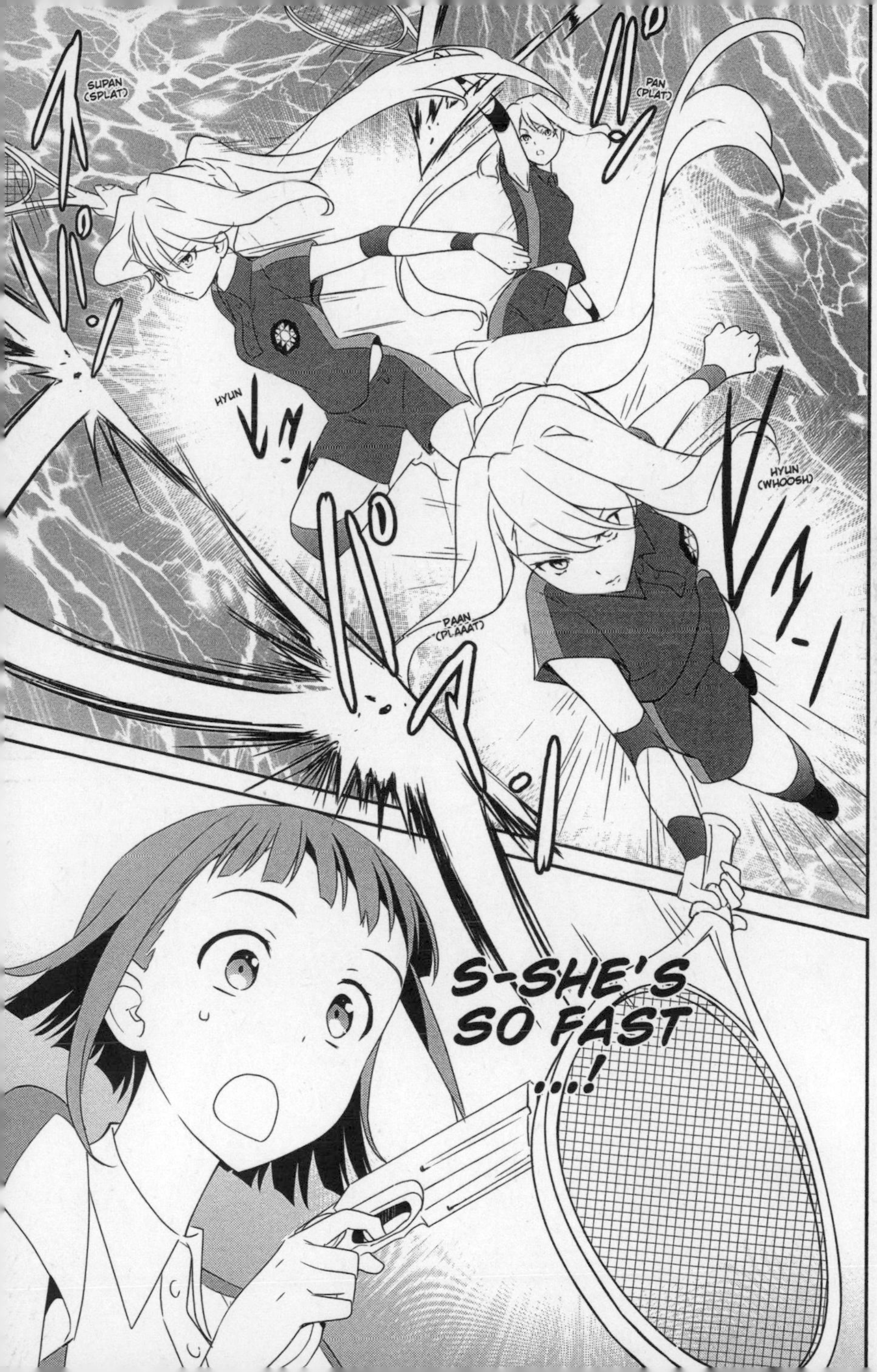
PAN (PLAT)
SUPAN (SPLAT)
HYUN (WHOOSH)
HYUN
PAAN (PLAAAT)
S-SHE'S SO FAST ...!

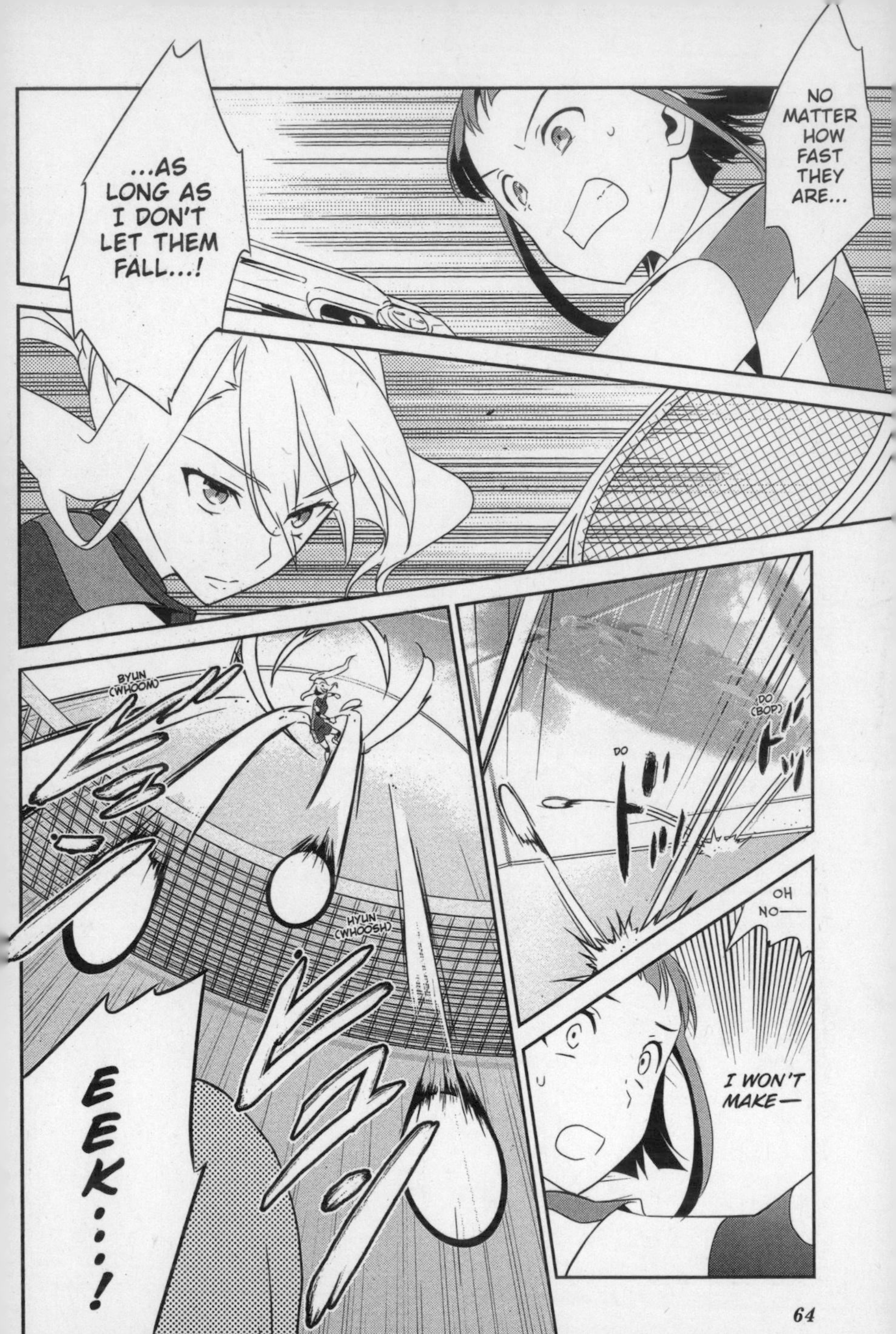
NO MATTER HOW FAST THEY ARE...
...AS LONG AS I DON'T LET THEM FALL...!
DO (BOP)
DO
OH NO—
I WON'T MAKE—
BYUN (WHOOM)
HYUN (WHOOSH)
EEK...!

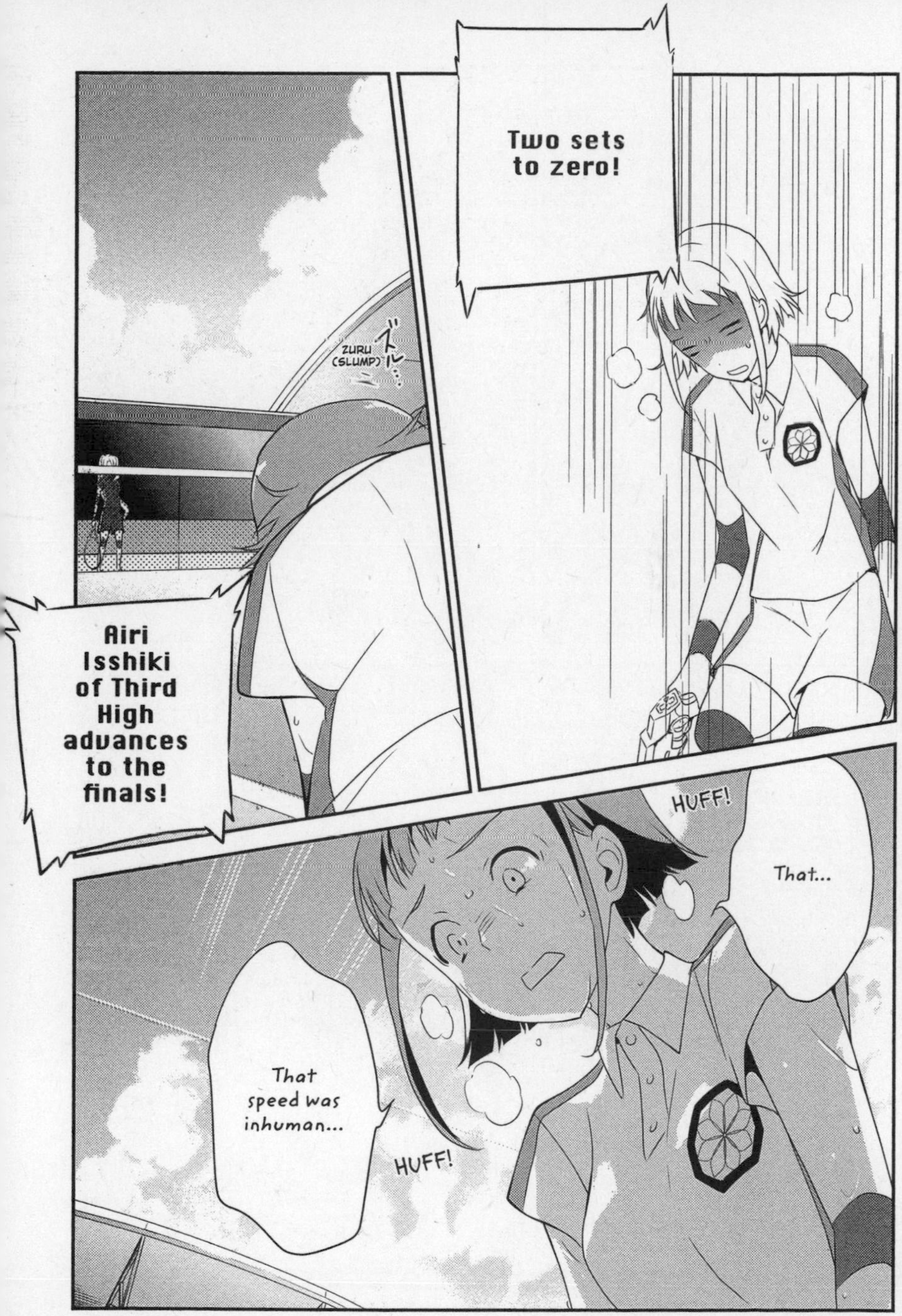
Two sets to zero!
ズル…
ZURU (SLUMP)
Airi Isshiki of Third High advances to the finals!
HUFF!
That...
That speed was inhuman...
HUFF!

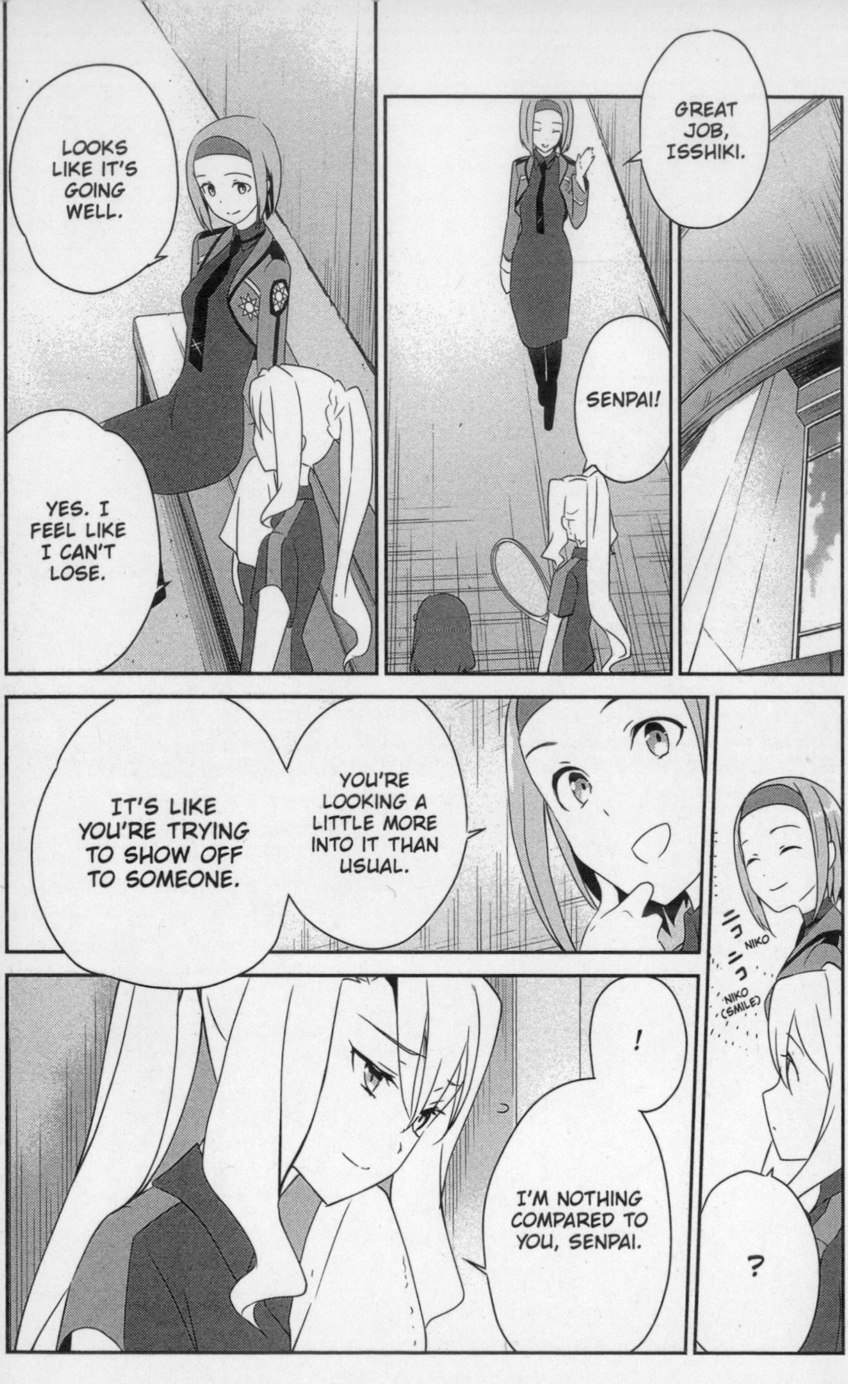
GREAT JOB, ISSHIKI.
SENPAI!
LOOKS LIKE IT'S GOING WELL.
YES. I FEEL LIKE I CAN'T LOSE.
NIKO
NIKO (SMILE)
?
YOU'RE LOOKING A LITTLE MORE INTO IT THAN USUAL.
IT'S LIKE YOU'RE TRYING TO SHOW OFF TO SOMEONE.
!
I'M NOTHING COMPARED TO YOU, SENPAI.

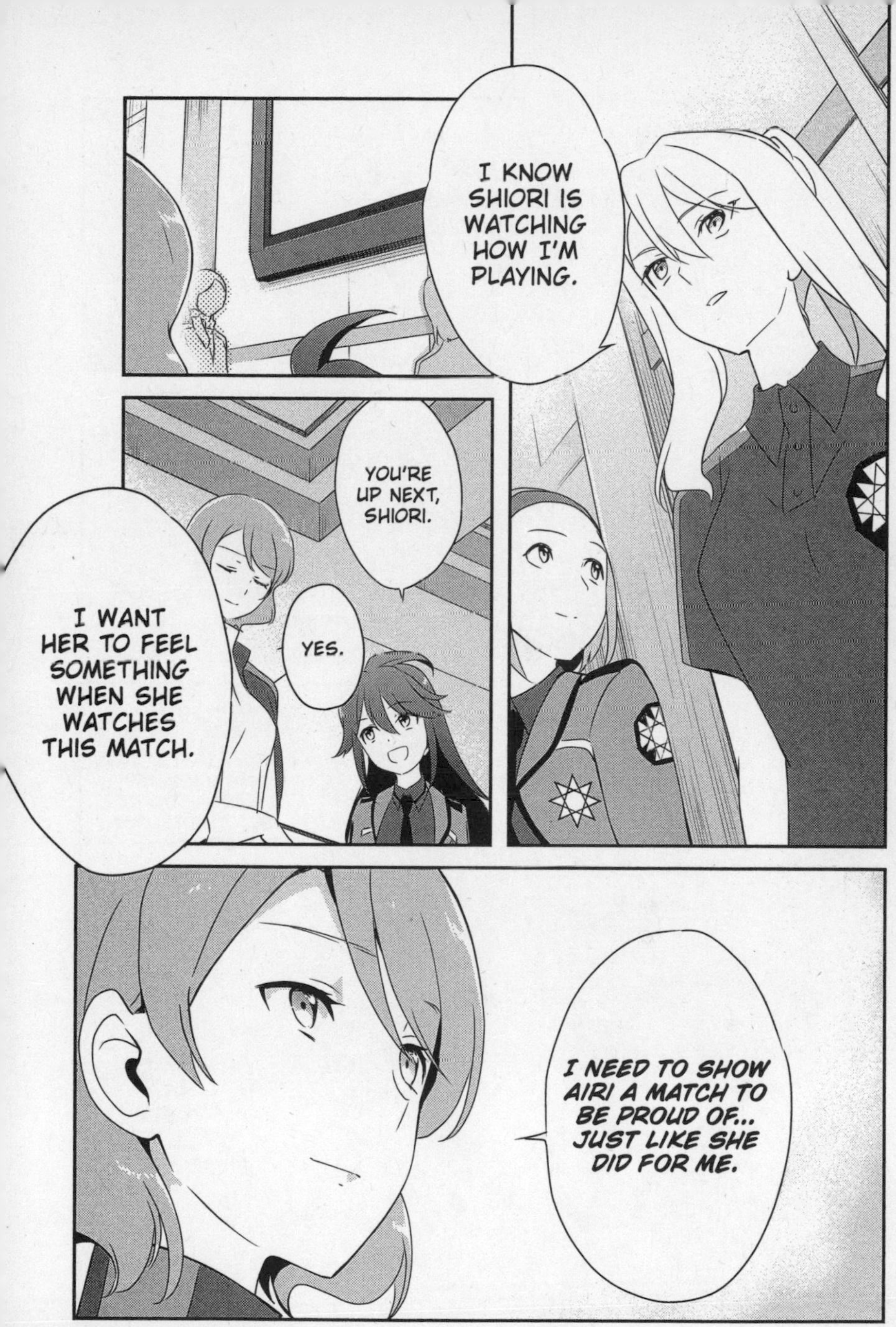
I KNOW SHIORI IS WATCHING HOW I'M PLAYING.
YOU'RE UP NEXT, SHIORI.
YES.
I WANT HER TO FEEL SOMETHING WHEN SHE WATCHES THIS MATCH.
I NEED TO SHOW AIRI A MATCH TO BE PROUD OF... JUST LIKE SHE DID FOR ME.

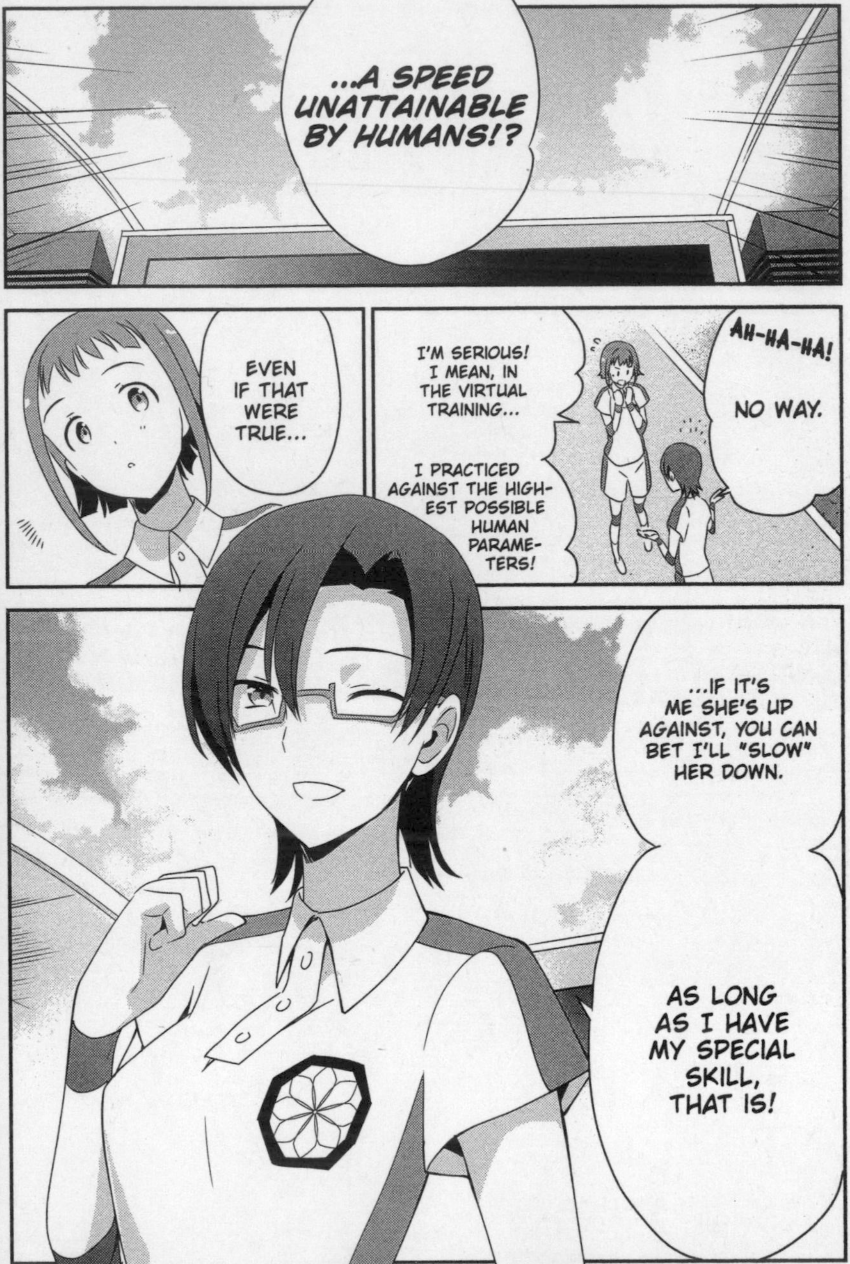
...A SPEED UNATTAINABLE BY HUMANS!?
AH-HA-HA!
NO WAY.
I'M SERIOUS! I MEAN, IN THE VIRTUAL TRAINING...
I PRACTICED AGAINST THE HIGH-EST POSSIBLE HUMAN PARAME-TERS!
EVEN IF THAT WERE TRUE...
...IF IT'S ME SHE'S UP AGAINST, YOU CAN BET I'LL "SLOW" HER DOWN.
AS LONG AS I HAVE MY SPECIAL SKILL, THAT IS!

THE
HONOR
STUDENT
AT
MAGIC HIGH
SCHOOL

VARIOUS HAIR-STYLES

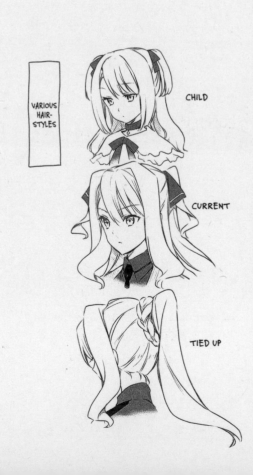

CHILD

CURRENT

TIED UP

CHAPTER 34

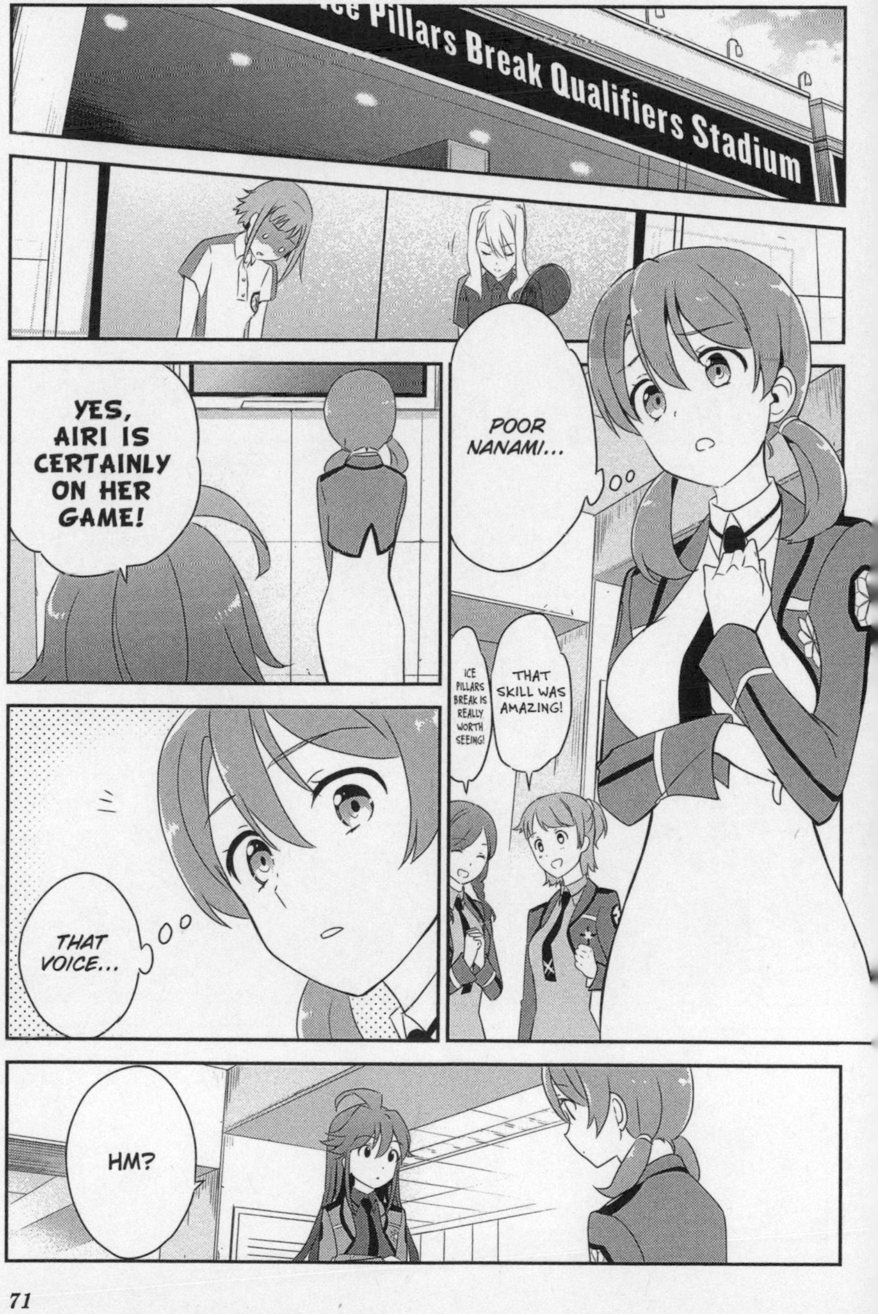

Pillars Break Qualifiers Stadium
POOR NANAMI...
THAT SKILL WAS AMAZING!
ICE PILLARS BREAK IS REALLY WORTH SEEING!
YES, AIRI IS CERTAINLY ON HER GAME!
THAT VOICE...
HM?

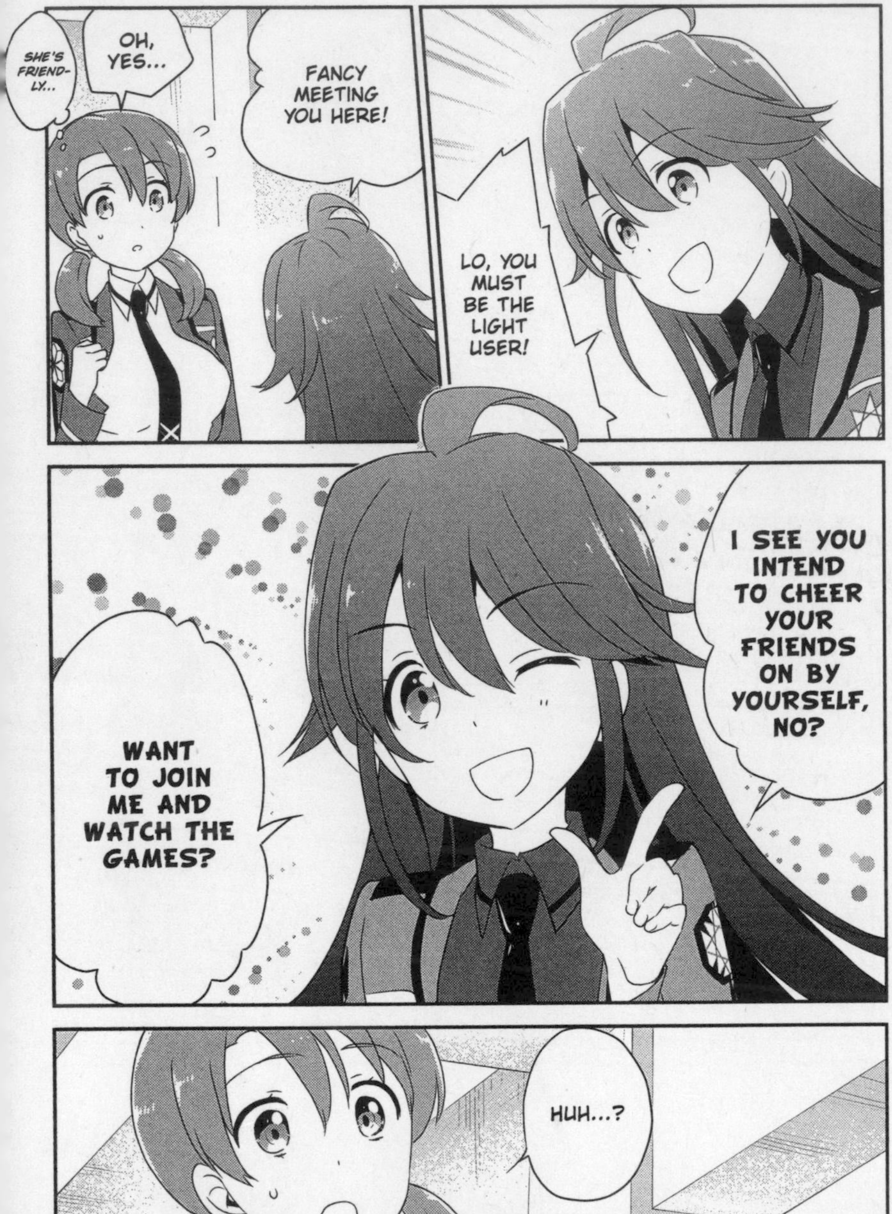
LO, YOU MUST BE THE LIGHT USER!
FANCY MEETING YOU HERE!
OH, YES...
SHE'S FRIEND-LY...
I SEE YOU INTEND TO CHEER YOUR FRIENDS ON BY YOURSELF, NO?
WANT TO JOIN ME AND WATCH THE GAMES?
HUH...?

CHAPTER 34

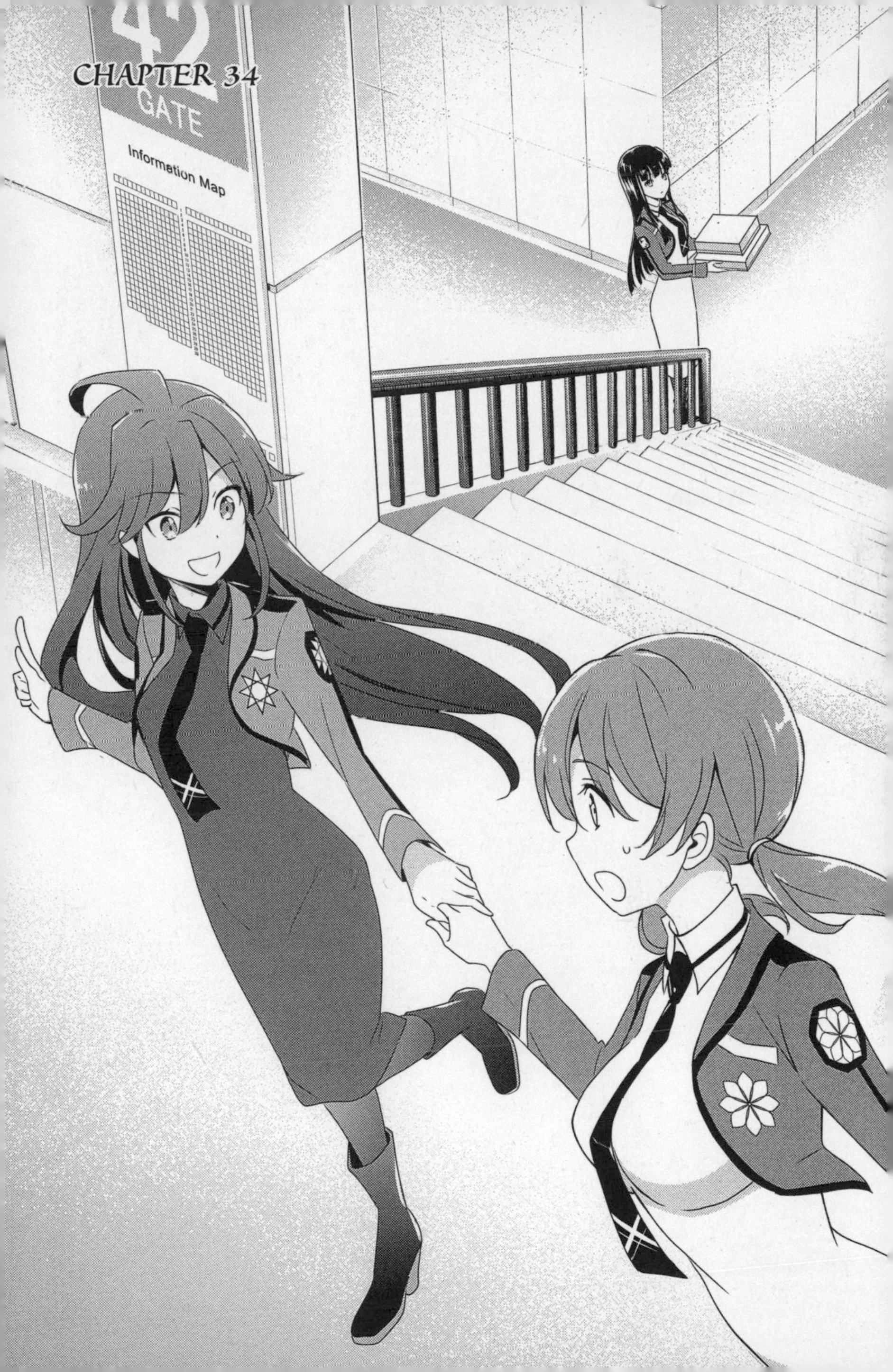
42
GATE
Information Map

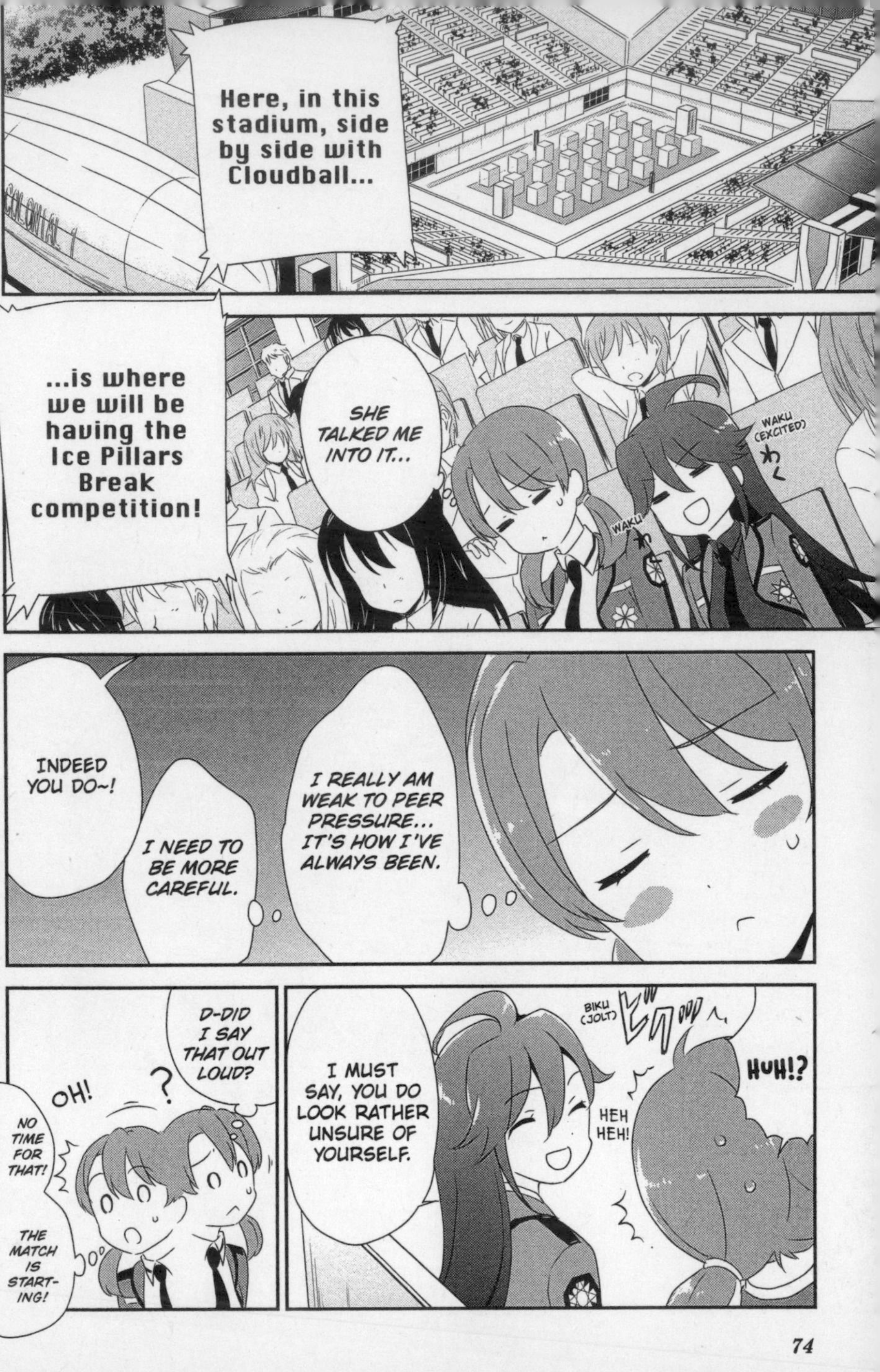
Here, in this stadium, side by side with Cloudball...
COLONIAL 1
...is where we will be having the Ice Pillars Break competition!
WAKU (EXCITED)
WAKU
SHE TALKED ME INTO IT...
I REALLY AM WEAK TO PEER PRESSURE... IT'S HOW I'VE ALWAYS BEEN.
I NEED TO BE MORE CAREFUL.
INDEED YOU DO~!
BIKU (JOLT)
HUH!?
HEH HEH!
I MUST SAY, YOU DO LOOK RATHER UNSURE OF YOURSELF.
D-DID I SAY THAT OUT LOUD?
?
OH!
NO TIME FOR THAT!
THE MATCH IS STARTING!

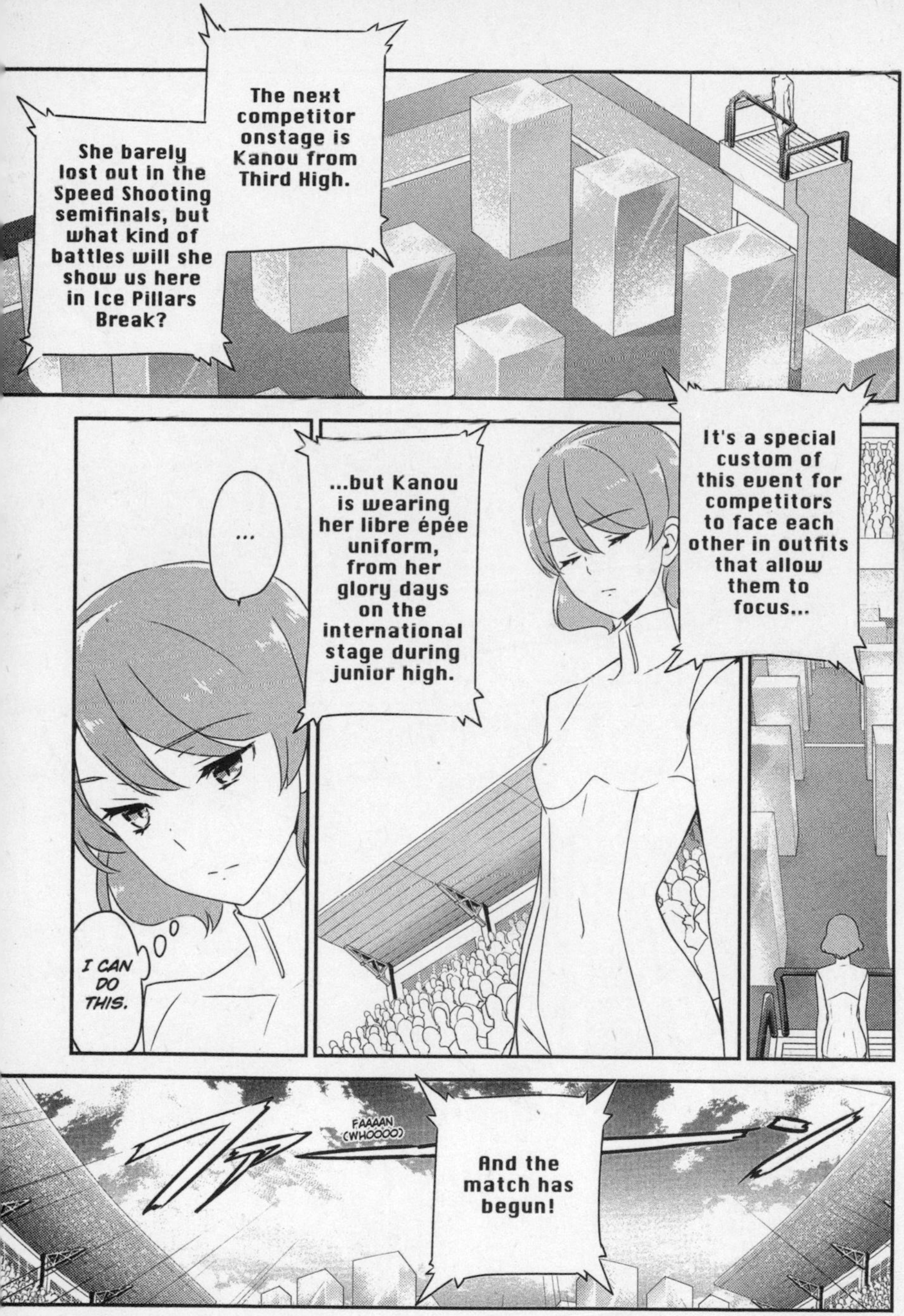
The next competitor onstage is Kanou from Third High.
She barely lost out in the Speed Shooting semifinals, but what kind of battles will she show us here in Ice Pillars Break?
It's a special custom of this event for competitors to face each other in outfits that allow them to focus...
...but Kanou is wearing her libre épée uniform, from her glory days on the international stage during junior high.
...
I CAN DO THIS.
FAAAAN (WHOOOO)
And the match has begun!

HUH!?

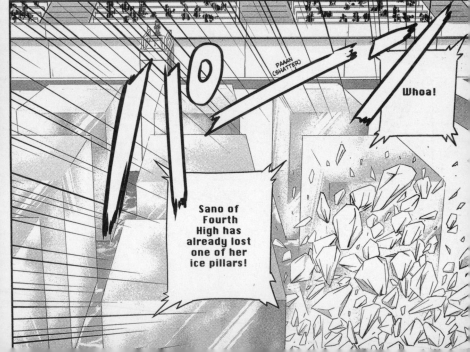
PAAAN (SHATTER)

Whoa!

Sano of Fourth High has already lost one of her ice pillars!

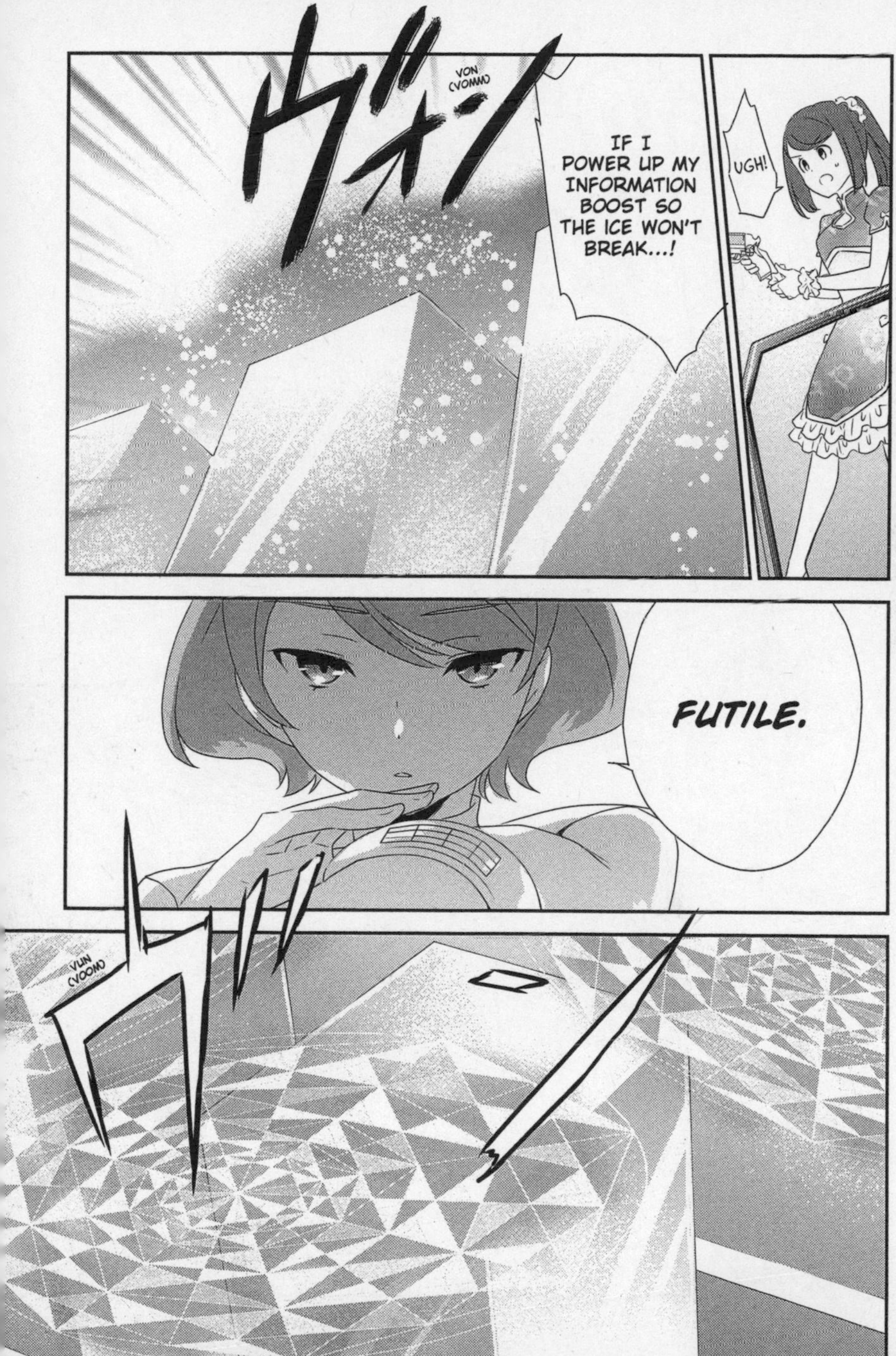
UGH!
VON (VOMM)
IF I POWER UP MY INFORMATION BOOST SO THE ICE WON'T BREAK...!
FUTILE.
VUN (VOOM)

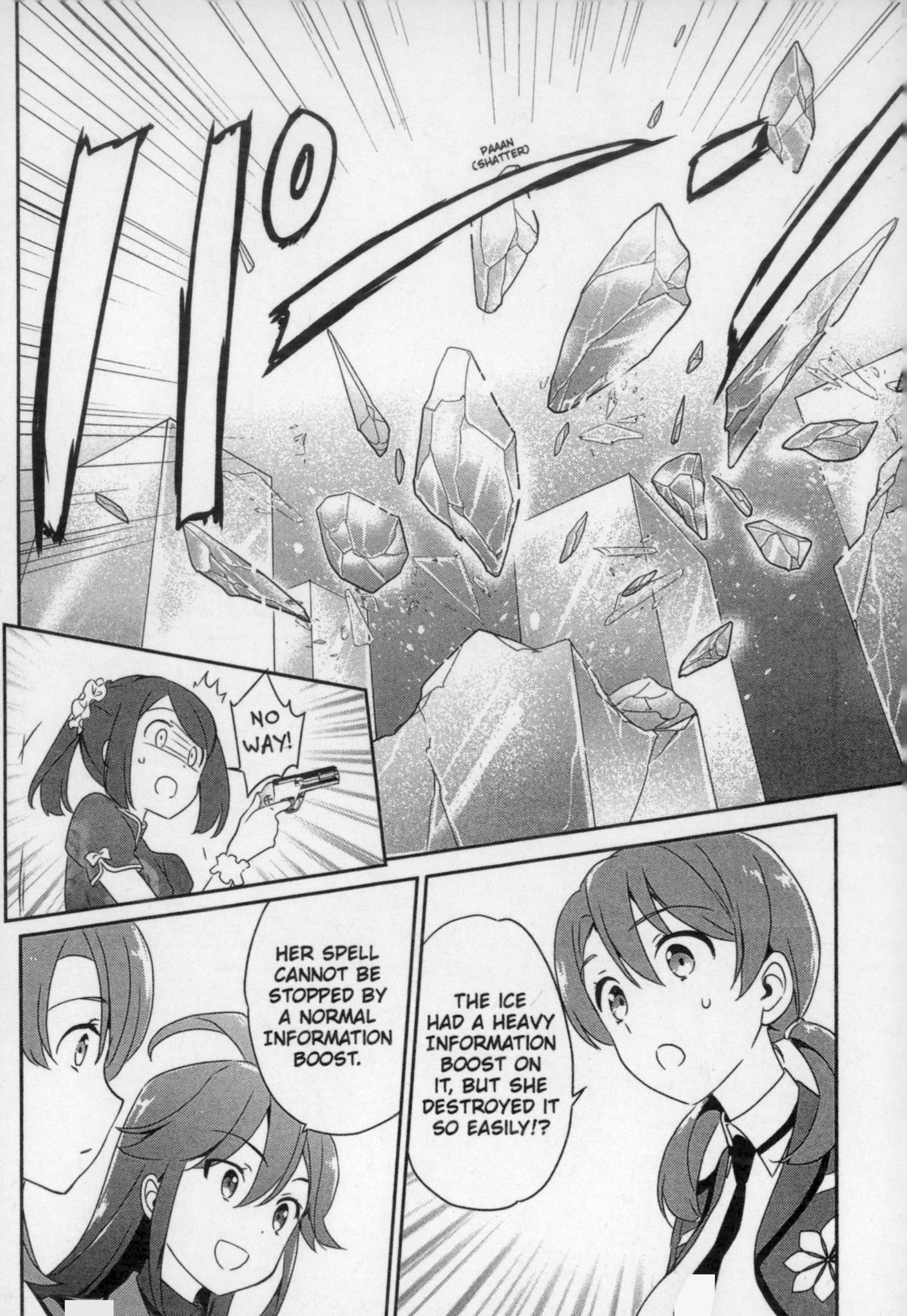
PAAAN (SHATTER)
NO WAY!
THE ICE HAD A HEAVY INFORMATION BOOST ON IT, BUT SHE DESTROYED IT SO EASILY!?
HER SPELL CANNOT BE STOPPED BY A NORMAL INFORMATION BOOST.

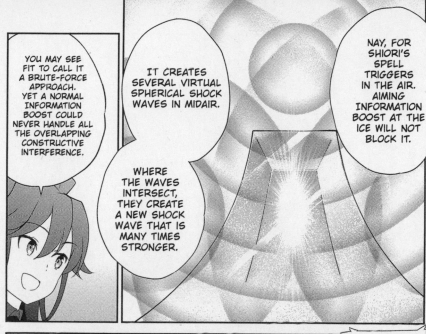

NAY, FOR SHIORI'S SPELL TRIGGERS IN THE AIR. AIMING INFORMATION BOOST AT THE ICE WILL NOT BLOCK IT.
IT CREATES SEVERAL VIRTUAL SPHERICAL SHOCK WAVES IN MIDAIR.
WHERE THE WAVES INTERSECT, THEY CREATE A NEW SHOCK WAVE THAT IS MANY TIMES STRONGER.
YOU MAY SEE FIT TO CALL IT A BRUTE-FORCE APPROACH. YET A NORMAL INFORMATION BOOST COULD NEVER HANDLE ALL THE OVERLAPPING CONSTRUCTIVE INTERFERENCE.
Kanou still hasn't allowed a single one of her own pillars to go down.
Sano only has five. She's lost over half!
URGH...
IT'S ALL OR NOTHING NOW.

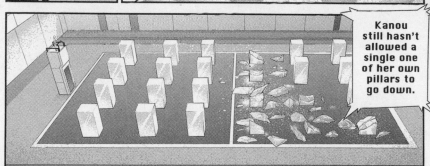

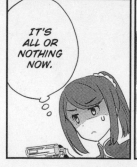

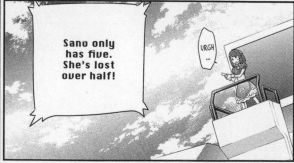

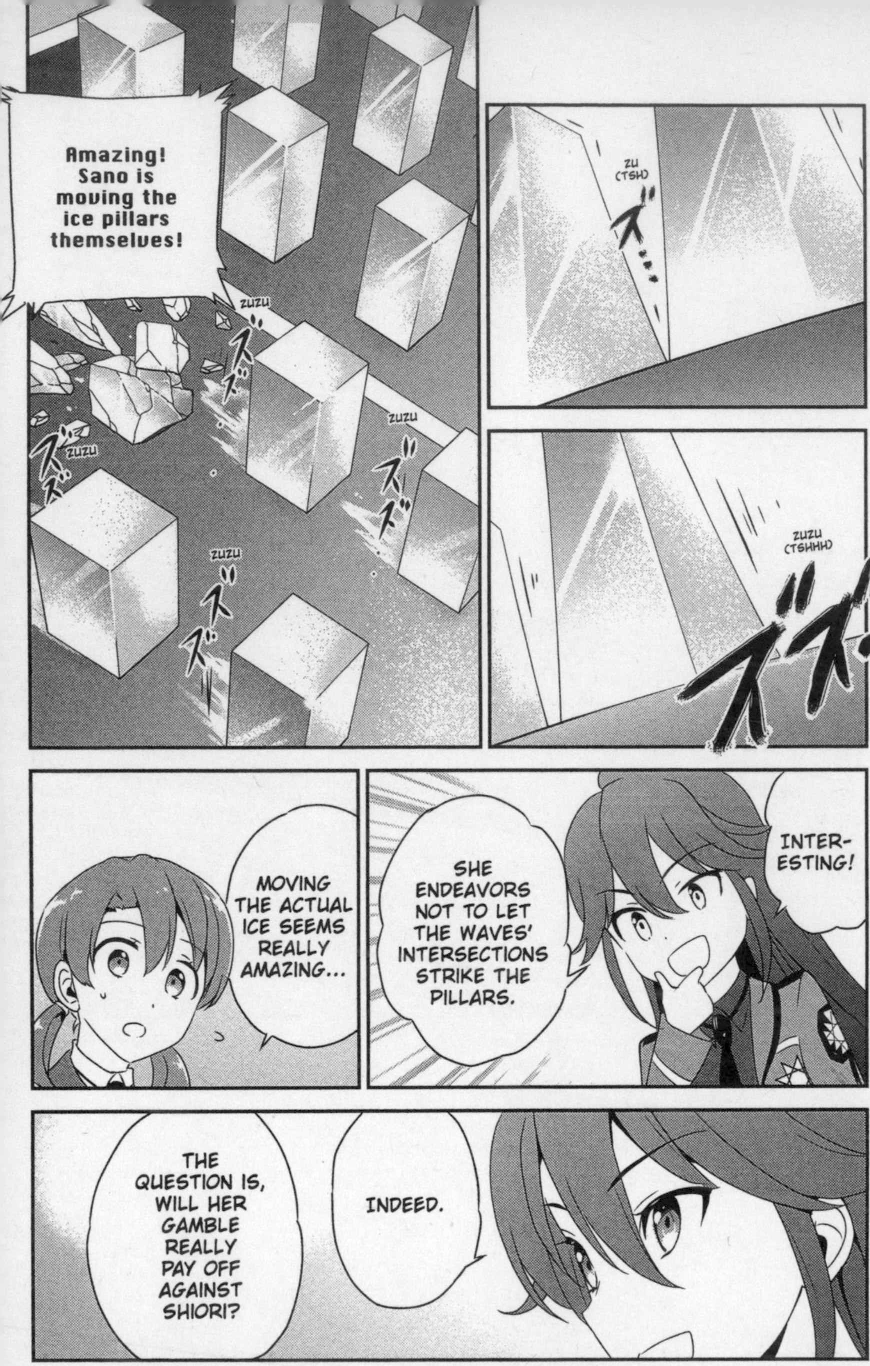
ZU (TSH)
ZUZU (TSHHH)
Amazing! Sano is moving the ice pillars themselves!
ZUZU
ZUZU
ZUZU
ZUZU
INTER-ESTING!
SHE ENDEAVORS NOT TO LET THE WAVES' INTERSECTIONS STRIKE THE PILLARS.
MOVING THE ACTUAL ICE SEEMS REALLY AMAZING...
INDEED.
THE QUESTION IS, WILL HER GAMBLE REALLY PAY OFF AGAINST SHIORI?

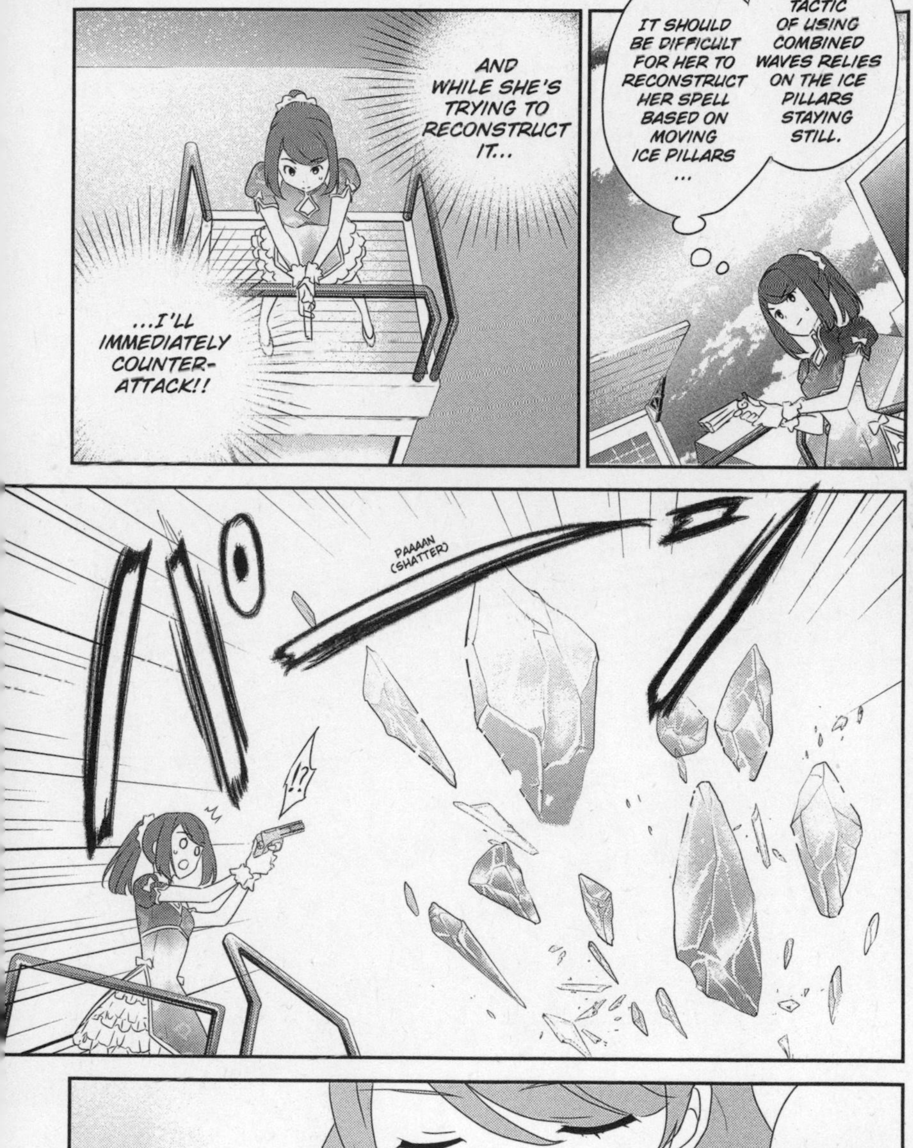
KANOU'S TACTIC OF USING COMBINED WAVES RELIES ON THE ICE PILLARS STAYING STILL.
IT SHOULD BE DIFFICULT FOR HER TO RECONSTRUCT HER SPELL BASED ON MOVING ICE PILLARS ...
AND WHILE SHE'S TRYING TO RECONSTRUCT IT...
...I'LL IMMEDIATELY COUNTER-ATTACK!!
PAAAAN (SHATTER)
!?
I THOUGHT AS MUCH.

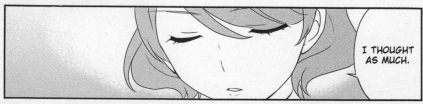

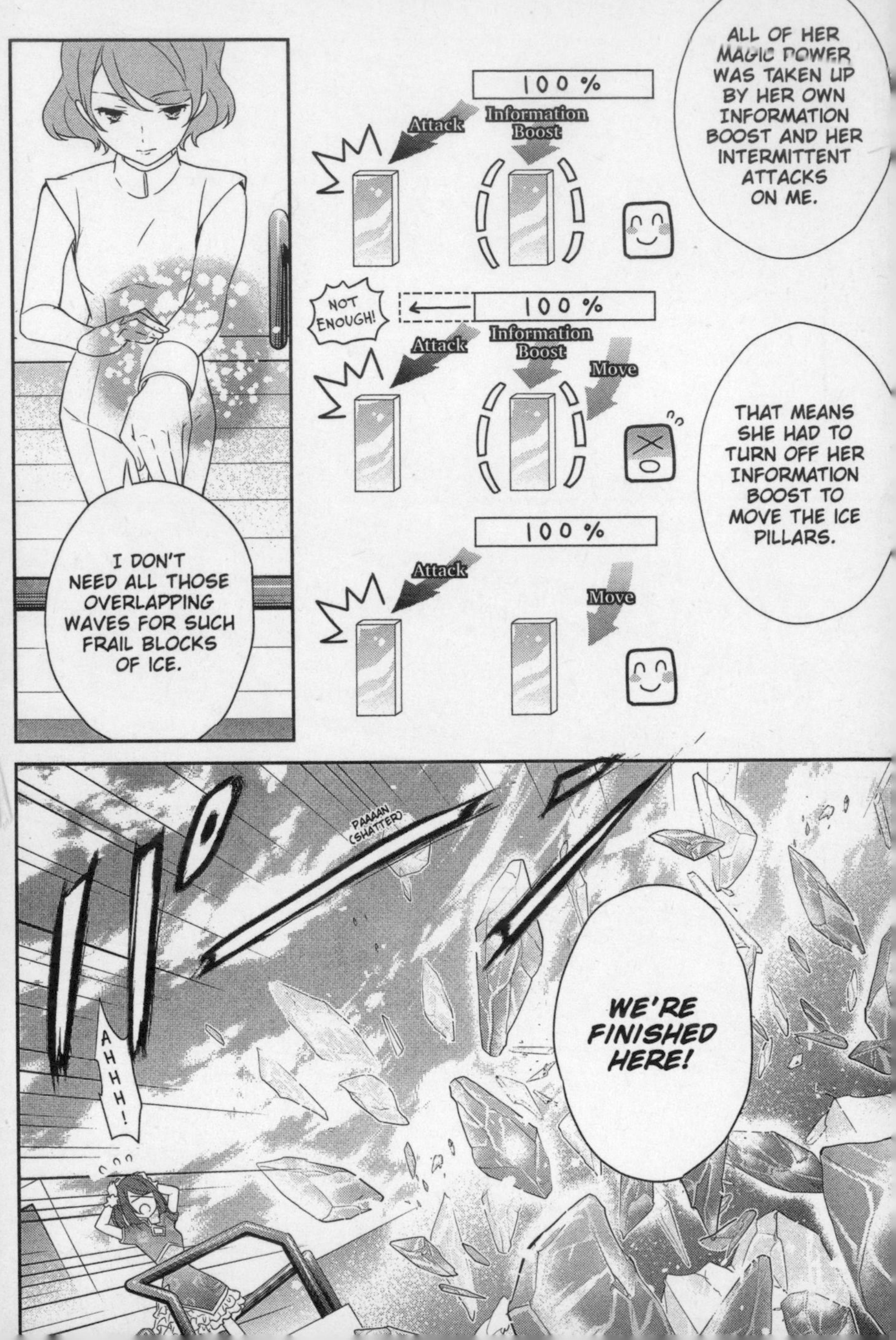
ALL OF HER MAGIC POWER WAS TAKEN UP BY HER OWN INFORMATION BOOST AND HER INTERMITTENT ATTACKS ON ME.
100 %
Information Boost
Attack
NOT ENOUGH!
100 %
Information Boost
Attack
Move
THAT MEANS SHE HAD TO TURN OFF HER INFORMATION BOOST TO MOVE THE ICE PILLARS.
100 %
Attack
Move
I DON'T NEED ALL THOSE OVERLAPPING WAVES FOR SUCH FRAIL BLOCKS OF ICE.
WE'RE FINISHED HERE!
PAAAAN (SHATTER)
AHHH!

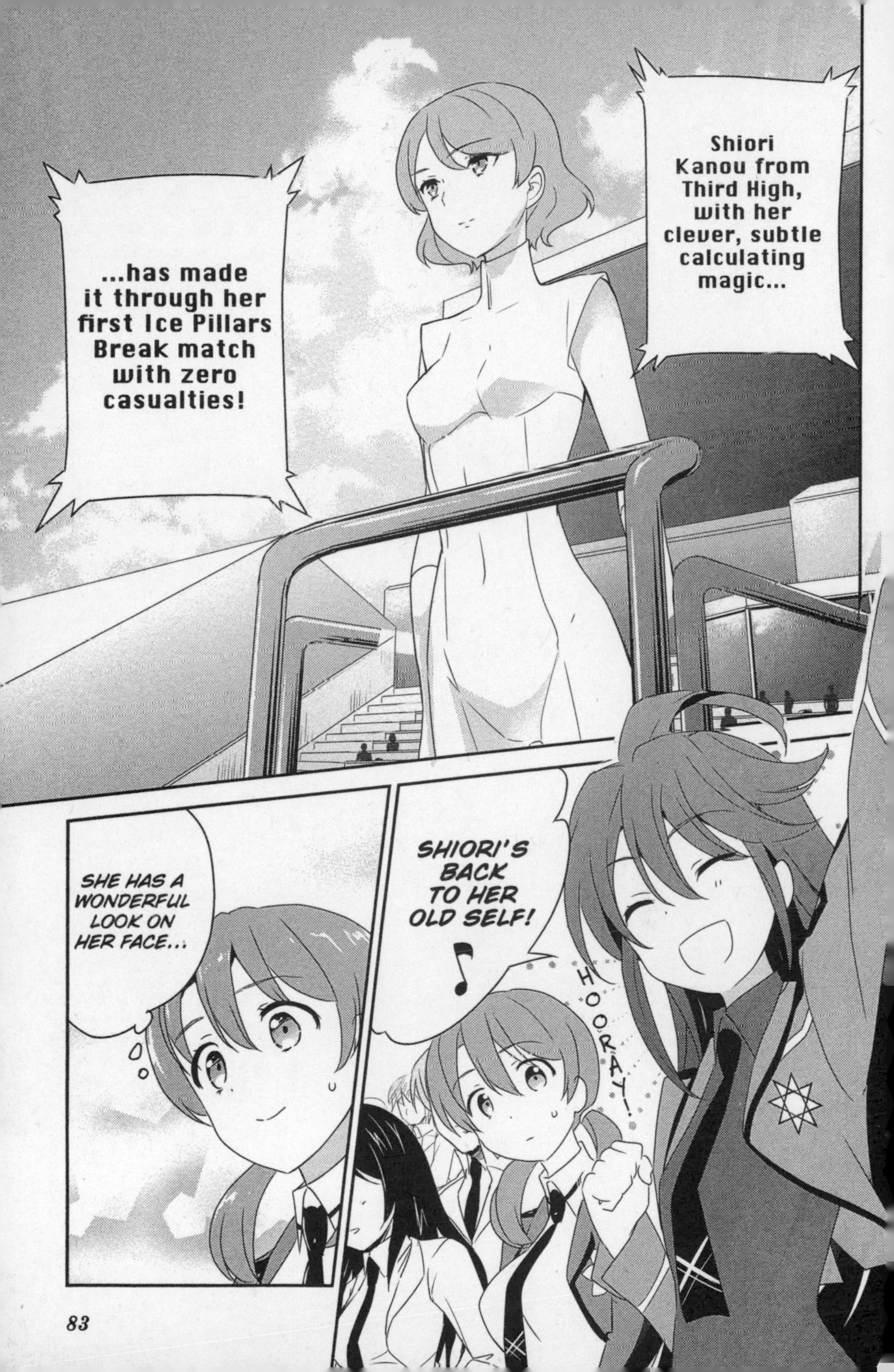
Shiori Kanou from Third High, with her clever, subtle calculating magic...
...has made it through her first Ice Pillars Break match with zero casualties!
SHIORI'S BACK TO HER OLD SELF! ♪
HOORAY!
SHE HAS A WONDERFUL LOOK ON HER FACE...

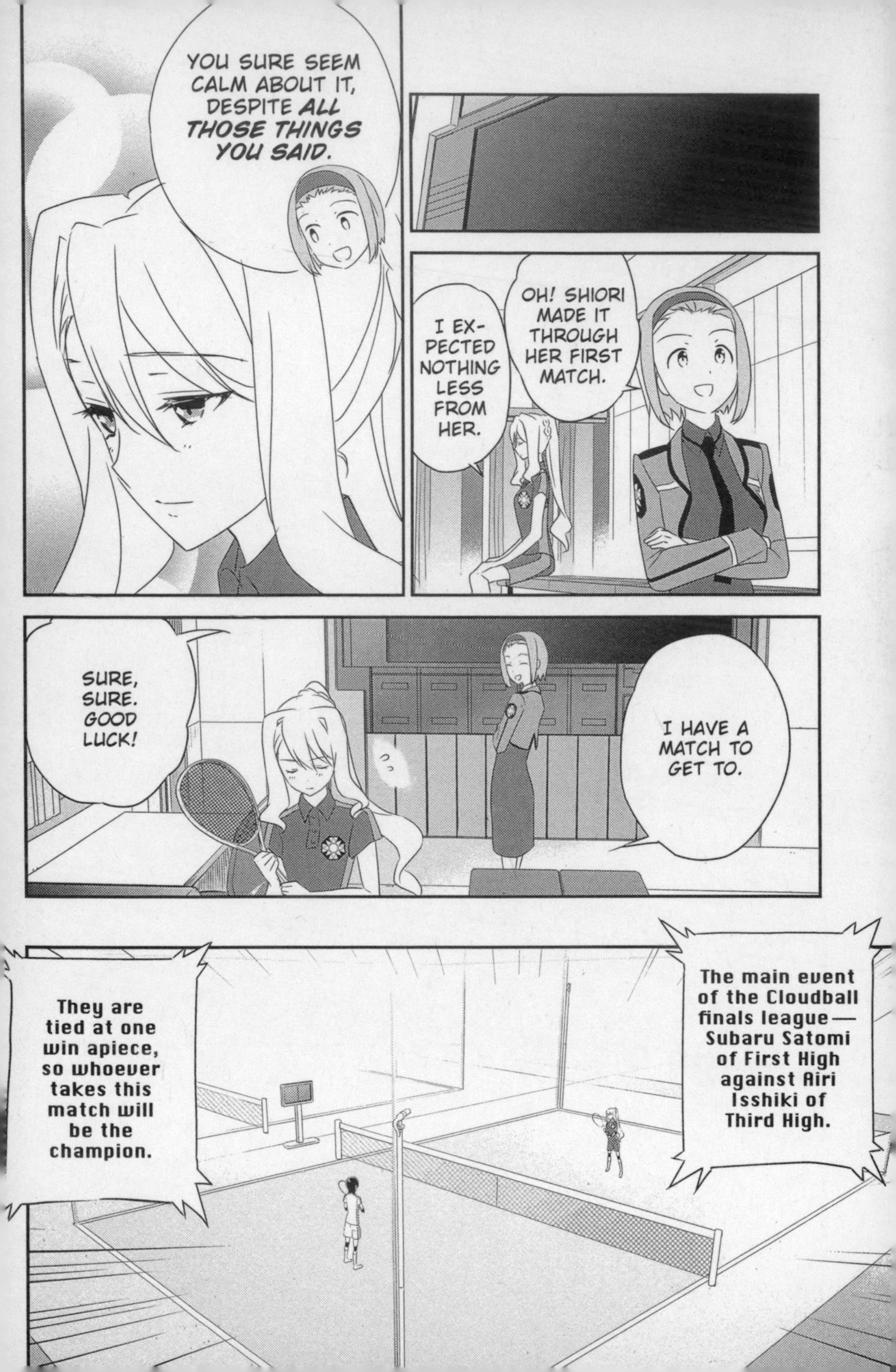
OH! SHIORI MADE IT THROUGH HER FIRST MATCH.
I EX-PECTED NOTHING LESS FROM HER.
YOU SURE SEEM CALM ABOUT IT, DESPITE ALL THOSE THINGS YOU SAID.
I HAVE A MATCH TO GET TO.
SURE, SURE. GOOD LUCK!
The main event of the Cloudball finals league—Subaru Satomi of First High against Airi Isshiki of Third High.
They are tied at one win apiece, so whoever takes this match will be the champion.

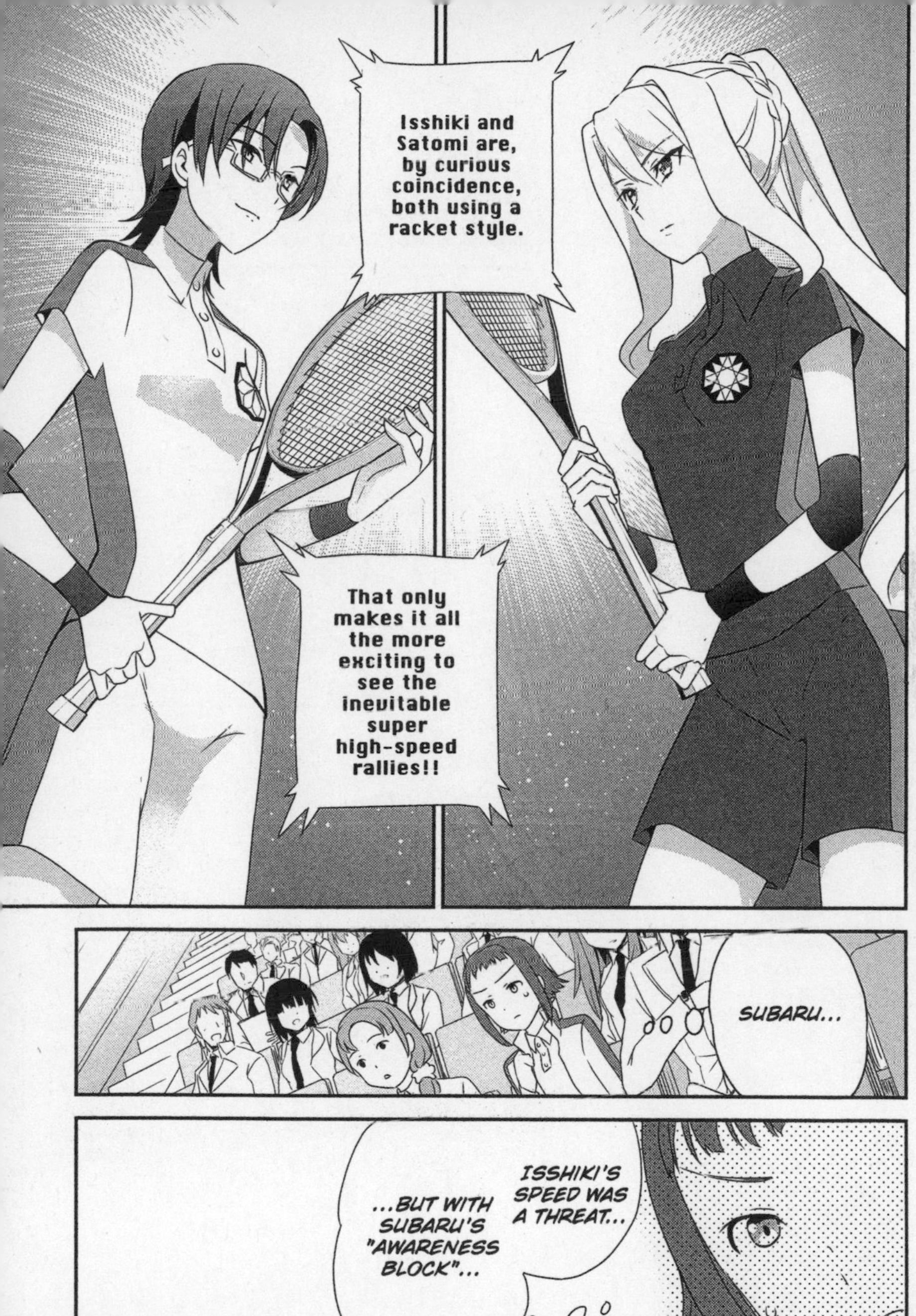
Isshiki and Satomi are, by curious coincidence, both using a racket style.
That only makes it all the more exciting to see the inevitable super high-speed rallies!!
SUBARU...
ISSHIKI'S SPEED WAS A THREAT...
...BUT WITH SUBARU'S "AWARENESS BLOCK"...

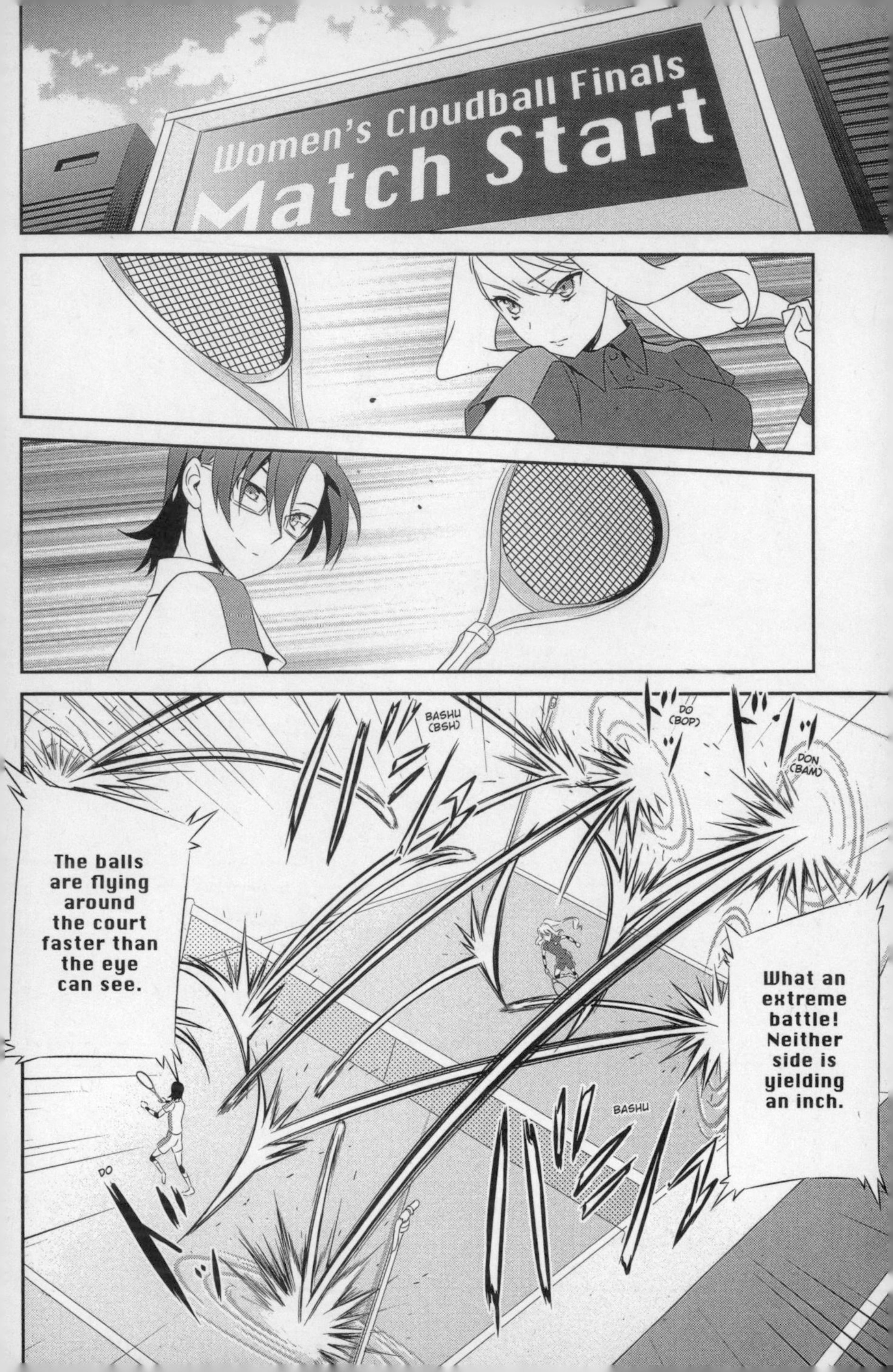

Women's Cloudball Finals
Match Start
DO (BOP)
DON (BAM)
BASHU (BSH)
The balls are flying around the court faster than the eye can see.
What an extreme battle! Neither side is yielding an inch.
BASHU
DO

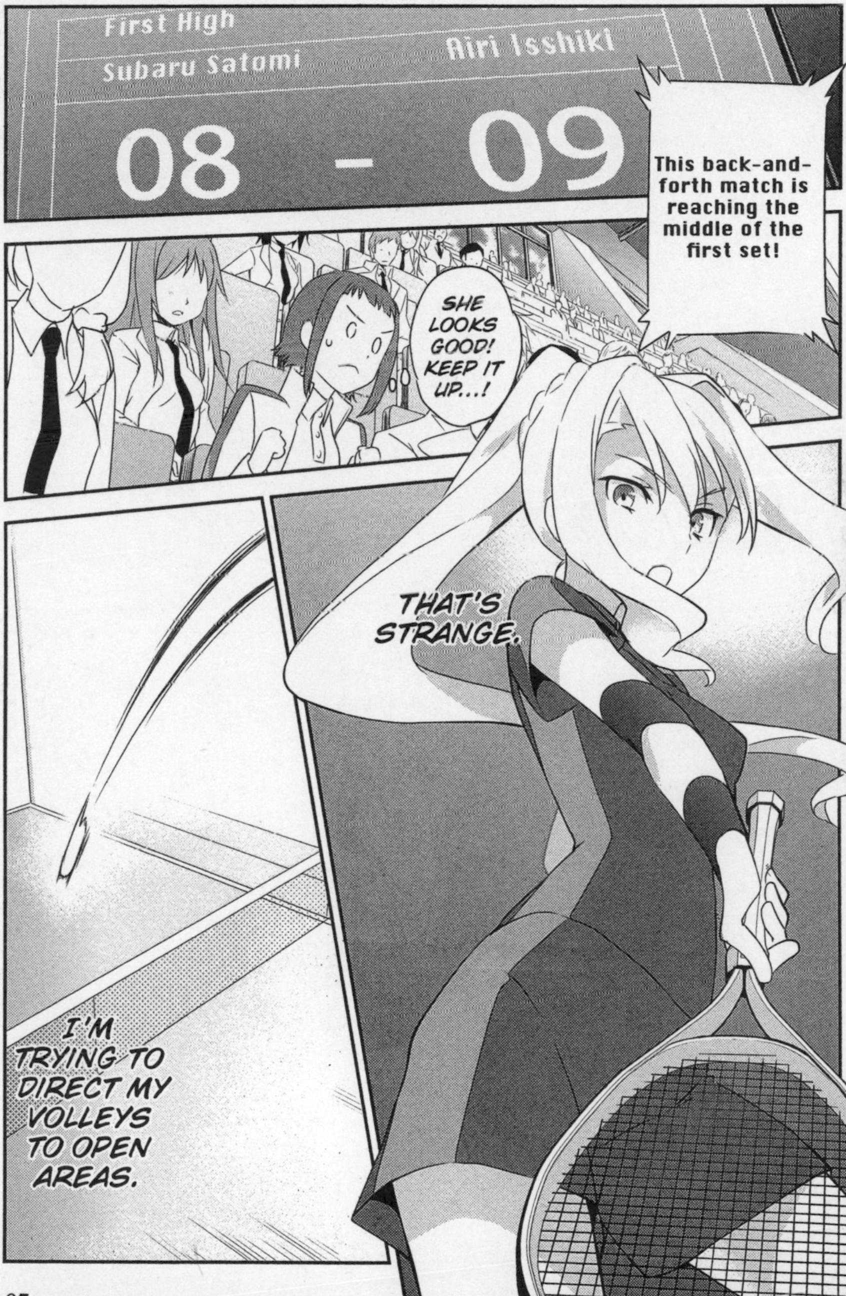
This back-and-forth match is reaching the middle of the first set!
First High
Subaru Satomi
Airi Isshiki
08 - 09
SHE LOOKS GOOD! KEEP IT UP...!
THAT'S STRANGE.
I'M TRYING TO DIRECT MY VOLLEYS TO OPEN AREAS.

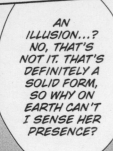

AN ILLUSION...? NO, THAT'S NOT IT. THAT'S DEFINITELY A SOLID FORM, SO WHY ON EARTH CAN'T I SENSE HER PRESENCE?

SHE'S GOOD— STILL SO FAST EVEN UNDER THE EFFECTS OF MY "AWARENESS BLOCK."

BUT HOW LONG CAN SHE KEEP UP WITH ME?

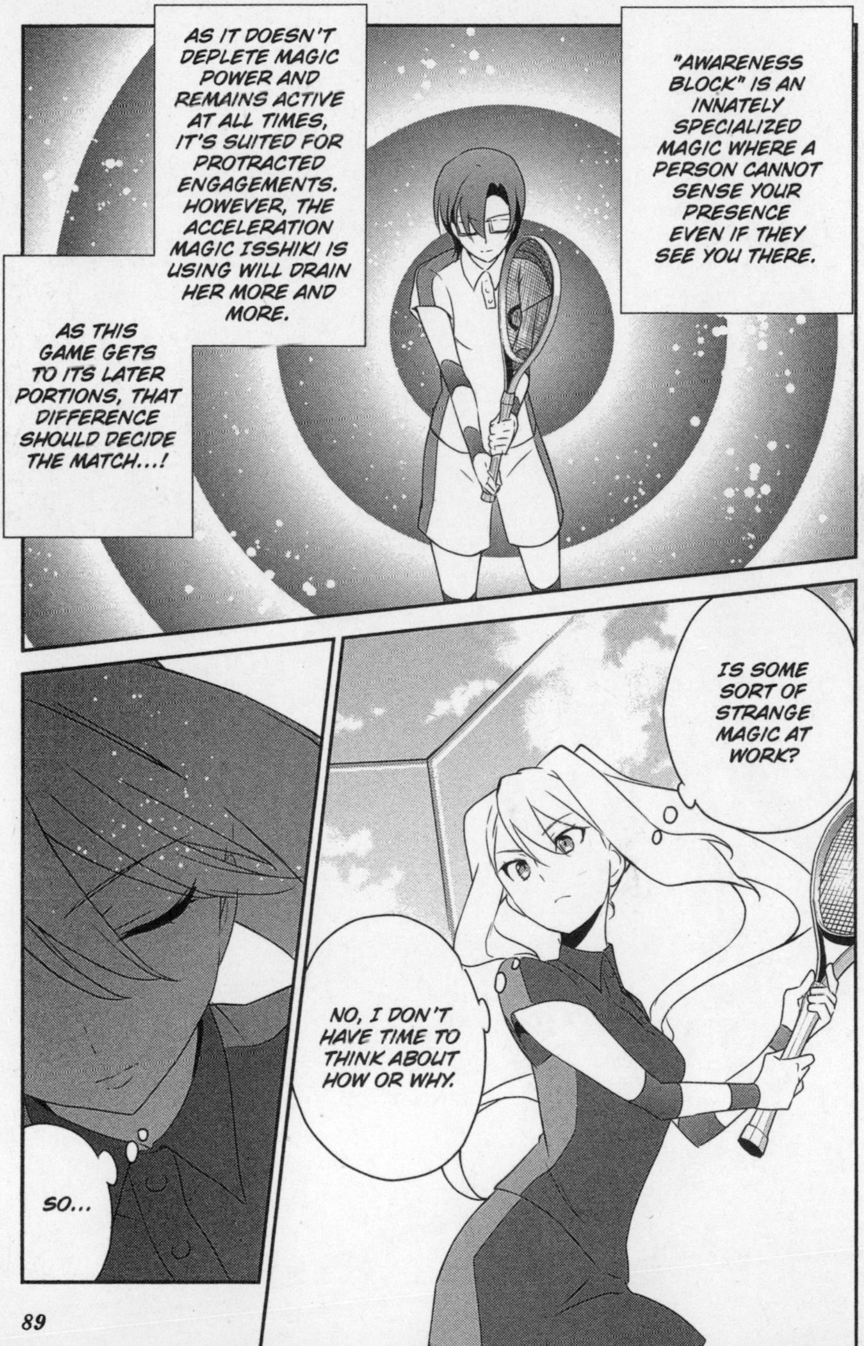
"AWARENESS BLOCK" IS AN INNATELY SPECIALIZED MAGIC WHERE A PERSON CANNOT SENSE YOUR PRESENCE EVEN IF THEY SEE YOU THERE.
AS IT DOESN'T DEPLETE MAGIC POWER AND REMAINS ACTIVE AT ALL TIMES, IT'S SUITED FOR PROTRACTED ENGAGEMENTS. HOWEVER, THE ACCELERATION MAGIC ISSHIKI IS USING WILL DRAIN HER MORE AND MORE.
AS THIS GAME GETS TO ITS LATER PORTIONS, THAT DIFFERENCE SHOULD DECIDE THE MATCH...!
IS SOME SORT OF STRANGE MAGIC AT WORK?
NO, I DON'T HAVE TIME TO THINK ABOUT HOW OR WHY.
SO...

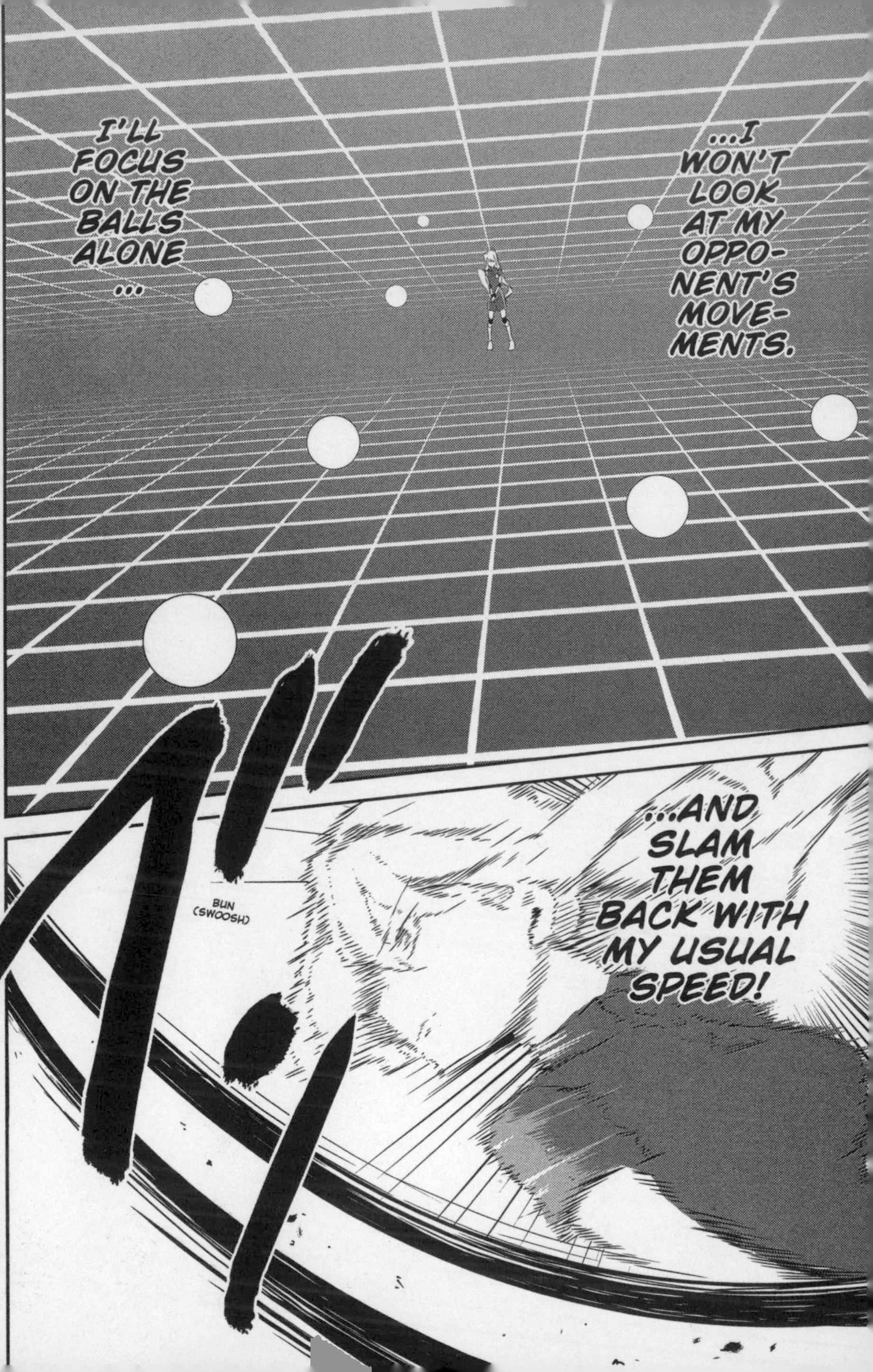
...I WON'T LOOK AT MY OPPONENT'S MOVEMENTS.
I'LL FOCUS ON THE BALLS ALONE...
...AND SLAM THEM BACK WITH MY USUAL SPEED!
BUN (SWOOSH)

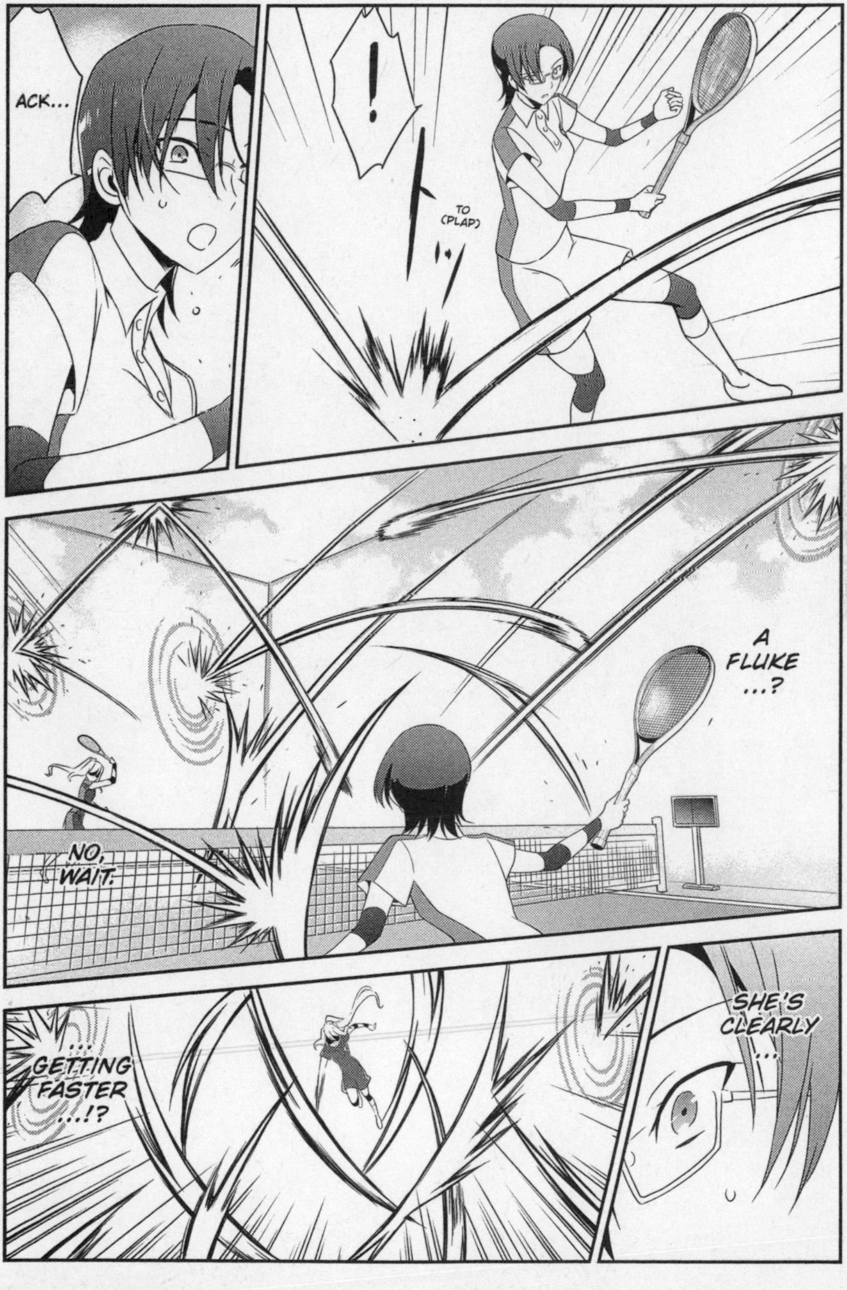
!
TO (PLAP)
ACK...
A FLUKE ...?
NO, WAIT.
SHE'S CLEARLY ...
... GETTING FASTER ...!?

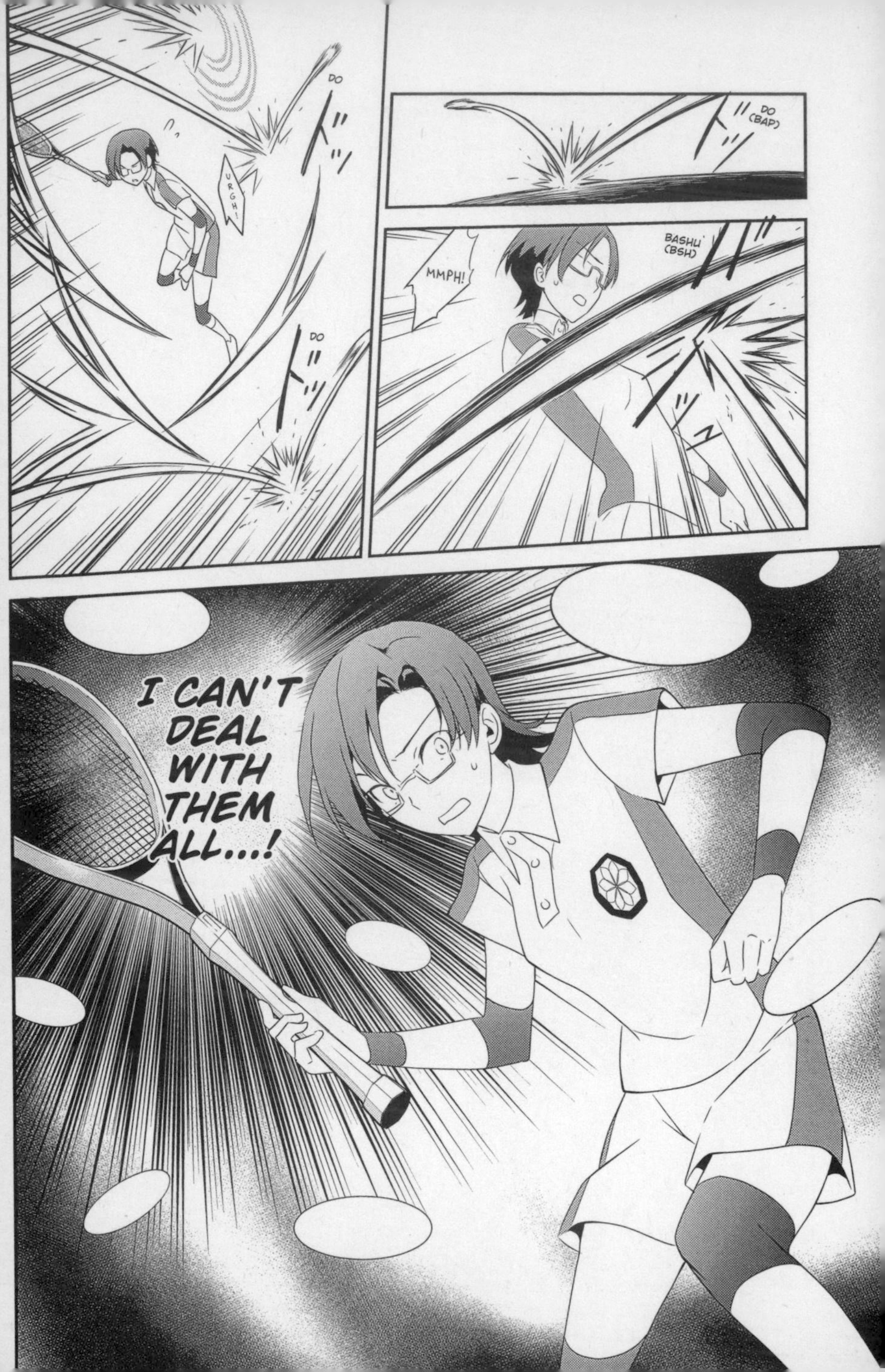
DO (BAP)
BASHU (BSH)
MMPH!
DO
URGH!
DO
I CAN'T DEAL WITH THEM ALL...!

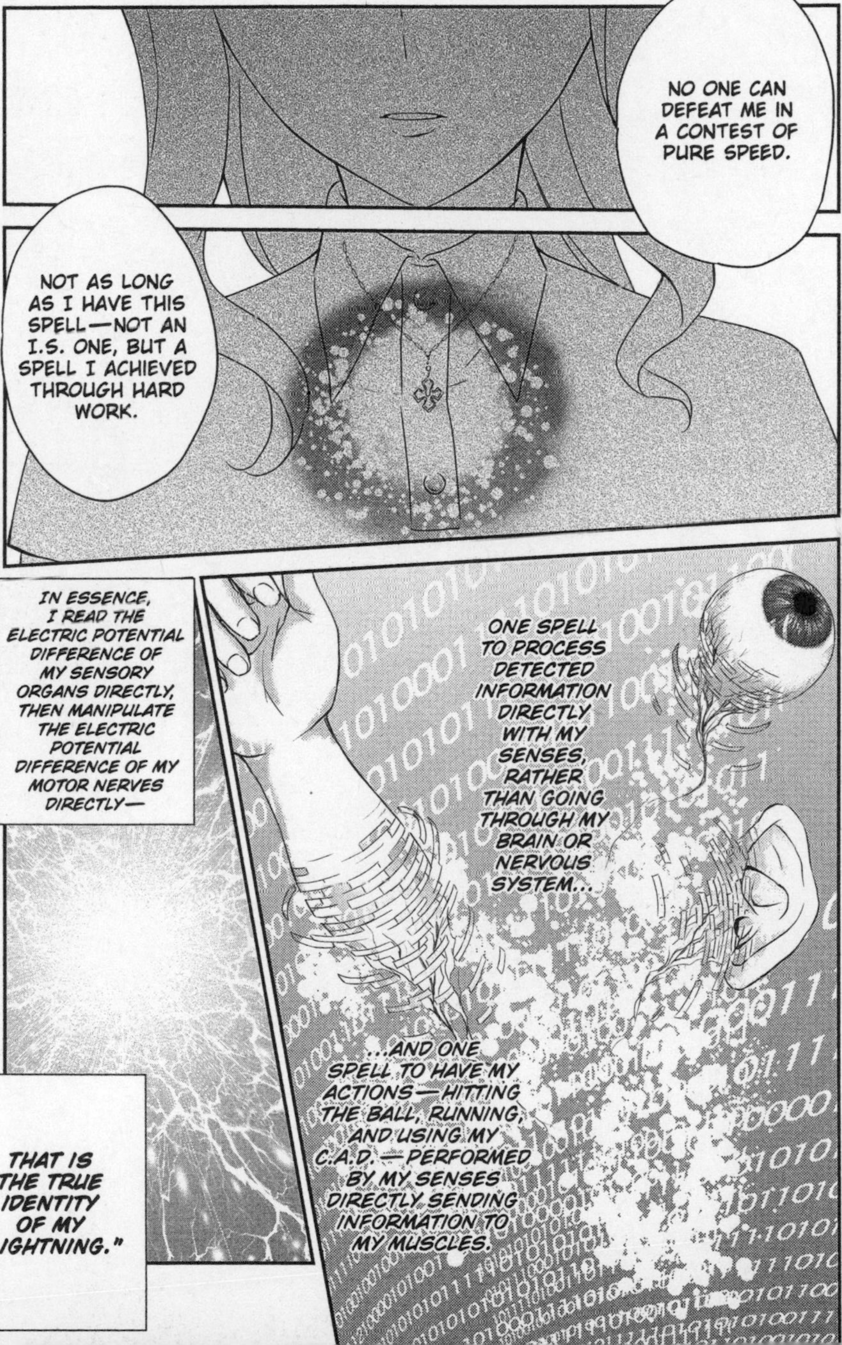

NO ONE CAN DEFEAT ME IN A CONTEST OF PURE SPEED.
NOT AS LONG AS I HAVE THIS SPELL—NOT AN I.S. ONE, BUT A SPELL I ACHIEVED THROUGH HARD WORK.
ONE SPELL TO PROCESS DETECTED INFORMATION DIRECTLY WITH MY SENSES, RATHER THAN GOING THROUGH MY BRAIN OR NERVOUS SYSTEM...
...AND ONE SPELL TO HAVE MY ACTIONS—HITTING THE BALL, RUNNING, AND USING MY C.A.D.—PERFORMED BY MY SENSES DIRECTLY SENDING INFORMATION TO MY MUSCLES.
IN ESSENCE, I READ THE ELECTRIC POTENTIAL DIFFERENCE OF MY SENSORY ORGANS DIRECTLY, THEN MANIPULATE THE ELECTRIC POTENTIAL DIFFERENCE OF MY MOTOR NERVES DIRECTLY—
THAT IS THE TRUE IDENTITY OF MY "LIGHTNING."

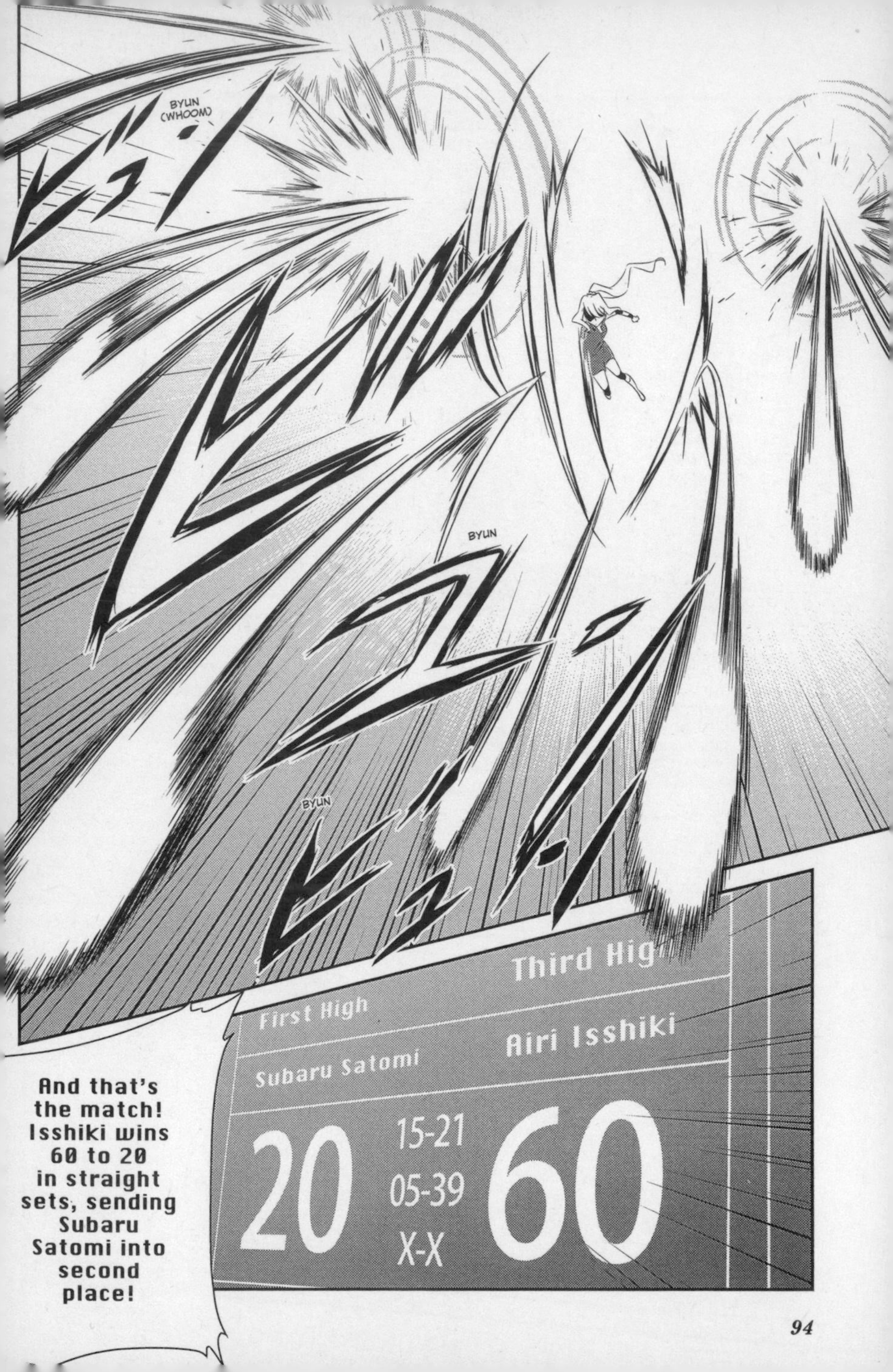
BYUN (WHOOM)
BYUN
BYUN
First High
Third High
Subaru Satomi
Airi Isshiki
20
15-21
05-39
X-X
60
And that's the match! Isshiki wins 60 to 20 in straight sets, sending Subaru Satomi into second place!

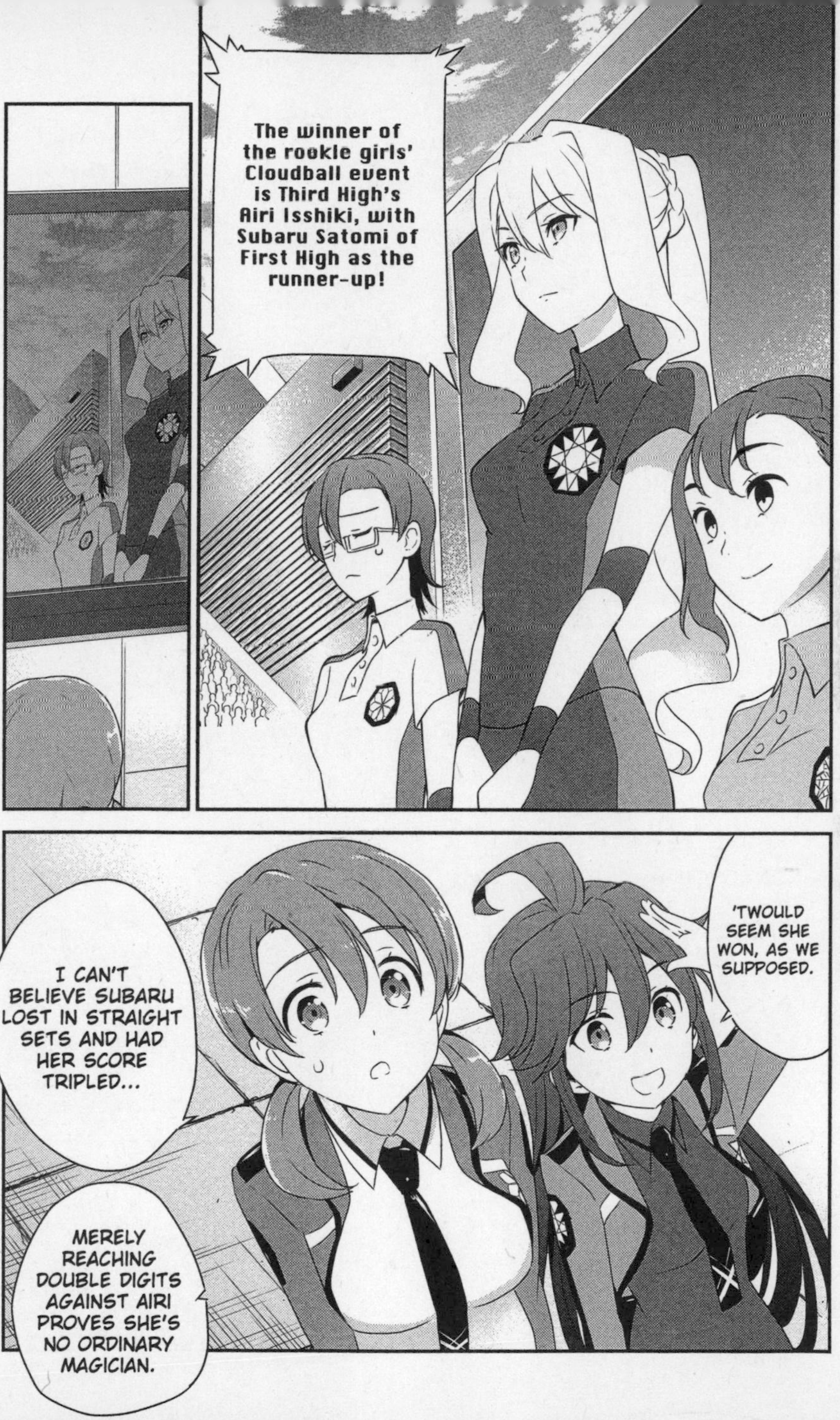
The winner of the rookie girls' Cloudball event is Third High's Airi Isshiki, with Subaru Satomi of First High as the runner-up!
'TWOULD SEEM SHE WON, AS WE SUPPOSED.
I CAN'T BELIEVE SUBARU LOST IN STRAIGHT SETS AND HAD HER SCORE TRIPLED...
MERELY REACHING DOUBLE DIGITS AGAINST AIRI PROVES SHE'S NO ORDINARY MAGICIAN.

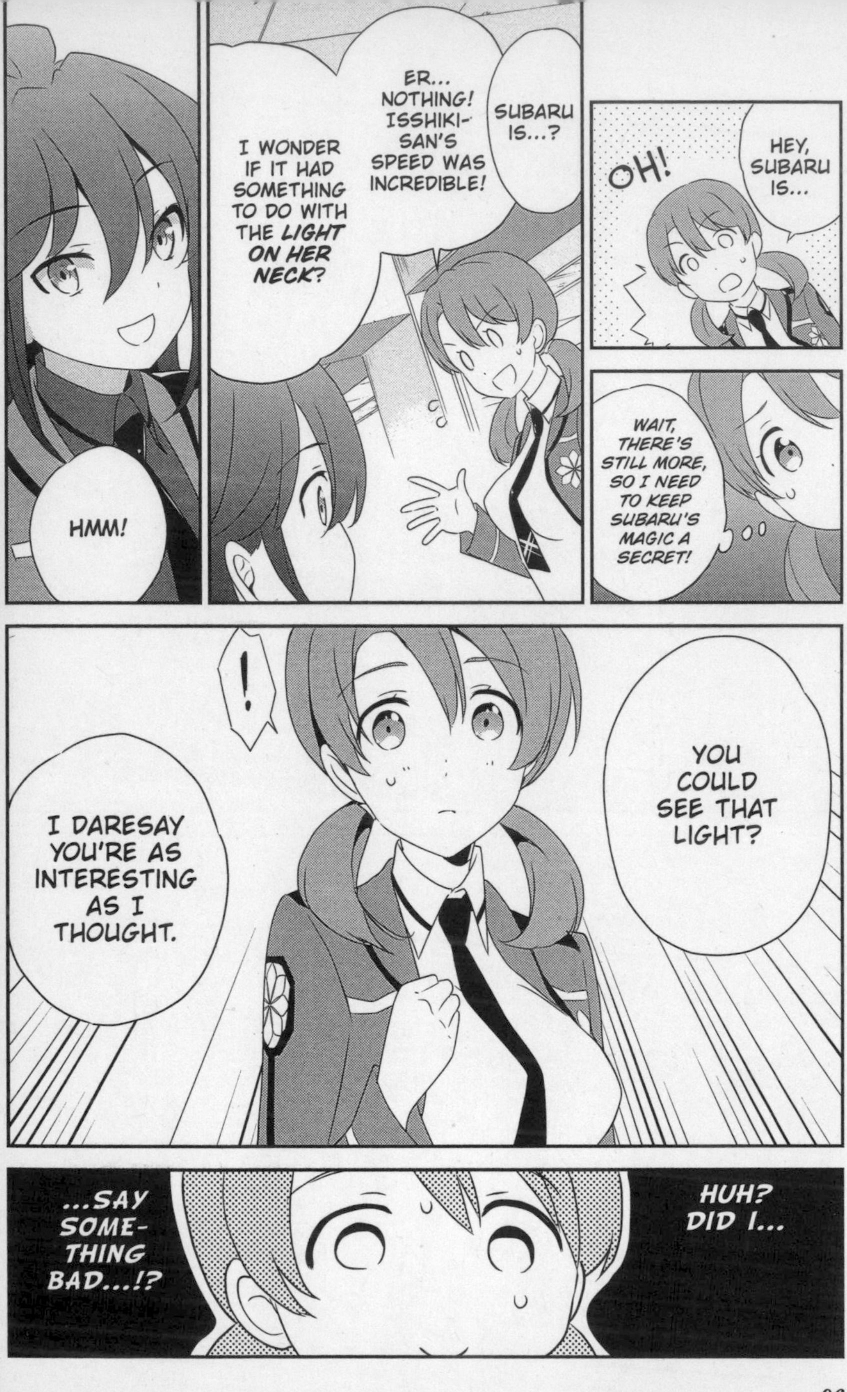
HEY, SUBARU IS...
OH!
WAIT, THERE'S STILL MORE, SO I NEED TO KEEP SUBARU'S MAGIC A SECRET!
SUBARU IS...?
ER... NOTHING! ISSHIKI-SAN'S SPEED WAS INCREDIBLE!
I WONDER IF IT HAD SOMETHING TO DO WITH THE LIGHT ON HER NECK?
HMM!
!
YOU COULD SEE THAT LIGHT?
I DARESAY YOU'RE AS INTERESTING AS I THOUGHT.
HUH? DID I...
...SAY SOME-THING BAD...!?

THE HONOR STUDENT AT MAGIC HIGH SCHOOL

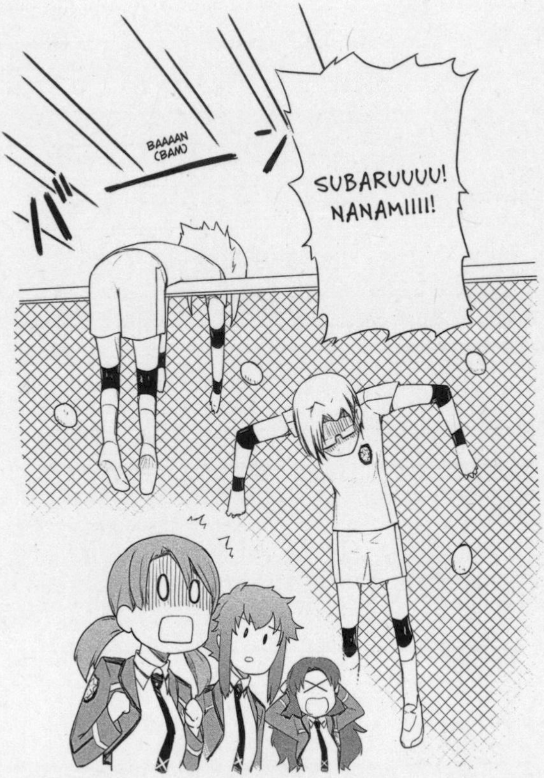
BAAAAN
(BAM)
SUBARUUUU!
NANAMIIIII!

CHAPTER 35

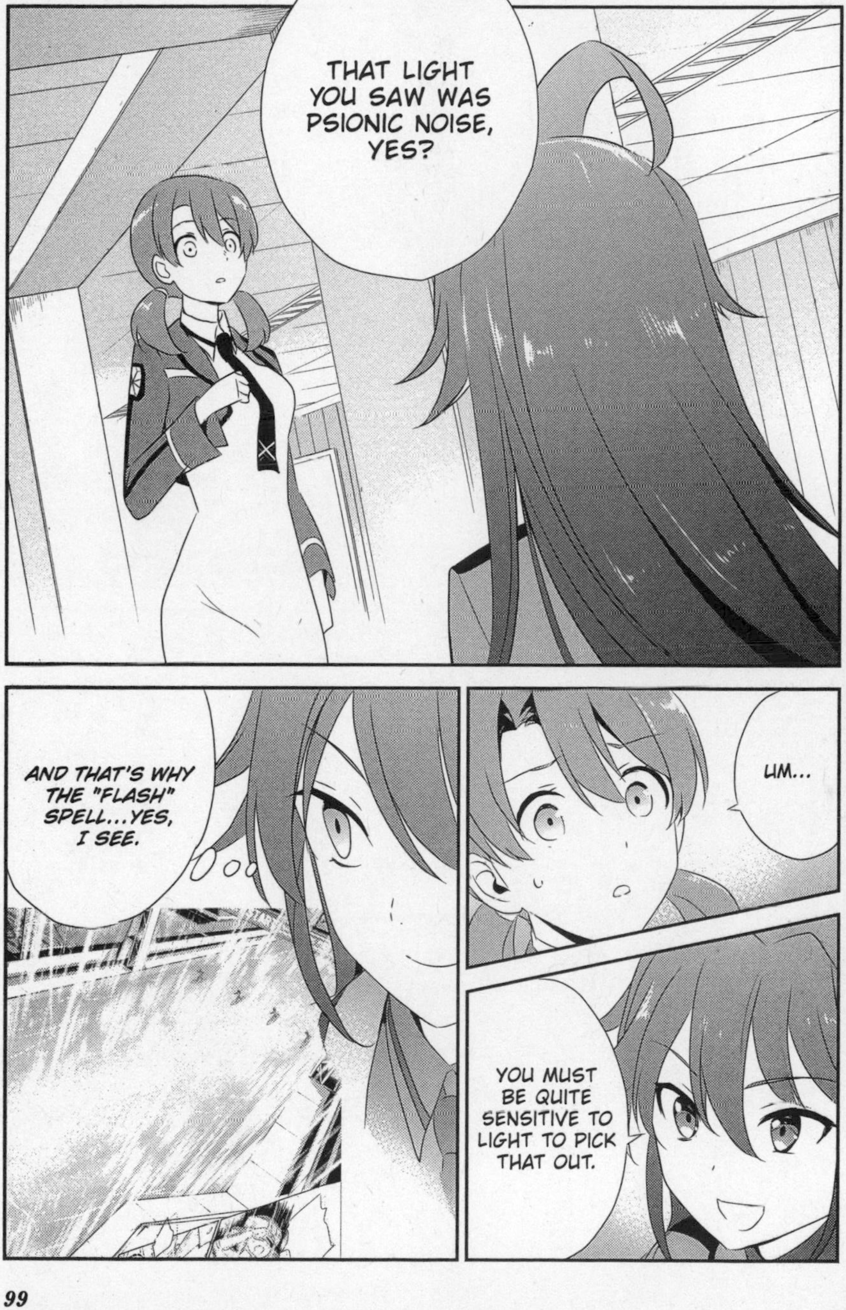
THAT LIGHT YOU SAW WAS PSIONIC NOISE, YES?
UM...
YOU MUST BE QUITE SENSITIVE TO LIGHT TO PICK THAT OUT.
AND THAT'S WHY THE "FLASH" SPELL...YES, I SEE.

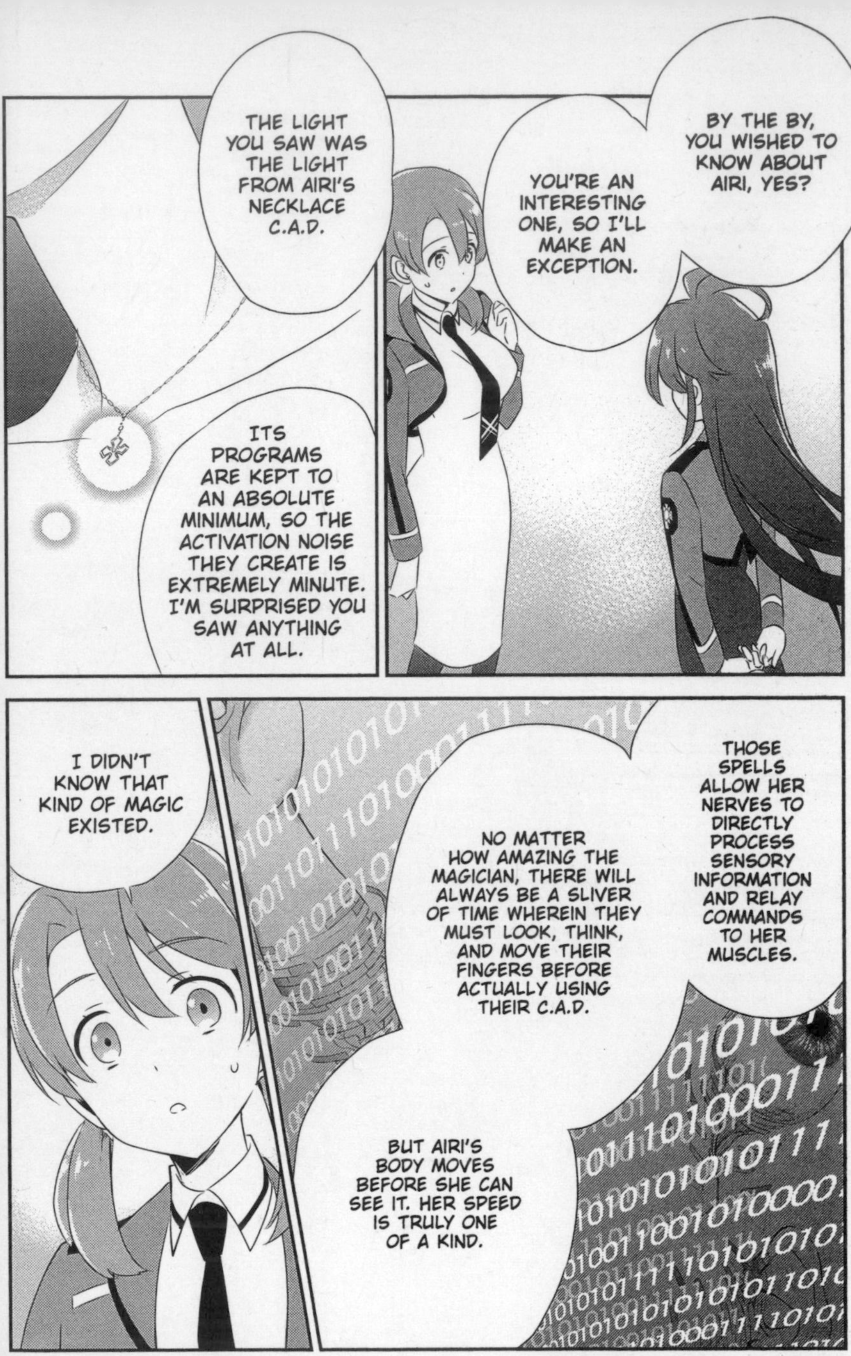
BY THE BY, YOU WISHED TO KNOW ABOUT AIRI, YES?
YOU'RE AN INTERESTING ONE, SO I'LL MAKE AN EXCEPTION.
THE LIGHT YOU SAW WAS THE LIGHT FROM AIRI'S NECKLACE C.A.D.
ITS PROGRAMS ARE KEPT TO AN ABSOLUTE MINIMUM, SO THE ACTIVATION NOISE THEY CREATE IS EXTREMELY MINUTE. I'M SURPRISED YOU SAW ANYTHING AT ALL.
THOSE SPELLS ALLOW HER NERVES TO DIRECTLY PROCESS SENSORY INFORMATION AND RELAY COMMANDS TO HER MUSCLES.
NO MATTER HOW AMAZING THE MAGICIAN, THERE WILL ALWAYS BE A SLIVER OF TIME WHEREIN THEY MUST LOOK, THINK, AND MOVE THEIR FINGERS BEFORE ACTUALLY USING THEIR C.A.D.
BUT AIRI'S BODY MOVES BEFORE SHE CAN SEE IT. HER SPEED IS TRULY ONE OF A KIND.
I DIDN'T KNOW THAT KIND OF MAGIC EXISTED.

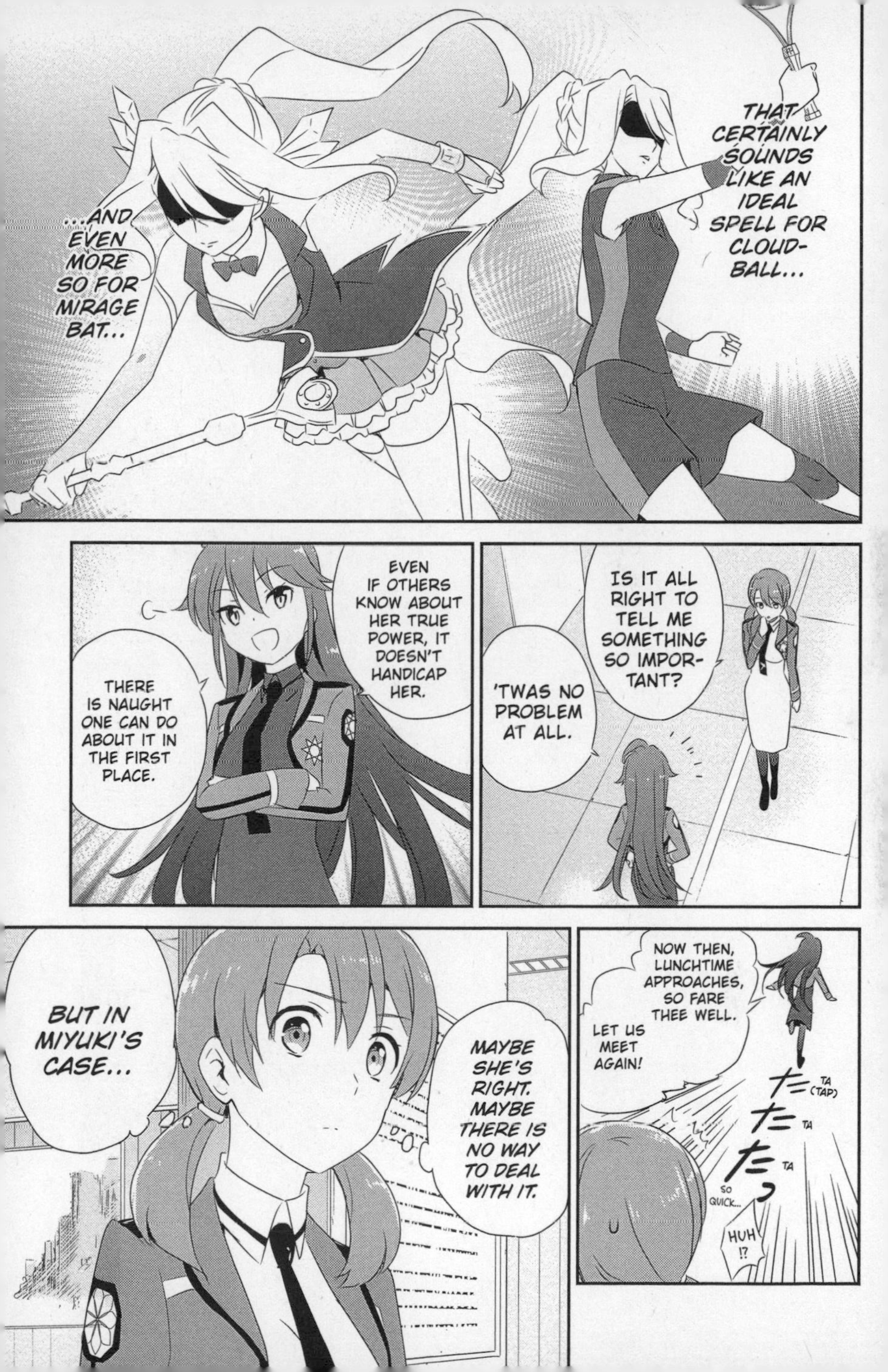
THAT CERTAINLY SOUNDS LIKE AN IDEAL SPELL FOR CLOUD-BALL...
...AND EVEN MORE SO FOR MIRAGE BAT...
IS IT ALL RIGHT TO TELL ME SOMETHING SO IMPORTANT?
'TWAS NO PROBLEM AT ALL.
EVEN IF OTHERS KNOW ABOUT HER TRUE POWER, IT DOESN'T HANDICAP HER.
THERE IS NAUGHT ONE CAN DO ABOUT IT IN THE FIRST PLACE.
NOW THEN, LUNCHTIME APPROACHES, SO FARE THEE WELL.
LET US MEET AGAIN!
TA (TAP)
TA
TA
SO QUICK...
HUH !?
MAYBE SHE'S RIGHT. MAYBE THERE IS NO WAY TO DEAL WITH IT.
BUT IN MIYUKI'S CASE...

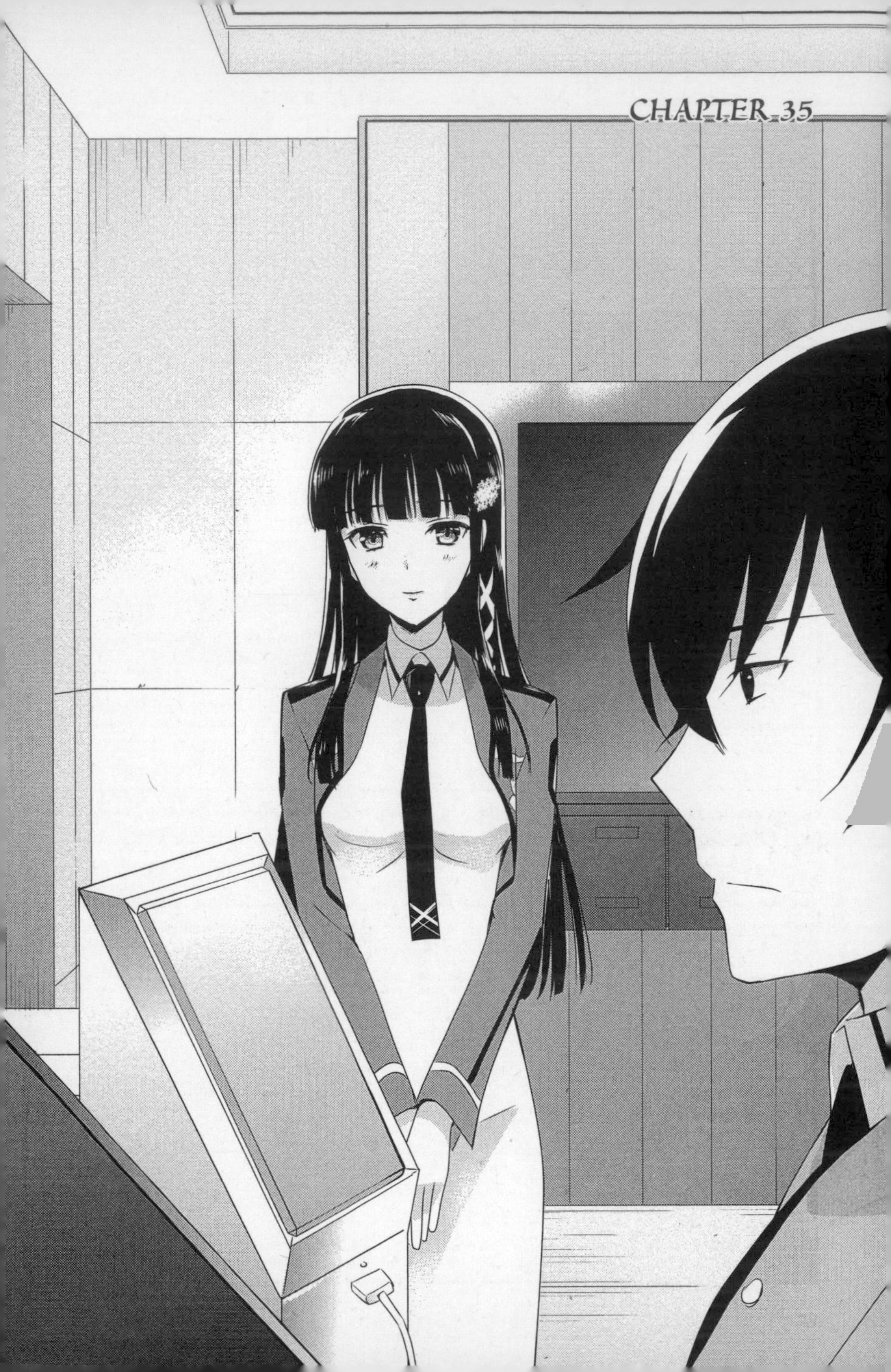
CHAPTER 35

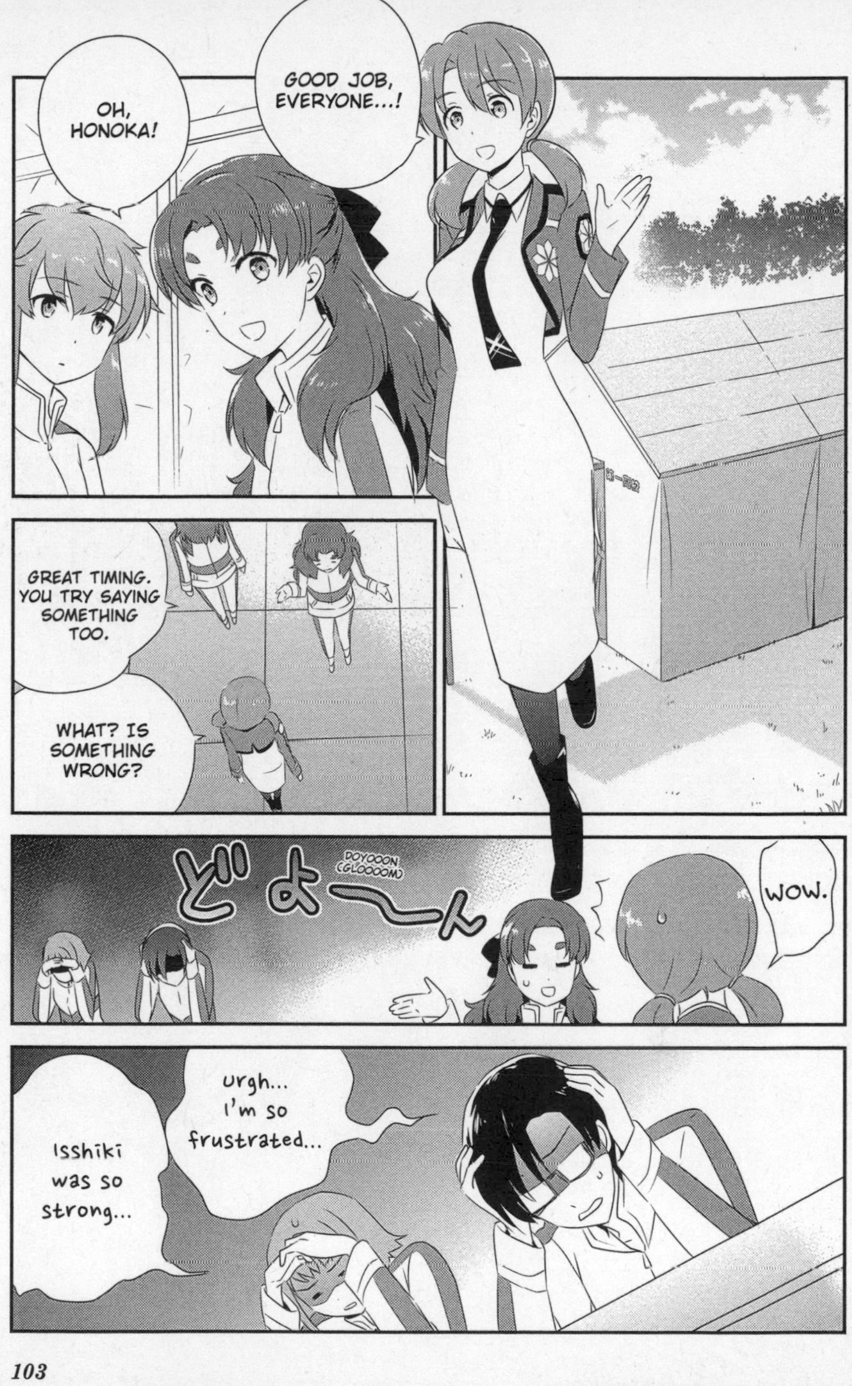
GOOD JOB, EVERYONE...!
OH, HONOKA!
GREAT TIMING. YOU TRY SAYING SOMETHING TOO.
WHAT? IS SOMETHING WRONG?
WOW.
どよ〜〜ん
DOYOOON (GLOOOOM)
Urgh... I'm so frustrated...
Isshiki was so strong...

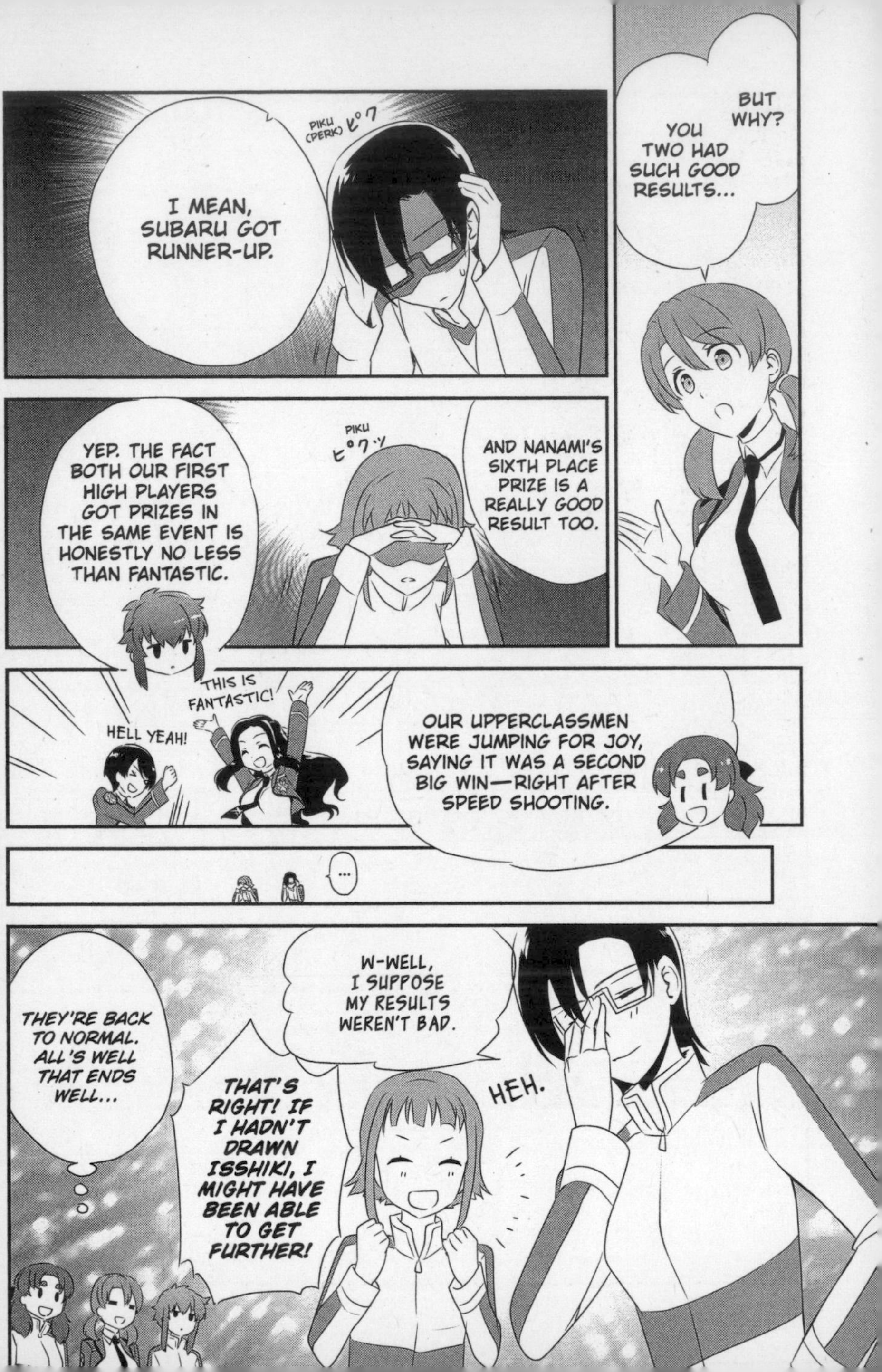
BUT WHY?
YOU TWO HAD SUCH GOOD RESULTS...
PIKU (PERK) ピク
I MEAN, SUBARU GOT RUNNER-UP.
PIKU ピクッ
AND NANAMI'S SIXTH PLACE PRIZE IS A REALLY GOOD RESULT TOO.
YEP. THE FACT BOTH OUR FIRST HIGH PLAYERS GOT PRIZES IN THE SAME EVENT IS HONESTLY NO LESS THAN FANTASTIC.
OUR UPPERCLASSMEN WERE JUMPING FOR JOY, SAYING IT WAS A SECOND BIG WIN—RIGHT AFTER SPEED SHOOTING.
THIS IS FANTASTIC!
HELL YEAH!
...
W-WELL, I SUPPOSE MY RESULTS WEREN'T BAD.
HEH.
THAT'S RIGHT! IF I HADN'T DRAWN ISSHIKI, I MIGHT HAVE BEEN ABLE TO GET FURTHER!
THEY'RE BACK TO NORMAL. ALL'S WELL THAT ENDS WELL...

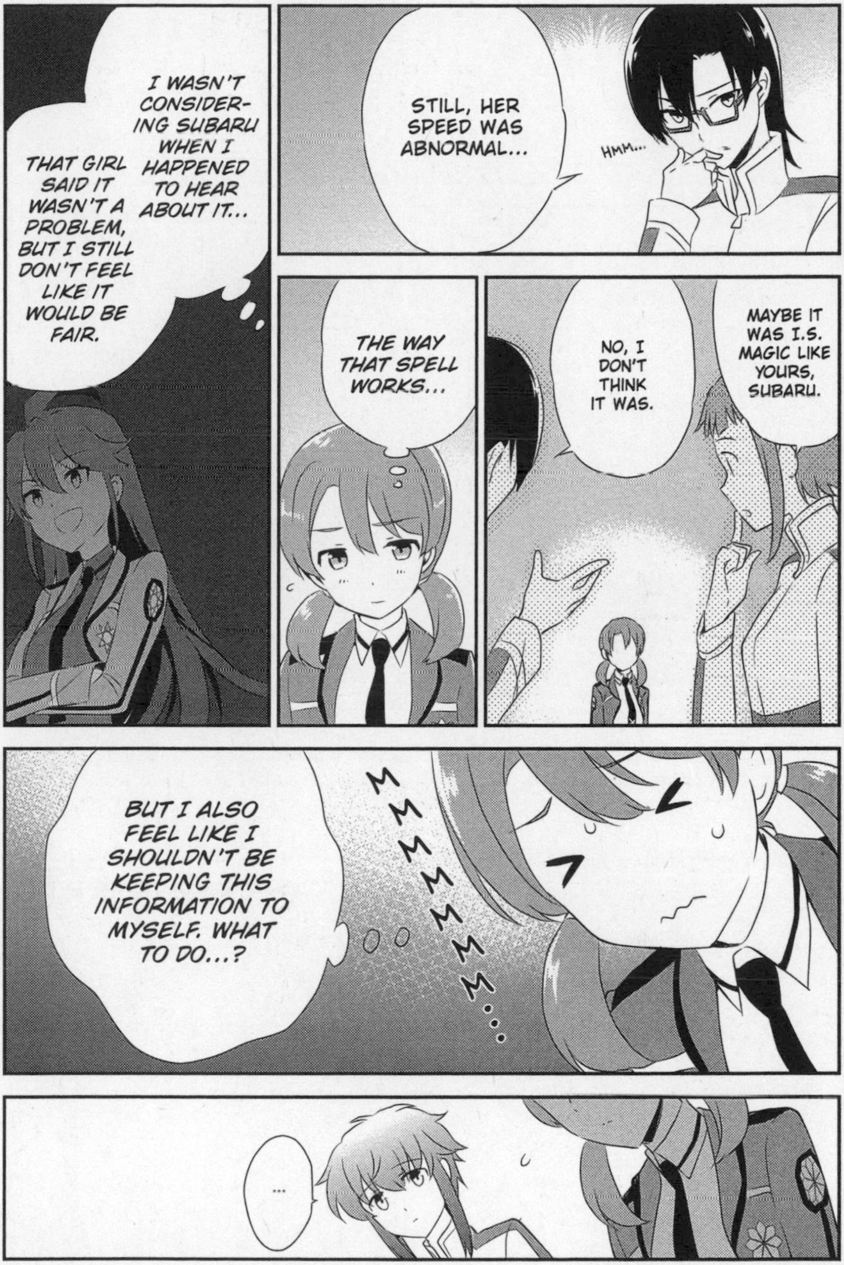
STILL, HER SPEED WAS ABNORMAL...
HMM...
MAYBE IT WAS I.S. MAGIC LIKE YOURS, SUBARU.
NO, I DON'T THINK IT WAS.
THE WAY THAT SPELL WORKS...
I WASN'T CONSIDERING SUBARU WHEN I HAPPENED TO HEAR ABOUT IT...
THAT GIRL SAID IT WASN'T A PROBLEM, BUT I STILL DON'T FEEL LIKE IT WOULD BE FAIR.
MMMMMMMM...
BUT I ALSO FEEL LIKE I SHOULDN'T BE KEEPING THIS INFORMATION TO MYSELF. WHAT TO DO...?
...

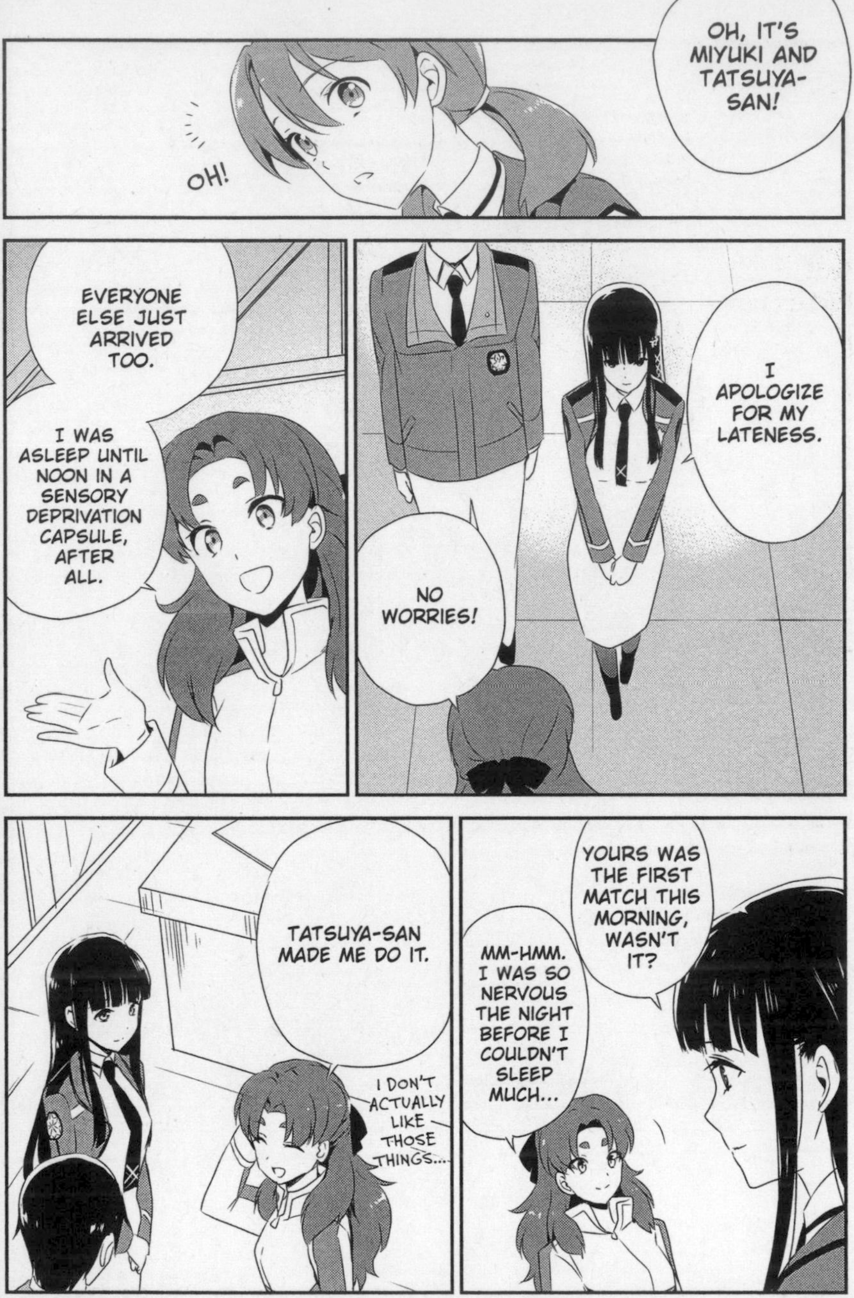
OH, IT'S MIYUKI AND TATSUYA-SAN!
OH!
I APOLOGIZE FOR MY LATENESS.
NO WORRIES!
EVERYONE ELSE JUST ARRIVED TOO.
I WAS ASLEEP UNTIL NOON IN A SENSORY DEPRIVATION CAPSULE, AFTER ALL.
YOURS WAS THE FIRST MATCH THIS MORNING, WASN'T IT?
MM-HMM. I WAS SO NERVOUS THE NIGHT BEFORE I COULDN'T SLEEP MUCH...
TATSUYA-SAN MADE ME DO IT.
I DON'T ACTUALLY LIKE THOSE THINGS...

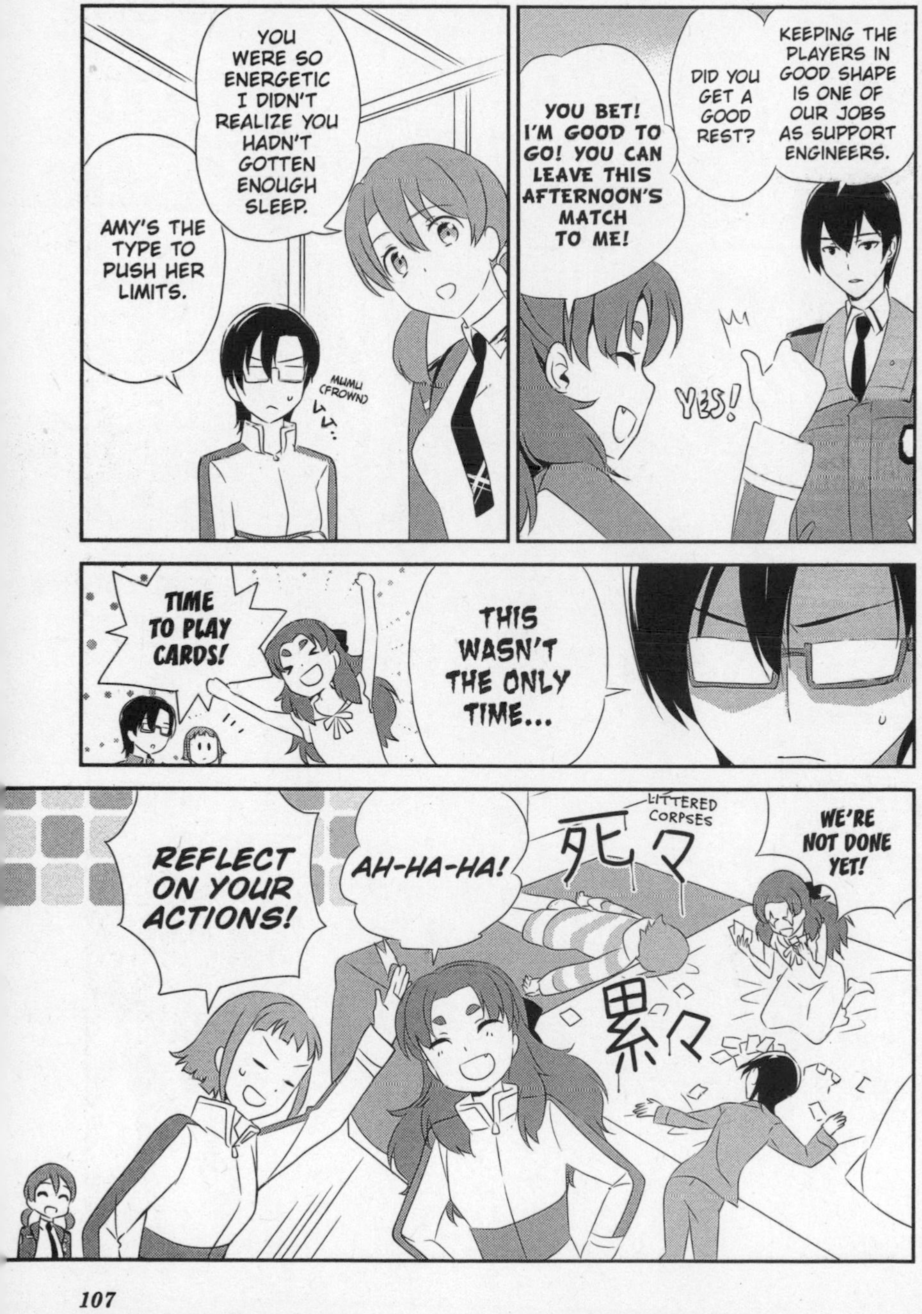
KEEPING THE PLAYERS IN GOOD SHAPE IS ONE OF OUR JOBS AS SUPPORT ENGINEERS.
DID YOU GET A GOOD REST?
YOU BET! I'M GOOD TO GO! YOU CAN LEAVE THIS AFTERNOON'S MATCH TO ME!
YES!
YOU WERE SO ENERGETIC I DIDN'T REALIZE YOU HADN'T GOTTEN ENOUGH SLEEP.
AMY'S THE TYPE TO PUSH HER LIMITS.
MUMU (FROWN)
THIS WASN'T THE ONLY TIME...
TIME TO PLAY CARDS!
WE'RE NOT DONE YET!
LITTERED CORPSES
死々
累々
AH-HA-HA!
REFLECT ON YOUR ACTIONS!

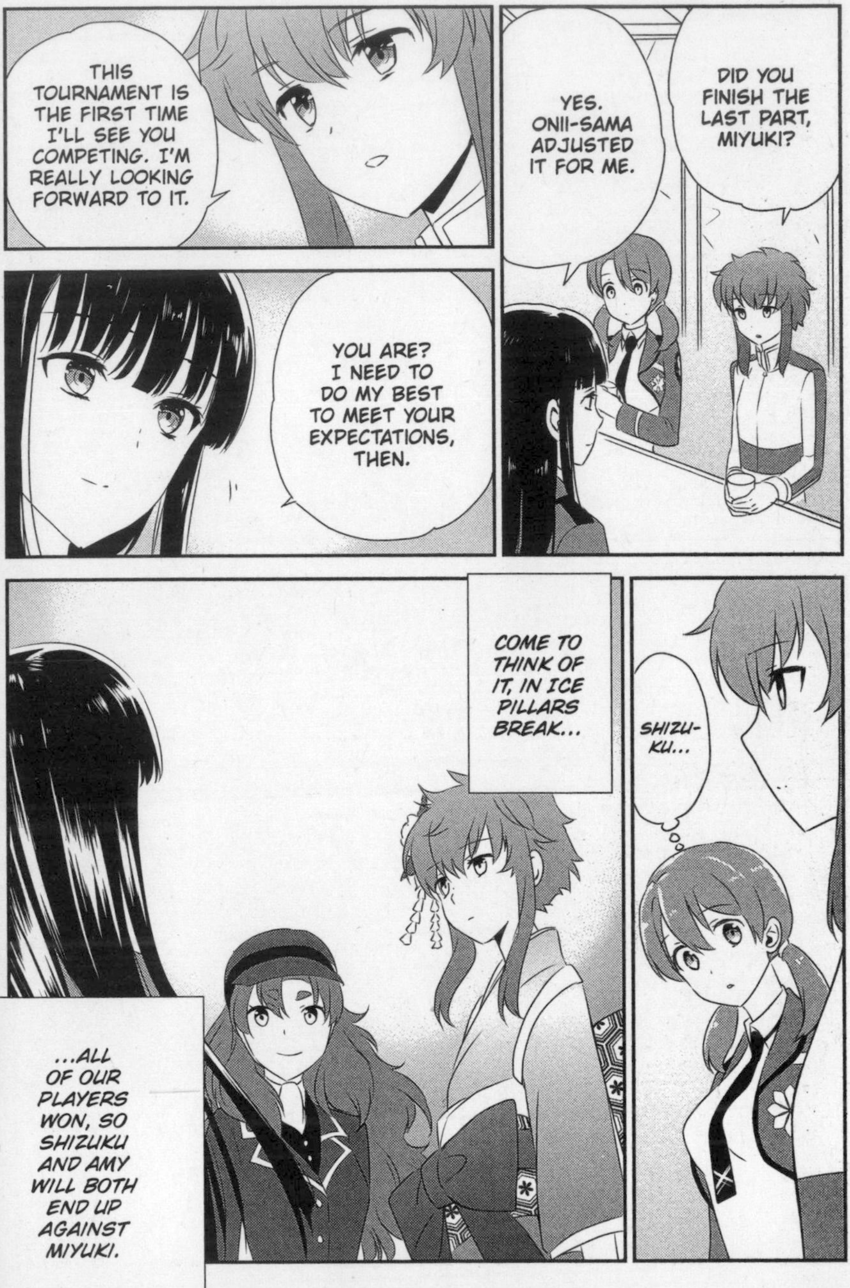
DID YOU FINISH THE LAST PART, MIYUKI?
YES. ONII-SAMA ADJUSTED IT FOR ME.
THIS TOURNAMENT IS THE FIRST TIME I'LL SEE YOU COMPETING. I'M REALLY LOOKING FORWARD TO IT.
YOU ARE? I NEED TO DO MY BEST TO MEET YOUR EXPECTATIONS, THEN.
SHIZU-KU...
COME TO THINK OF IT, IN ICE PILLARS BREAK...
...ALL OF OUR PLAYERS WON, SO SHIZUKU AND AMY WILL BOTH END UP AGAINST MIYUKI.

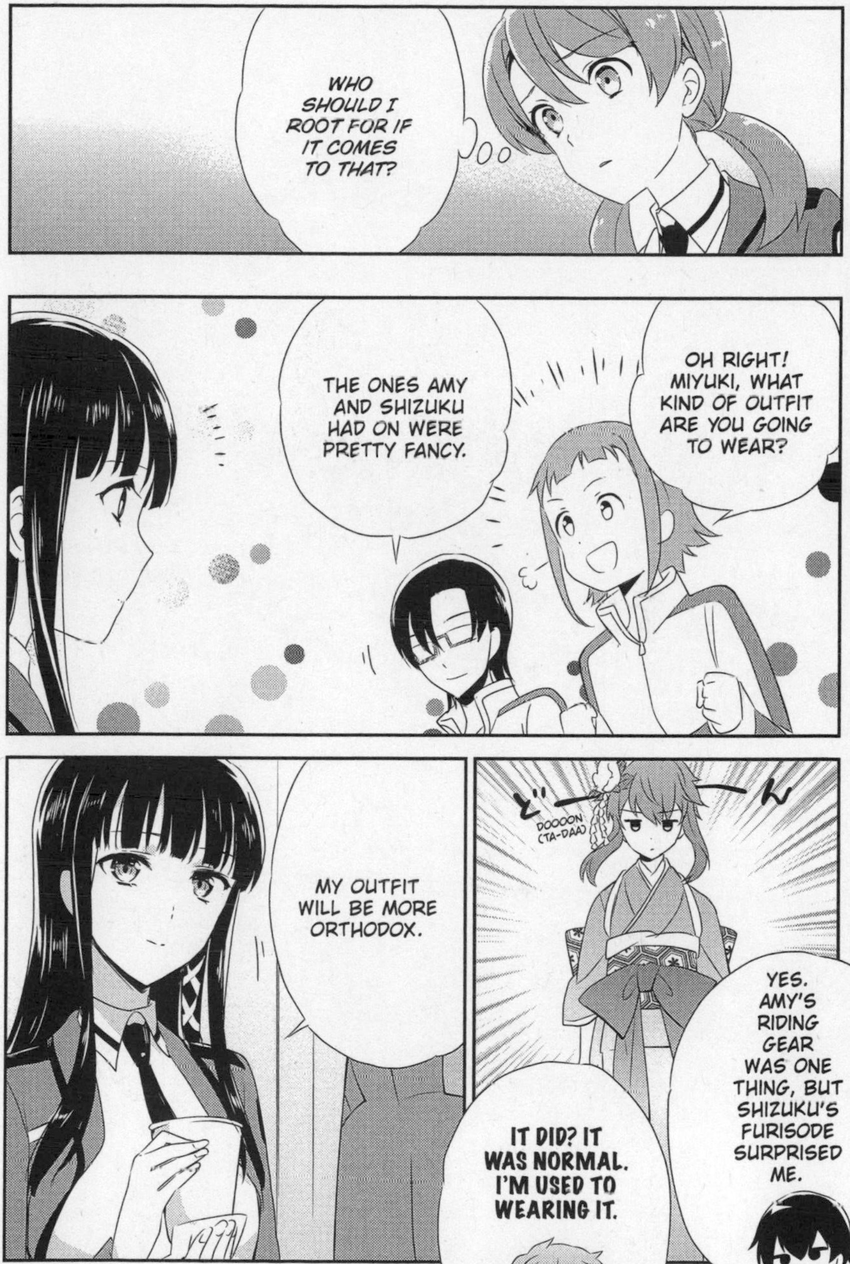
WHO SHOULD I ROOT FOR IF IT COMES TO THAT?
OH RIGHT! MIYUKI, WHAT KIND OF OUTFIT ARE YOU GOING TO WEAR?
THE ONES AMY AND SHIZUKU HAD ON WERE PRETTY FANCY.
DOOOON (TA-DAA)
YES. AMY'S RIDING GEAR WAS ONE THING, BUT SHIZUKU'S FURISODE SURPRISED ME.
IT DID? IT WAS NORMAL. I'M USED TO WEARING IT.
MY OUTFIT WILL BE MORE ORTHODOX.

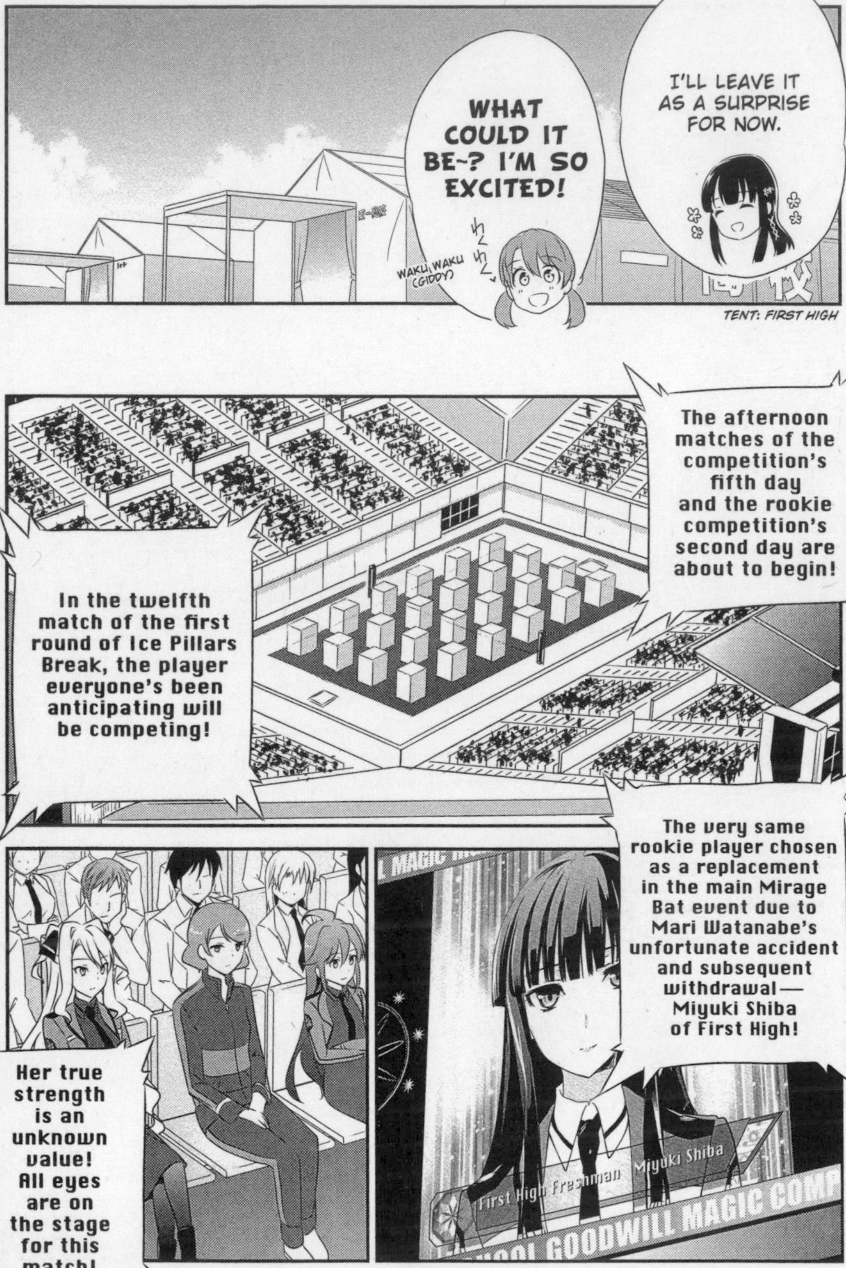
I'LL LEAVE IT AS A SURPRISE FOR NOW.
WHAT COULD IT BE~? I'M SO EXCITED!
WAKU WAKU (GIDDY)
TENT: FIRST HIGH
The afternoon matches of the competition's fifth day and the rookie competition's second day are about to begin!
In the twelfth match of the first round of Ice Pillars Break, the player everyone's been anticipating will be competing!
The very same rookie player chosen as a replacement in the main Mirage Bat event due to Mari Watanabe's unfortunate accident and subsequent withdrawal— Miyuki Shiba of First High!
First High Freshman Miyuki Shiba
GOODWILL MAGIC COMP
Her true strength is an unknown value! All eyes are on the stage for this match!

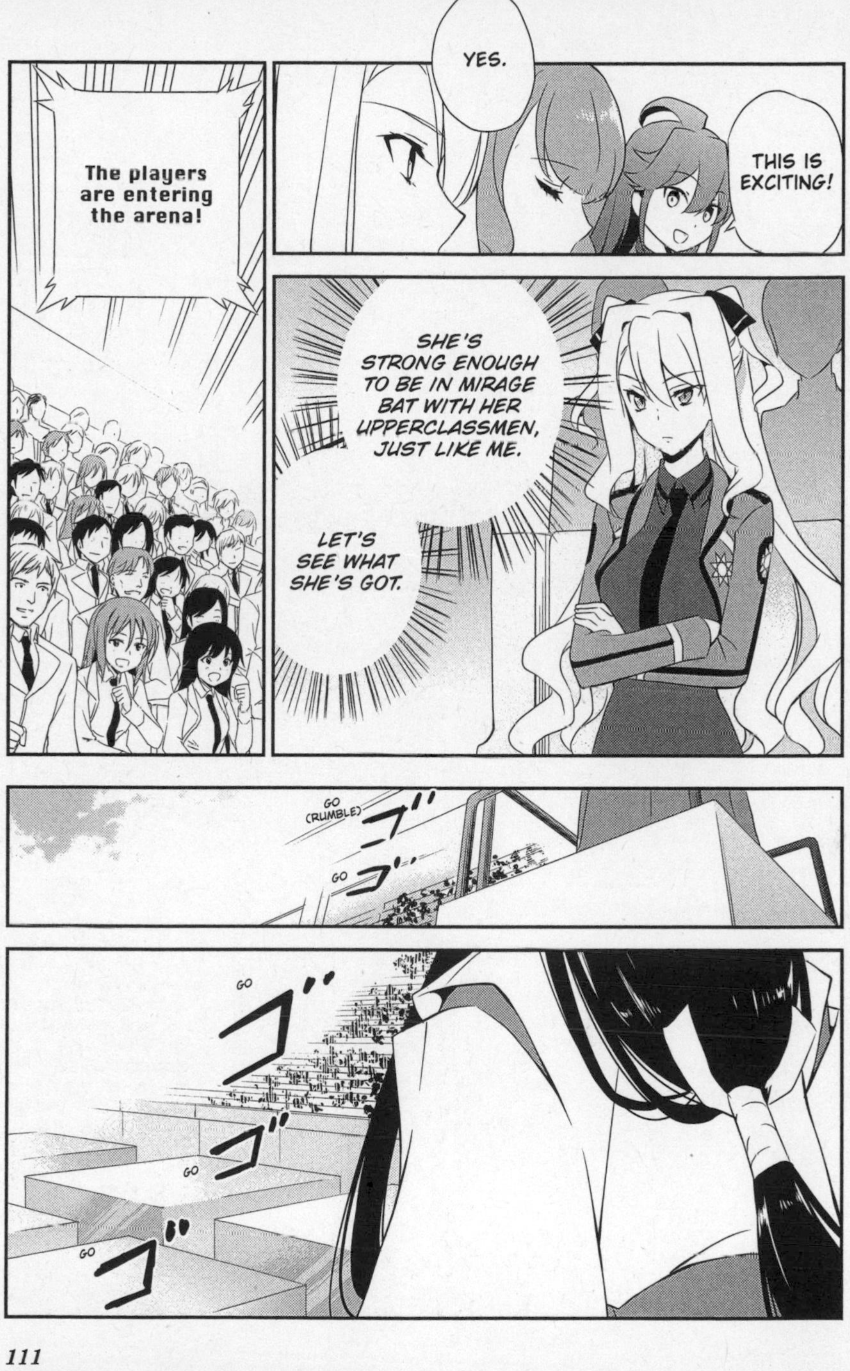
THIS IS EXCITING!
YES.
SHE'S STRONG ENOUGH TO BE IN MIRAGE BAT WITH HER UPPERCLASSMEN, JUST LIKE ME.
LET'S SEE WHAT SHE'S GOT.
The players are entering the arena!
GO (RUMBLE)
GO
GO
GO
GO

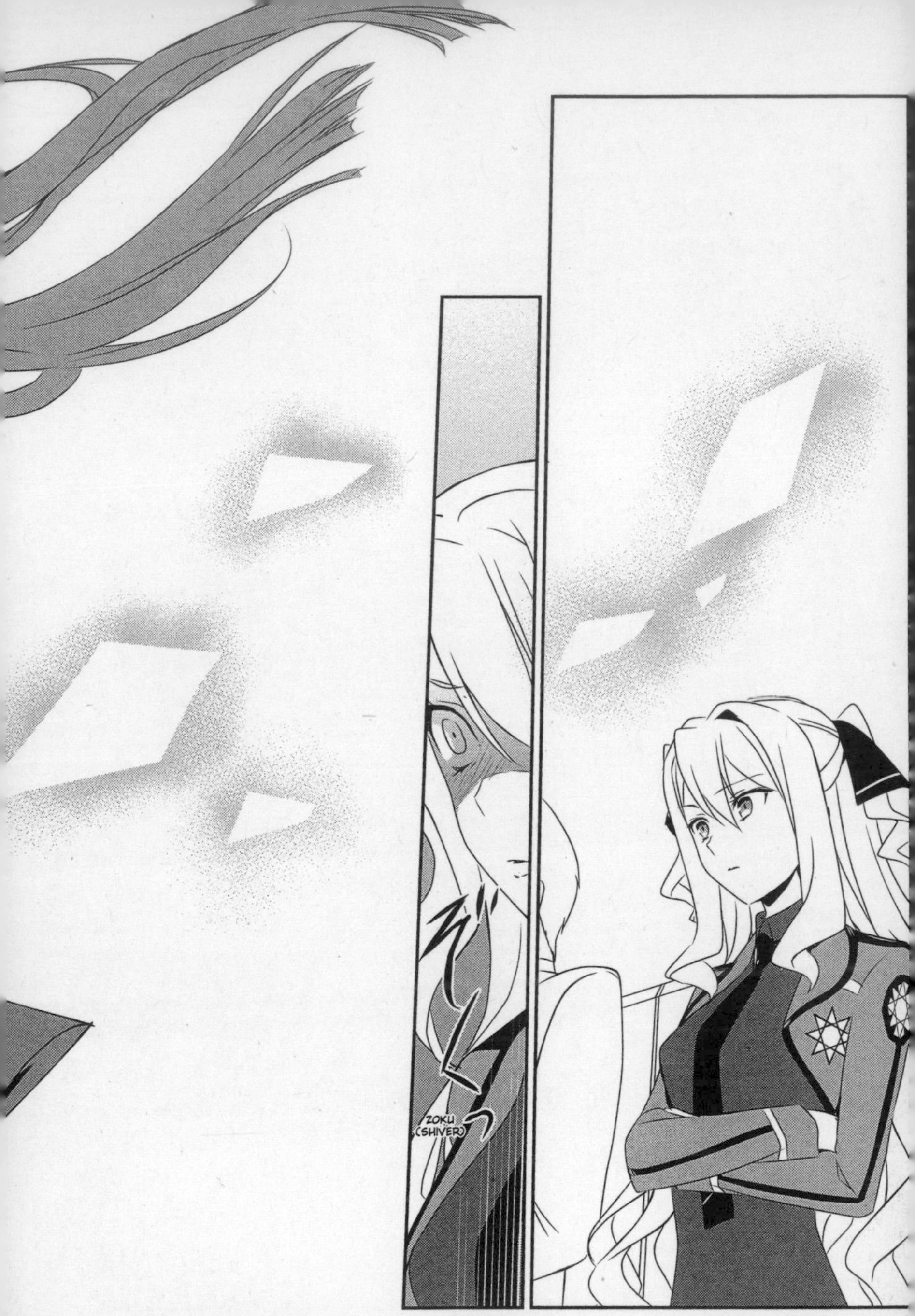
ZOKU
(SHIVER)

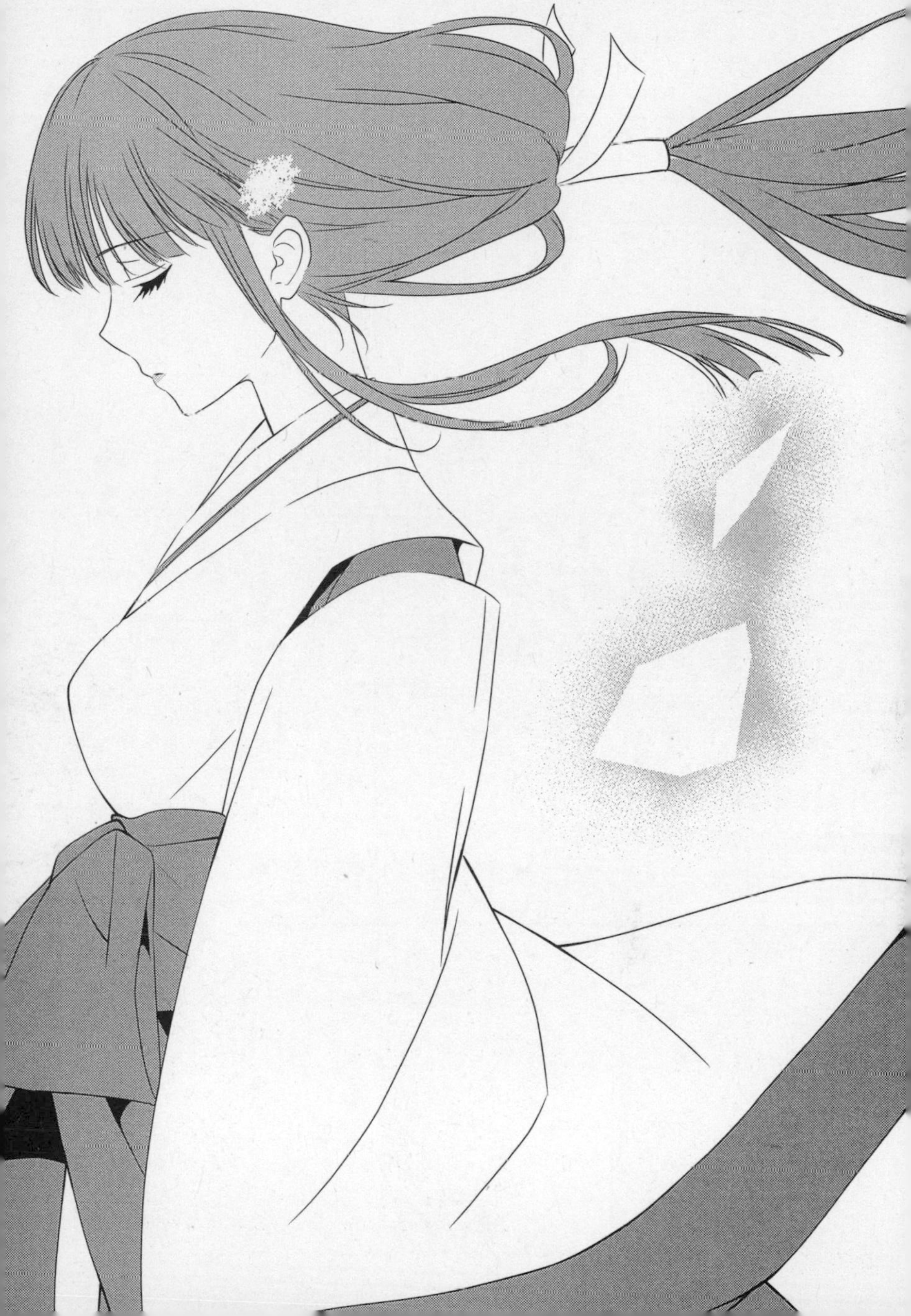

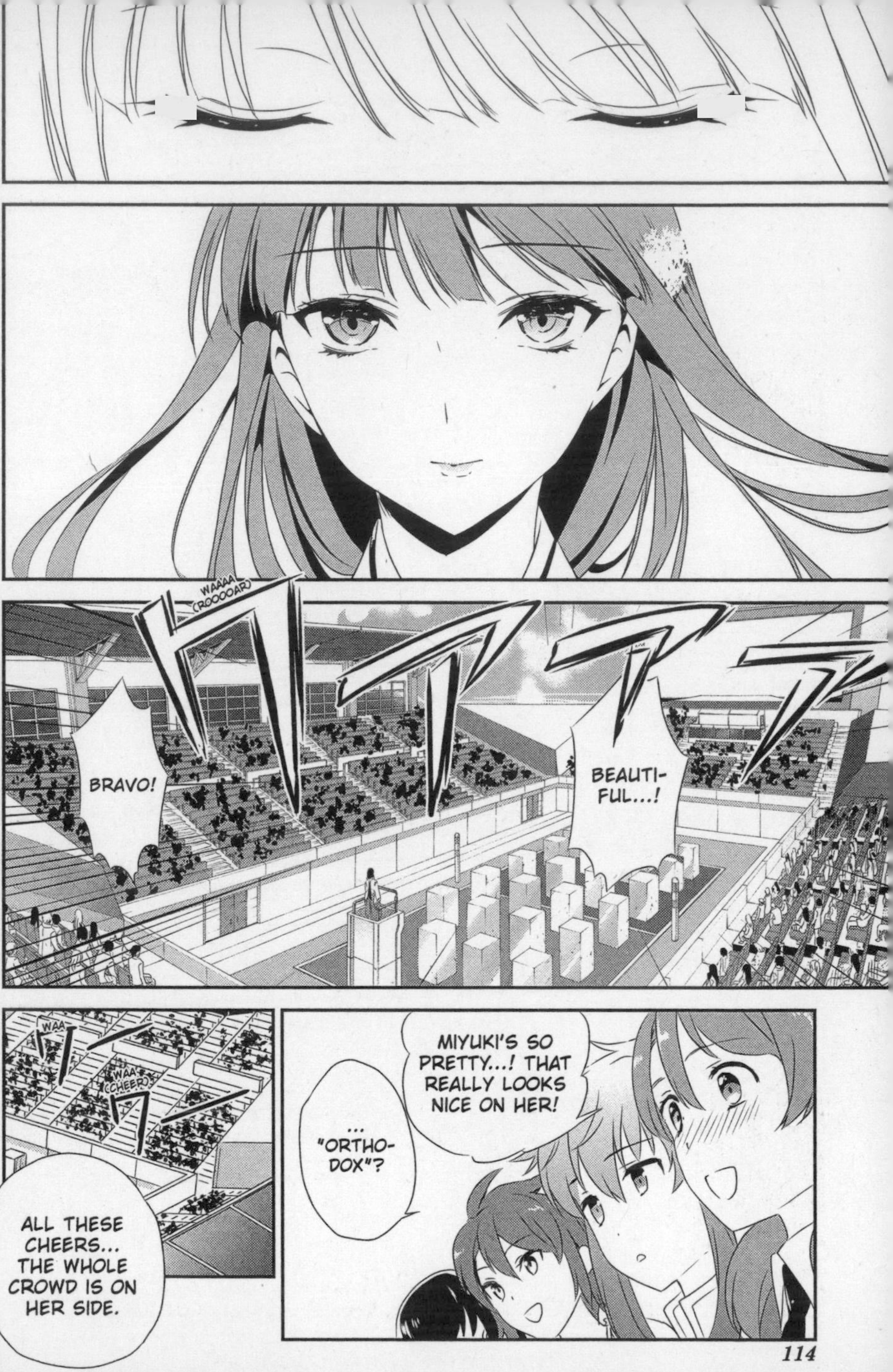
WAAAA (ROOOOAR)
BEAUTIFUL...!
BRAVO!
MIYUKI'S SO PRETTY...! THAT REALLY LOOKS NICE ON HER!
... "ORTHODOX"?
WAA
WAA (CHEER)
ALL THESE CHEERS... THE WHOLE CROWD IS ON HER SIDE.

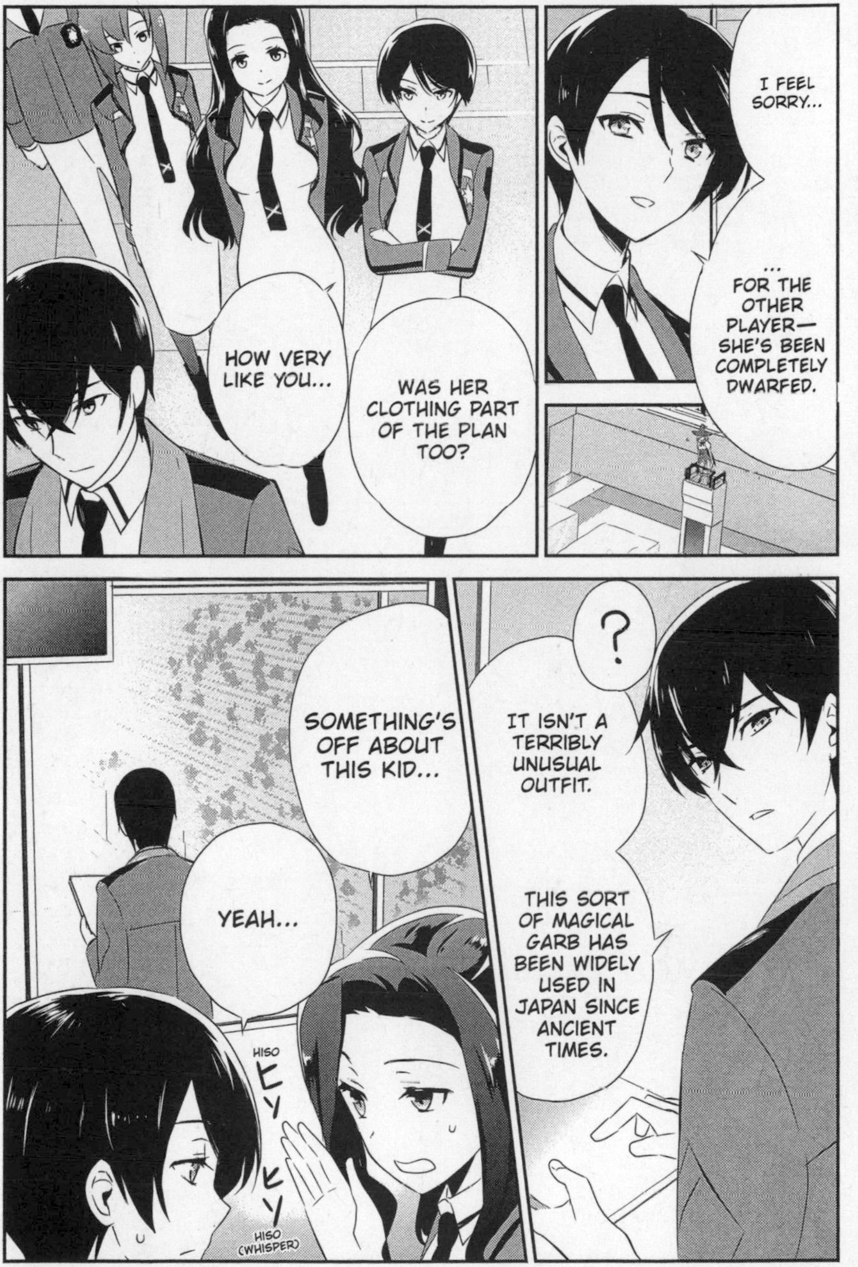
I FEEL SORRY...
... FOR THE OTHER PLAYER—SHE'S BEEN COMPLETELY DWARFED.
HOW VERY LIKE YOU...
WAS HER CLOTHING PART OF THE PLAN TOO?
?
IT ISN'T A TERRIBLY UNUSUAL OUTFIT.
THIS SORT OF MAGICAL GARB HAS BEEN WIDELY USED IN JAPAN SINCE ANCIENT TIMES.
SOMETHING'S OFF ABOUT THIS KID...
YEAH...
HISO
ヒソ
ヒソ
HISO (WHISPER)

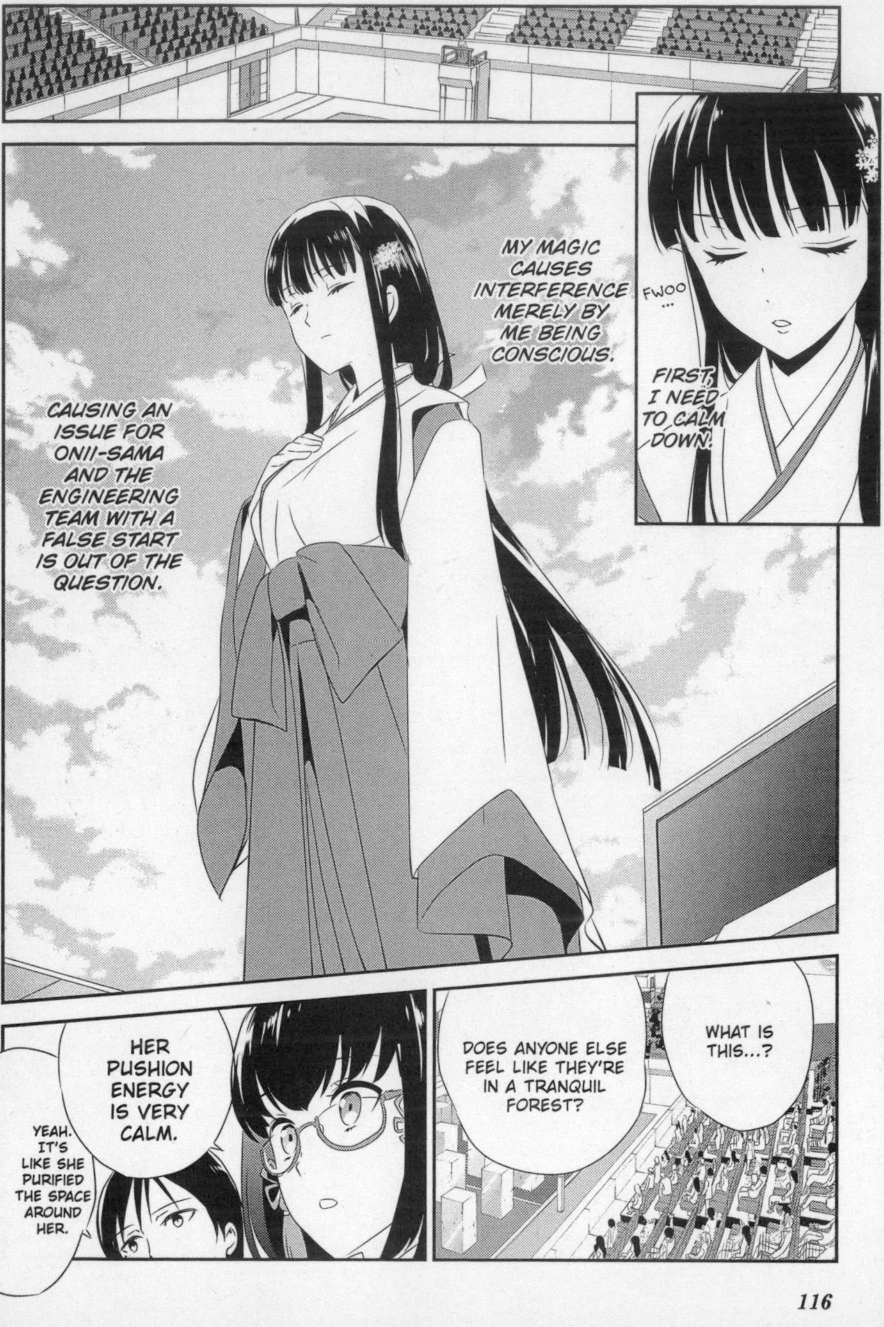
FWOO...
FIRST, I NEED TO CALM DOWN.
MY MAGIC CAUSES INTERFERENCE MERELY BY ME BEING CONSCIOUS.
CAUSING AN ISSUE FOR ONII-SAMA AND THE ENGINEERING TEAM WITH A FALSE START IS OUT OF THE QUESTION.
WHAT IS THIS...?
DOES ANYONE ELSE FEEL LIKE THEY'RE IN A TRANQUIL FOREST?
HER PUSHION ENERGY IS VERY CALM.
YEAH. IT'S LIKE SHE PURIFIED THE SPACE AROUND HER.

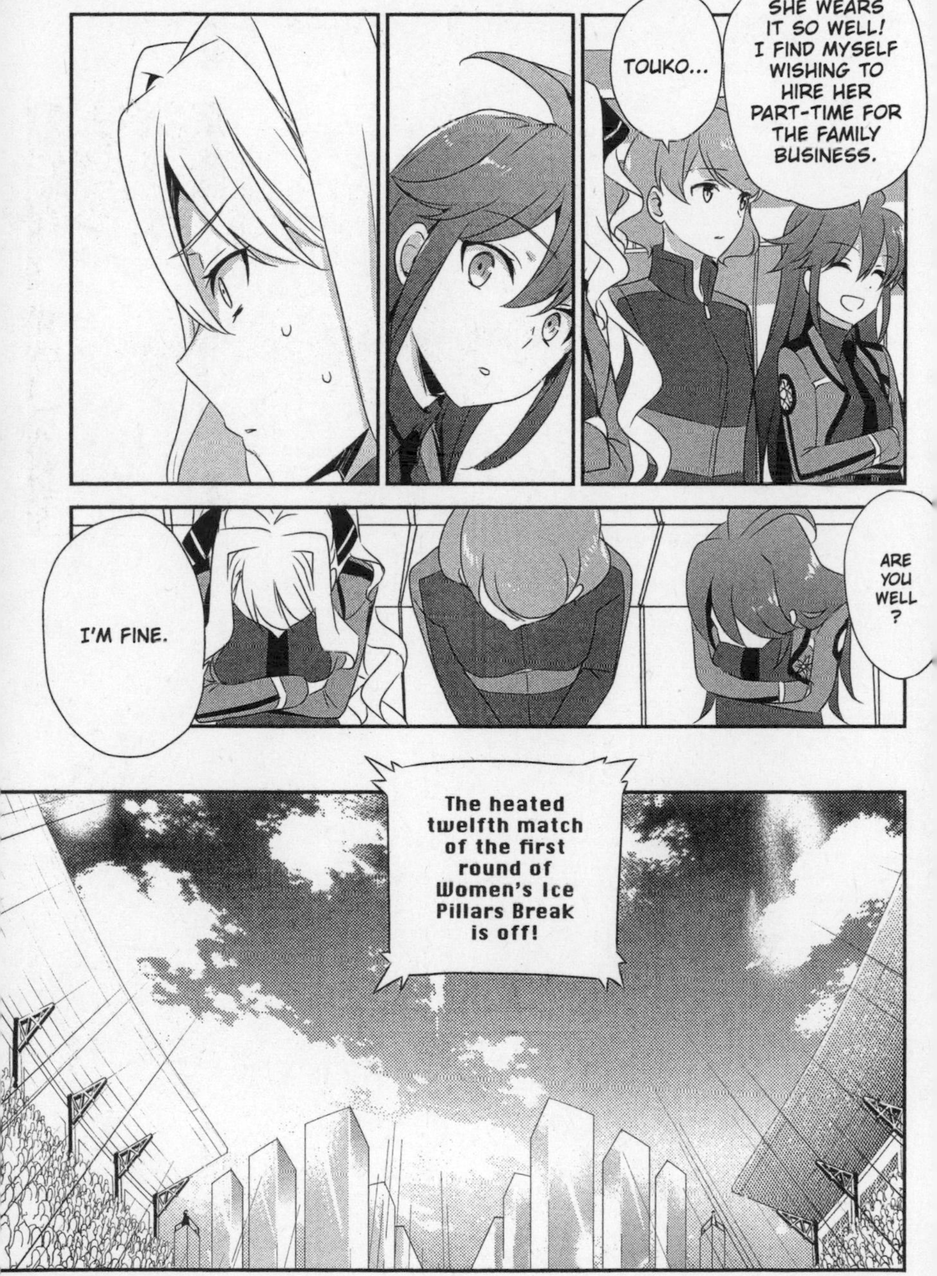
SHE WEARS IT SO WELL! I FIND MYSELF WISHING TO HIRE HER PART-TIME FOR THE FAMILY BUSINESS.
TOUKO...
ARE YOU WELL?
I'M FINE.
The heated twelfth match of the first round of Women's Ice Pillars Break is off!

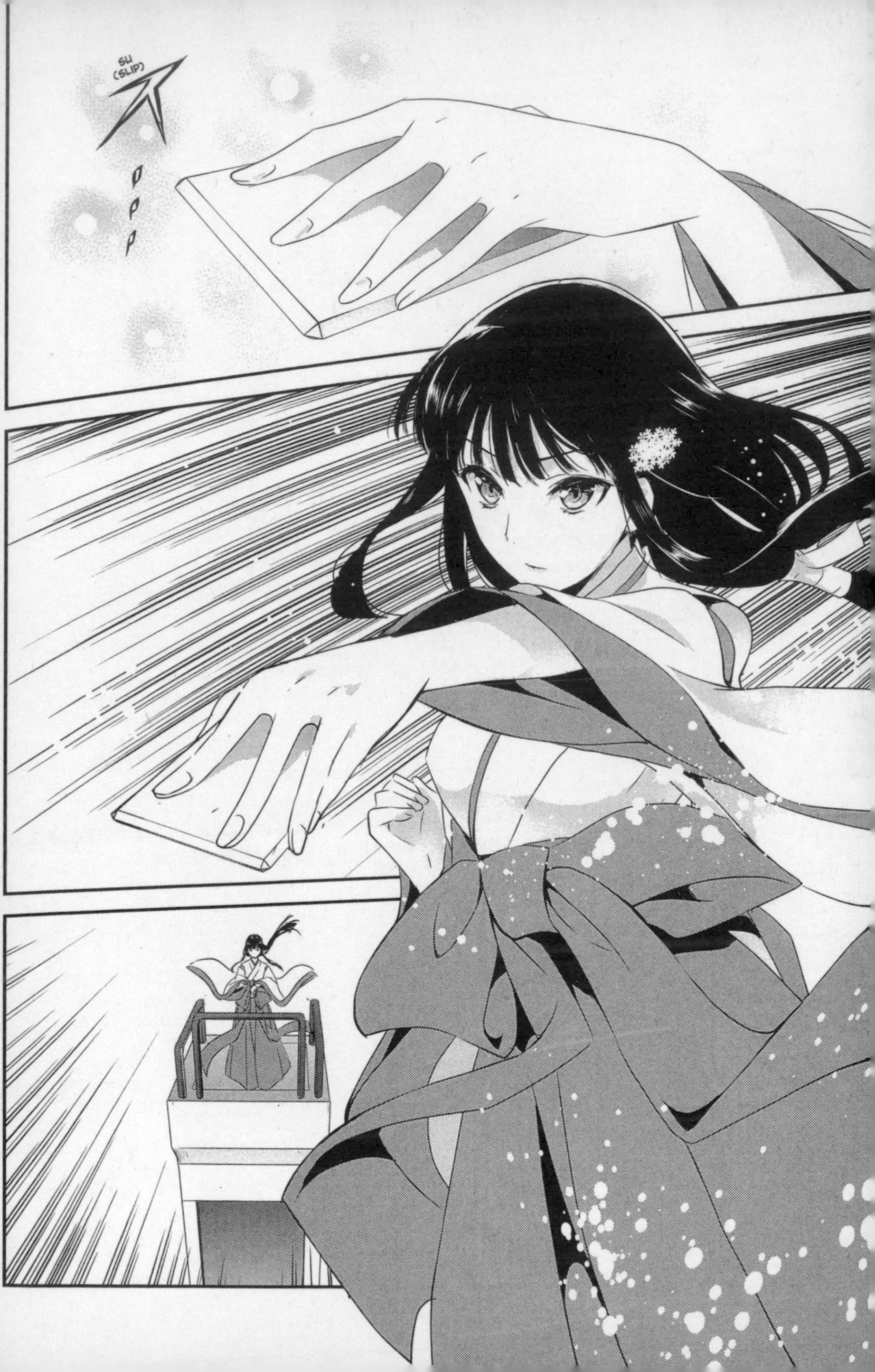
SU
(SLIP)

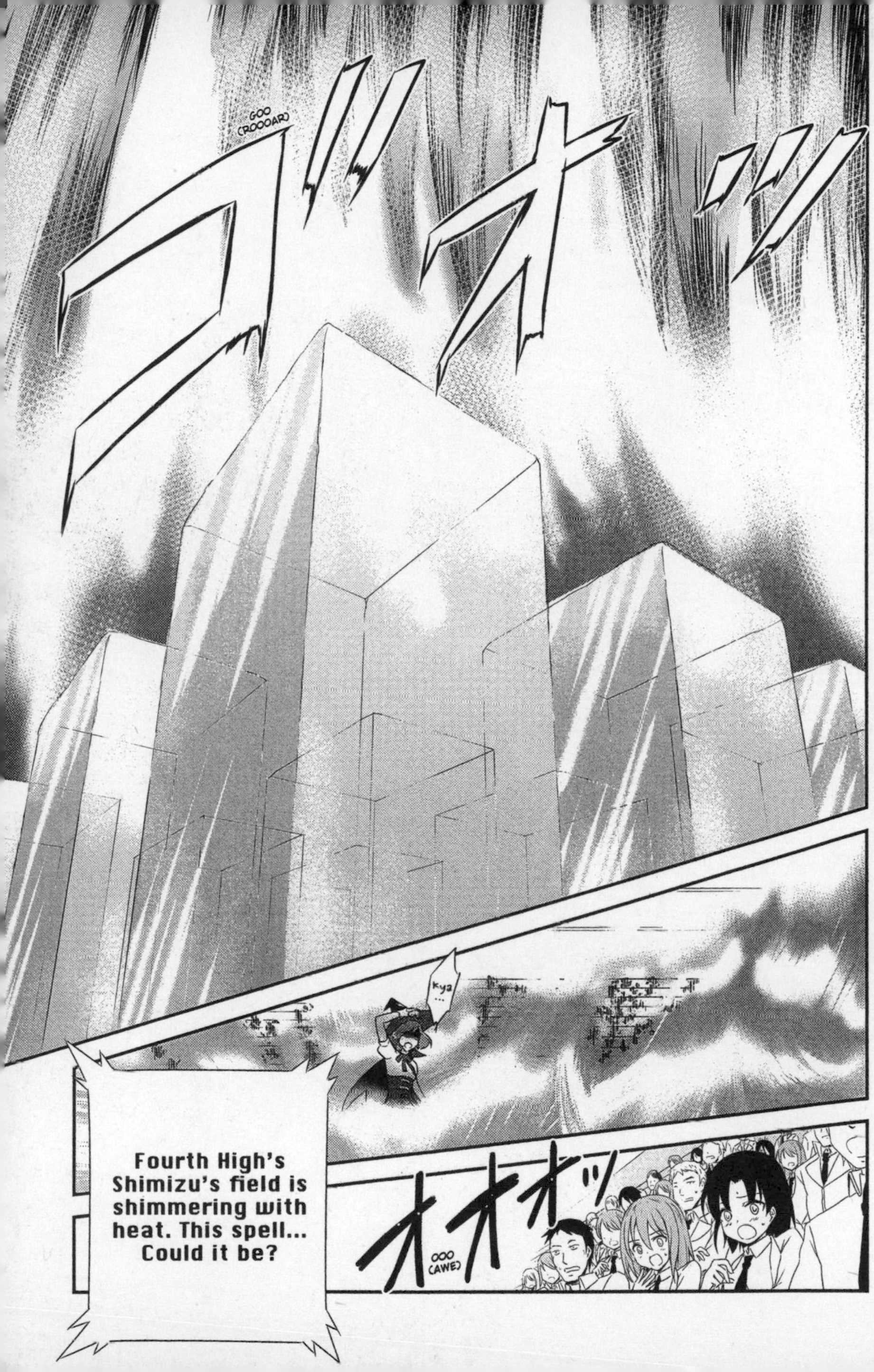

GOO
(ROOOAR)
Kya...
オオオッ
OOO
(AWE)
Fourth High's Shimizu's field is shimmering with heat. This spell... Could it be?

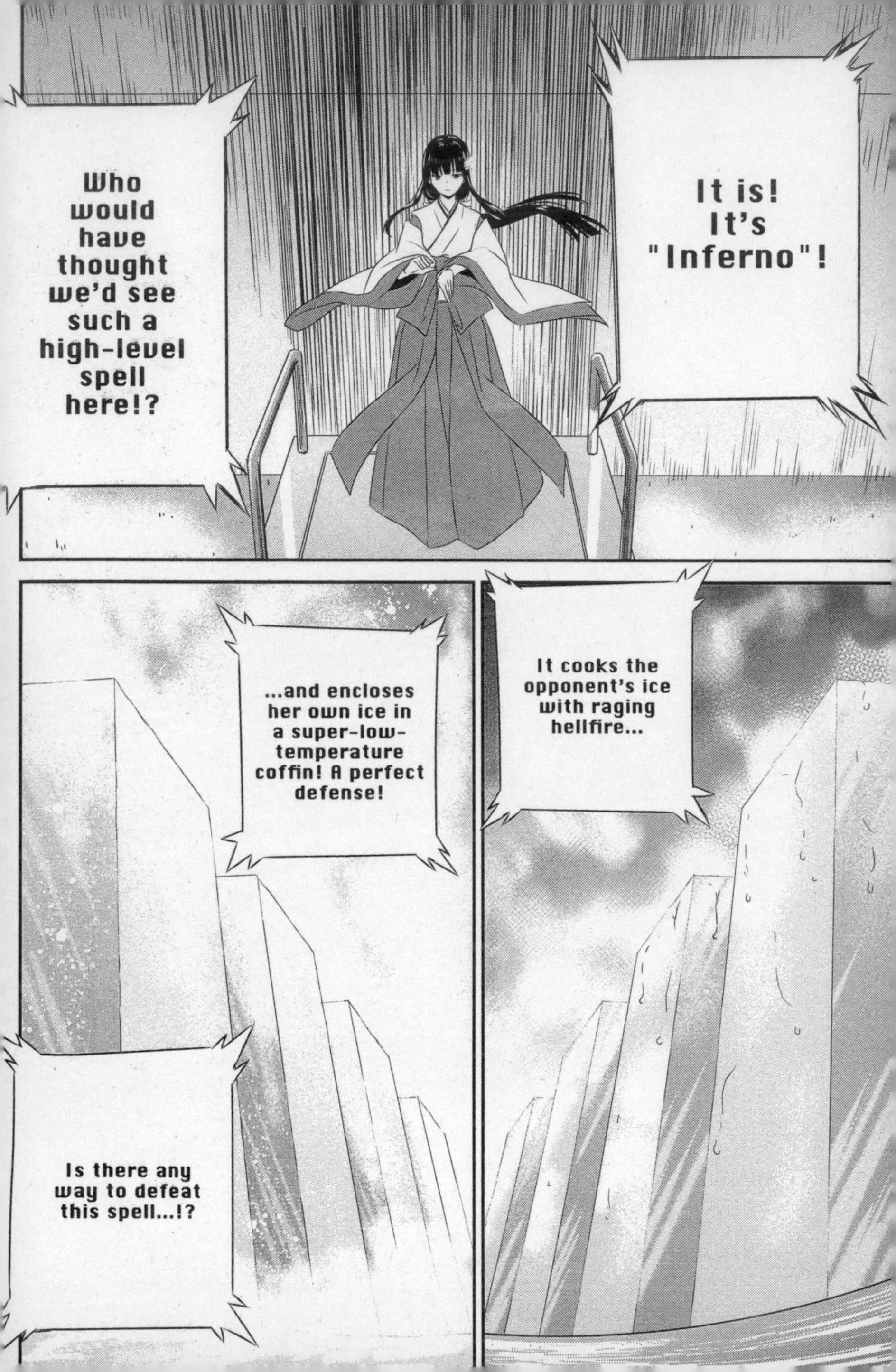
It is! It's "Inferno"!
Who would have thought we'd see such a high-level spell here!?
It cooks the opponent's ice with raging hellfire...
...and encloses her own ice in a super-low-temperature coffin! A perfect defense!
Is there any way to defeat this spell...!?

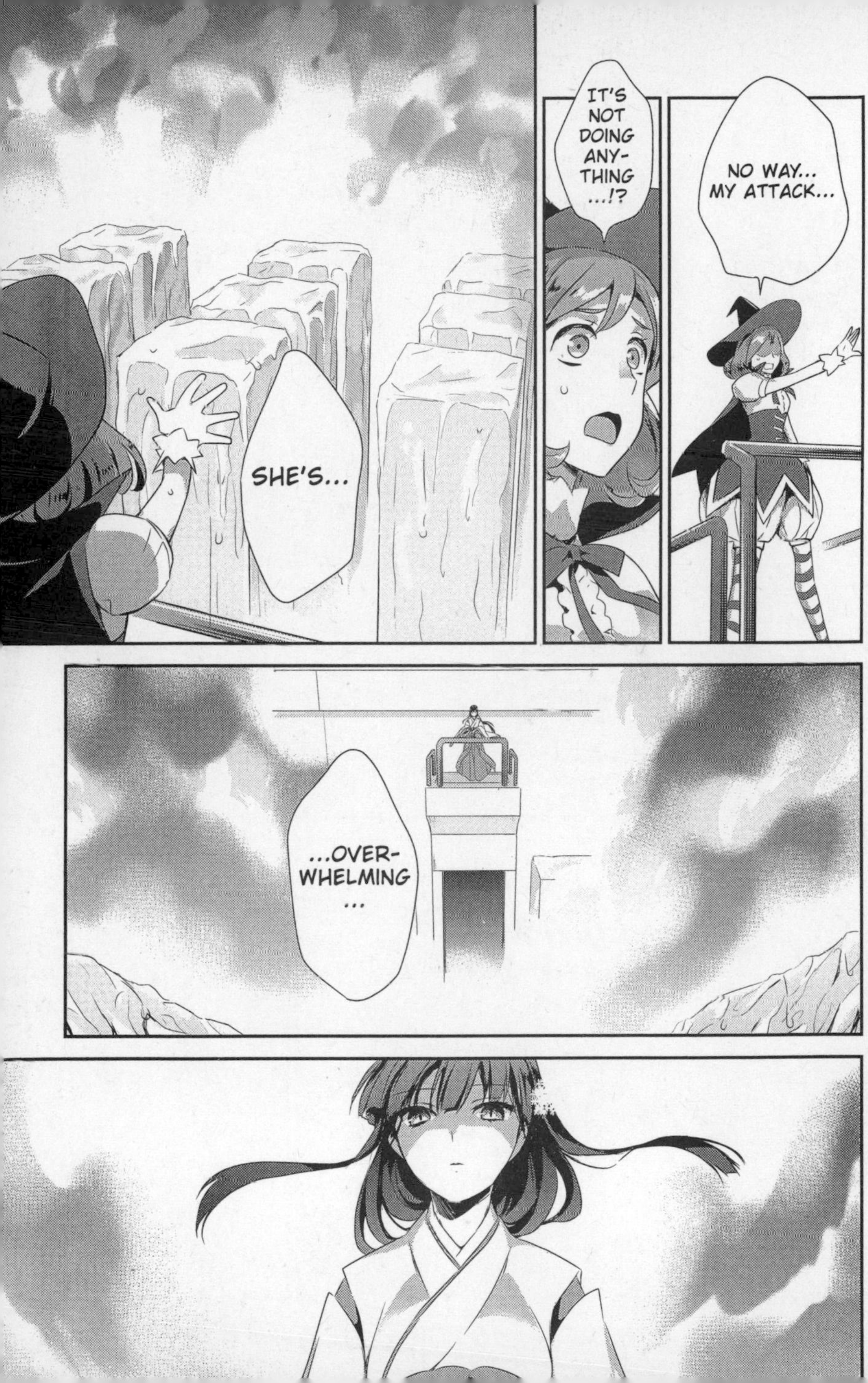
NO WAY... MY ATTACK...
IT'S NOT DOING ANY-THING ...!?
SHE'S...
...OVER-WHELMING ...

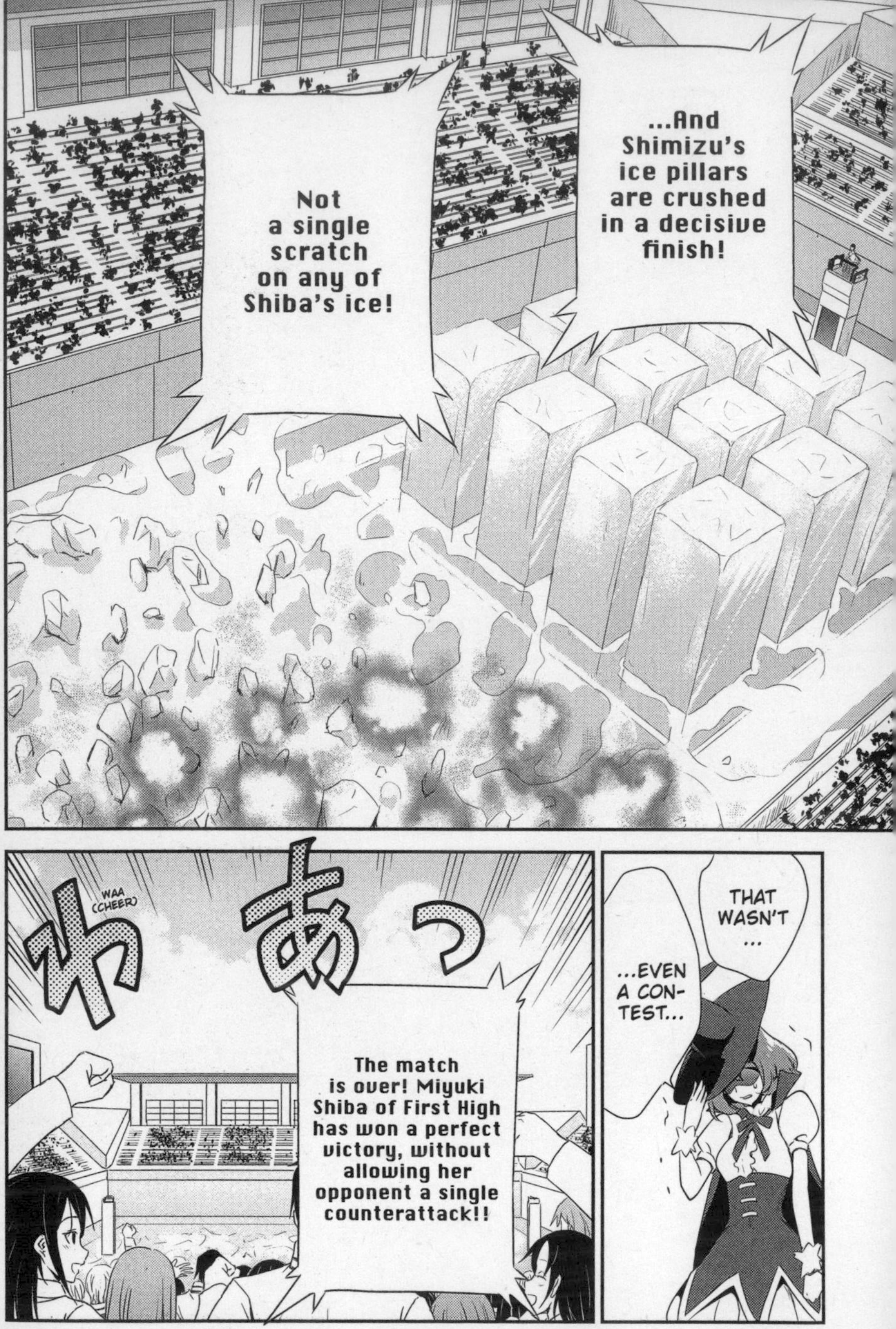

Not a single scratch on any of Shiba's ice!
...And Shimizu's ice pillars are crushed in a decisive finish!
THAT WASN'T ...
...EVEN A CON-TEST...
わあっ
WAA (CHEER)
The match is over! Miyuki Shiba of First High has won a perfect victory, without allowing her opponent a single counterattack!!

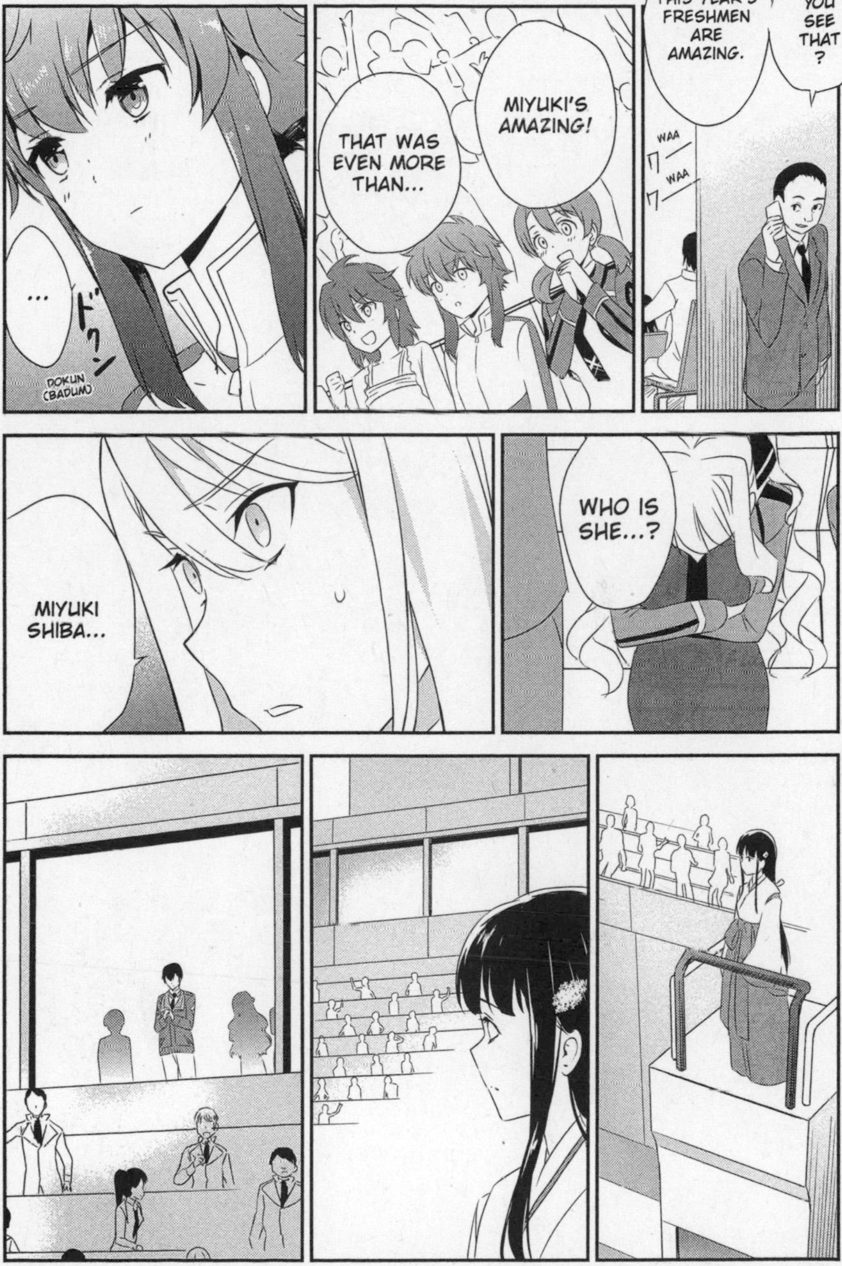
DID YOU SEE THAT?
THIS YEAR'S FRESHMEN ARE AMAZING.
ワ WAA
ワ WAA
MIYUKI'S AMAZING!
THAT WAS EVEN MORE THAN...
...
ドクン
DOKUN (BADUM)
WHO IS SHE...?
MIYUKI SHIBA...

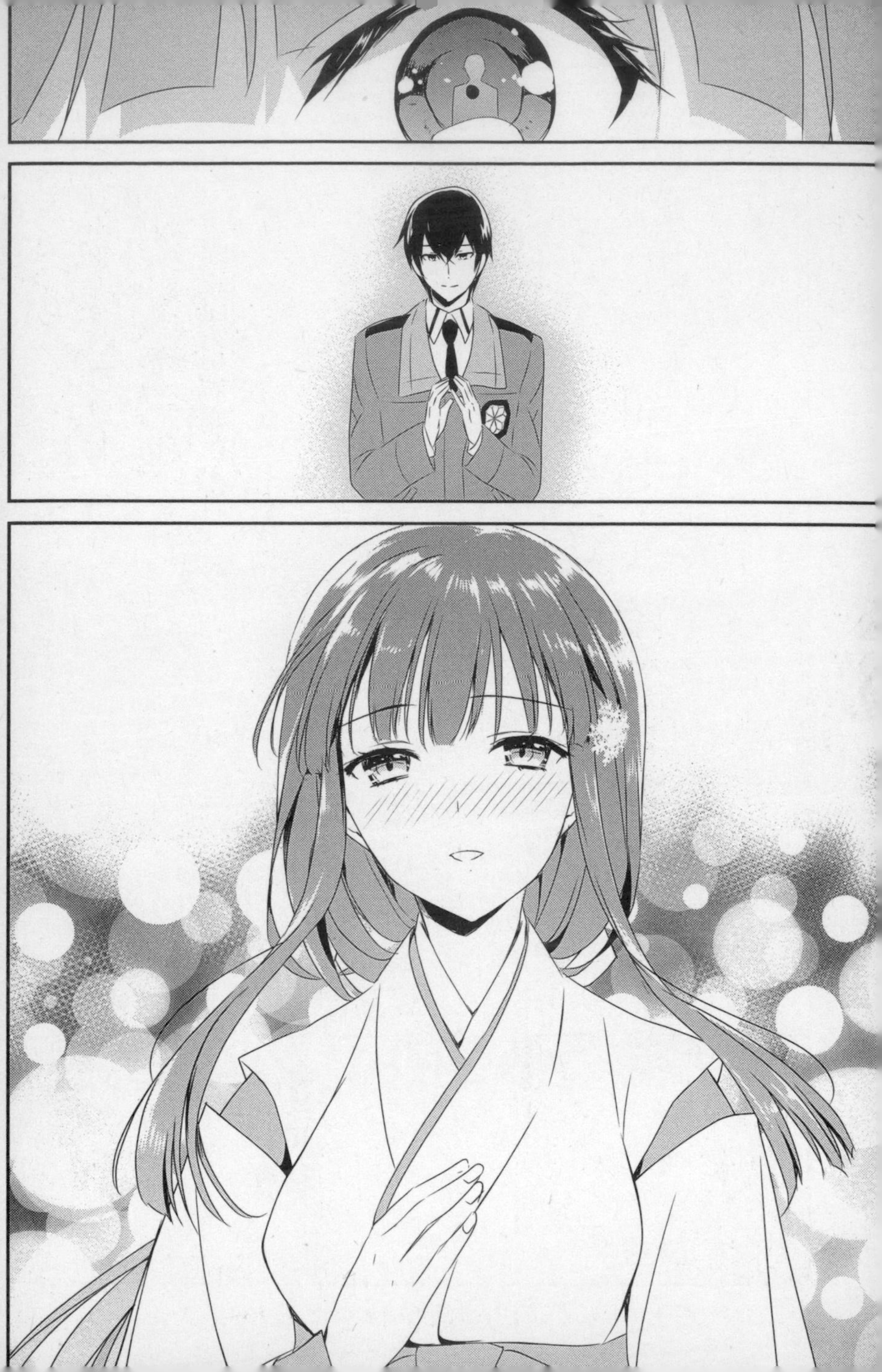

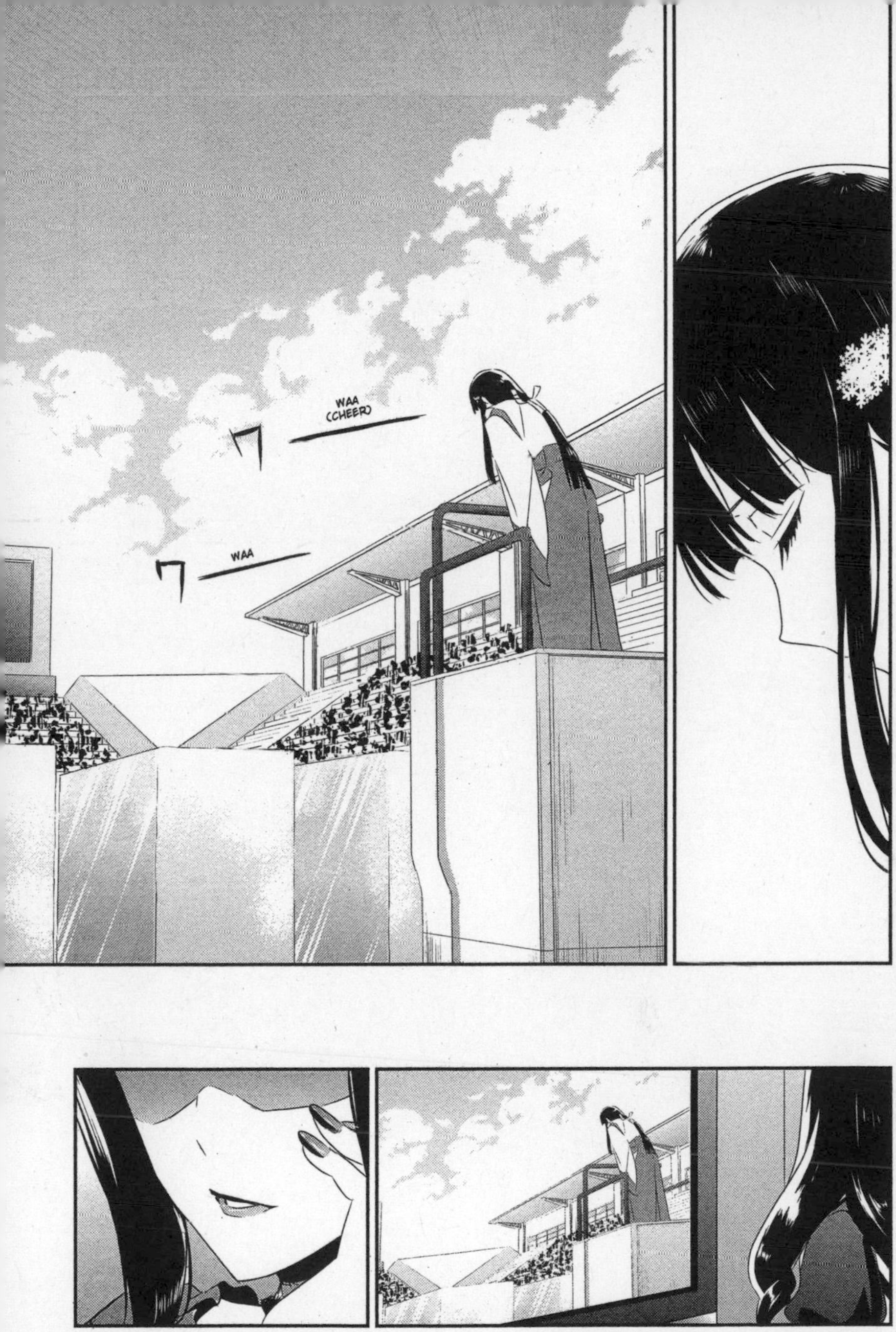
WAA
(CHEER)
WAA

TO BE CONTINUED IN VOLUME 7

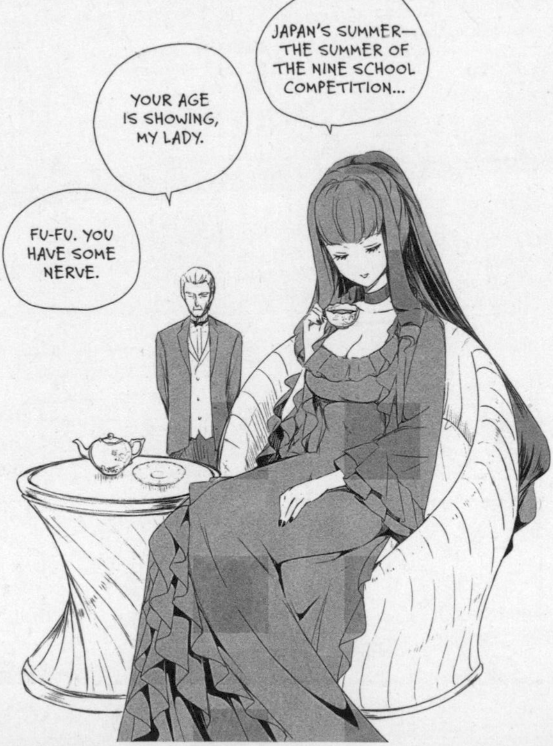
JAPAN'S SUMMER—THE SUMMER OF THE NINE SCHOOL COMPETITION...
YOUR AGE IS SHOWING, MY LADY.
FU-FU. YOU HAVE SOME NERVE.

EXTRA CHAPTER: SHIZUKU'S FIERCE NINE SCHOOL COMPETITION

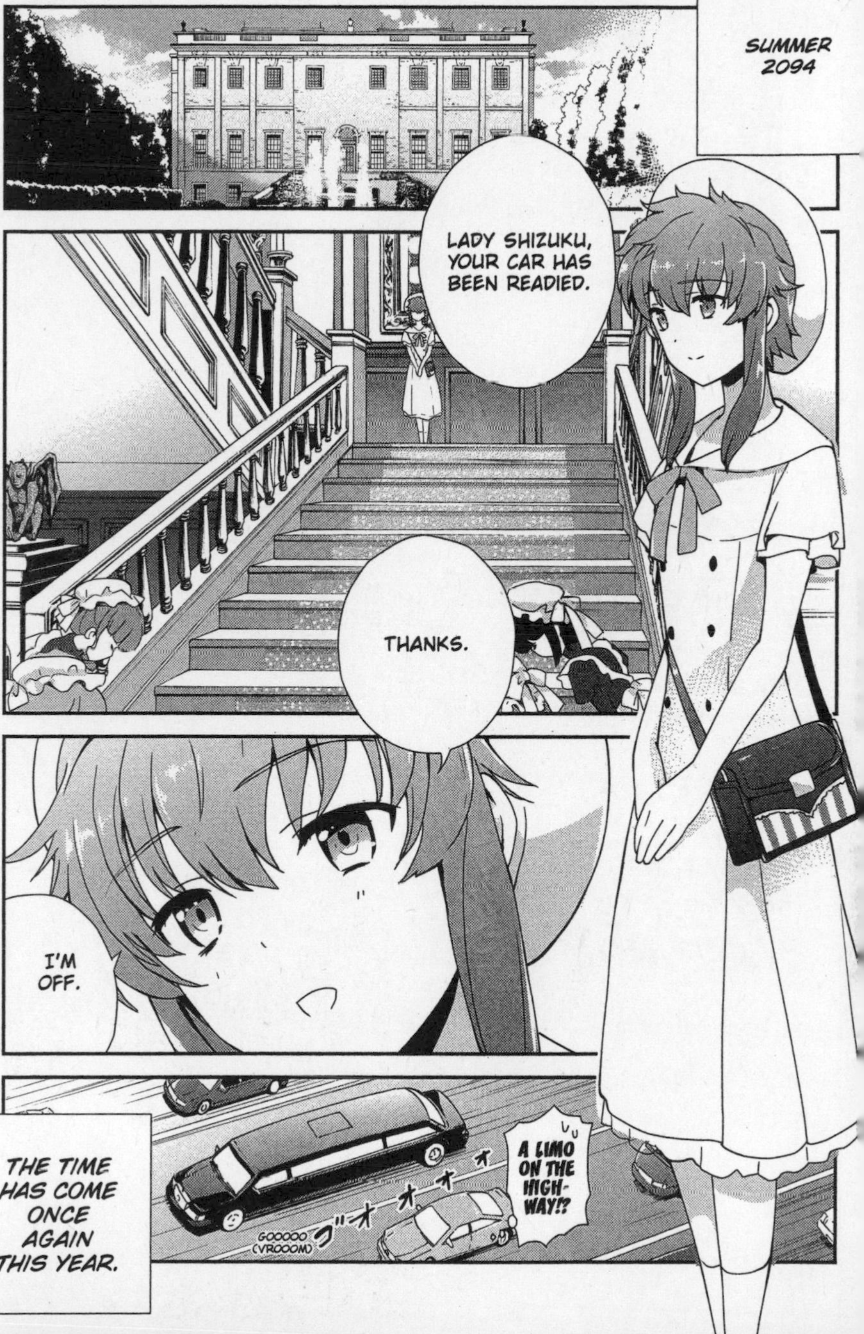
SUMMER 2094
LADY SHIZUKU, YOUR CAR HAS BEEN READIED.
THANKS.
I'M OFF.
A LIMO ON THE HIGH-WAY!?
GOOOOO (VROOOM)
THE TIME HAS COME ONCE AGAIN THIS YEAR.

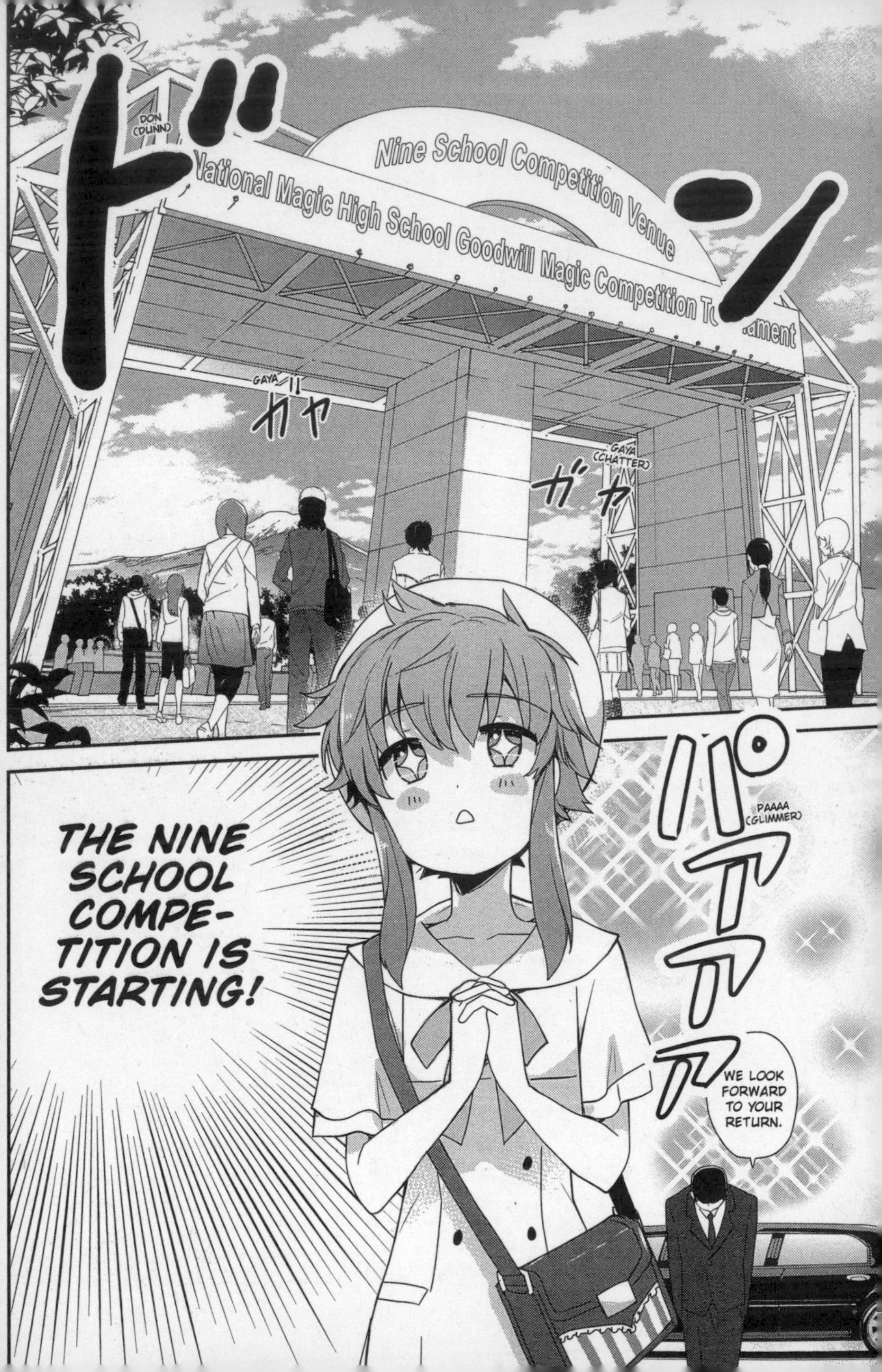
DON (DUNN)
Nine School Competition Venue
ational Magic High School Goodwill Magic Competition To
ament
GAYA
GAYA (CHATTER)
PAAAA (GLIMMER)
WE LOOK FORWARD TO YOUR RETURN.
THE NINE SCHOOL COMPE-TITION IS STARTING!

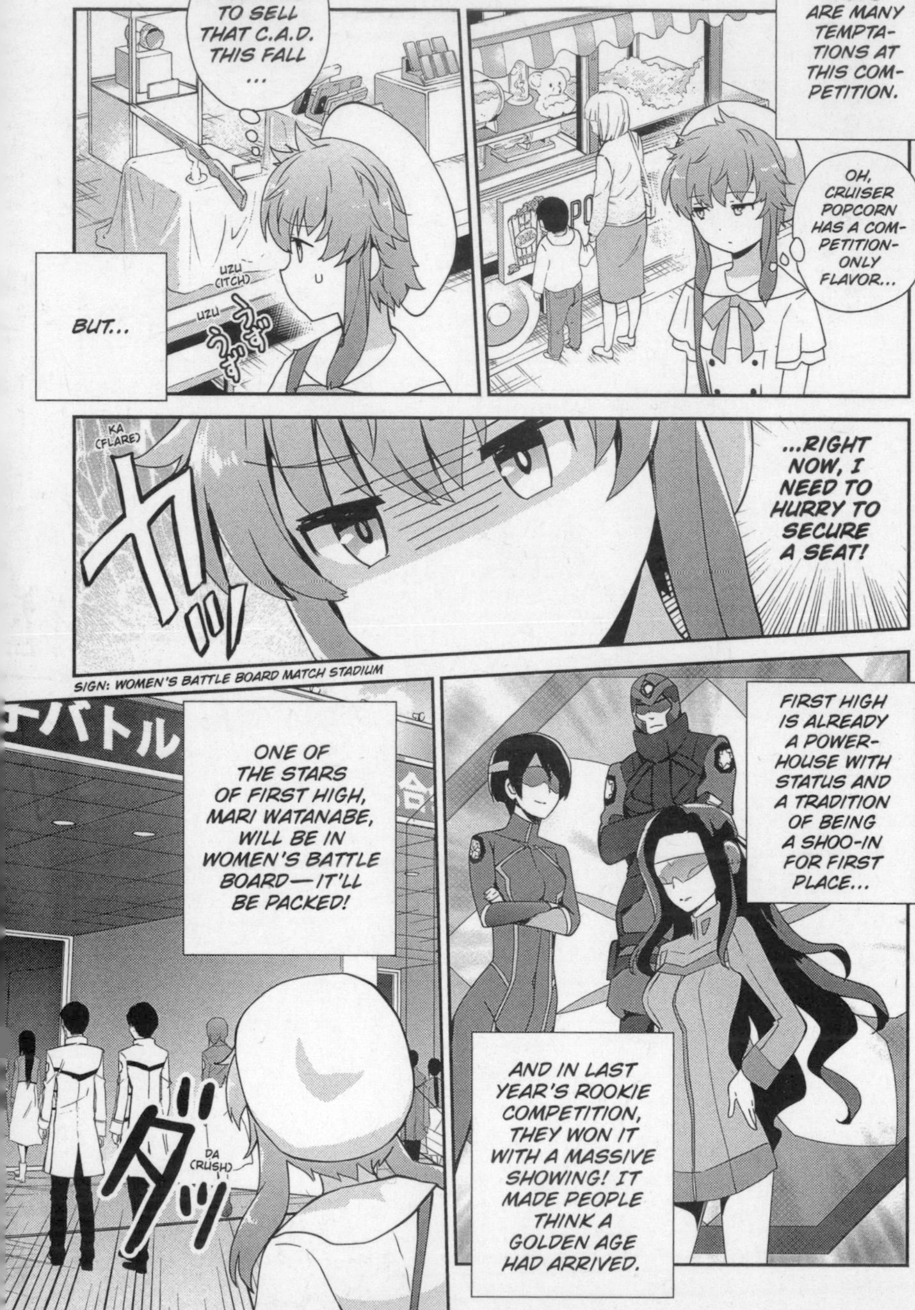
THERE ARE MANY TEMPTATIONS AT THIS COMPETITION.
OH, CRUISER POPCORN HAS A COMPETITION-ONLY FLAVOR...
ROSEN IS PLANNING TO SELL THAT C.A.D. THIS FALL...
UZU (ITCH)
UZU
BUT...
...RIGHT NOW, I NEED TO HURRY TO SECURE A SEAT!
KA (FLARE)
FIRST HIGH IS ALREADY A POWERHOUSE WITH STATUS AND A TRADITION OF BEING A SHOO-IN FOR FIRST PLACE...
AND IN LAST YEAR'S ROOKIE COMPETITION, THEY WON IT WITH A MASSIVE SHOWING! IT MADE PEOPLE THINK A GOLDEN AGE HAD ARRIVED.
SIGN: WOMEN'S BATTLE BOARD MATCH STADIUM
ONE OF THE STARS OF FIRST HIGH, MARI WATANABE, WILL BE IN WOMEN'S BATTLE BOARD—IT'LL BE PACKED!
DA (RUSH)

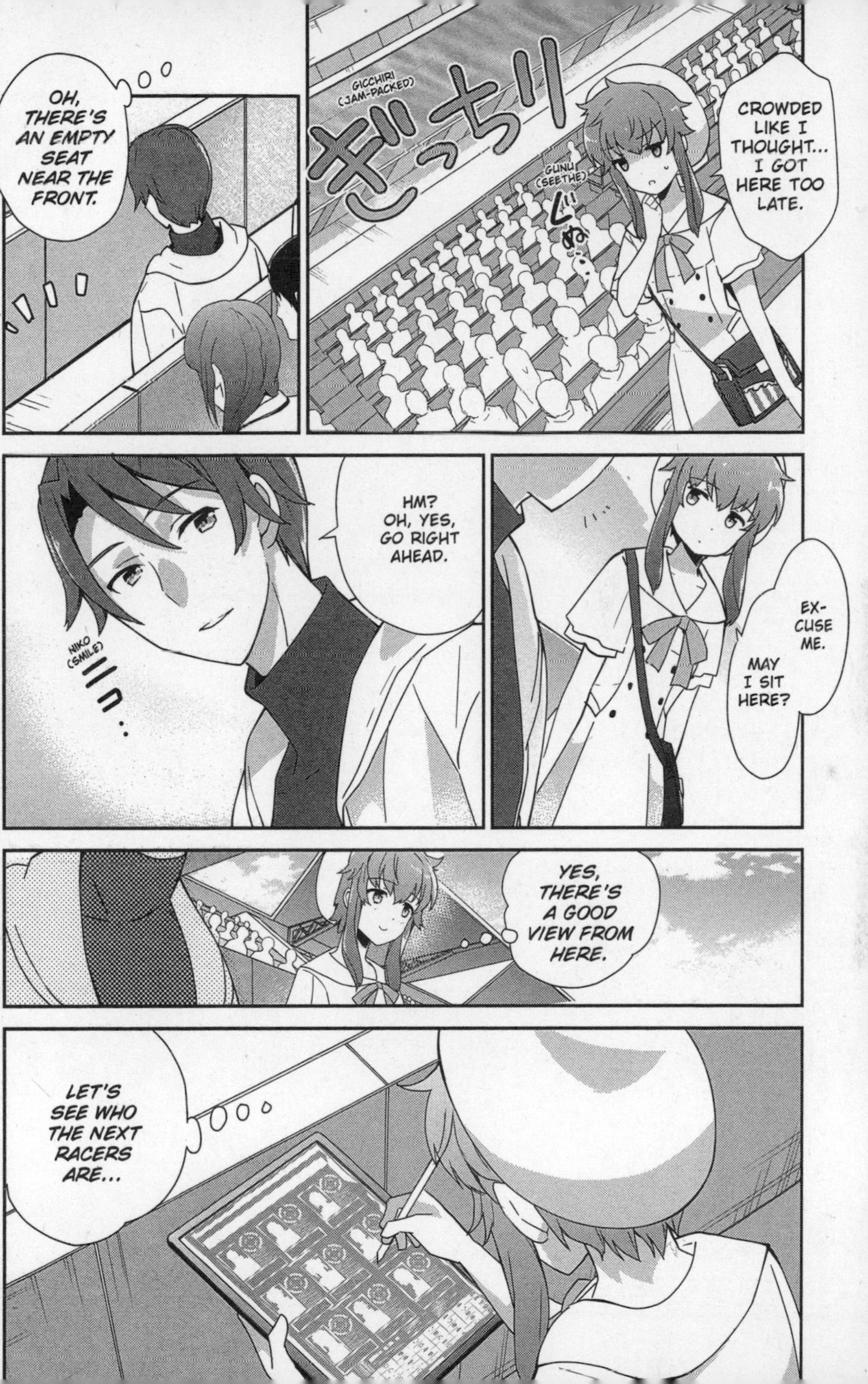
GICCHIRI (JAM-PACKED)
ぎっちり
CROWDED LIKE I THOUGHT... I GOT HERE TOO LATE.
GUNU (SEETHE)
ぐぬ
OH, THERE'S AN EMPTY SEAT NEAR THE FRONT.
EX-CUSE ME.
MAY I SIT HERE?
HM? OH, YES, GO RIGHT AHEAD.
NIKO (SMILE)
ニコ
YES, THERE'S A GOOD VIEW FROM HERE.
LET'S SEE WHO THE NEXT RACERS ARE...

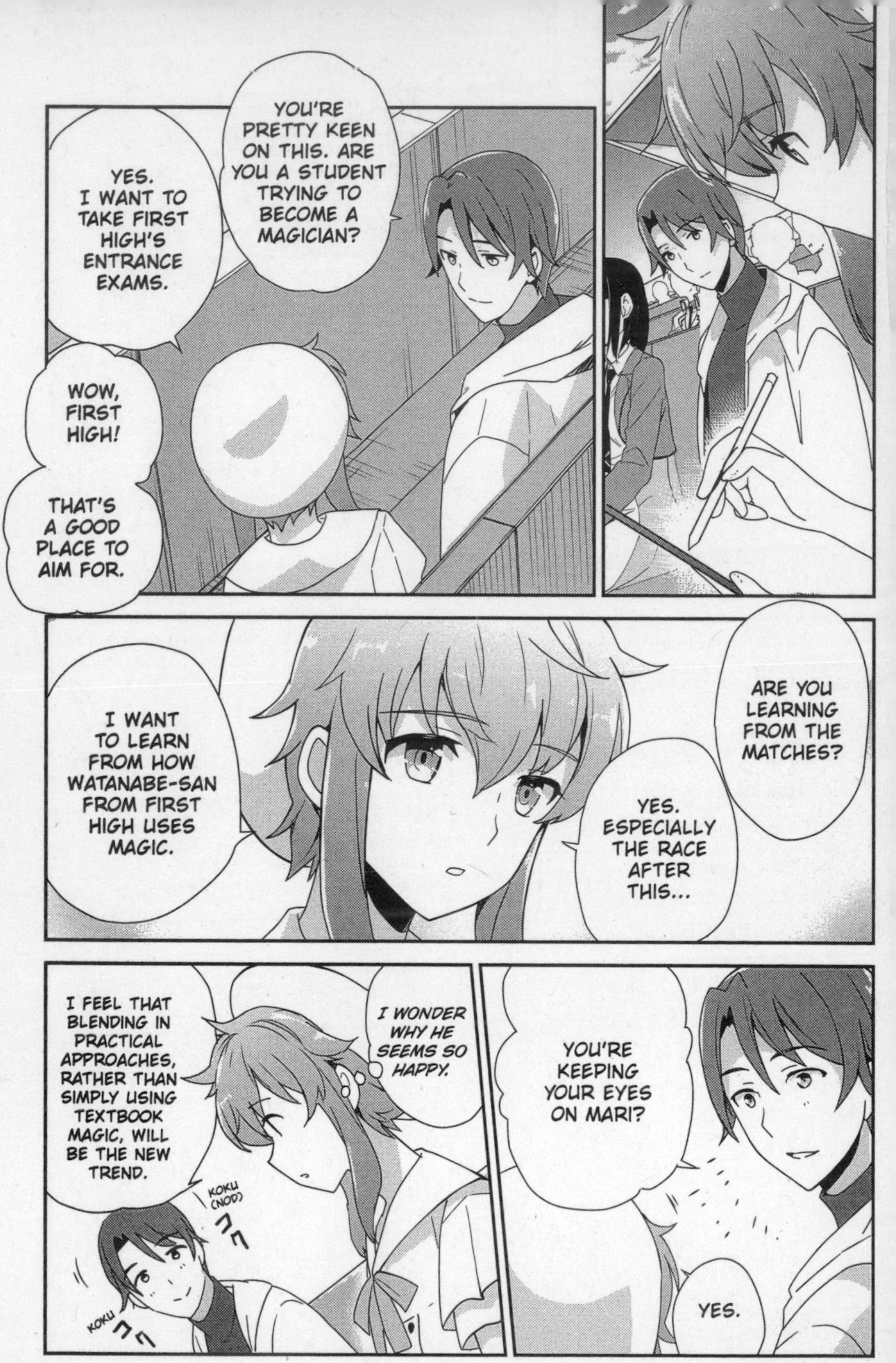
YOU'RE PRETTY KEEN ON THIS. ARE YOU A STUDENT TRYING TO BECOME A MAGICIAN?
YES. I WANT TO TAKE FIRST HIGH'S ENTRANCE EXAMS.
WOW, FIRST HIGH!
THAT'S A GOOD PLACE TO AIM FOR.
ARE YOU LEARNING FROM THE MATCHES?
YES. ESPECIALLY THE RACE AFTER THIS...
I WANT TO LEARN FROM HOW WATANABE-SAN FROM FIRST HIGH USES MAGIC.
YOU'RE KEEPING YOUR EYES ON MARI?
YES.
I WONDER WHY HE SEEMS SO HAPPY.
I FEEL THAT BLENDING IN PRACTICAL APPROACHES, RATHER THAN SIMPLY USING TEXTBOOK MAGIC, WILL BE THE NEW TREND.
KOKU (NOD)
KOKU

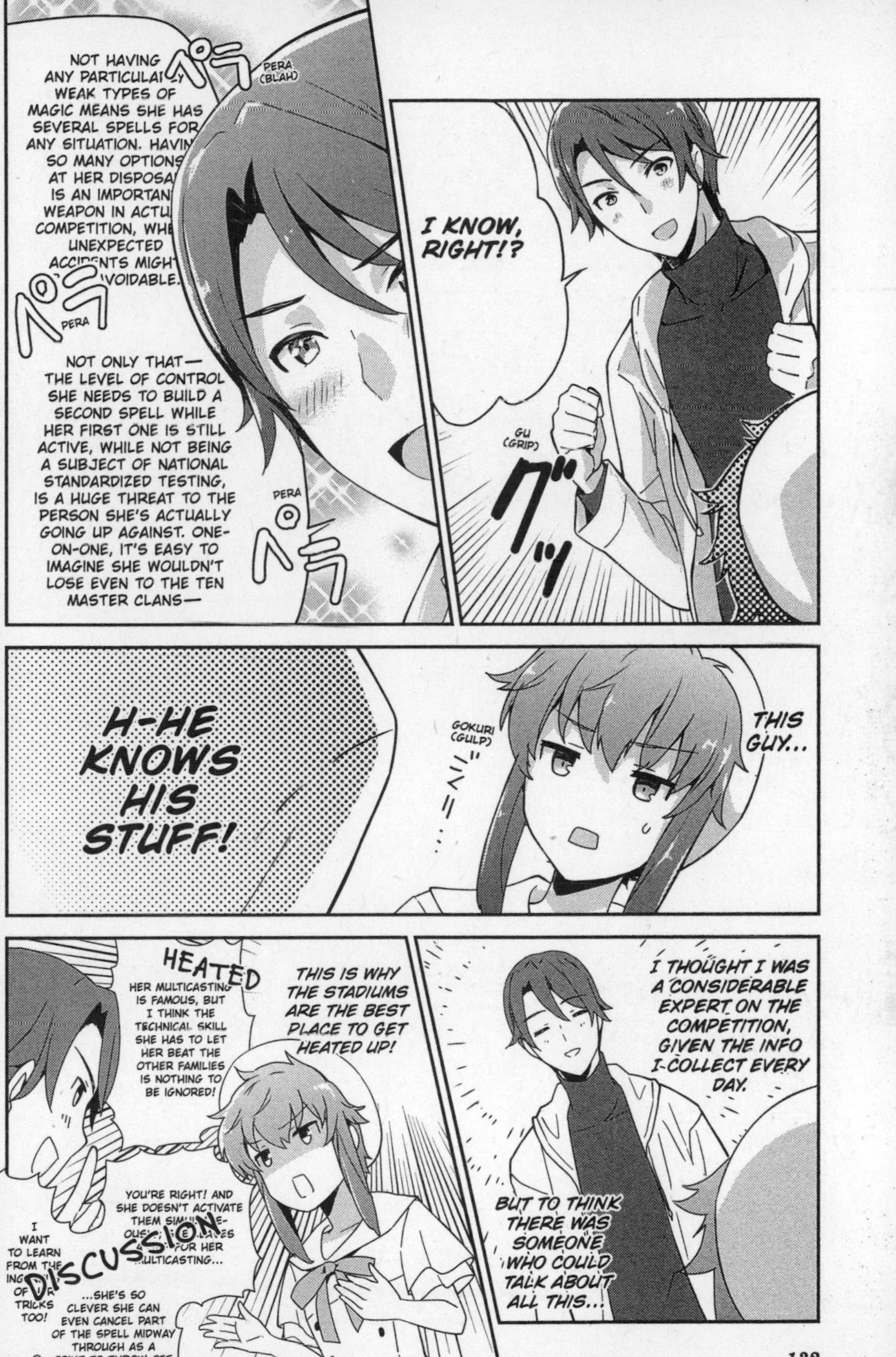

I KNOW, RIGHT!?
GU (GRIP)
PERA (BLAH)
NOT HAVING ANY PARTICULARLY WEAK TYPES OF MAGIC MEANS SHE HAS SEVERAL SPELLS FOR ANY SITUATION. HAVING SO MANY OPTIONS AT HER DISPOSAL IS AN IMPORTANT WEAPON IN ACTUAL COMPETITION, WHERE UNEXPECTED ACCIDENTS MIGHT BE UNAVOIDABLE.
PERA
NOT ONLY THAT—THE LEVEL OF CONTROL SHE NEEDS TO BUILD A SECOND SPELL WHILE HER FIRST ONE IS STILL ACTIVE, WHILE NOT BEING A SUBJECT OF NATIONAL STANDARDIZED TESTING, IS A HUGE THREAT TO THE PERSON SHE'S ACTUALLY GOING UP AGAINST. ONE-ON-ONE, IT'S EASY TO IMAGINE SHE WOULDN'T LOSE EVEN TO THE TEN MASTER CLANS—
PERA
THIS GUY...
GOKURI (GULP)
H-HE KNOWS HIS STUFF!
I THOUGHT I WAS A CONSIDERABLE EXPERT ON THE COMPETITION, GIVEN THE INFO I COLLECT EVERY DAY.
BUT TO THINK THERE WAS SOMEONE WHO COULD TALK ABOUT ALL THIS...
THIS IS WHY THE STADIUMS ARE THE BEST PLACE TO GET HEATED UP!
HEATED
HER MULTICASTING IS FAMOUS, BUT I THINK THE TECHNICAL SKILL SHE HAS TO LET HER BEAT THE OTHER FAMILIES IS NOTHING TO BE IGNORED!
YOU'RE RIGHT! AND SHE DOESN'T ACTIVATE THEM
MULTICASTING...
I WANT TO LEARN FROM THE
TRICKS TOO!
DISCUSSION
...SHE'S SO CLEVER SHE CAN EVEN CANCEL PART OF THE SPELL MIDWAY THROUGH AS A FEINT TO THROW OFF HER OPPONENT!

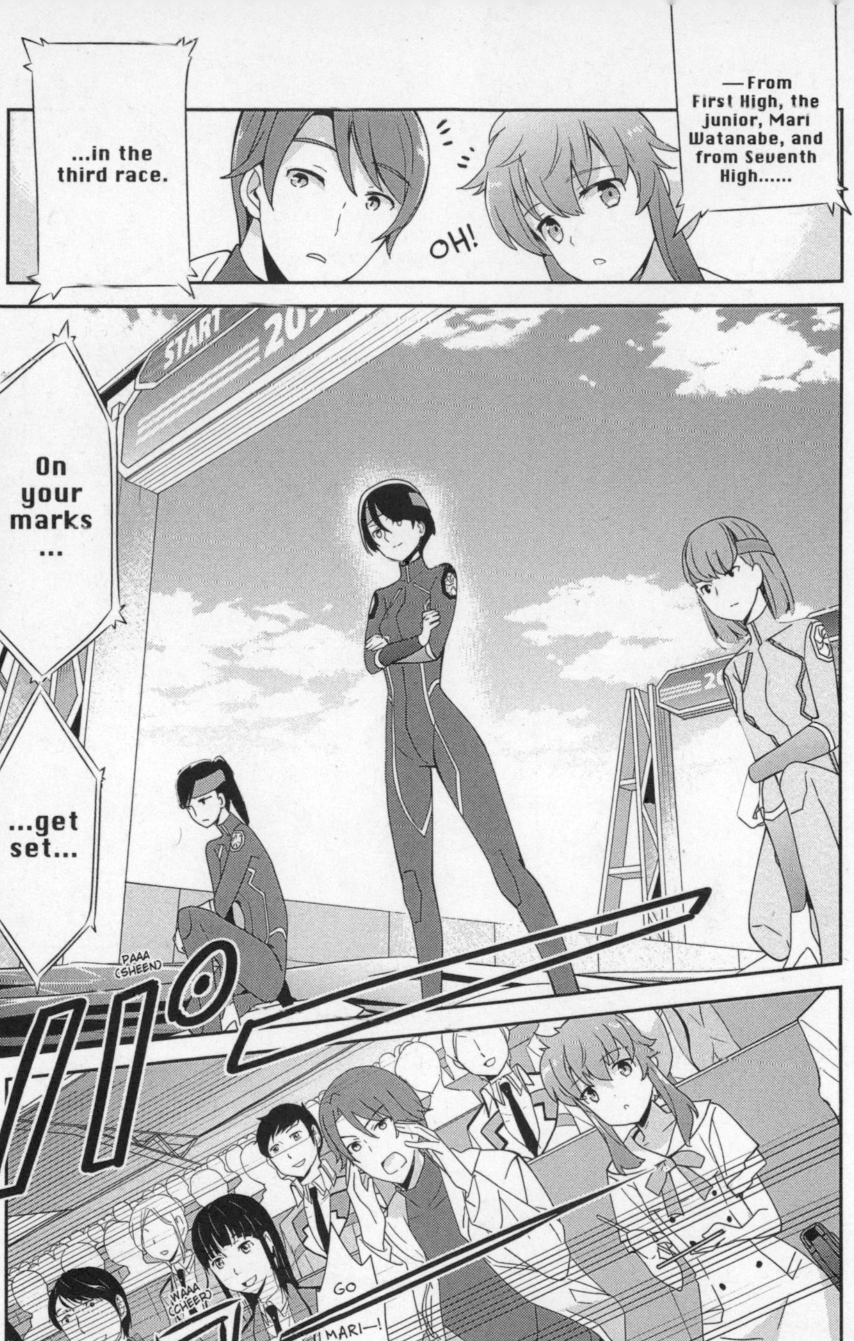
—From First High, the junior, Mari Watanabe, and from Seventh High......
OH!
...in the third race.
On your marks...
...get set...
PAAA (SHEEN)
GO MARI—!
WAAA (CHEER)

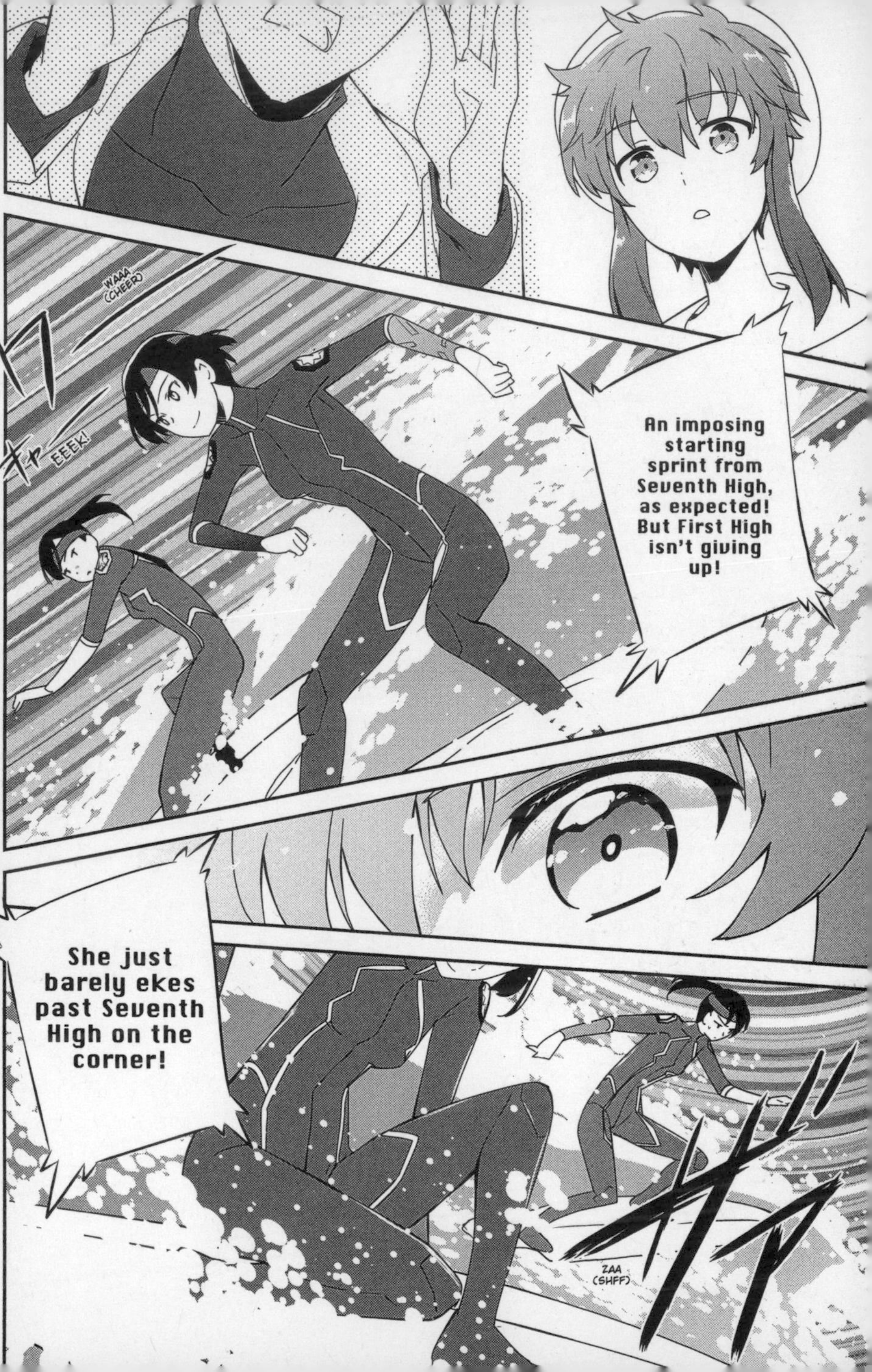
An imposing starting sprint from Seventh High, as expected! But First High isn't giving up!
WAAA (CHEER)
EEEK!
She just barely ekes past Seventh High on the corner!
ZAA (SHFF)

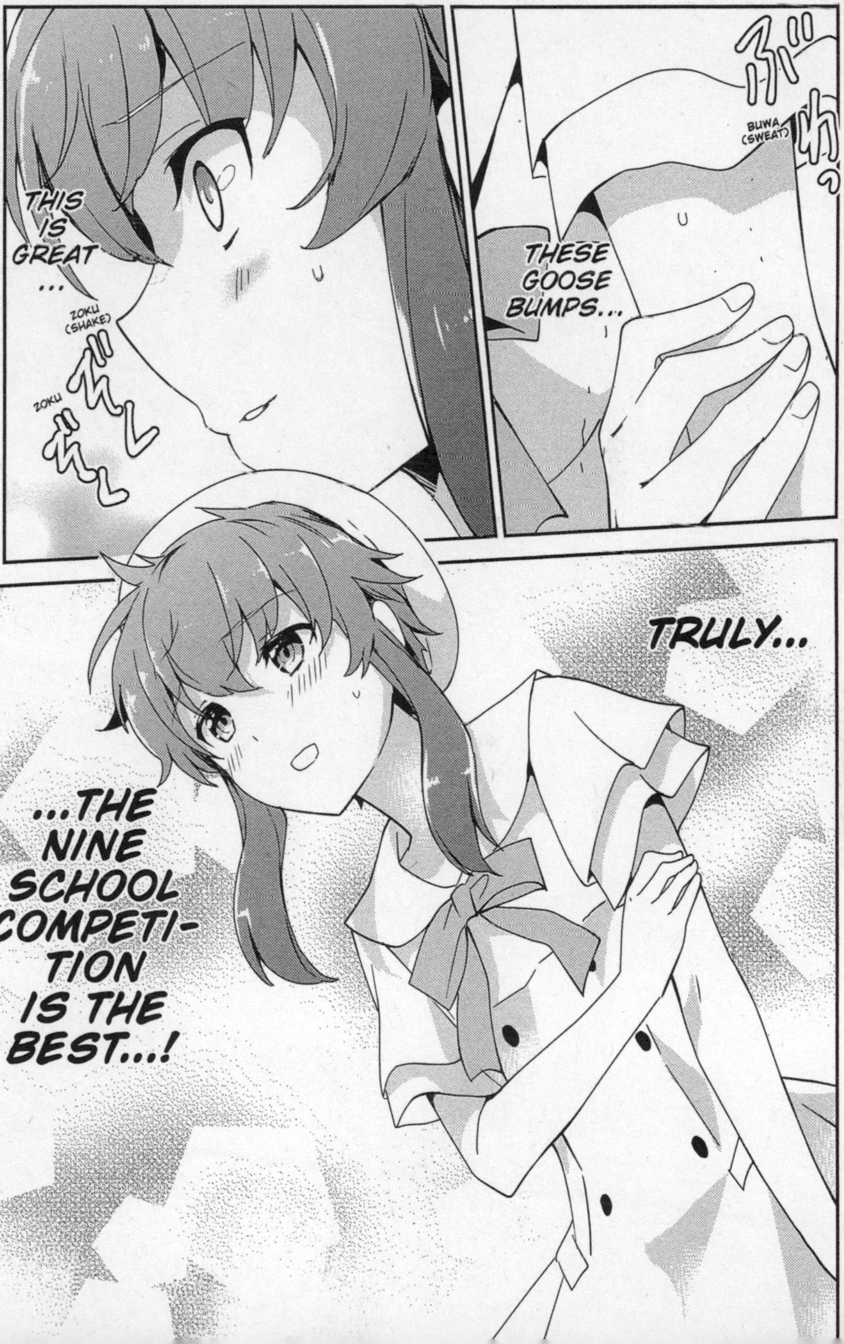
ぶわっ
BUWA (SWEAT)
THESE GOOSE BUMPS...
THIS IS GREAT...
ZOKU (SHAKE)
ZOKU
ぞくぞく
TRULY...
...THE NINE SCHOOL COMPETI-TION IS THE BEST...!

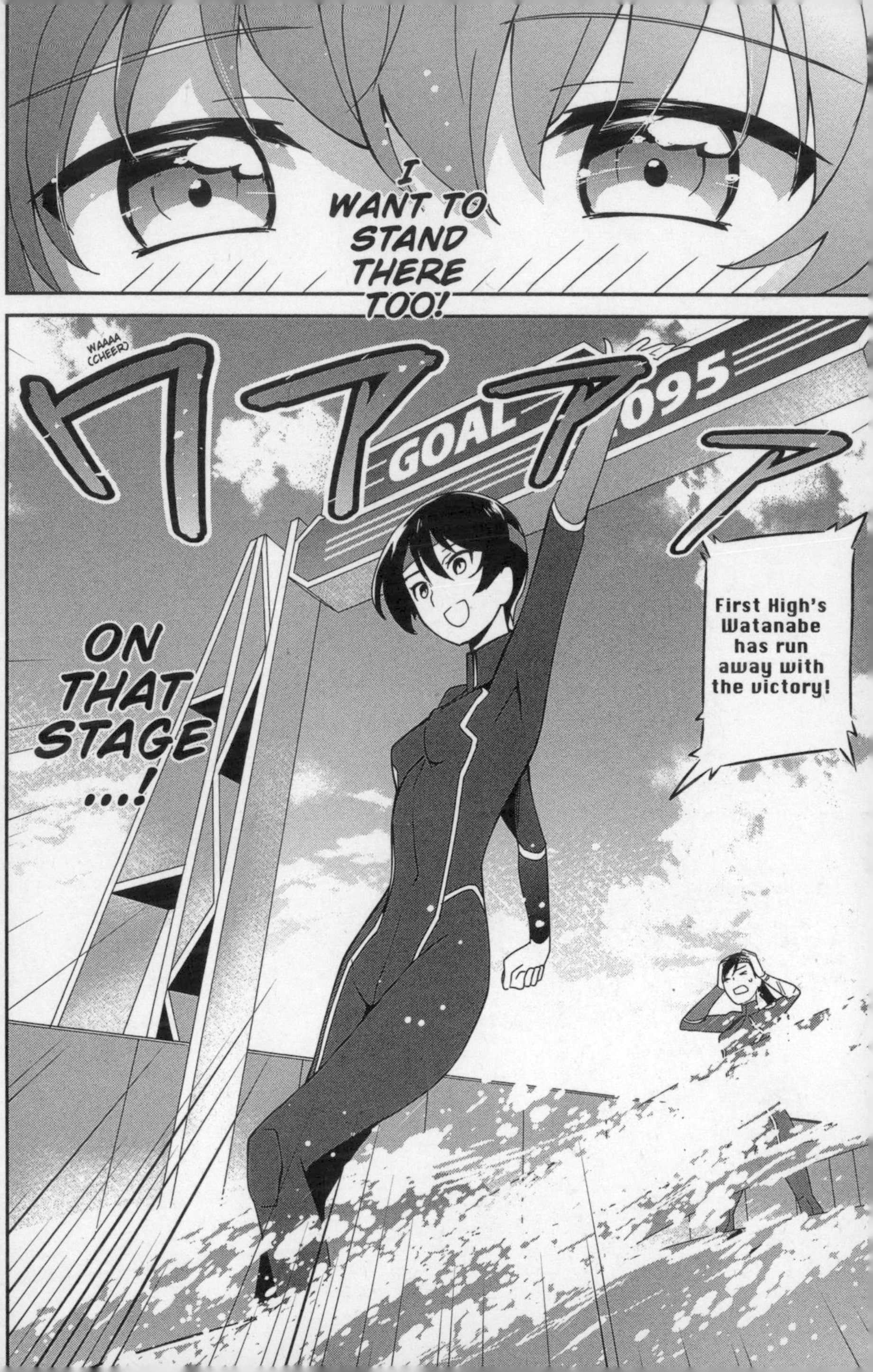
I WANT TO STAND THERE TOO!
WAAAA (CHEER)
GOAL 095
First High's Watanabe has run away with the victory!
ON THAT STAGE ...!

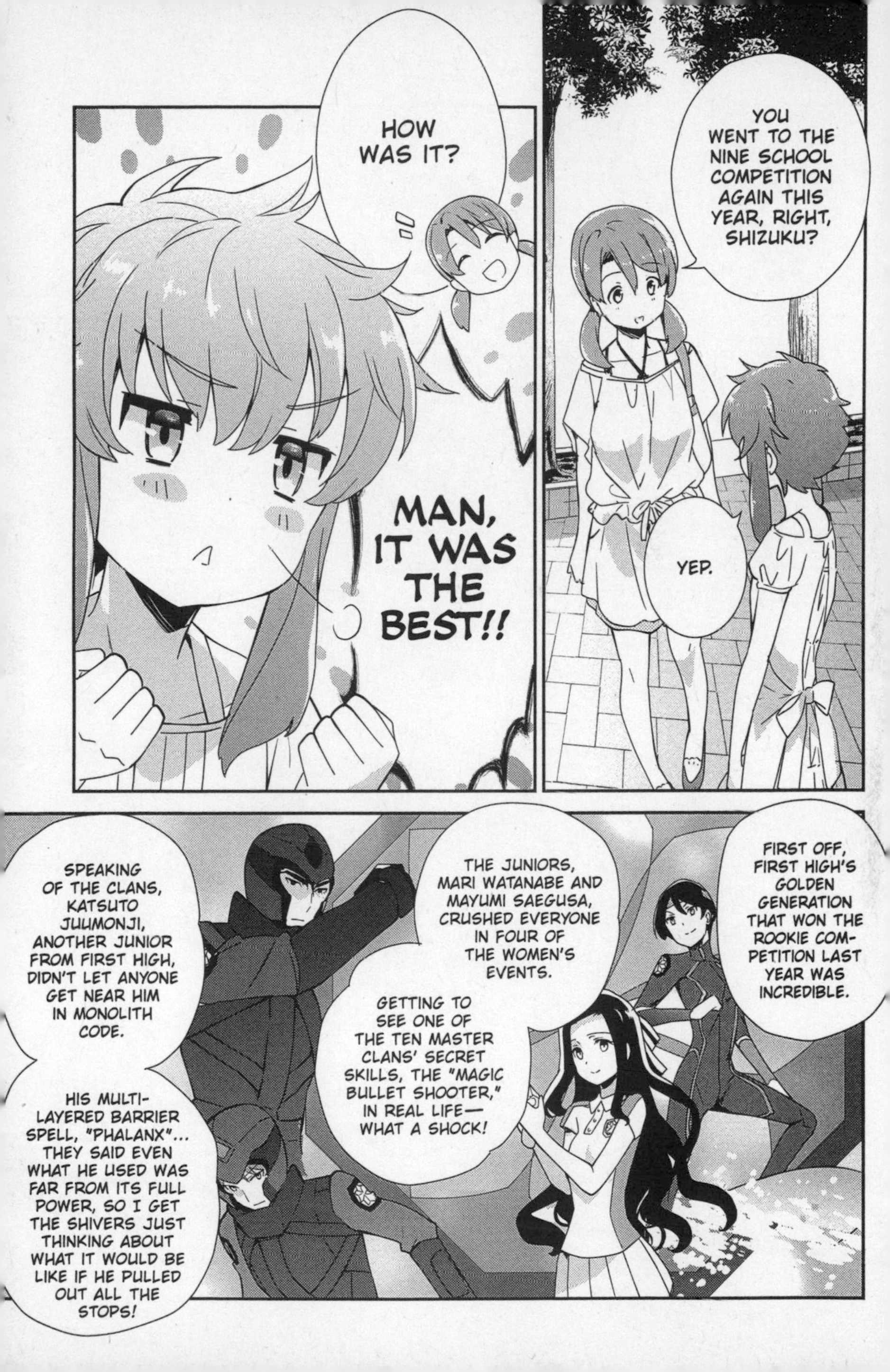
YOU WENT TO THE NINE SCHOOL COMPETITION AGAIN THIS YEAR, RIGHT, SHIZUKU?
YEP.
HOW WAS IT?
MAN, IT WAS THE BEST!!
FIRST OFF, FIRST HIGH'S GOLDEN GENERATION THAT WON THE ROOKIE COMPETITION LAST YEAR WAS INCREDIBLE.
THE JUNIORS, MARI WATANABE AND MAYUMI SAEGUSA, CRUSHED EVERYONE IN FOUR OF THE WOMEN'S EVENTS.
GETTING TO SEE ONE OF THE TEN MASTER CLANS' SECRET SKILLS, THE "MAGIC BULLET SHOOTER," IN REAL LIFE—WHAT A SHOCK!
SPEAKING OF THE CLANS, KATSUTO JUUMONJI, ANOTHER JUNIOR FROM FIRST HIGH, DIDN'T LET ANYONE GET NEAR HIM IN MONOLITH CODE.
HIS MULTI-LAYERED BARRIER SPELL, "PHALANX"... THEY SAID EVEN WHAT HE USED WAS FAR FROM ITS FULL POWER, SO I GET THE SHIVERS JUST THINKING ABOUT WHAT IT WOULD BE LIKE IF HE PULLED OUT ALL THE STOPS!

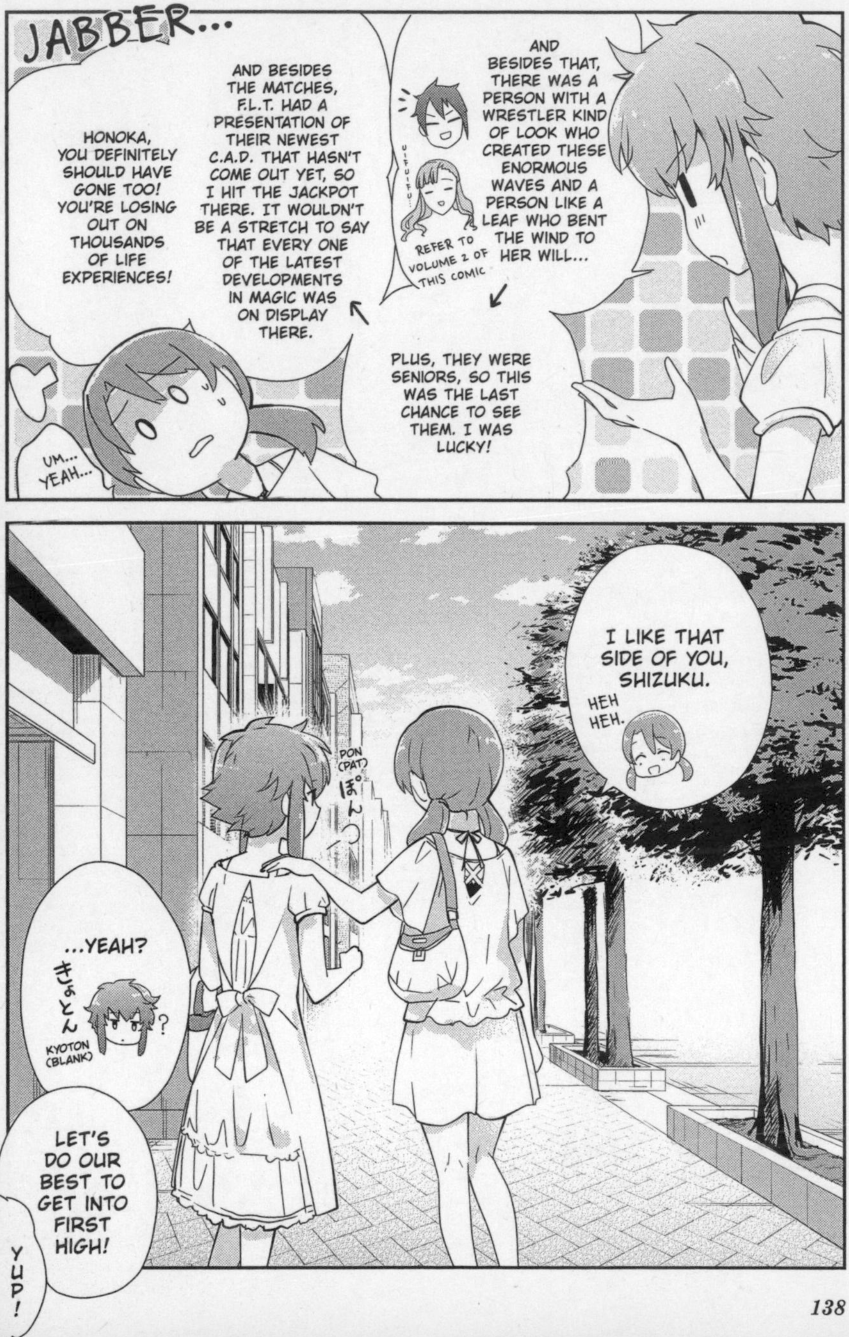
AND BESIDES THAT, THERE WAS A PERSON WITH A WRESTLER KIND OF LOOK WHO CREATED THESE ENORMOUS WAVES AND A PERSON LIKE A LEAF WHO BENT THE WIND TO HER WILL...
UFUFUFU...
REFER TO VOLUME 2 OF THIS COMIC
PLUS, THEY WERE SENIORS, SO THIS WAS THE LAST CHANCE TO SEE THEM. I WAS LUCKY!
AND BESIDES THE MATCHES, F.L.T. HAD A PRESENTATION OF THEIR NEWEST C.A.D. THAT HASN'T COME OUT YET, SO I HIT THE JACKPOT THERE. IT WOULDN'T BE A STRETCH TO SAY THAT EVERY ONE OF THE LATEST DEVELOPMENTS IN MAGIC WAS ON DISPLAY THERE.
HONOKA, YOU DEFINITELY SHOULD HAVE GONE TOO! YOU'RE LOSING OUT ON THOUSANDS OF LIFE EXPERIENCES!
JABBER...
UM... YEAH...
I LIKE THAT SIDE OF YOU, SHIZUKU.
HEH HEH.
PON (PAT)
ぽん
...YEAH?
きょとん
KYOTON (BLANK)
LET'S DO OUR BEST TO GET INTO FIRST HIGH!
YUP!

THE
HONOR
STUDENT
AT
MAGIC HIGH
SCHOOL

THE STORY ABOUT THE NAOTSUGU-MARI COUPLE UNEXPECTEDLY SNUCK INTO THIS EXTRA CHAPTER. APPARENTLY, THEY FELL IN LOVE WHILE TRAINING AT THE CHIBA DOJO.

GOOOO
(RAAAAGE)
ゴオオオ

EXTRA CHAPTER TWO: HONOKA AND THE STUDY GROUP OF LOVE

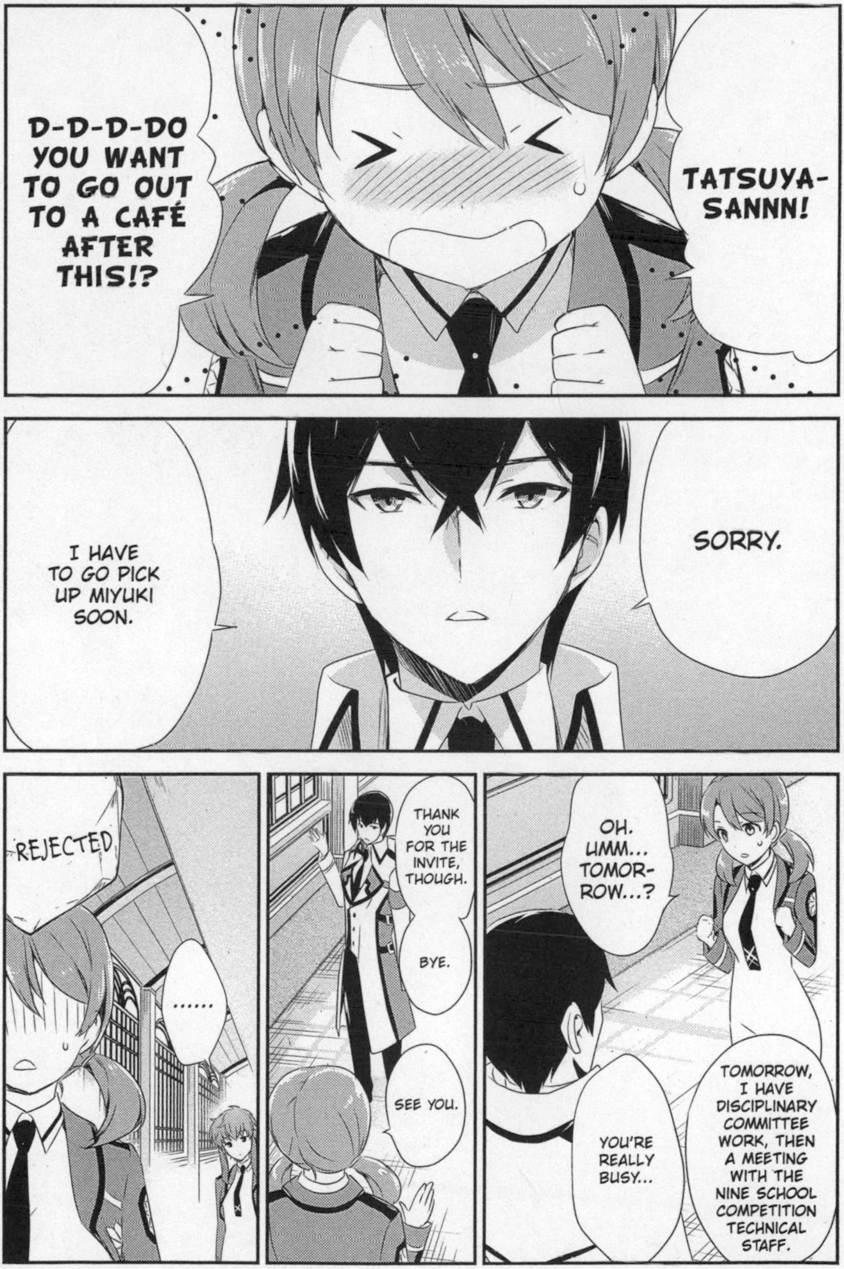
TATSUYA-SANNN!
D-D-D-DO YOU WANT TO GO OUT TO A CAFÉ AFTER THIS!?
SORRY.
I HAVE TO GO PICK UP MIYUKI SOON.
OH. UMM... TOMOR-ROW...?
TOMORROW, I HAVE DISCIPLINARY COMMITTEE WORK, THEN A MEETING WITH THE NINE SCHOOL COMPETITION TECHNICAL STAFF.
YOU'RE REALLY BUSY...
THANK YOU FOR THE INVITE, THOUGH.
BYE.
SEE YOU.
REJECTED
......

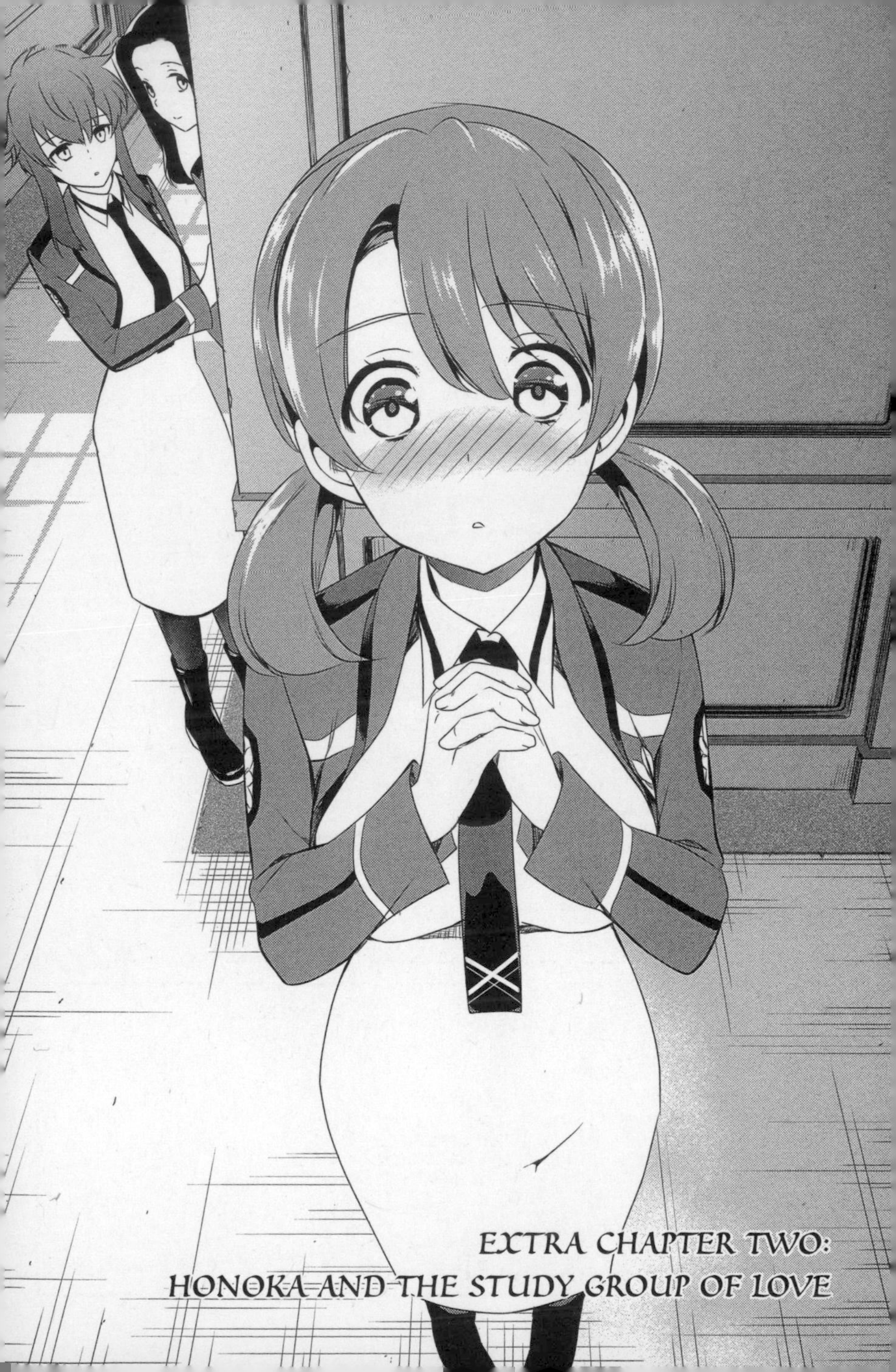
EXTRA CHAPTER TWO:
HONOKA AND THE STUDY GROUP OF LOVE

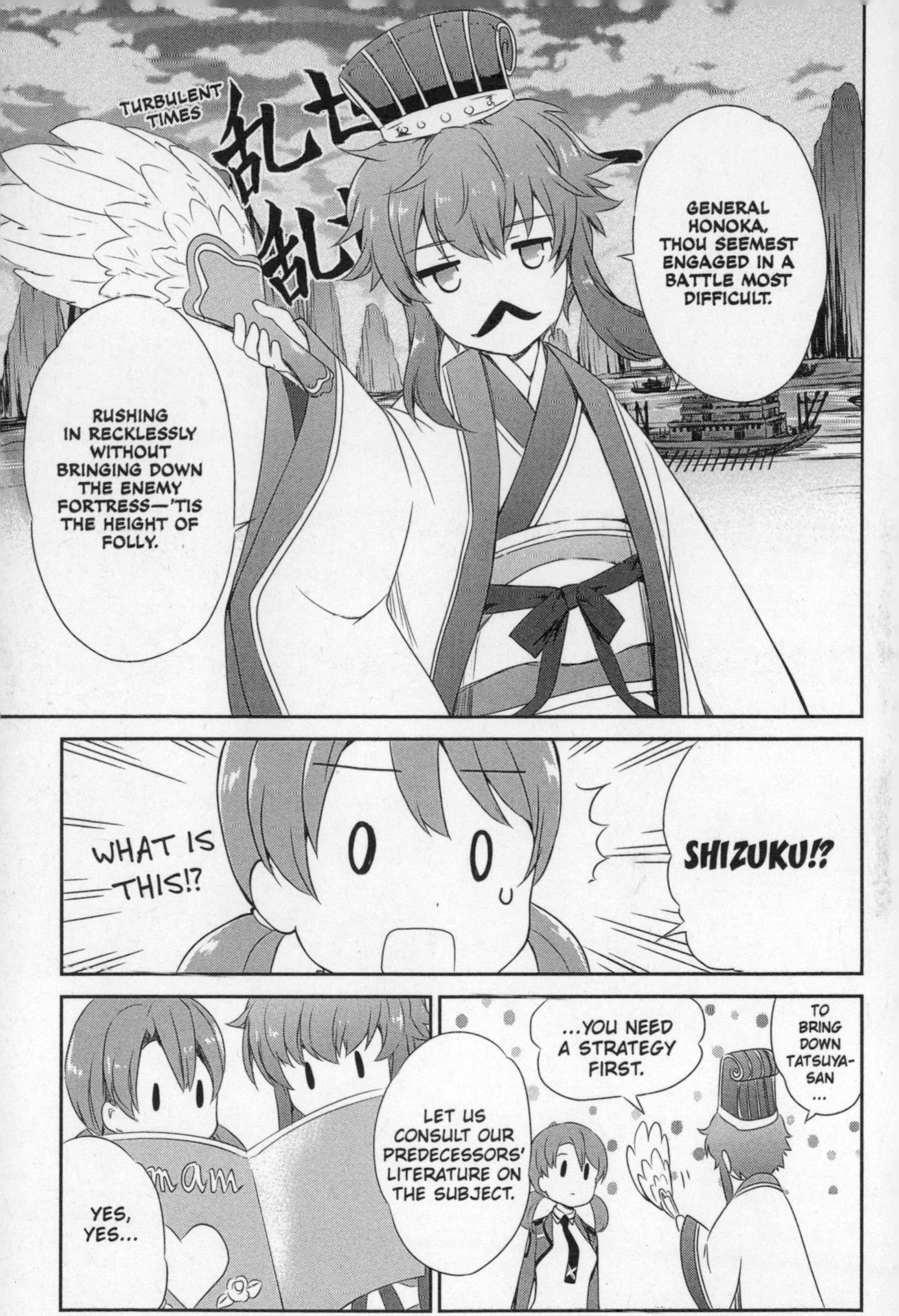
GENERAL HONOKA, THOU SEEMEST ENGAGED IN A BATTLE MOST DIFFICULT.
TURBULENT TIMES
RUSHING IN RECKLESSLY WITHOUT BRINGING DOWN THE ENEMY FORTRESS—'TIS THE HEIGHT OF FOLLY.
SHIZUKU!?
WHAT IS THIS!?
TO BRING DOWN TATSUYA-SAN ...
...YOU NEED A STRATEGY FIRST.
LET US CONSULT OUR PREDECESSORS' LITERATURE ON THE SUBJECT.
YES, YES...

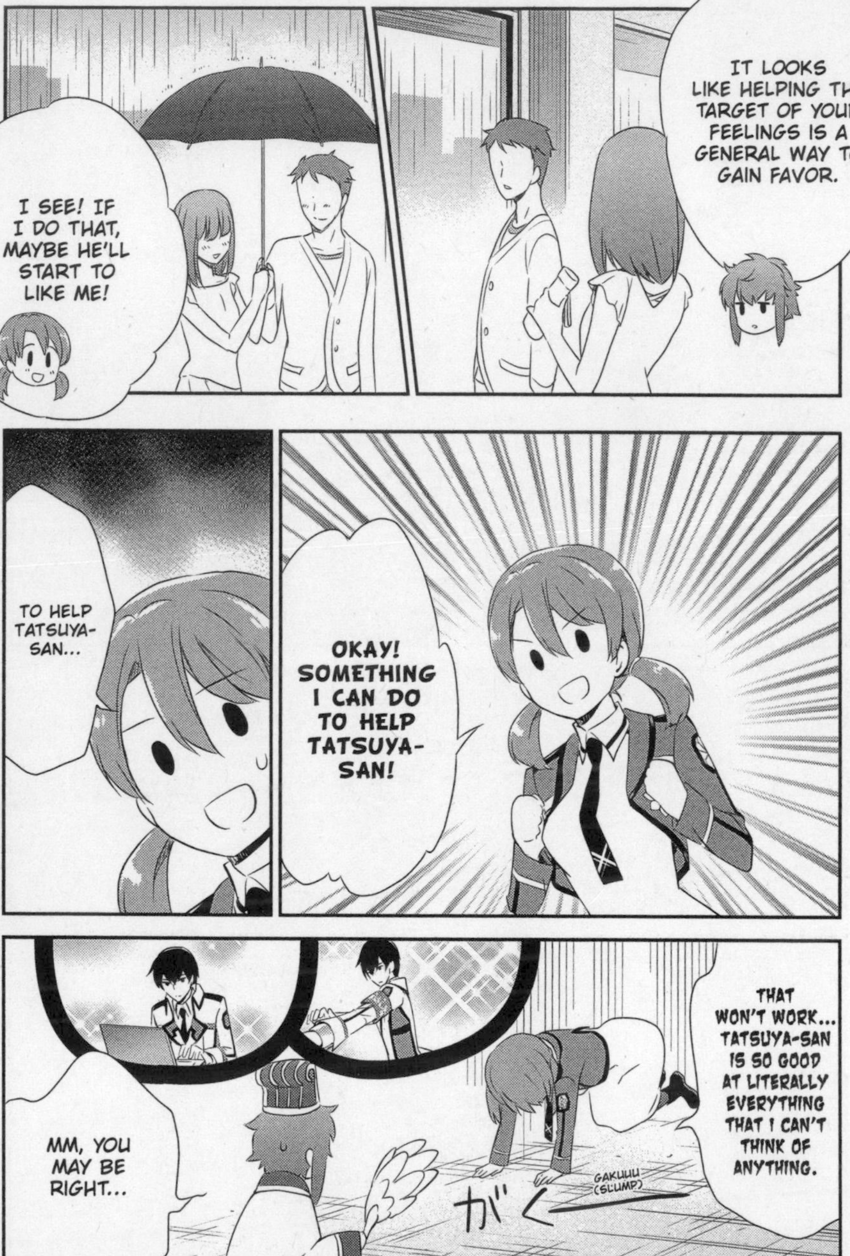
IT LOOKS LIKE HELPING THE TARGET OF YOUR FEELINGS IS A GENERAL WAY TO GAIN FAVOR.
I SEE! IF I DO THAT, MAYBE HE'LL START TO LIKE ME!
OKAY! SOMETHING I CAN DO TO HELP TATSUYA-SAN!
TO HELP TATSUYA-SAN...
THAT WON'T WORK... TATSUYA-SAN IS SO GOOD AT LITERALLY EVERYTHING THAT I CAN'T THINK OF ANYTHING.
GAKUUU (SLUMP)
がく
MM, YOU MAY BE RIGHT...

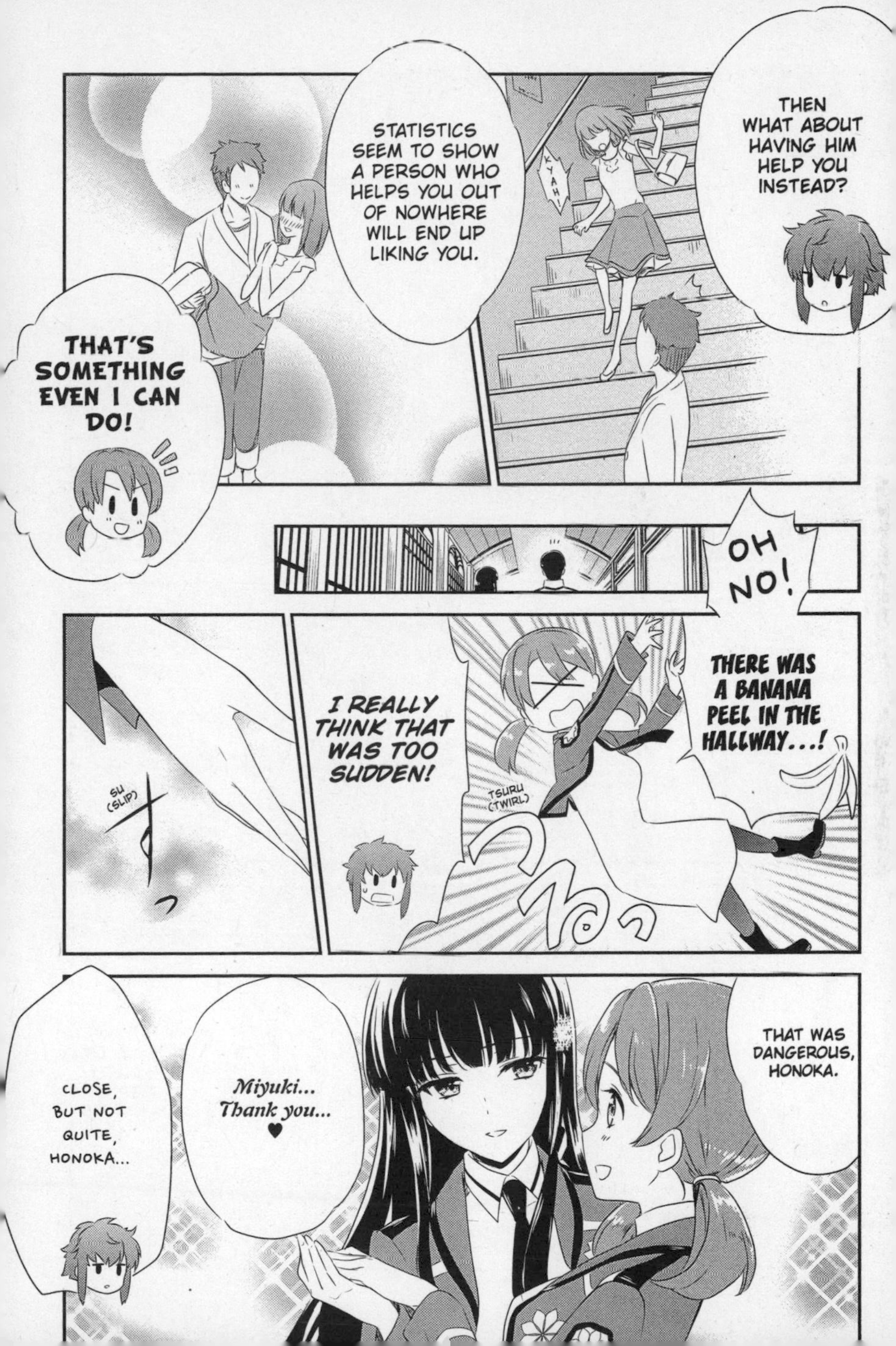

THEN WHAT ABOUT HAVING HIM HELP YOU INSTEAD?
KYAH!
STATISTICS SEEM TO SHOW A PERSON WHO HELPS YOU OUT OF NOWHERE WILL END UP LIKING YOU.
THAT'S SOMETHING EVEN I CAN DO!
OH NO!
THERE WAS A BANANA PEEL IN THE HALLWAY...!
TSURU (TWIRL)
I REALLY THINK THAT WAS TOO SUDDEN!
SU (SLIP)
THAT WAS DANGEROUS, HONOKA.
Miyuki... Thank you... ♥
CLOSE, BUT NOT QUITE, HONOKA...

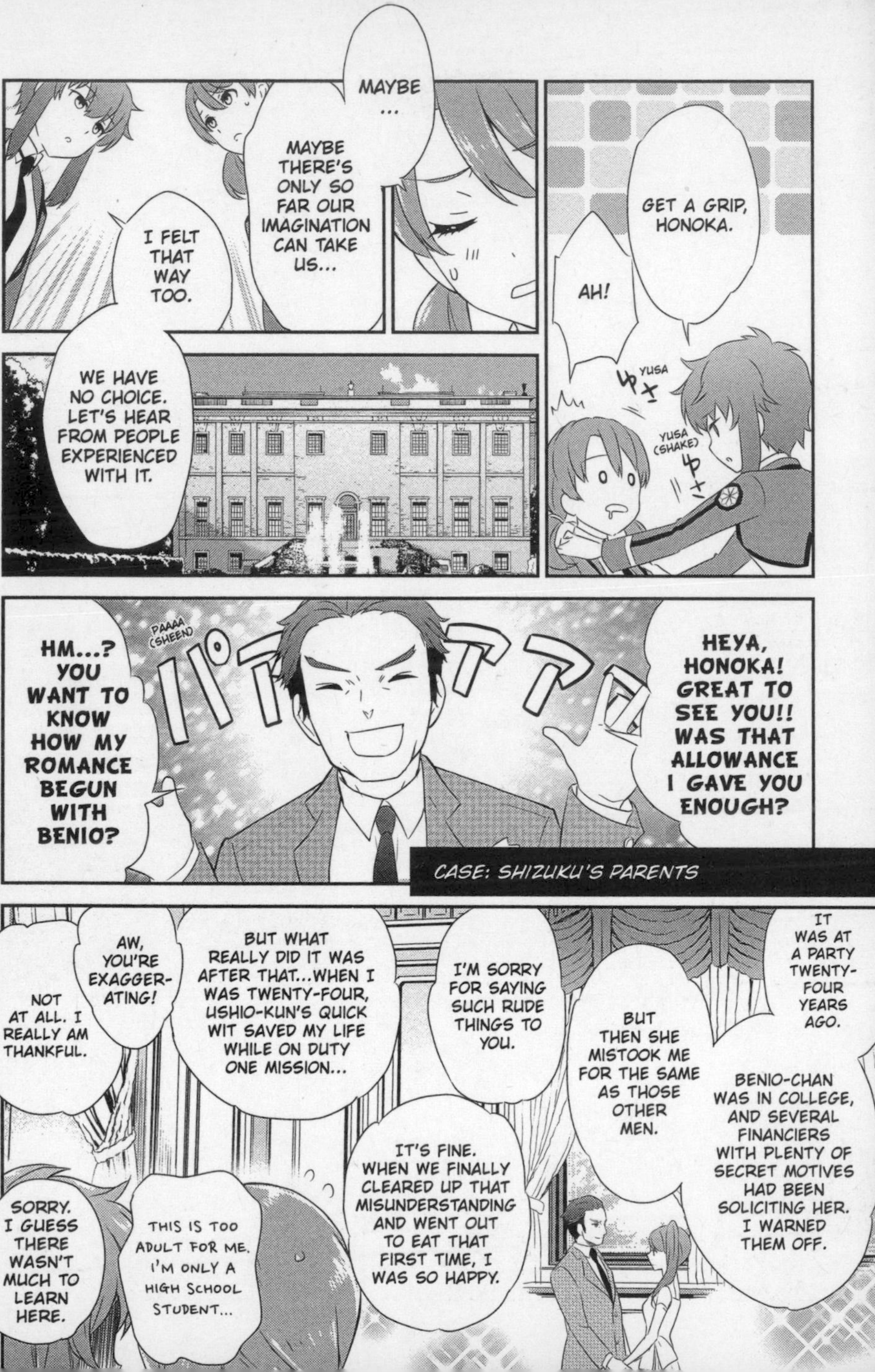
GET A GRIP, HONOKA.
AH!
YUSA
YUSA (SHAKE)
MAYBE ...
MAYBE THERE'S ONLY SO FAR OUR IMAGINATION CAN TAKE US...
I FELT THAT WAY TOO.
WE HAVE NO CHOICE. LET'S HEAR FROM PEOPLE EXPERIENCED WITH IT.
HEYA, HONOKA! GREAT TO SEE YOU!! WAS THAT ALLOWANCE I GAVE YOU ENOUGH?
PAAAA (SHEEN)
HM...? YOU WANT TO KNOW HOW MY ROMANCE BEGUN WITH BENIO?
CASE: SHIZUKU'S PARENTS
IT WAS AT A PARTY TWENTY-FOUR YEARS AGO.
BENIO-CHAN WAS IN COLLEGE, AND SEVERAL FINANCIERS WITH PLENTY OF SECRET MOTIVES HAD BEEN SOLICITING HER. I WARNED THEM OFF.
BUT THEN SHE MISTOOK ME FOR THE SAME AS THOSE OTHER MEN.
I'M SORRY FOR SAYING SUCH RUDE THINGS TO YOU.
IT'S FINE. WHEN WE FINALLY CLEARED UP THAT MISUNDERSTANDING AND WENT OUT TO EAT THAT FIRST TIME, I WAS SO HAPPY.
BUT WHAT REALLY DID IT WAS AFTER THAT...WHEN I WAS TWENTY-FOUR, USHIO-KUN'S QUICK WIT SAVED MY LIFE WHILE ON DUTY ONE MISSION...
AW, YOU'RE EXAGGER-ATING!
NOT AT ALL. I REALLY AM THANKFUL.
THIS IS TOO ADULT FOR ME. I'M ONLY A HIGH SCHOOL STUDENT...
SORRY. I GUESS THERE WASN'T MUCH TO LEARN HERE.

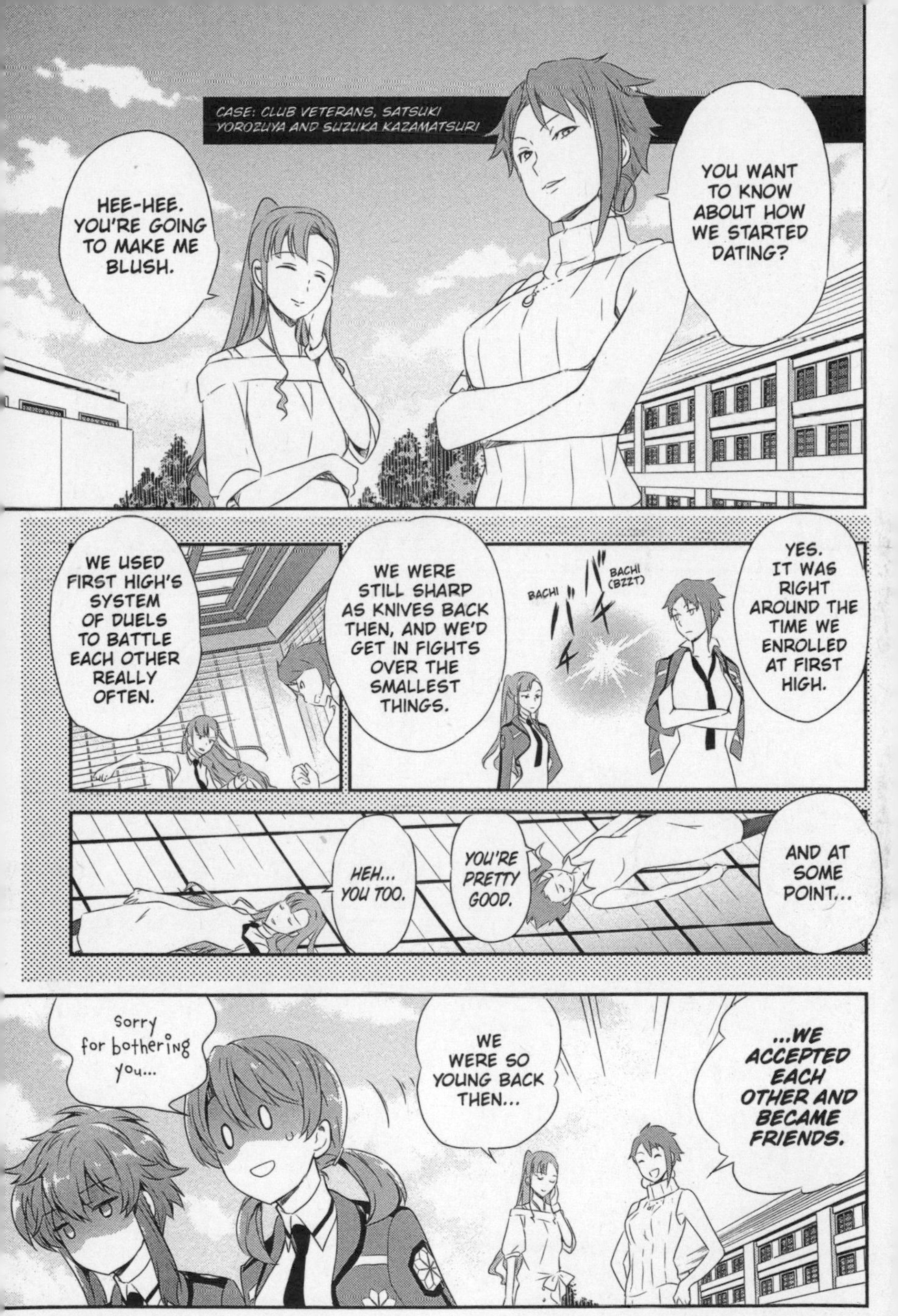
CASE: CLUB VETERANS, SATSUKI YOROZUYA AND SUZUKA KAZAMATSURI
YOU WANT TO KNOW ABOUT HOW WE STARTED DATING?
HEE-HEE. YOU'RE GOING TO MAKE ME BLUSH.
YES. IT WAS RIGHT AROUND THE TIME WE ENROLLED AT FIRST HIGH.
BACHI (BZZT)
BACHI
WE WERE STILL SHARP AS KNIVES BACK THEN, AND WE'D GET IN FIGHTS OVER THE SMALLEST THINGS.
WE USED FIRST HIGH'S SYSTEM OF DUELS TO BATTLE EACH OTHER REALLY OFTEN.
AND AT SOME POINT...
YOU'RE PRETTY GOOD.
HEH... YOU TOO.
...WE ACCEPTED EACH OTHER AND BECAME FRIENDS.
WE WERE SO YOUNG BACK THEN...
Sorry for bothering you...

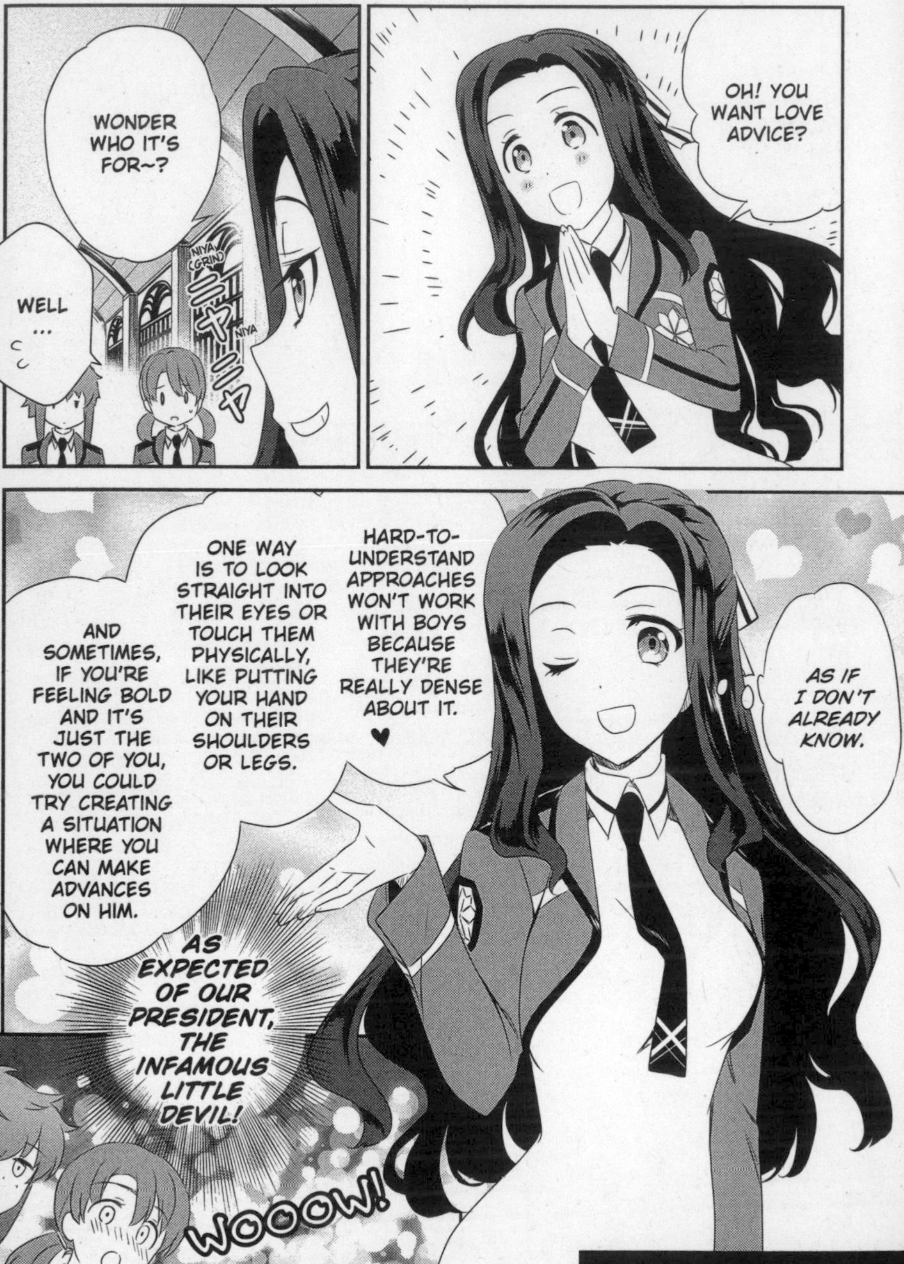
OH! YOU WANT LOVE ADVICE?
WONDER WHO IT'S FOR~?
NIYA GRIND
ニヤニヤ
NIYA
WELL ...
AS IF I DON'T ALREADY KNOW.
HARD-TO-UNDERSTAND APPROACHES WON'T WORK WITH BOYS BECAUSE THEY'RE REALLY DENSE ABOUT IT. ♥
ONE WAY IS TO LOOK STRAIGHT INTO THEIR EYES OR TOUCH THEM PHYSICALLY, LIKE PUTTING YOUR HAND ON THEIR SHOULDERS OR LEGS.
AND SOMETIMES, IF YOU'RE FEELING BOLD AND IT'S JUST THE TWO OF YOU, YOU COULD TRY CREATING A SITUATION WHERE YOU CAN MAKE ADVANCES ON HIM.
AS EXPECTED OF OUR PRESIDENT, THE INFAMOUS LITTLE DEVIL!
WOOOW!
CASE: MAYUMI SAEGUSA

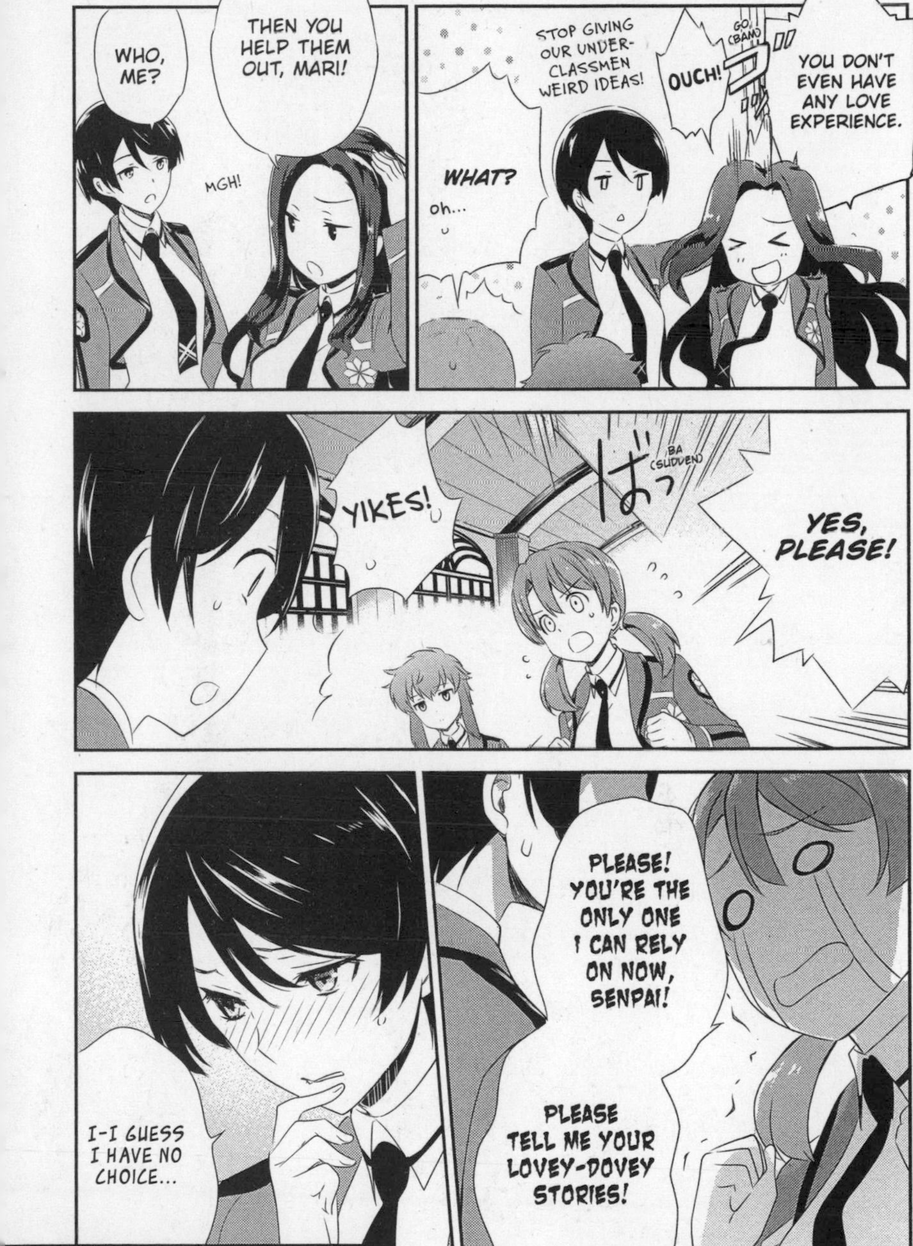
YOU DON'T EVEN HAVE ANY LOVE EXPERIENCE.
GO (BAM)
OUCH!
STOP GIVING OUR UNDER-CLASSMEN WEIRD IDEAS!
WHAT?
oh...
THEN YOU HELP THEM OUT, MARI!
WHO, ME?
MGH!
ばっ
BA (SUDDEN)
YES, PLEASE!
YIKES!
PLEASE! YOU'RE THE ONLY ONE I CAN RELY ON NOW, SENPAI!
PLEASE TELL ME YOUR LOVEY-DOVEY STORIES!
I-I GUESS I HAVE NO CHOICE...
CASE: MARI WATANABE

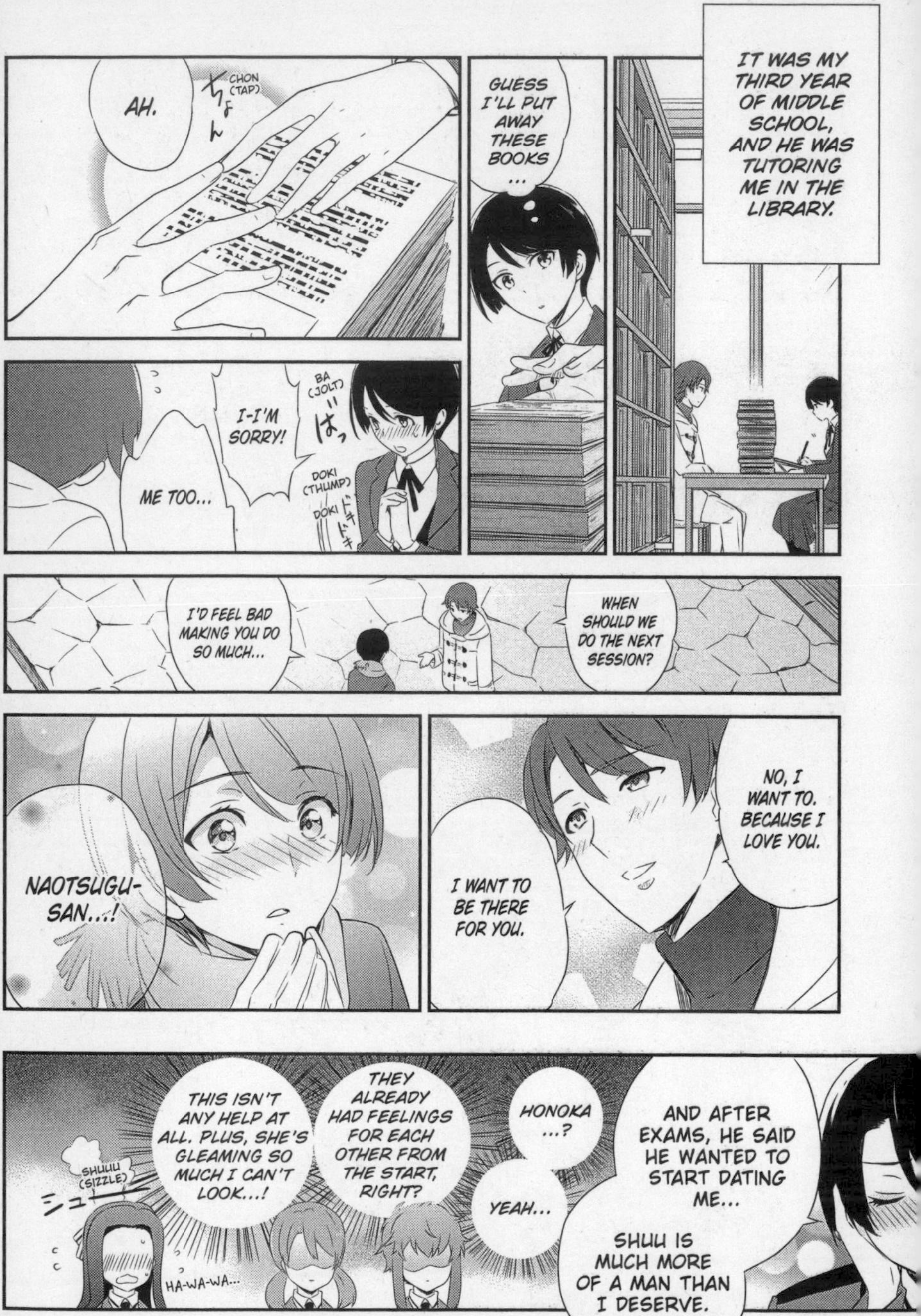
IT WAS MY THIRD YEAR OF MIDDLE SCHOOL, AND HE WAS TUTORING ME IN THE LIBRARY.
GUESS I'LL PUT AWAY THESE BOOKS ...
CHON (TAP)
ちょん
AH.
BA (JOLT)
ばっ
I-I'M SORRY!
DOKI (THUMP) DOKI
ドキドキ
ME TOO...
WHEN SHOULD WE DO THE NEXT SESSION?
I'D FEEL BAD MAKING YOU DO SO MUCH...
NO, I WANT TO. BECAUSE I LOVE YOU.
I WANT TO BE THERE FOR YOU.
NAOTSUGU-SAN...!
AND AFTER EXAMS, HE SAID HE WANTED TO START DATING ME...
SHUU IS MUCH MORE OF A MAN THAN I DESERVE.
HONOKA ...?
YEAH...
THEY ALREADY HAD FEELINGS FOR EACH OTHER FROM THE START, RIGHT?
THIS ISN'T ANY HELP AT ALL. PLUS, SHE'S GLEAMING SO MUCH I CAN'T LOOK...!
SHUUU (SIZZLE)
シュー
HA-WA-WA...

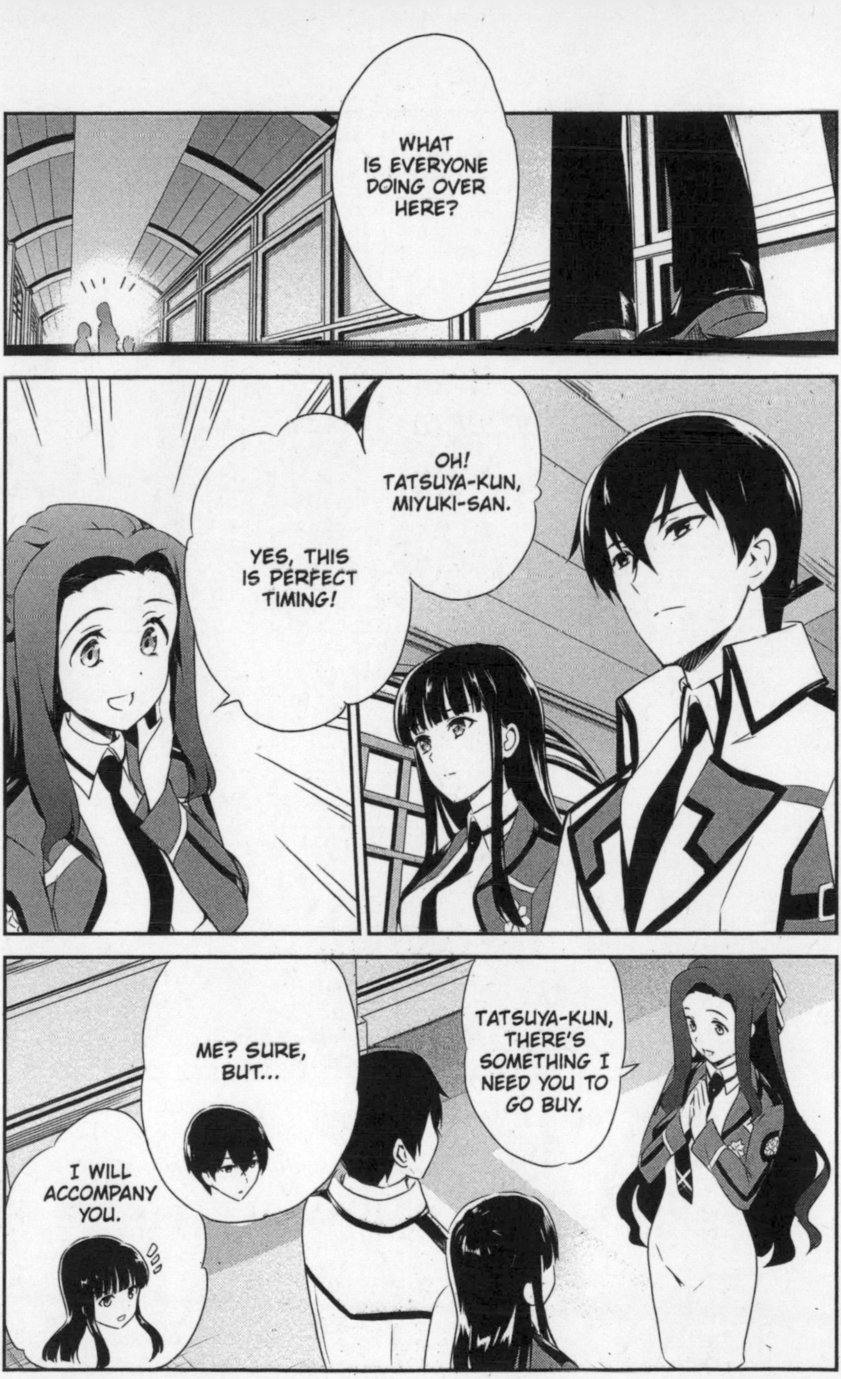
WHAT IS EVERYONE DOING OVER HERE?
OH! TATSUYA-KUN, MIYUKI-SAN.
YES, THIS IS PERFECT TIMING!
TATSUYA-KUN, THERE'S SOMETHING I NEED YOU TO GO BUY.
ME? SURE, BUT...
I WILL ACCOMPANY YOU.

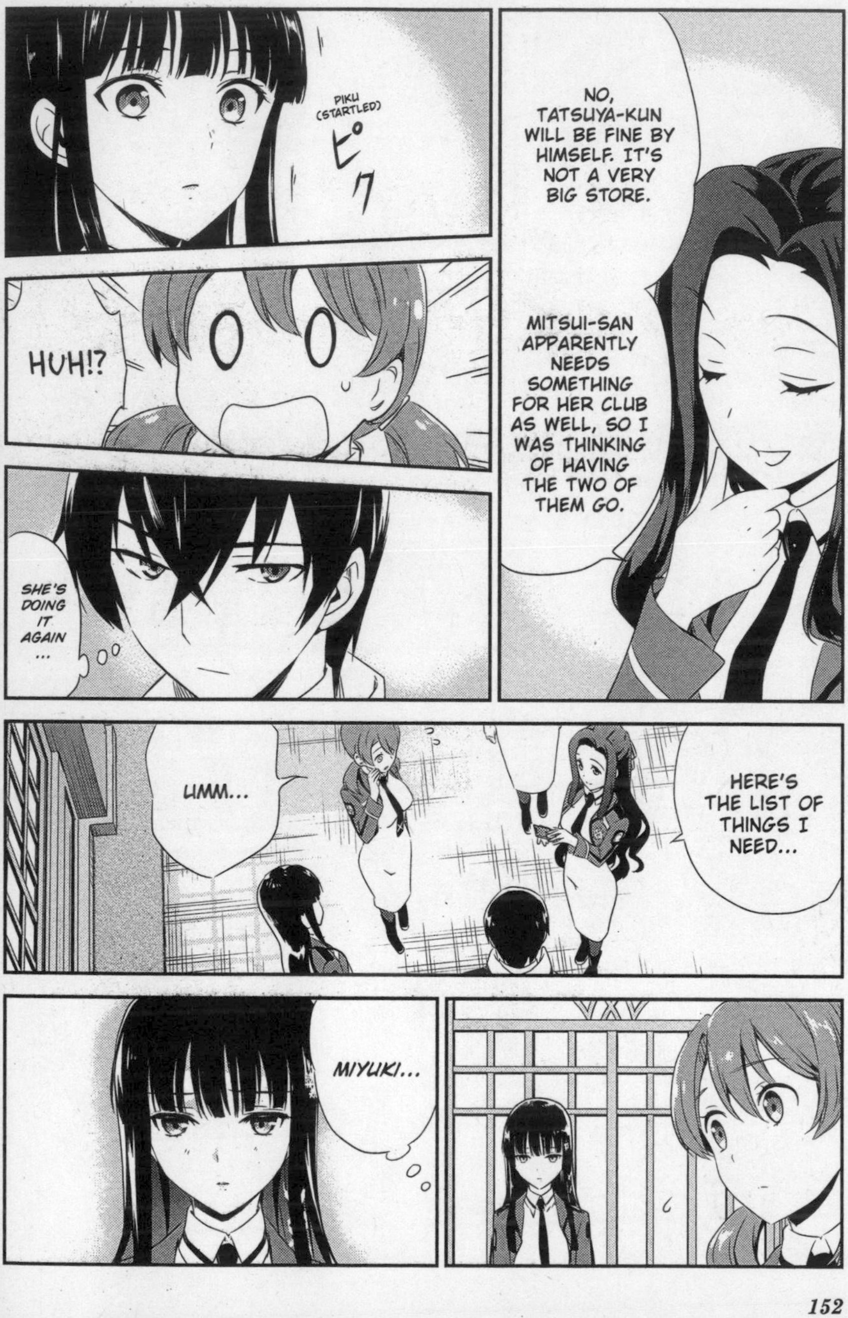
NO, TATSUYA-KUN WILL BE FINE BY HIMSELF. IT'S NOT A VERY BIG STORE.
MITSUI-SAN APPARENTLY NEEDS SOMETHING FOR HER CLUB AS WELL, SO I WAS THINKING OF HAVING THE TWO OF THEM GO.
PIKU (STARTLED)
ピク
HUH!?
SHE'S DOING IT AGAIN...
HERE'S THE LIST OF THINGS I NEED...
UMM...
MIYUKI...

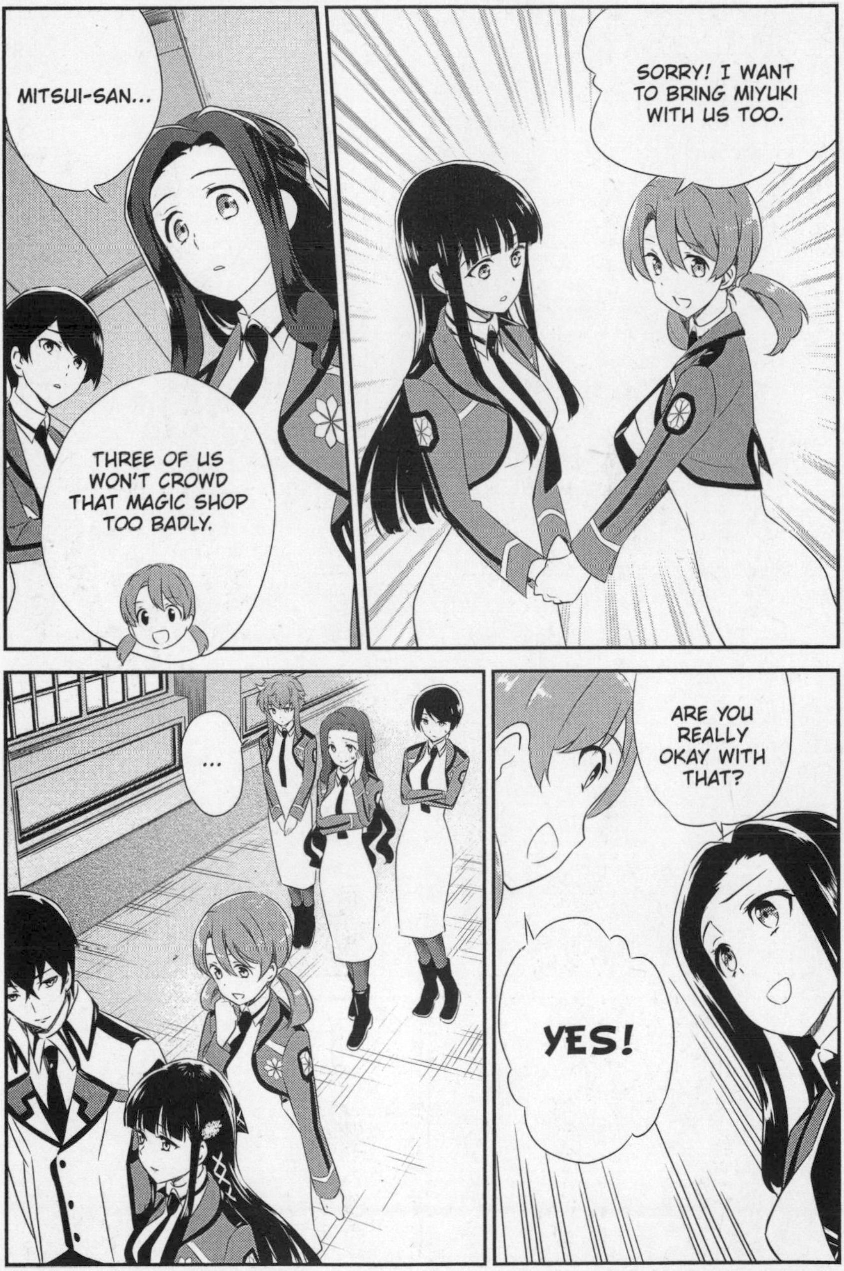
SORRY! I WANT TO BRING MIYUKI WITH US TOO.
MITSUI-SAN...
THREE OF US WON'T CROWD THAT MAGIC SHOP TOO BADLY.
ARE YOU REALLY OKAY WITH THAT?
YES!
...

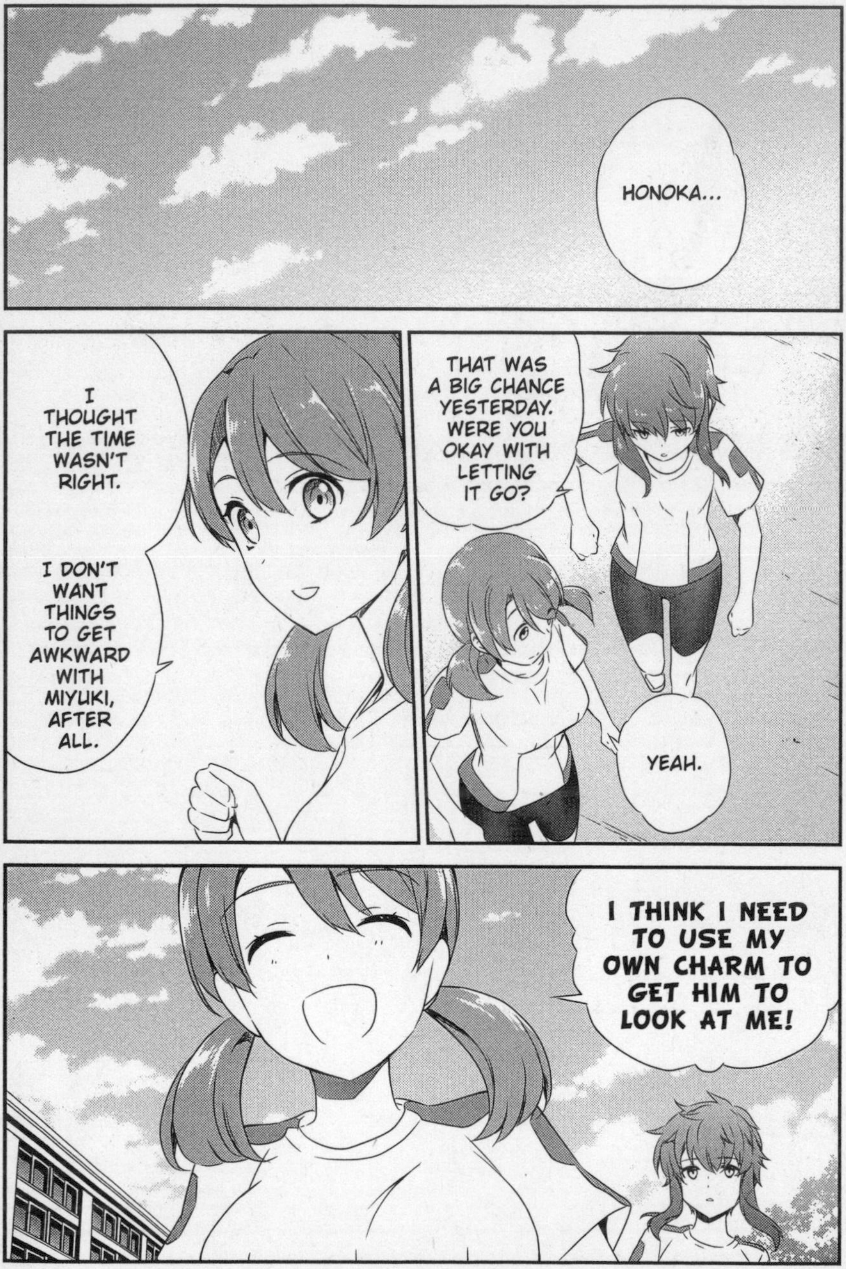
HONOKA...
THAT WAS A BIG CHANCE YESTERDAY. WERE YOU OKAY WITH LETTING IT GO?
YEAH.
I THOUGHT THE TIME WASN'T RIGHT.
I DON'T WANT THINGS TO GET AWKWARD WITH MIYUKI, AFTER ALL.
I THINK I NEED TO USE MY OWN CHARM TO GET HIM TO LOOK AT ME!

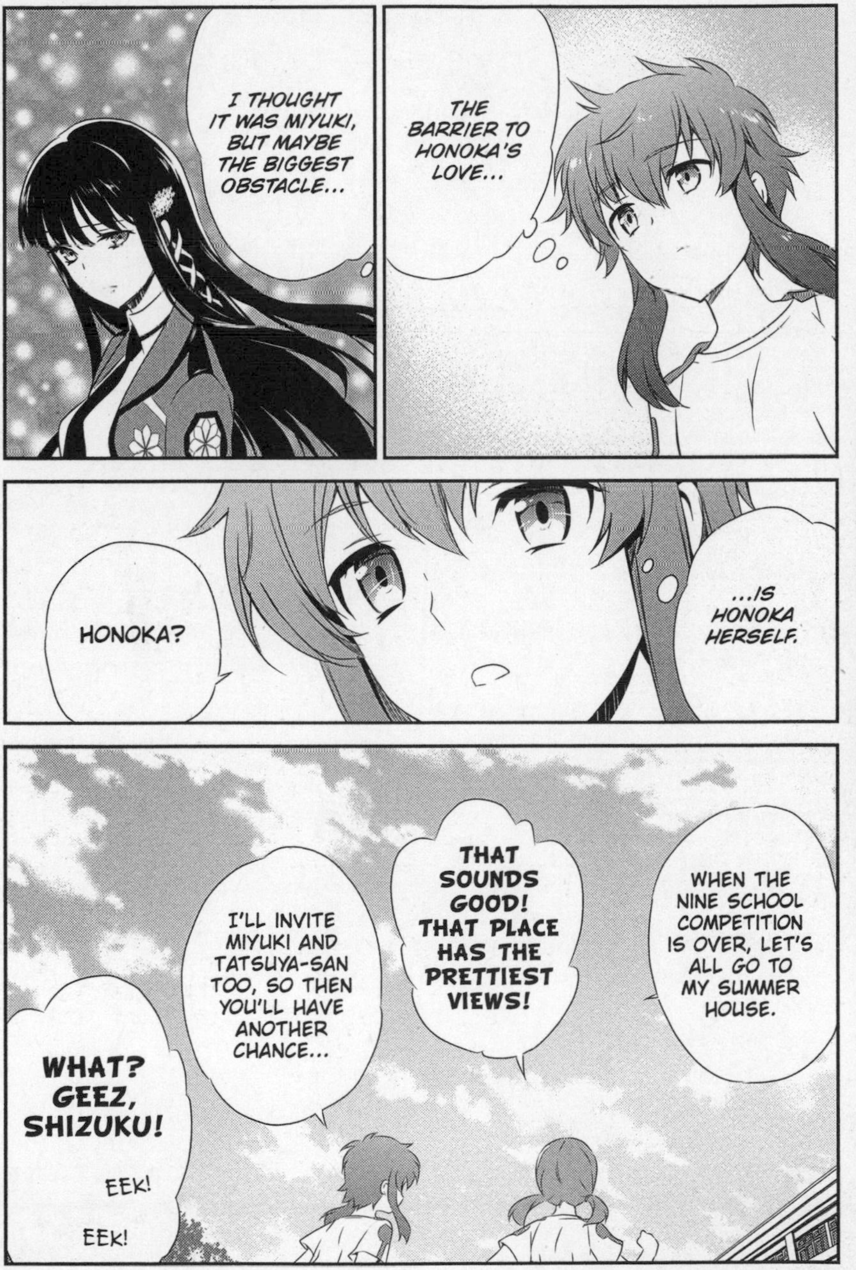
THE BARRIER TO HONOKA'S LOVE...
I THOUGHT IT WAS MIYUKI, BUT MAYBE THE BIGGEST OBSTACLE...
...IS HONOKA HERSELF.
HONOKA?
WHEN THE NINE SCHOOL COMPETITION IS OVER, LET'S ALL GO TO MY SUMMER HOUSE.
THAT SOUNDS GOOD! THAT PLACE HAS THE PRETTIEST VIEWS!
I'LL INVITE MIYUKI AND TATSUYA-SAN TOO, SO THEN YOU'LL HAVE ANOTHER CHANCE...
WHAT? GEEZ, SHIZUKU!
EEK!
EEK!

Activation sequence

The blueprints for magic and the programs used to construct it. Activation sequence data is stored in a compressed format in C.A.D.s. Design waves are sent from the magician to the device, where they're converted into a signal according to the decompressed data and returned to the magician.

Antinite

A military-grade commodity only produced in lands where ancient alpine civilizations prospered, such as part of the Aztec Empire and the Mayan countries and regions. Extremely valuable due to its limited production quantity and impossible for civilians to acquire.

Blanche

A national anti-magic political organization with the objective of uprooting discrimination in society based on magical ability. They hold protest activities based on the criticism of the fictional concept of the current system giving special political treatment to magicians. Behind the scenes, they engage in terrorism and other illegal activities and are strictly watched by the public peace agency.

Blooms, Weeds

Terms displaying the gap between Course 1 students and Course 2 students in First High. The left breast of Course 1 student uniforms is emblazoned with an eight-petaled emblem, but it is absent from the Course 2 uniforms.

Cabinets

Small, linear vehicles holding either two or four passengers and controlled by a central station. Used for commuting to work and school as a public transportation replacement for trains.

Cardinal George

Shinkurou Kichijouji's nickname. Given to him for having discovered one of the Cardinal Codes, which only existed in theory beforehand, at the young age of thirteen.

Cast jamming

A variety of typeless magic that obstructs magic sequences from exerting influence on Eidos. It weakens the process by which magic sequences affect Eidos by scattering large amounts of meaningless psionic waves.

C.A.D. (Casting Assistant Device)

A device that simplifies the activation of magic. Magical programming is recorded inside. The main types are specialized and multipurpose.

Crimson Prince

Masaki Ichijou's nickname. Given to him for having fought through a battle at the young age of thirteen "drenched in the blood of enemy and ally alike" during the Sado Invasion of 2092 as a volunteer soldier on the defensive line.

Égalité

A branch organization of Blanche. They take in young people who hate politics, so they don't reveal that they're directly related to Blanche.

Eidos (Individual information body)

Originally a term from Greek philosophy. In modern magic, Eidos are the bodies of information that accompany phenomena. They record the existence of those phenomena on the world, so they can also be called the footprints that phenomena leave on the world. The definition of "magic" in modern magic refers to the technology that modifies these phenomena by modifying Eidos.

Four Leaves Technology (F.L.T.)

A domestic C.A.D. manufacturer. Originally famous for its magic engineering products, rather than finished C.A.D.s, but with the development of its Silver line of models, its fame skyrocketed as a C.A.D. manufacturer.

Idea (Information body dimension)

Pronounced "ee-dee-ah." Originally a term from Greek philosophy. In modern magic, "Idea" refers to the platform on which Eidos are recorded. Magic's primary form is a technology wherein a magic sequence is output onto this platform, thus rewriting the Eidos recorded within.

The Index

A table of the proper names of spells recorded in the encyclopedia of magic created by the National Magic University. Its full name is the "National Magic University's Compiled Magic Encyclopedia Name Index." Researchers in Japan who are involved in magical research and development work hard every day with the grand goal of being chosen for the Index.

I.S. Magic

Unique abilities that are difficult to systematize as magic. "I.S." stands for "innately specialized."

Loopcast system

Activation sequences made so that a magician can continually execute a spell as many times as their calculation capacity will permit. Normally, one must re-expand activation sequences every time one executes the same spell, but the loopcast system makes it possible by automatically duplicating the activation sequence's final state in the magician's magic calculation region.

Magician

An abbreviation of "magical technician," referring to anyone with the skill to use magic at a practical level.

Magic Association of Japan

A social group of Japanese magicians based in Kyoto. The Kantou branch location is established within Yokohama Bay Hills Tower.

Magic calculation region

A mental region for the construction of magic sequences. The substance, so to speak, of magical talent. It exists in a magician's unconscious, and even if a magician is normally aware of using his or her magic calculation region, he or she cannot be aware of the processes being conducted within. The magic calculation region can be called a "black box" for the magician himself.

◉ Magic engineer
Refers to engineers who design, develop, and maintain apparatuses that assist, amplify, and strengthen magic. Their reputation in society is slightly worse than that of magicians. However, magic engineers are indispensable for tuning the C.A.D.s, indispensable tools for magicians, so in the industrial world, they're in higher demand than normal magicians. A first-rate magic engineer's earnings surpass even that of first-rate magicians.

◉ Magic high school
The nickname for the high schools affiliated with the National Magic University. There are nine established throughout the country. Of them, the first through the third have two hundred students per grade and use the Course 1/Course 2 system.

◉ Magic sequence
An information body for the purpose of temporarily altering information attached to phenomena. They are constructed from the Psions possessed by magicians.

◉ Nine School Competition
An abbreviation of "National Magic High School Goodwill Magic Competition Tournament." Magic high school students across the country, from First through Ninth High, are gathered to compete with their schools in fierce magic showdowns. There are six events: Speed Shooting, Cloudball, Battle Board, Ice Pillars Break, Mirage Bat, and Monolith Code.

◉ Psions
Non-physical particles belonging to the dimension of psychic phenomena. Psions are elements that record information on consciousness and thought products. Eidos — the theoretical basis for modern magic — as well as activation sequences and magic sequences — supporting its main framework — are all bodies of information constructed from Psions. Also referred to as "thought particles."

◉ Pushions
Non-physical particles belonging to the dimension of psychic phenomena. Their existence has been proven, but their true form and functions have yet to be elucidated. Magicians are generally only able to "feel" the pushions being activated through magic. Also referred to as "spirit particles."

◉ The Ten Master Clans
The strongest group of magicians in Japan. Ten families from a list of twenty-eight are chosen during the Ten Master Clans Selection Conference that happens every four years and are named as the Ten Master Clans. The twenty-eight families are Ichijou, Ichinokura, Isshiki, Futatsugi, Nikaidou, Nihei, Mitsuya, Mikazuki, Yotsuba, Itsuwa, Gotou, Itsumi, Mutsuzuka, Rokkaku, Rokugou, Roppongi, Saegusa, Shippou, Tanabata, Nanase, Yatsushiro, Hassaku, Hachiman, Kudou, Kuki, Kuzumi, Juumonji, and Tooyama.

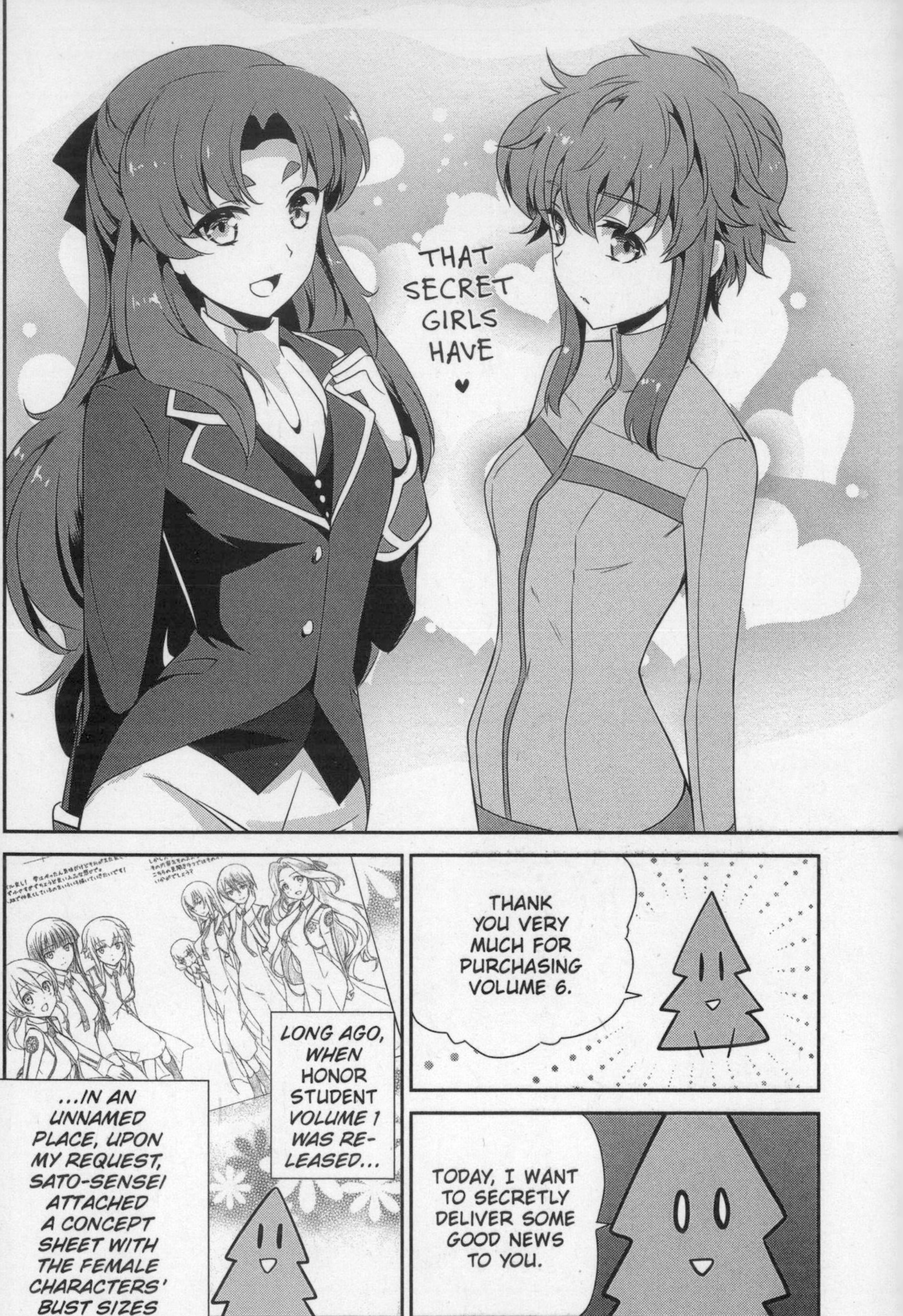
THAT SECRET GIRLS HAVE ♥
THANK YOU VERY MUCH FOR PURCHASING VOLUME 6.
TODAY, I WANT TO SECRETLY DELIVER SOME GOOD NEWS TO YOU.
LONG AGO, WHEN HONOR STUDENT VOLUME 1 WAS RE- LEASED...
...IN AN UNNAMED PLACE, UPON MY REQUEST, SATO-SENSEI ATTACHED A CONCEPT SHEET WITH THE FEMALE CHARACTERS' BUST SIZES ON IT.

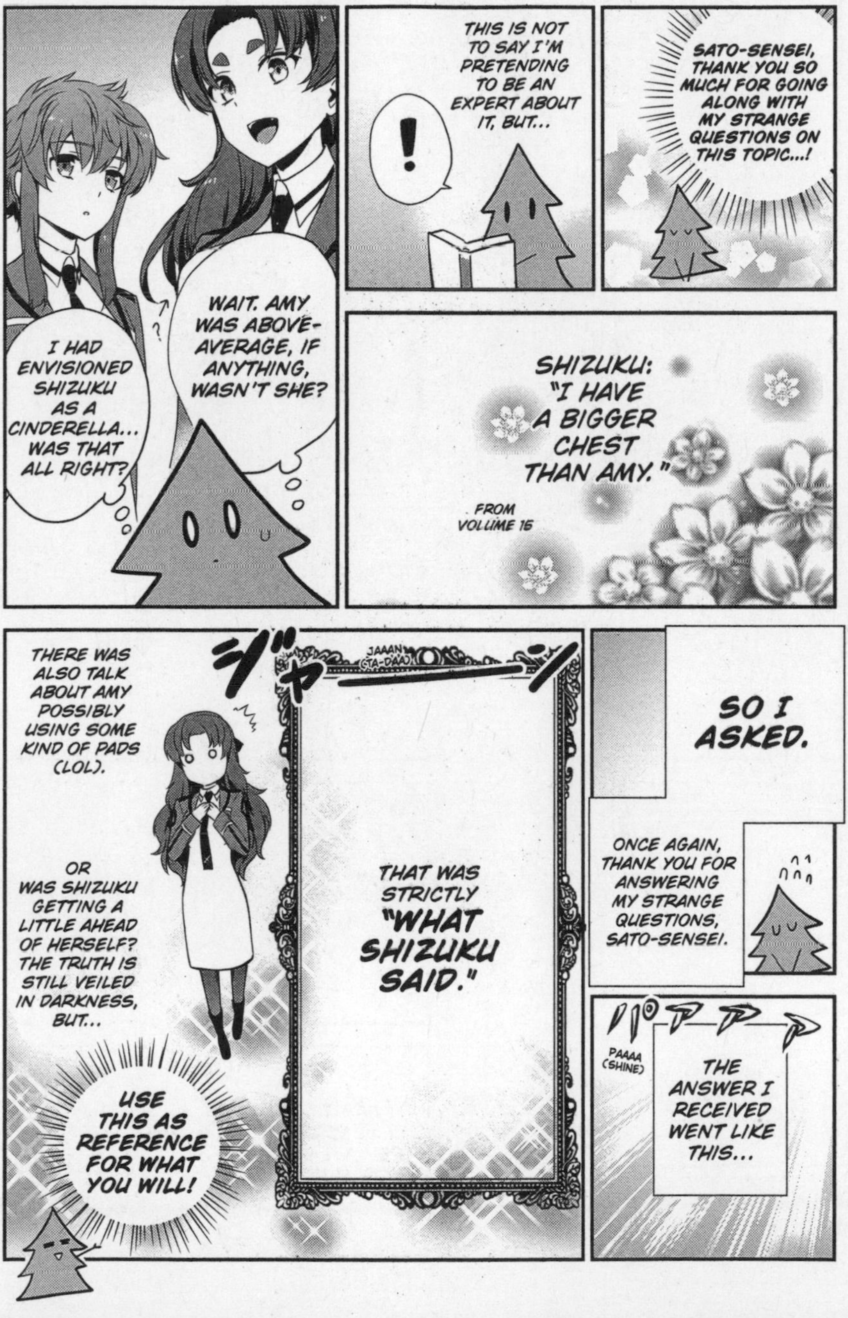
SATO-SENSEI, THANK YOU SO MUCH FOR GOING ALONG WITH MY STRANGE QUESTIONS ON THIS TOPIC...!
THIS IS NOT TO SAY I'M PRETENDING TO BE AN EXPERT ABOUT IT, BUT...
!
SHIZUKU: "I HAVE A BIGGER CHEST THAN AMY."
FROM VOLUME 15
WAIT. AMY WAS ABOVE-AVERAGE, IF ANYTHING, WASN'T SHE?
?
I HAD ENVISIONED SHIZUKU AS A CINDERELLA... WAS THAT ALL RIGHT?
SO I ASKED.
ONCE AGAIN, THANK YOU FOR ANSWERING MY STRANGE QUESTIONS, SATO-SENSEI.
PAAAA (SHINE)
THE ANSWER I RECEIVED WENT LIKE THIS...
JAAAN (TA-DAA)
THAT WAS STRICTLY "WHAT SHIZUKU SAID."
THERE WAS ALSO TALK ABOUT AMY POSSIBLY USING SOME KIND OF PADS (LOL).
OR WAS SHIZUKU GETTING A LITTLE AHEAD OF HERSELF? THE TRUTH IS STILL VEILED IN DARKNESS, BUT...
USE THIS AS REFERENCE FOR WHAT YOU WILL!

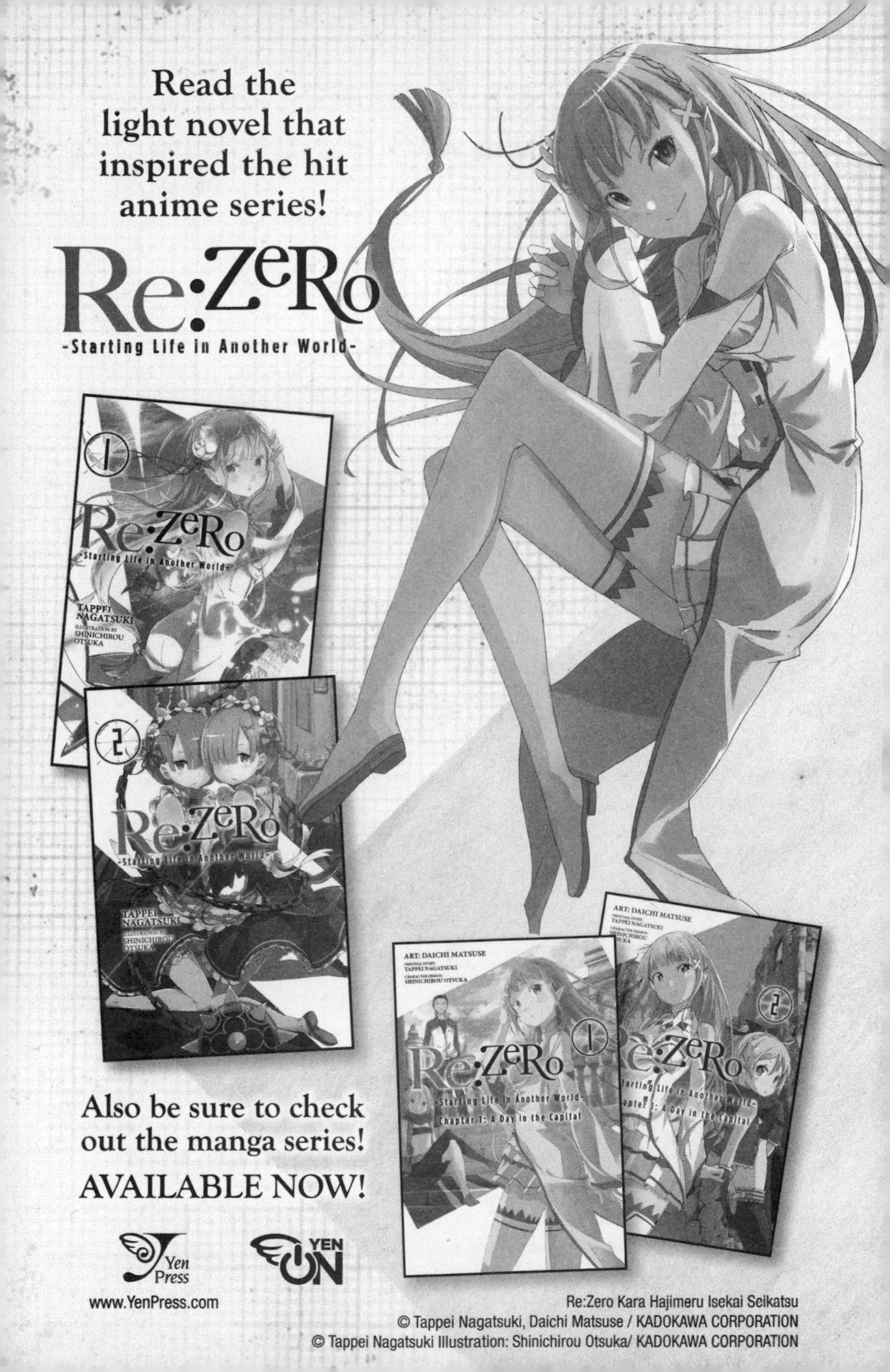

THE HONOR STUDENT
AT MAGIC HIGH SCHOOL ❻

YU MORI
Original Story: **TSUTOMU SATO**
Character Design: **KANA ISHIDA**

Translation: Andrew Prowse
Lettering: Phil Christie

MAHOUKA KOUKOU NO YUUTOUSEI Volume 6
© TSUTOMU SATO / YU MORI 2015
All rights reserved.
Edited by ASCII MEDIA WORKS
First published in Japan in 2015 by KADOKAWA CORPORATION, Tokyo.
English translation rights arranged with KADOKAWA CORPORATION, Tokyo,
through Tuttle-Mori Agency, Inc., Tokyo.

English translation © 2017 by Yen Press, LLC

Yen Press
1290 Avenue of the Americas
New York, NY 10104

Visit us at yenpress.com
facebook.com/yenpress
twitter.com/yenpress
yenpress.tumblr.com
instagram.com/yenpress

First Yen Press Edition: March 2017

Yen Press is an imprint of Yen Press, LLC.
The Yen Press name and logo are trademarks of Yen Press, LLC.

Library of Congress Control Number: 2016932699

ISBNs: 978-0-316-46604-2 (paperback)
       978-0-316-46617-2 (ebook)

10 9 8 7 6 5 4 3 2 1

BVG

Printed in the United States of America